A CURRENT AFFAIR

A JAMESON FAMILY NOVEL -BOOK 2

TRACEE LYDIA GARNER

TRACEE GARNER

A Current Affair

© Copyright 2020 by Tracee Lydia Garner

www.TraceeGarner.com

Published by Tracee Lydia Garner

ISBN: 978-0-9981099-8-5

Formatting by Tracee Lydia Garner / Vellum

© Editing by Best Words Editing

© Cover Design by Ally Hastings

SPECIAL NOTE TO READERS

TRIGGER WARNING: This story includes potentially triggering themes of miscarriage, gun violence, suicide and assault.

1

When Chyna Lockhart found herself at the front of the church she felt tears sting the back of her eyes. One statement replayed itself over and over again in her cluttered head: *Joseph Jameson Sr. is dead.* Her entire future might as well have died with him.

All the children of the late Mr. Jameson were seated at the front. A small crowd of fellow mourners surrounded them, paying their last respects and offering their condolences for the loss. Chyna wouldn't be doing any of that. She wouldn't speak to anybody at all. In fact, she didn't want them to see her, or even to know she was there.

Chyna was clothed head to toe in black for the occasion, large mirrored sunglasses covering her eyes. She had spent almost an hour that morning combing her thick mane of natural shoulder-length hair around her face. She'd debated wearing a veil, but had eventually decided that this was unfeasible in Virginia's muggy, oppressive heat. Joseph Jameson Sr. had died during the final days of the notoriously hot summer in Springfield, Virginia. Now, wearing a small black hat courtesy of her own deceased mother, Chyna sat and sweltered.

Still, she had to manage only a few more minutes until the long slow train of people moved on and she could escape, walking out with her head down, holding a crumpled handkerchief to her face at every opportunity. Despite having known the Jameson family all her life, she hoped fervently that the family would be too distracted in their grief to notice her. She knew she should have said something, offered words of sorrow to the family like the others, but right then she felt like nothing more than a casual acquaintance. Dean Jameson had made sure of that.

Mrs. Jameson, of course, would insist she was family. As a girl, Chyna had practically lived in the home of her well-respected neighbors. She had often sought refuge there from her own family - that bunch of socially defunct misfits. She was more than a friend, almost a second sister to Jina and Tish. They had often referred to Chyna as such, and she always felt as if their inclusion and open expressions of love for her were genuine and true. Their home life was so different than her own. No one ever yelled or raised their voice, and they always seemed to have just enough love to embrace one more child: Chyna.

When Mr. Jameson fell ill years earlier, she had become his nurse. She patiently waited on him hand and foot - Mrs. Jameson, too - and she had done so gladly. The Jamesons had given her so much happiness in her youth, it felt only fair to return the favor in their old age. With both her parents dead, the Jamesons were the only family she had left. It didn't matter that she wasn't really related to them. But Dean... he'd brought that feeling to a halt, hadn't he?

Chyna shook her head absently. The longer she stood in line waiting to say goodbye, the more she felt a heavy and overwhelming numbness trying to swallow her. Unsuccessfully, she struggled to escape the strong arms of grief and sadness that threatened to envelope her.

As she looked at Mr. Jameson's still frame, she chanced a quick look at Dean from the side of her concealing glasses. Dean's eyes were blank and expressionless as he stared off into space. His slumped posture and distant gaze tugged at Chyna's heart. She hated Dean for what he'd done to her, but despite it all she still cared.

When his eyes seemed about to lift and drift toward her, Chyna quickly turned away. Dean Jameson was the thing she had wanted most in her life: more than almost anything else. The one thing she wanted more, he'd caused her to lose.

Out of the corner of her eye, Chyna saw Tish. Her best friend's belly now swollen with twins, she was leaning against her big husband for support, his arm around her shoulders and his large right hand resting over her taut stomach as if holding them all together through her grief. They deserved to be happy, Chyna thought. They had been through so much together. Mr. Jameson's Alzheimer's had taxed the family's emotions over the years, especially over the last few months. Then he died. It was a great deal to bear.

She wished she could tuck herself securely under Dean's shoulder just the way Tish sat under her own husband's arm. Didn't she deserve a happy ending, too? She and Dean would have been perfect together, she thought. But that was not her fate.

She stared at the elderly man lovingly and took a deep breath, suppressing the nauseous angst rising from her stomach. Bowing her head, she prayed no one in the family would notice her as she quickly stooped and pressed her lips to the forehead of Joe Jameson Sr.

"Rest in peace," she whispered as tears sprang to her eyes. She felt so silly that as a nurse and freelance medical writer, she still couldn't come up with something more original than *rest in peace*.

She erected herself and, turning to face the door, noticed Dean out of the corner of her eye.

Moving as if pushed by an unseen hand, she stood up straight and walked as fast as she could on leaden legs down the burgundy-carpeted aisle of the church toward the exit. She pretended not to see Dean as he stood and turned to face her.

As she neared the crowded exit, Chyna successfully pushed her way through the throng, all the while chastising herself for being identified. She was almost out the door at last when she bumped an older woman, nearly knocking her to the floor. Instinctively, she reached out with both arms to steady the toppling figure.

She watched as the elderly woman's eyes moved slowly up to focus on her dark shades. Her disguise was that bad. When the woman peered closer, Chyna fought the urge to rear back, as if doing so could keep her from being recognized. Such an action would only be a dead giveaway. She mumbled an apology for bumping the woman.

"My goodness, honey. Is that you, Chyna?" the older woman exclaimed, grasping Chyna's arms with her withered hands. "Where you been?" It was Loretta Jenkins, a neighbor and a friend of her deceased mother. Chyna hesitated. She could simply deny it was her, but once Ms. Jenkins heard her voice, the lady would know. Chyna could never lie convincingly anyway, so she just squirmed mutely out of the woman's boney grasp.

Looking toward the front of the church, she saw Dean following her. He would have reached her by now if he had not been continually stopped by mourners offering their condolences. Why he was pursuing her, she didn't know. He'd made it quite obvious he didn't care for her. Plus, this was his father's funeral. Certainly it was neither the time nor the place to discuss their unsolvable problems. She turned and walked quickly outside into the oppressive heat.

In the parking lot, the cars were practically stacked one on top of the other. She pushed her glasses higher up on her nose, praying someone hadn't blocked her in; and her prayers were answered. As she prepared to drive away, Chyna noticed how the sun shone brightly: as if this were a cheery day, as if the past week hadn't been so full of one piece of bad news after the other, as if her dear friend and lone father figure hadn't just died.

She looked around the lot one last time as she worked the key. She hated this car. The engine never turned on the first try.

Suddenly, Dean Jameson's tall frame filled the church doorway. In a panic, Chyna ducked. She'd seen his hand held to his brow, shielding his eyes from the sun as he searched the dense array of cars: looking for her, it seemed. He walked down the concrete steps and out of her view. Had he seen her?

She sprang straight up in her seat and frantically twisted the key once more. To her relief, the engine finally revved. Placing her foot on the gas pedal, she turned the wheel sharply, narrowly missing the tail end of a car parked ridiculously close as she barreled out of the lot. In her rearview mirror, she saw Dean waving his hands rapidly, motioning for her to stop. She didn't.

2

D ean Jameson stared at the space that used to be his
office. It was now gutted: charred rubble. The once
brand new furniture he'd picked out himself was
reduced to hollow charcoal shells of black ash. Nothing was
left. The burned-out roof let pale streaks of sunlight in.

Police and detectives might eventually find the culprits
behind the arson of his building, but truth be told, there had
been a series of arsons in the area lately, and his building was
just the latest in the string of casualties.

He was so very glad that no one was hurt, but the person
who had taken a torch to his building might have actually done
him a favor. He hadn't admitted that to anyone, and he wouldn't
ever: it was his secret.

Dean wished he could summon the emotion to be more
upset about it, but there was something bothering him even
more than someone having burned down his entire building. A
few weeks ago, Chyna Lockhart had run from him - literally.
Why?

He stood and slapped his hands again the side of his jeans,
gray ash clinging to everything in sight including his pant legs.

The last time he'd talked to Chyna, she had promised to return and tell him what happened with her supposed ex. Only Dean had recently heard that she wasn't an ex-anything, but that she was in fact still married. She had assured him that she could give a complete explanation; but, Dean reflected glumly, the fact that she had avoided talking to or even looking at him at any point during his father's funeral surely meant it was over. What else could it mean?

He had thought his life was on an upswing when he'd seen Chyna at the funeral, but before he knew what was happening she'd practically run out of the church, leaving him standing alone and confused in the parking lot that day, the hot dust lifting from the graveled lot and wafting onto his shiny black shoes. He'd tried calling her several times after that, but Chyna stopped taking his phone calls. This had become another mystery that he just couldn't solve.

He ducked under the yellow police tape at the entrance to his former office building, from the sidewalk of a strip mall that was pretty much dead save for one shabby grocery store. If it did decide to rain, Dean surmised, it was two days too late to make a difference here. This side of the three-storey structure, or what was left of it, was the place he'd called work for the last twelve years. The practice where people could find "Dr. J" six days a week, Monday through Saturday, was now nothing.

"Yo, Deanie? How does it - uh, how is it looking in there?"

Jojo Jameson approached, placing a comforting hand on his brother's shoulder. "You all right, bro?"

Dean shrugged as he looked up. Jojo, the gentle giant who never normally looked concerned, seemed to cast those eyes on him. He hated it: the look was more than just his space being burnt out. It was for his relationship, for his mother relocating... Dean reflected sadly that it was like he had nothing and no one to care about anymore.

"Yeah, what's up?" Dean shrugged, standing up to his full height which nonetheless didn't quite match his brother's.

"Nothing, just checking..." Joseph trailed off, placed his hands in his pockets and moved to walk beside him.

"Well you can quit checking up on me," Dean snapped as his brother hesitated. "I told you I'm all right," Dean added testily, wishing everyone would leave him alone.

"Yeah, well, you know," was all Jojo offered in return, as he shrugged his broad shoulders.

After all these years, Dean still felt inadequate around Jojo, and not just physically. He couldn't have a practice, couldn't have a woman – even his own Momma left him. Dean had the urge to give a wry, bitter laugh, but he didn't want to add to Jojo's or anyone else's concern about his mental health. He saw Jojo's girlfriend, Angel, approach, and stepped off the curb ready to greet her.

"Hey, Angel," Dean greeted the woman who gave him a hug and stepped back quickly.

"Hello, Dean, how are you?"

"Doing fine, thanks." He tried not to roll his eyes. "Where are Casey and Cassie?" Dean looked around for the van, then at his brother expectantly. The Velenti twins were never far from Jojo's or Angel's side: since they'd had Jojo in their lives, they were like his little shadows. Dean studied the minivan his brother now drove, reflecting in wonder at the changes he'd seen in his brother over the last year. The eldest Jameson, much to everyone's astonishment, had allowed love to take him by storm. Dean tried to smile, knowing his big brother had fought falling in love 110 percent, but in the end hadn't seemed to stand a chance.

"There," Jojo pointed with a small chuckle. Casey, a lanky boy with bronzy cheeks, waved frantically back at them. "And Cassie, over there."

Dean nodded and lifted his hand to wave back at the two.

They were waiting in line at a rusty-looking old ice cream van and skipped back over once they had their treats in hand.

The boy, Casey, didn't seem to talk and barely communicated in any other fashion. That said, he had made a considerable progression since Jojo had entered his life. In any case, his twin sister, Cassie, talked enough for everyone.

"So what you gonna do about your place?" Jojo asked, nodding back to the child.

Dean stared at them, wondering, considering, weighing everything it seemed of late: everything and everyone moving on. *Such is life: it moves on.* He took a deep breath.

The kids got into the van but the door remained open and while Cassie pretended to be absorbed in opening her treat, he knew she waited as eagerly as Jojo for an answer to the question that hung in the air.

"No idea," Dean shrugged a shoulder. He really didn't know. He was already knee-deep in fixing up the home he'd grown up in: he had a list of projects a mile long for that. A part of him had hoped he'd be getting reacquainted with Chyna, only that wasn't happening.

True, the current situation with his gutted workplace was forcing him to look at the possibilities quicker than he had wanted to. He'd never been at such a loss regarding what to do before, and it was both depressing and scary.

"You can let the insurance rebuild it," Jojo offered, "then sell it like you wanted – or do something else entirely. Do you know what direction you were headed, uh – before?"

Dean shrugged again. "I don't care if it's built back up or not," he said dully. "It's not in me anymore."

"Well, you know what I think?" Jojo continued.

Dean looked at his brother and rolled his eyes. He didn't care, but he knew Jojo would tell him anyway.

"You need a vacation," his brother continued matter-of-factly. "Rest up, check out your options, see what's what."

"This from the man who hasn't taken a vacation in twenty years?" Dean replied skeptically. A vacation sounded good to his mind, but his body barely rejoiced. The word *vacation* took on a "spring break" connotation. That had been what it was called the last time he'd had anything close to one. "So what exactly did you have in mind for this little find-my-direction trip?"

"Hey, Uncle Dean!" Cassie called out; her little lips stained red and blue from her rocket ice pop.

"Yes, Short Stuff?" Dean replied enthusiastically.

"I think you should come with us to Disney World! We have room in our van."

Dean lifted his eyebrows, a genuine laugh crinkling his eyes and nose for the first time in a long while. While he didn't know the twins that well, Cassie always seemed to say something to lift his spirits and make him think. The comedic aspect was simply that he *couldn't* go to Disney World. He just couldn't imagine being a part of the family unless Chyna or someone – *anyone*, for that matter - was with him. The momentary laughter over what had struck him as a funny scenario died moments later, leaving him feeling way too serious and, yes, remorseful again.

"I appreciate your invitation sweetheart, but I, uh, gotta stick around to hear from the investigators," he lied. Cassie looked disappointed but didn't continue her line of suggestion, returning to the task of licking her frozen pop.

"You know that's not true, right?" interjected Jojo. "They can call you from anywhere."

Dean shrugged. He knew that, of course, but he had no comment. He could see how the twins - and perhaps even Angel, though he didn't know much about her yet - could have captured his brother's heart so easily. Cassie was funny and optimistic, a child without adult issues, and the family just seemed ready-made. It was like a meal that you just heated up and ate. The table was already set; they were just waiting for Jojo.

Dean gave his head a little shake and grinned wryly to himself. He wasn't entirely sure when he'd taken to making up bad analogies, but they kept coming unbidden to his brain.

"Talked to Chyna yet?"

Dean stared at his brother.

"Hey, don't get upset with me!"

"Why not?" Dean retorted.

"It's an honest question."

"Well, the honest answer is 'no.'"

"Relationships work two ways, Dean. You have to make an effort too. I know everything comes easily to you..."

"That's not true," Dean protested.

"Sure it is. Grades, women, money... you can do whatever you want." Jojo paused. "Well - not women, not the women you want, I should clarify. The *easy* women come easily, but the one you really want – well, you can't just think her to you..."

"Who says I ever 'thought Chyna to me'?" Dean retorted, then bit his lip. To admit anything was to confirm he was thinking about her at all. He wasn't. Okay, he knew he was, but he at least didn't want anyone else to know that.

"I've known you my whole life, Deanie - get over yourself," Jojo chuckled. "Make a move already! Time is a'wasting and life is short. Stop being so stubborn. We gotta go."

"Good." Dean said it before he could stop himself.

Jojo just laughed. Dean watched as all the doors to the black minivan slid closed with finality. Jojo got in the driver's seat. All the windows were rolled down and Cassie was waving at him frantically, yelling her goodbyes.

Dean waved and nodded in a less-than-enthusiastic way but somewhere deep down inside he was happy for his brother.

He wasn't that stubborn, he thought. He did want to find happiness, of course he did. Turning around, he looked at his office building one last time before walking over to his luxury sedan. Fine, he told himself, he'd see about Chyna one last time - but if it didn't work, if she dodged him yet again, it really was the end. His heart held out hope as he cranked the engine and sped away.

"DID YOU SEE THAT, son? Did you?" Chauncey Hardig, hard-core business tycoon and lawyer, used a thick stubby finger to jab the window button in the back of his blue Town And Country Buick. "Look at that, son!"

Chauncey tapped the arm of his son, who sat just inches from him. Warren Hardig looked over as if he'd just arrived, when in fact they'd been sitting there with the AC blasting and the car running for the better part of a long and tortuous thirty minutes. Warren had long since lost interest in the monotony of his father's subject matter. He leaned forward disinterestedly to see what his father was indicating: the Jamesons talking, then Dean Jameson standing all alone for a moment before getting into his car and leaving. Warren had never been so happy to see them all disperse. Now he could finally get back to the office, instead of watching this latest episode of The Restless Jamesons. He sat back in relief as his father motioned to the driver and the car cruised off.

"Warren, surely I tell you, I need you remember this scene," Chauncey continued animatedly. "It will drive you. It will give you purpose in the morning and fill your bones with fire. Are you listening to me, boy?" Chauncey shouted. "That there's a Jameson. Did you see how despondent he looked?" he crowed, checking his three-thousand-dollar watch in satisfaction. "I wish it could have been his old man sitting there, but, well, a man's offspring, that's the next best thing."

Chauncey looked at his son again, with wariness and some

contempt. "Dean Jameson. He'll have to do," he emphasized. "Now, how's that contact you got? Lisa Stephens, is that her name?"

Warren looked up, finally paying some scant attention to what his father said. "Mmm?"

"Whatever her name is, you tell her my contact at the bank is in place. She's to send those papers over, and he'll handle the rest." Chauncey took a deep breath. "You know, son, I said I was going to stay out of your personal affairs, but... well, Lisa Stephens might be the girl who does it for you behind closed doors, but she is not the kind of character you let hang on your arm at respectable functions. Got that?"

Warren shrugged, not bothering to listen further. His old man was right in some respects, of course. Lisa Stephens did serve a man's purpose well, but another woman held Warren Hardig's attention. That was who he really wanted.

"Are you listening to me?" his father snapped. "I'm getting tired of this silent treatment. Please tell me you are not sleeping with this girl!"

"My private life is none of your business," replied Warren smoothly.

"It is when you're flaunting that trash all over town! You cut her loose, you hear? She is to serve one purpose only and that is to advance our cause of ruining the Jamesons: nothing more. You keep your pants zipped. I'll find someone else for you to attend the function with."

"Chyna Lockhart is in town," Warren offered.

"And how do you know this?" Chauncey boomed.

"I hired someone to find her."

"You're not serious!" his father exclaimed. "You are wasting your time. You were supposed to contact her ex-husband for an endorsement in the new Hardig buildings in the downtown Springfield, not sniff after his ex."

"I've always liked her a lot, Dad. You knew this when we

started." Warren shrugged in response to his father's withering stare, instantly sorry he'd revealed his intentions. He did like her a lot.

"You listen to me and you listen good: you relinquish this stupid crush you have on Chyna Lockhart," his father exclaimed. "She was Gary Williams's wife, for crying out loud. Now, here's what I want you to do. You ask Gary for a soundbite for reconstruction of this Springfield area. You scratch his back and give him someone to keep our California properties in good light. He's slipping in the polls, so a small check will keep him hanging on with us: a hundred grand or so should do the trick. Nothing talks like cold, hard Hardig cash, all right? I'll have a check ready for you. And while I think of it, what's with this DuPont Circle apartment I saw a line item for? Are you moving again? Listen to me - and get back on your medication, boy. You're getting a little all over the place, yet again."

Warren's lip curled.

"That's right," his father said, "I'll have you revaluated. I signed papers for you under the strict belief that you would adhere to the life I'm trying to create for you. If you still can't seem to get it together – well, we'll just have to take a little trip upstate."

Chauncey raised a finger, ticking off the things he meant for his son to do. "Your orders are as follows: Let go of this Lisa character, or see her out of the state. I don't want the press to get wind of your affair with her if she should mess up. What possessed you to take her in the first place?" Chauncey waved his hand as if he didn't want Warren to answer. "Two. Call off the person you've hired to find Lockhart. Lastly, ask Senator Gary Williams for endorsement on the Springfield Transition Project Phase 2, and take him the check."

Chauncey took a deep disapproving breath after his rant before hammering on.

"Now, back to the Jameson matter at hand."

He looked out the window again as the ramp to Washington disappeared: a sign that they'd soon be back in their DC high rise. "I want you to pay Jameson your respects in a bit, over the death of his father. Let things die down, then after a while you'll ask him to join your team. If he seems resistant, you'll use whatever he cares about. I'll research that in a bit."

Warren nodded, as he always did when he was no longer paying attention or no longer cared. The portly man sitting across from him was his bread and butter, but Warren had a plan of his own. Once he inherited his father's fortune, he'd tell the press all about this man named Chauncey Hardig. His story would be a million-dollar tale: a surefire best-seller. Of course, no-one knew Chauncey Hardig was an abusive, mean-spirited and bitter old man. Warren was simply biding his time. He would appease his father for only so long before he planned to cut him out of his life entirely. Warren's only desires were to own a nice piece of the Hardig Empire and to wed Chyna Lock-hart. He did wonder, however, what exactly the Jamesons had done to warrant his father's intense hatred of them.

Warren snapped back to the present when his father barked orders to the driver, but went back to planning his own life and schemes as his father droned on about how unfair life was and how the Jameson's were the root of all evil. This was a familiar story Warren had grown tired of many years ago.

3

"I'm fine, Samson. Yes, I'm sure. I know that painkillers can become habit-forming. I haven't taken them for a week and I've been feeling fine." *Physically,* Chyna thought to herself. Emotionally she was still a wreck. "Thank you for your concern, but I've been through this before."

Chyna blinked fast after the last sentence as tears threatened to spill over. "I just don't want to talk... to anyone. Or think about it right now," she continued. "I know you're only concerned about me. Yes, thank you. Goodbye."

She placed the receiver back in its cradle. She'd called Samson Godfrey, a good friend of hers as well as of her ex-husband, in a moment of panic. He'd tried to pursue more than a friendship after she and Gary had separated, but she'd politely turned him down. Despite that potentially awkward history, Samson still tried to show the numerous ways he cared for her. He always called to check on her, all the while making it quietly clear that he was still interested in her as more than a friend.

Chyna thought she had mastered the ability to put up a strong front, but as soon as she heard his familiar voice on the phone, it brought back the reason for her return home, all that she'd lost and the feelings she had for someone - but that someone wasn't Samson. Something inside her just wanted to blurt out all the messy details of her breakup with Dean, as well as her recent confrontation with Gary back in California. She mentioned her miscarriage to Samson, but immediately regretted telling him. She couldn't involve Samson, or anyone else for that matter, in her affairs. It was a mess of her own making - and all because she'd lied. If she wanted it cleaned up, she'd have to do it herself.

Samson offered to come over and cheer her up, whatever that meant. She declined. She needed time alone and refused to use Samson as the recovery man.

For the last week, she'd done absolutely nothing to exert energy, but still she felt drained. She looked at the bottle sitting on the nightstand. The sleeping pills had been prescribed by her doctor to help her get through the night, but they weren't working, and more often than not they left her feeling woozy. Pulling the information sheet from the white prescription bag, she took a moment to read the side effects and rolled her eyes when she came across the word *dizziness*. She tossed the bottle into the trash, disgusted.

She'd been through a similarly major loss with Gary, too. What made her feel even worse was that she had wanted a child, but after finding out what kind of person he was, she hadn't wanted a child with *him*. She dealt with that one the same way she dealt with this one: by shutting herself away, not telling anyone where she was and doing the best she could to get through her grief. Alone.

Technology was a wonderful convenience as far as Chyna was concerned. She didn't have to talk to anyone to get anything in this day and age. Although she wasn't the greatest cook, even getting food was something she didn't have to leave the house for, thanks to food delivery services. Her only communication and connection to the outside world was the Internet and her television. She could become a total hermit if she wanted.

"What is happening in the world today?" Chyna said out loud as she moved to the television. She didn't watch much television, but sometimes the place was too quiet and she turned it on just to hear talking in the background, like there were other live beings there with her. She pressed the power button and stared blankly as the screen grew with color. She had always watched the news with Mr. and Mrs. Jameson. Her and Mrs. Jameson talked about the issues of the world and every now and then, when he was lucid and present and despite his failing mind, Mr. Jameson would chime in with something so timely that it seemed he wasn't lost at all but still in there somewhere. She and Mrs. Jameson would laugh, and for a few minutes it felt normal.

"No more of that!" Chyna turned up the volume, hating herself for what seemed like constant trips down memory's painful lane. Then she realized that the newscaster was standing outside a building she recognized. Chyna sat down abruptly, her thoughts forgotten and her ears and mind now tuned in to whatever was being said, wishing right then that she'd upgraded to DVR like the Jamesons had so she could run back the story.

Absently Chyna rubbed her chest, realizing it was Dean's building that had been the latest building to be affected by devastating fires: not just affected but deliberately targeted. Whatever her feelings toward him, Chyna was never in doubt that he loved his practice and the people he served. He gave free exams to children no matter what their parents' status; he had even done overseas outreach missions with Doctors Without Borders. Just because he seemed to have rejected her and the fact that it had hurt didn't mean she wanted anything bad to happen to him or his livelihood. This would hurt him, and so soon after his father's death too. She knew first-hand that loss often seemed to come in double, triple, sometimes quadruple waves. As soon as you recovered or dodged one, another came and knocked you down suddenly and unexpectedly.

He had his family, a voice told her, and they would surround one another; and she had no one, another more selfish voice reminded her.

Chyna muted the television and stood. She moved to the kitchen window and stared out. Another downpour loomed. She looked around the space and hated it. It was her childhood home but it had never felt as such. It was a dump. As a child, she had wished to live anywhere but there.

When she'd returned from California, she'd been devastated to see her items boxed up and on the street, right as she'd been served a hasty eviction notice from the landlord. She thought it was Gary's doing at the time, and part of her still believed that it was. She wanted to believe he wouldn't be so callus, but he also knew she had her mother's home still in her possession... Perhaps, she had thought, this was a way for her to move back home and deal with her feelings.

Until she found the motivation to either fix it up for herself or prepare it for sale, this sorry place would have to do in its current state for the foreseeable future. It needed some renovations and a ton of repairs, but Chyna knew she could do it - her and YouTube, of course. If being married to a senator had taught her anything, it was that she didn't fit in as a high-society wife. She didn't like getting dressed up or attending fancy parties, and above all the experience had taught her that no matter how immaculate, large and well-stocked a house was, these things alone couldn't ever make it a home.

This was what she wanted, she told herself: a quiet life, without all the frills and catering. She'd learned the hard way how those things couldn't improve her marriage – as well as the fact that bringing a child into an unhappy marriage wouldn't improve it, either. She'd lost her first baby and everything else too.

She wanted a family so badly. She flushed at the memory of the joy she had felt when she first discovered she was carrying Dean's child. *Her baby.* She liked the sound of those words, but doubted she'd ever be a mother. Her track record was zero-for-two. She knew now for sure that she could do without her husband, without cocktail parties and fundraising events, without smiling falsely at people with deep pockets just to get them to dig deeper into those pockets and hand over the donations. But she didn't know if she could live without being a mother.

Chyna took a seat at the rickety table to rifle through her mail, most of it junk, before she reached the folded newspaper. It contained a recent article she'd written about loss, grief, and coping. Ironically, she'd written it before she lost her baby and prior to Mr. Jameson's death. She had plenty to draw from now, and still felt like she had even more to write about.

She looked away as tears cascaded down her face. Absently, she put aside the other mail that held no interest for her and swiped at a fruit fly that buzzed around her head.

The hole in her heart would heal eventually, and while Dean might always be in the back of her mind, she would have to stop loving him. She doubted that would happen all at once today, but she'd continue trying.

When the doorbell rang, she moved to open it without thinking, glad for any interruption whatsoever. The only person that normally visited her was her mother's old friend the mailman with something to sign. Her brain nearly short-circuited at the sight of Dean standing in the doorway. *Nope: definitely not getting over him today.*

4

Dean had expected that finding Chyna Lockhart would take longer, but all this time he'd never even thought to look in his own backyard.

Although he had his own apartment, days and nights found him at his Mother and Father's house doing what could be best described as puttering around. He certainly wasn't doing much else productive: his thumb was still smarting from his hammer's recent miss. Frustrated, he had spontaneously decided to take a walk around his block, to clear his mind and just force himself to leave well enough alone before he broke something more important than a digit.

Dean's parents lived in a very old neighborhood where more than a handful of the locals had been his patients at some point, so he knew most of the houses and their residents quite well. When he stopped at the one he knew to be Chyna's old house, just one street over, at first he just looked hesitantly from the sidewalk. After moving up the driveway, he found himself peeking furtively into the garage, noticing her compact Honda. *She was still living here?*

Incredulous that she'd been right here all this time, he tried to pace himself for the short walk to her front door and rang the doorbell, holding his breath until she appeared.

"Uh, hi hey, uh, hello Chyna." *For goodness sakes, how many ways could one say hi?* While his eyes took in the sight of her for the first time in forever, he reminded himself that it was really not that long ago that he saw her last. Then again, the funeral hadn't really counted: he hadn't really seen her there, only the back of her hastening to get away from him. His brain felt confused and slightly alarmed on many fronts.

"I've been thinking about – er, wondering how you are doing?"

"Dean, hi... Uh, how did you know I was here?" Chyna relaxed the arm that was obscured by the partially open door: it held a sledgehammer. She ducked down and laid it against the wall before reappearing.

"I didn't, I didn't," Dean replied hurriedly, flustered. "I just, uh - I had no idea you were here, truthfully. I went for a walk." Well, that was partly true. He was searching for phrasing that didn't make it obvious he'd been on the lookout for clues of her whereabouts ever since he'd arrived back in his old neighborhood. The decision to come over today, though, really had just kind of... *happened.*

"I'm doing good, thanks."

Dean was thoughtful. She looked fragile and that shocked him. Chyna Lockhart was tough, strong; and the woman standing before him was weak and weary. The light that usually twinkled in her eye was somewhat dim and if he looked closer he would swear she'd been crying.

"Okay," Dean said. "Well, can I come in?"

He watched to his dismay as she crossed her arms warily over her chest to regard him before answering.

"Now's not really a good time. The place is a mess. I'm - I was doing some teardown work in the back. Maybe some other time."

He saw her shrug and felt annoyed at the casual disregard. It was true, then: they didn't mean anything to one another. He tried to shrug like she did, but it wasn't easy. He sensed from her an urgency to be done with him.

"I'm sorry to hear about your office. Are there any leads on the culprits?"

Dean felt a sliver of hope. "No, uh, uh, it's just - there's been a few in the area. This person is very good: probably a rogue firefighter, someone who knows the business well and can stay one step ahead of his fellow firefighters."

"Really - you think so? That's quite the story."

Dean shrugged. He really didn't know, but he was glad to at least be engaging with her about anything. They could talk about the weather and it would be good with him.

"You look uh, thin," he ventured. "Uh, have you been feeling okay?" Dean felt a genuine concern as he watched her hand move up to her midsection but slowly drift down to her side before she shook her head.

"Doing good. Everything is A-Okay," she replied firmly.

There was an awkward pause. "Mom, uh, went to be with Tisha until the babies come, so I'm fixing up the house and doing some repairs," Dean offered, attempting to restart the conversation.

"Oh, babies? Oh, right."

"Yeah. I thought she would have told you. They're having twins."

"Oh okay. Yes, she did tell me - I remember now." Chyna nodded at him. "That's so great," she whispered.

Dean moved closer. "Chyna, what happened to..."

"Nothing, nothing, Dean, there's nothing," Chyna replied, the pitch of her voice rising thinly. "It's just best, okay... I gotta go." With that, she closed the door in his face.

～

CHYNA LEANED against the closed door, taking deep gulps of needed air. She would have slid down the door to the floor and stayed there, but she couldn't let herself slip away again. She was working on coming up and out of her issues and she knew that she could do it: she just had to be Dean-free. At least that was what she kept telling herself.

Moving down the hall, Chyna remembered with a pang of embarrassment that she hadn't done much of anything with the space as yet. She had planned to gut the room, to knock down one wall, and the rest of the plan... well it was in her brain. She should probably write it out but she wanted to make at least a little practical headway first.

She heard the door click, realizing in frustration that she forgot to lock the front door, and saw Dean re-enter.

"Fortunately for you, Chyna, I'm not the type to be so easily put off – but that was rude," Dean said, pointing over his shoulder to indicate the previously slammed door.

She ignored the comment and turned away. She hoped her silent treatment would get him to leave sooner than if she engaged in the conversational banter he seemed to want.

"Mrs. Jenkins next door said you were making a lot of racket," he continued. "You should be careful. Our houses are about the same, so I know some of the pipes leading from the bathroom are right about here," - he looked up and motioned to a section of the ceiling above their heads. "They lead to the septic pipes," he added.

Chyna nodded, looking at him but trying hard not to notice everything about him, like how tall he was. The ceilings seemed lower and the room smaller with him in it.

Dean lowered his hand. "Where are your safety goggles?" he asked Chyna. "Isn't the dust making your eyes water?"

She shrugged. "I wear my glasses."

"You're lying. Anyway, even if you did wear your glasses, they're not the same. Debris falls, lands on your lashes, and gets into your eyes. It can scratch your retinas," Dean chided. "And you should use gloves. You could get calluses on your hands and that can hurt after a while."

Chyna looked down to the floor but nodded. She knew he was right: she needed goggles, gloves, a tool belt, a drop cloth if she planned to save the rug, and a host of other things if she was going to do this job right.

He was always right, and she hated it.

"Thanks," she said and crossed her arms, preparing for whatever other notes of caution he had.

"I'm serious, Chyna."

"I just said thanks."

"Is this how it's going to be with us?"

"How what is going to be?"

"Man, I don't know," Dean exploded. "This attitude, this silent treatment, your sulking around when you said you were coming back after talking with Gary... You didn't come back and tell me anything at all about why you lied about your divorce. Then at my father's funeral, rather than have a conversation, you just ran. You act like I did something to you - I didn't do anything. I was waiting for you and you never showed."

5

D ean had thought he knew her, could read her like a book; but it was fast becoming evident that he didn't really know her at all. Her anger radiated off her like tongues of fire aimed straight at him. He stood his ground. Not knowing what had happened, having heard no explanation, caused him to conjure way too many thoughts: all bad.

"Did you and Gary reconcile, Chyna?" he persisted.

"You sure do have a lot of questions that seem painfully evident, don't they?" she retorted.

"Uh, they're not 'evident', hence my asking. I'm trying, Chyna."

"You're trying, you're trying – really, you're *trying*? What were you *trying* to do the night I returned to our favorite restaurant to see you and Lisa huddled up in a corner booth, locking lips? Is that how you *try*? If so, then I want no part of it, you got me? And no: for the record, Gary and I are *not* together. We will never be together again. I lied about being divorced, and I shouldn't have, to help his career and campaign. In return, he gave me my freedom when I thought I wanted to be with you, but then you were... busy."

She raised a hand to point at his chest, but instead of going in for the next round, he took her hand gently in his.

"I would never lie to you," he replied softly. "I was drunk and Lisa tried to force herself on me. I asked her to take me home because I was in no shape to drive, and that was it, okay?" He moved closer. "That was it," he repeated. "She and I talked a lot that night. Yes, I chose the wrong person to pour my heart out to, but I'd seen the six o'clock news and heard the report that Chyna Lockhart was with her husband for some kind of fundraiser and, excuse my ignorance, but I thought I'd lost you. I should not have been with her, granted; but I wasn't with her in any way like that. I was in mourning, truly: two losses in the span of a couple of weeks, my dad, and y-o-u."

Chyna shrugged her shoulders. "Well, good for you."

"Why are you crying?" he asked.

"Because it's all I do, okay? That's what I do."

"Let me help you tomorrow with this, uh, renovation, okay?"

"No! No." Chyna couldn't imagine that this was some form of reconciliation. She still kept secrets, even though she shouldn't have. Even these new revelations didn't change her mind. They only made it hurt worse. She was resolute that nothing could change her mind now: it seemed too far gone. It was for the best.

"I'm not giving up, Chyna," Dean said with finality.

She hated to think what that meant. She already knew he was the determined type, but she would have to maintain that what she needed was time and plenty of it. Her wounds were raw. Yes, she'd jumped to some conclusions and made some mistakes, but she couldn't just put them down so easily and jump right back into his arms. She had still more things she kept to herself, and no real way of letting all the truth out. Plus, if Gary, her ex, was so bent on ruining her life, he would probably put Dean on his hit list too, knowing Chyna had loved him for so long. Chyna didn't want to believe her husband could be so vindictive, but her marriage taught her that she didn't truly know anyone. *But you know Dean*, her mind whispered.

She just stared him.

"Get some goggles," he said one last time. "I'm leaving, but I want you know it's only to give you time. Make no mistake: this isn't a concession, it's space."

She couldn't fight. All the energy was zapped from her.

"Get some goggles," he repeated. "Wait, no, I'll bring you some tomorrow morning, so don't demolish anything else before then."

To Chyna's surprise, he leant down and kissed her on the cheek. His perfectly trimmed goatee was just prickly enough to tickle as his breath caressed her cheek. It took all she had not to lean into him, but she managed.

Removing a hand from his pocket, he quickly grabbed her free hand. "And I have some gloves that should fit you. I'll bring those too," he added.

He caressed her hand with his thumb before Chyna withdrew it.

"These hands build up and care for people," Dean whispered. "They don't tear down and destroy things."

"Sometimes things need tearing down and clearing out," she returned evenly.

"You can just paint over it: the old cracks won't show," Dean parried. They spoke in a kind of code, the real meaning of which both parties knew had nothing to do with home improvement. His heart hoped, but he had more convincing to do if Chyna's look of resignation was any indication of what lay ahead. "Never give up on love," he whispered. It was his mother's mantra and it came to him now. Still she said nothing.

He smiled tightly and when he got back to the front of the house and opened the door, he turned to her. "Lock this door, please. I'll be back tomorrow," was all he said before closing it.

Dean walked back to his parents' house, his energy and determination back to full throttle. The loss of his father and his business were two unfortunate things that happened so recently in his life, but he would never lose hope. He just had to have enough of it so some could rub off on Chyna and pray the rest would work itself out.

6

D emolition work was new to Chyna, but the revelations of the day before renewed her motivation to smash things with each swing of the sledgehammer. Her new work gloves that fit her like a second skin - quite nice, she conceded begrudgingly - helped her get a good grip on the hammer, and she felt still more confident with them on: so much so that if she wasn't careful she'd probably knock down the entire house.

Although Chyna wanted to stay mad at Dean, most of the rage had left her when she found a box full of items she desperately needed on her doorstep earlier that day. She had barely sat down to drink her morning coffee when a knock sounded on her door, and it might as well have been Christmas when she'd found not only a new pair of gloves, medium and small with the Home Depot tags still attached, but a tool box with a drill, a tool belt complete with floral-handled hammers in two sizes, and a pair of pink goggles. She wasn't so much a frilly girl type, but she did like to look stylish and competent even if she truly had no idea what she was doing. She hated to think of it, but those small touches had her in Dean's back pocket.

It was her error all along – but it was his error too about her love life. With that annoyance at the front of her mind, Chyna mentally plastered Lisa Stephens's face onto the next wall and swung hard. When the wall finally fell, something inside her eased. She could feel a shift, a release in tension... and a redoubled desire to keep pounding.

She had no idea what she wanted to do with the room. She just knew she wanted to make the place as barren and as empty as she felt. When that was done, she'd create something new from scratch, updating and replacing everything.

Her parents' home was a mess, but when hadn't it been? Her father had been a drunken musician and when he'd left them, her mother had slipped into a devastating depression that she never recovered from. Now that they were both dead, she'd decided she would make this place livable after all these years. It was paid for, after all, and the awful times could be buried at last with the people who had caused them. She didn't have to just exist: now she could live.

Under the agreement, she'd let Gary have everything so she could have her freedom. He could have used infidelity against her. Even though she hadn't been unfaithful in the actual act of cheating, her heart surely had belonged to someone else, and she felt ashamed for that. Emotional infidelity, she'd heard it called. Rather than stay and fight, she'd simply packed a bag; and that was all she had from their shared residence to this day. Gary knew a dozen lawyers in his circle, not to mention the many media folks in his contact list, and that bunch would not only conjure up tales of a torrid love triangle, but because she was the one that had eventually left, Gary would naturally be cast in the role of jilted lover. She wished she could just tell the truth about him, but it would only cause her more pain - and Dean might be dragged into the fire, when he already had a real fire to contend with. She felt something for Dean, certainly. She wished him no pain, far from it; but she didn't know if what she felt was akin to happily ever after or if she were simply delusional.

Chyna took another swing at the lower part of the offending wall before using both her gloved hands to yank at the plaster and the wood behind it as she continued to think. A month ago, Chyna had thought she had one last chance to see all her dreams come true. She swore she had told Dean that it was over between her and Gary, so she wondered how Dean could honestly think she would have reconciled with that man and have continued their farce of a marriage? She and Dean had known each other virtually all their lives. Ultimately, what she didn't like about this whole situation was his questioning of her integrity. Gary had a right to question her about their marriage; Dean didn't, she thought indignantly, because he was the only one she really had told everything to. *Everything except that one thing*, her mind reminded her, and she held her belly as the memories of the pain came rushing back.

When Chyna had left Virginia, her plan had been to make a public announcement in California that she and Gary were divorced and express her regret about lying in order to help him in the polls. She hadn't told anyone about this plan, but before she'd left she had told Dean she was coming back. During the divorce proceedings, more than a year ago now, Gary had promised to give her everything she asked for if she promised to keep all that a secret. All he ever cared about was his image, his prominent position in politics. He wanted to make people think everything was fine in his personal life: to stay married in order to increase his chances for reelection. Chyna had agreed because it was the only bargaining chip she had left to get him to sign the divorce papers.

There had been no sense in trying to explain all that to Dean that night. Had he heard a different story? She wasn't sure. She hadn't appeared on any talk shows after all, so where did he get the idea that she and Gary were still married? The two fo them had argued, he'd yelled, and she'd left not wanting to talk to him until after he'd calmed down, when she returned from California. Dean had angrily forbidden her to go, but Chyna had left anyway to secure her future and to end the charade.

Chyna could deal with having fooled the Californian public, but she couldn't have Dean believing she was an adulterer or that she didn't love him with all her heart. Added to that, if Dean knew the type of man Gary was, she was truly worried about what Dean might do to him.

Her second plan had been to meet with an up-and-coming young news reporter, in hopes that she could talk candidly with someone just a little more likely to tell the truth. Later, though, it transpired that the young reporter in question was also on Gary's payroll. It turned out she couldn't trust anyone to tell the truth and to help her.

Nothing was resolved. Things just hadn't worked out like she'd planned. They never did. *And you gave up everything much too easily,* a voice niggled.

Forgetting that her gloved hand was still covered in plaster dust and tiny white particles, Chyna absentmindedly rubbed her tear-clouded eyes, then winced as particles scratched her face. Dust mixed with her fresh tears so she could barely see anything. She removed the glove quickly and went to the bathroom just down the hall, spluttering and coughing on dust particles. She hadn't used the facemask that Dean had also thoughtfully bought for her because she it made her claustrophobic, but as she now saw, she should have. Trying to wash her hands and remove the stubborn dust while coughing, she was suddenly quiet, listening intently to what sounded like gears grinding in the pipes overhead. She quickly turned off the water and the noise grew louder. As she stepped out into the hall, the ceiling burst with a crash, spilling water everywhere.

Horrified, Chyna ran to get a bucket, trying to contain the water; but within moments it was full to the brim, and she didn't have any other vessels. As she started trying to lug the bucket to the door, she stumbled over the ladder and tripped, right as the toilet crashed through the ceiling, narrowly missing her head but glancing off her shoulder and landing with full force on her leg. She tried to scream, knowing instantly that it was broken, but managed only a rush of breath whooshing from her lungs. Unbidden, she thought of Dean: a big *I told you so* was coming, she thought dizzily, yet above all she hoped he found her alive. Then another crash: another section of wall broke loose, a blinding pain in her temple, and all went dark.

7

D ean hadn't made much progress on his parents' house. He puttered around the house hoping for some odd reason that Chyna might call him, or that she might just need help with her own house project. He hoped his tool-kit olive branch was one small step toward repairing their relationship as well as her house - that is, if they still had one left to repair.

Two days later, he still couldn't believe that she'd not only returned to Virginia but that she was now sans husband. He finally got it: she'd been *looking* for him the night she came back to town, and he'd obviously messed everything up. Clearly feeling sorry for himself about his deceased father, he'd been in the process of pouring his soul out to the wrong woman that night: a point made all too clear by the fact that he hadn't even seen Lisa Stephens again since that night. Although she did some financial work for his parents and could easily have paid her condolences in person, she'd simply sent a glib group text with a less-than-heartfelt "sorry for your loss."

What a joke.

Dean looked out the window, wishing he could look into

the future just as easily. He scrolled idly through the messages on his phone. He wasn't in a talking mood, and he had a decision to make about his office. His lawyer had been calling every day to ask him if he wanted to rebuild, yet he was hesitant: the police seemed as if they were still investigating whatever substance it was that had been used to burn the place down to begin with. Sadly, he felt certain they weren't going to be successful in finding the culprits. Dean didn't know what he should feel, but ambivalence was what he felt about it all at present.

Other days, he felt freed by the material loss: liberated from obligation. Another doctor had taken the majority of his patients – and he'd had fewer and fewer the last few years, owing to his largely aging clientele. The work hadn't been making him any happier when he'd had it, anyway.

Dean looked at the pile of mail that had burgeoned in his mother's absence. Bills needed to be paid, records filed, and issues regarding his father's estate secured. Things that should've been taken care of when the Alzheimer's had first been diagnosed had just been put on hold. Right up until his father's death, Dean had automatically paid the bills each month, ensured any checks were deposited from his estate, his account consolidated to his mother, all the while hoping beyond hope that Joe Jameson, Sr. would miraculously heal. He hadn't.

When the doorbell rang, Dean stacked the mail neatly and put it aside, somewhat glad for an interruption that would keep him from confronting the fresh pain. He hoped it was Chyna, even though he knew it likely wouldn't be. She was just too stubborn to come knocking at his door.

Opening the door, he was surprised to see Lisa Stephens.

"Hi, sweetheart," she said cheerily and walked through the door without Dean's invitation. He stepped back mutely and let her proceed. He wasn't in the mood for her, although he noted that he'd just thought about her moments ago and now here she was. He had to hand it to her: she was better than Google at profiling him.

"Hi," Dean said, shutting the door. He followed her into the kitchen. She always came over like she owned the place. With his mother present he hadn't thought much about it; now it was just weird.

"Oh, honey," Lisa pouted. "I hate to see you this way."

Dean sat down at the kitchen table and wondered if he looked that bad. He was actually fine. Chyna was just down the street, so they were at least able to talk. Despite wanting to return to his own reverie about Chyna, he forced himself to respond aloud.

"I'm doing all right," he said.

"No, you're not!" Lisa insisted. She placed her hands on her hips and regarded him. Lisa never really asked you questions, she just seem to babble endlessly and her voice got on his nerves at times. This was definitely one of those times.

After poking through all the cabinets, she moved to the refrigerator and took out two eggs. "I'll make you something to eat," she said decisively, as she cracked them over a bowl and began to beat them vigorously. Over a heated skillet she dropped them into the pan and swirled them around.

"I'm really not hungry," he said, but she placed the plate before him anyway. The eggs weren't cooked through and they looked unappetizing. He decided that now was the moment to talk. "Listen, Lisa, you know that night when I was drunk?"

Taking a seat across from him, she produced a packaged salad she'd brought with her and drenched it with a runny red vinaigrette before opening a plastic utensil kit. She began to attack her food, shoving the leafy greens into her mouth. "Oh honey, you were a mess," she mumbled with her mouth full. "I'm so glad you have moved on. Chyna Williams does not deserve you. Just be glad she went back to her husband so you can move on with your life."

"Who said she went back to her husband?"

"Well, Senator Williams talks about her all the time and refers to her as his wife, and I never heard her deny it," Lisa replied innocently. "I'm so sorry to tell you this, I know it's painful..."

"Just because he refers to her as his wife doesn't mean she is," Dean retorted.

"Well then why wouldn't she go on television and set the record straight, honey? *I'm* certainly not about to let *my*self be called some man's woman when I'm not. Silence is complicity, right? I mean, that's what people say, you know. You're just hopelessly in love. I know. I am too," she said coyly, and looked away from him.

"Really?" Dean stood. That was news to him. He placed a napkin over the soggy eggs: he didn't see her put any salt or pepper in them, and half the mess was still stuck to the pan. "You sweet on someone? That's great, do I know him?"

"Oh, nah, I don't think so," Lisa said, as she turned around to look at him. She smiled sadly and stood to move closer to him. She wrapped her arms around his waist and laid her head on Dean's chest.

Dean stiffened and gently pushed her away.

"Oh honey, I know more than you realize," Lisa murmured. "It is so very hard loving someone who doesn't really know you exist. I've done that a long time, but one day this person is going to truly see me, as soon as he gets... other people out of his handsome head." She looked into his eyes, but Dean looked away.

He hated her double speak and it sent his mind to paying more attention, scrutinizing her a little bit more closely.

"Listen, I've got to get back to the office. I love..." - she hesitated - "what you've done to the place so far. And Dean, I'd love it if you'd give me a call sometime, when you're ready, okay? I can, uh, help you go through your dad's things. If you need help." Lisa backed toward the door.

Dean nodded. "Oh hey, before you go, Mom said you had some paperwork to be signed. Can I take a look and sign it for her?"

"Oh no, you shouldn't worry with that, I've got everything all taken care of," said Lisa breezily. "I'll get copies for you though, if you want, and send them to you via email - is that okay?"

Dean nodded but felt uneasy. He'd check the copies and make sure everything was in order.

He was startled and caught off guard when Lisa turned back to face him and leaned in, but he managed to rear back just in time: she was headed straight for his mouth.

"Sometimes you have to look closely, Dean, to see what's right in front of you. Remember the people who do all they can for you and your family," she breathed. "I'm sorry Chyna's gone, but facing the truth will make things so much better."

Lisa smiled up at him before she turned. Dean held the door for her. "Oh," she said, turning to face him again with a hungry look, "and sometimes *friends*, Dean, can be... a great comfort to each other when they're feeling low."

With that Lisa turned and left quickly.

Dean was restless and on edge as soon as Lisa left his house, so much so that he decided to give Chyna a visit. He didn't walk quickly, but he did feel a small sense of urgency to see her. He couldn't place it, but Lisa's visit had put a weird feeling over him. While it was amply clear that she liked him a lot, he also couldn't help but guess she was talking about him with all the 'he doesn't know I exist' and 'friends could be of great comfort to one another' hints. He hadn't thought her to be much of a threat, but now he knew better. Chyna saw her as a threat and that mattered to him: he wanted to assure Chyna that there was nothing, yet what he had just witnessed from Lisa Stephens had seemed very much like a come on. He wanted to make sure and reassure Chyna one more time that whatever Lisa's designs may be, he certainly didn't share them.

He didn't want to pressure Chyna but he was going to stay on her radar for as long as it took, and if that meant welfare checks while she did whatever it was she wanted to her home, he would make that happen just to make sure she was all right. He'd gladly rebuild her as many homes as she wanted if she would just let him know why his ultimate goal for them to be together was so difficult to realize.

He hadn't ever really pursued anyone before. As much as he hated to think of it, his brother's comment might have been somewhat true: things just sort of came naturally to him. He didn't normally work at his relationships: they just sort of worked by themselves. At some point, he and Chyna had worked... and then they didn't. Come to think of it, this had been the one instance he could recall in his adult life when a relationship wasn't going his way. He realized right then that he would not only have to start paying more attention to what was going on, but also put in work to orchestrate a few things and make stuff happen. Instead of this constant parrying, they needed to sit down like two civil adults, air it all out and get to the truth, whatever that was.

Standing at her front door, Dean took a deep breath and knocked. When there was no answer, he reached for the knob and turned. It opened. He made a mental note to chastise her about leaving her door unlocked, yet again. While this was a relatively safe neighborhood, break-ins and home invasions happened all the time.

Once inside, Dean called her name and listened for a response or footsteps on the upper level. He didn't hear anything except the faint trickle of water in the distance.

Unnerved, Dean moved down the hall toward the running

water sound. When he reached the doorway, he felt as well as saw a flood of water rush over his feet and seep up his pant leg. The beat of his heart slowed in dismay, and he quickly sent up a prayer that Chyna wasn't anywhere near this disastrous scene.

The place looked as if a hurricane had struck. Wood chips floated in the soupy water like globs of giant oatmeal. Dust danced through the air like smoke. Dean yelled for Chyna and started to leave the room in search of her, when his eye caught the brown skin of Chyna's fingertips, covered in dust, poking up through the rubble, gripping a piece of wall that rested on top of her body.

It seemed to take him days to wade through the water that slowed each footstep. Dean took larger steps, hiking his feet up higher as if he sloshed through two feet of snow, and finally he was there.

"Oh God. Chyna," he whispered.

Rubble and large wall pieces covered her. He felt the pulse of her exposed wrist. TO his relief, it surged lightly under the pad of his middle finger.

Desperately, Dean began to move pieces of drywall, chunks of concrete and soaked wood off of her. He looked over at the porcelain toilet lying on its side just inches from her and thanked God that it hadn't crushed her. He knew that if it had, she wouldn't have survived.

When he finally uncovered her face, she looked as if she'd dropped a bag of flour. She was ghostly white. Thick white flakes made their way onto her long lashes and sprinkled her eyebrows. Now that he knew she was alive, Dean grew angry. He'd told her to be careful. Her lips were dry and cracked, or perhaps it was the film of dust from the debris.

"Chyna, answer me - look at me," he pleaded, and with shaky hands smoothed the chips from her eyes and gently patted her face. It was all he could do not to shake her, to yell at her for being so careless, so stupid, and for not knowing what on earth she was doing. After an eternity, her eyes flickered open. They were red-rimmed and irritated from the dust.

"Dean?" she whispered.

"Yes, I'm here," he answered softly. "I need you to tell me if you can move."

Quickly, Dean assessed the rest of her still-buried lower half and realized he couldn't just pull her out for fear she'd broken something. Still, he kicked the large pieces off her and bent to remove the smaller ones. With every piece he lifted or pulled, Dean felt a zillion nicks and scrapes of the raggedy-edged scraps bite into the flesh of his own gloveless hands.

"Chyna, can you move your legs at all?" He instantly felt stupid for asking such a question when it was perfectly evident that a large piece of wall he wouldn't be able to move by himself lay across her whole lower body.

"It hurts."

"Where? Baby, tell me where it hurts."

"My shoulder," she whispered. "And my leg."

Her face distorted in pain when she twisted her body to move her leg. She bit her lower lip and stilled as the pain increased.

"Don't try to move it," Dean said, alarmed. "Just one of your legs or both of them?"

"My right one," she gasped.

Dean reached for his cell phone and dialed 911. After telling them the location of the house he hung up. He pushed away as much of the rubble as he could, cursing his stupid pride for not coming to see her sooner. It was tempting to blame Lisa and her untimely visit that once again seemed to deter him from Chyna.

Lifting the last piece, Dean ensured that Chyna's head was supported and that she didn't drown in the water covering the floor. Silently he cursed her for not being more careful.

Dean paused when he heard a man's voice call for Chyna from the front of the house.

"Chyna?" the voice called again. Dean heard the footsteps quicken down the hall until they encountered the water and the stomps turned into a sloshing sound.

When Samson Godfrey stood at the door, Dean looked up, only slightly irritated, before returning his attention to Chyna.

"What the hell are you doing?" Samson exclaimed as he moved inside the door. "Haven't you caused enough trouble already?" He bent down by Chyna and tried to shove Dean away. "Chyna, dear heart, I'll call the ambulance."

"I already called them," Dean said heatedly. Samson Godfrey's proprietary manner where Chyna was concerned only reaffirmed Dean's dislike of him.

"What the hell happened?" Samson demanded, shooting an evil look in Dean's direction.

"It's not his fault, Samson," Chyna whispered in Dean's defense. She had enough coherence to sense the tension between Dean and Samson.

They both looked at Chyna when she spoke. Dean kept his eyes low and silently sized up Samson Godfrey. He wondered if he had any actual muscle under the peacock display of expensive attire and a cologne that made itself known in a room before he did. Strong or not, Dean dismissed Samson as a complete fool when he stood, reached under Chyna's arms, and attempted to pull her from the rubble.

Dean was on his feet immediately. With a shove against Samson's chest, he pushed the ignorant man away from her. "Are you crazy? Don't pull her! Her leg is stuck and she said it hurts."

Samson looked down, belatedly noticing the thickness of the wall that covered most of her lower body. "What would you have me do? Sit here and twiddle my thumbs?" he said heatedly.

"I *said* don't pull on her and I meant it. Her legs are stuck under a truckload of rubble and if you'd taken a moment to observe, you'd have seen that." Dean looked down at Chyna and changed his tone. "Chyna, sweetheart, I need you to stay awake, okay?" he said gently. "I need you to look at me. You're going to be okay, I promise."

"She already knows your promises don't mean anything," Samson sneered.

Dean looked away, chagrined. Chyna had probably shared a lot with this man when Dean himself was unavailable. Granted, whatever Samson thought of him was probably true, but he was on a mission to change all that.

Taking her cold hand in his, Dean pretended Samson wasn't in the room at all. He focused on trying to think of a way to get Chyna out of the mess he, sadly, had helped to create. Where the hell was the ambulance?

He stood abruptly. "Chyna, stay awake! I know you're tired." And to Samson, "Keep her head supported. I'll be right back."

"Where in God's name are you going?" Samson's voice rose an octave, but Dean was already at the door.

In a matter of seconds, Dean rushed from Chyna's house down the street to his own. On the way back, he heard the sirens of the approaching ambulance. Again he waded through the shallow lake of Chyna's back room, taking a moment to pull the cord from the chainsaw he had grabbed.

"Put the goggles over her eyes and cover yours with your hand," he ordered Samson as he reentered. To be honest, he didn't care what the man did to protect himself so long as he listened to the instructions Dean gave for protecting Chyna.

"What?" Samson yelled over the roaring sound of the power machine - but Chyna had understood and reached onto her head to pull down the goggles for herself. Finally cottoning on, Samson shielded his own eyes just in time as the chainsaw's quick blade sliced through the fallen wood. It sent chips flying everywhere and stirred up yet more dust, but it was the only solution. Eventually, Dean was able to carve the large wall into smaller and more manageable pieces, which he tossed aside one by one until he could see Chyna's legs. They were twisted painfully inward, intertwined with one of the ladder's rungs.

When the ambulance finally arrived, Dean had set her leg as best he could. In doing so, he'd felt each of her painful whimpers pierce his heart. He didn't say anything when Samson helped the paramedics carefully lift her and secure her to the gurney. And he could only look on as Samson got into the ambulance with her before it sped away.

Running back to his own home, Dean hurriedly locked the doors. He put the chainsaw back into the garage, grabbed the keys to his car, and headed for the hospital.

8

C hyna blinked her eyes rapidly and tried to bring herself into a sitting position. She noticed her leg first. The white cast started just below her knee and stopped to allow her toes to peek out. Her shoulder ached but seemed okay overall, as she gingerly lifted it to test it out. Her wrist was wrapped in a brown bandage. She hadn't realized she'd hurt it at all. "At least it's not broken too," she said aloud, flexing it tentatively.

What a fool she had been: first in her relationship errors with Dean and now in her house. Both separate incidents, and both completely ramshackle and in desperate need of repair. She looked up at the ceiling with its brown-stained boards. The hospital room had ugly curtains that made it a contender for the most unfeeling, sterile institution she had ever seen. Being there brought back memories of her last visit.

"Hey, you're awake," Dean said, as he entered the room cheerily.

She gave a sigh. Had it not been for him, she knew she'd probably still be lying under the weight of her second floor.

She looked toward the window, away from him. She needed

to get out of there. Before she could do that, however, she'd need to find a way to get Dean to leave. It would prove difficult, but then again everything concerning Dean Jameson usually was.

"How are you, Chyna?" Dean moved closer to the bed and placed his hands on the bed's safety railing.

"Fine," she replied.

"Don't lie," Dean retorted.

"If you know so much about my state already, why bother to ask?" Chyna returned, turning her head angrily to face him. She hated his deep-set eyes and the way his brows knitted together, showing her his sincere concern.

"'Cause for once, I'd like you to tell me the truth about your feelings."

Dean took a breath and changed subjects. "I brought you a gift." He reached for the fern on her bedside tray table and held it up briefly for her to see.

"Thank you," she whispered. She did like plants and the fact that he remembered that counted in his favor.

"Chyna, dear heart, are you decent?" a voice called from the door.

Chyna pounded her head on the pillow in utter frustration. Her plan to exit the facility had just gained one more deterrent. She could tack on another whole two hours.

"Yes, Samson, I'm decent," she said exasperatedly.

Samson waltzed into the room as if he owned the place and set down two vases. One was filled with red roses and the other with yellow ones.

"How are you, dear?" He leaned down to touch his lips to her cheek, then noticed Dean standing at the other side of her bed. His eyes narrowed.

"I'm all right, Samson," Chyna replied. "Thank you for the flowers, they're beautiful." The flowers were beautiful, but she knew he only brought two bouquets so he wouldn't be outdone by anyone, especially Dean.

"Listen," Samson said, "I just came by to say hey. See how you were doing this morning. I'll pick you up whenever Charlie says you can be released. Just page me. I imagine you'll be here a few more days for observation?" he questioned.

Chyna started to shake her head in protest. *Not if I can help it.* Instead, she kept thoughts of her plot to herself and merely nodded.

"By the way, you owe me two hundred dollars for the new shoes I ruined," he chuckled. Although Samson was clearly joking about the repayment, Chyna knew the price of the plush leather moccasins was probably accurate. She noted with distaste how Samson's materialistic tendencies reminded her of her ex-husband - and any reminder of him was never a good thing. She smiled politely to acknowledge his poor attempt at humor. He was a good friend and she was thankful for his attention, but never in the years she had known him would she have called him funny.

"I'd say you were ripped off," Dean muttered.

"What?" Samson looked up at Dean with something akin to a snarl, and Chyna might have laughed at the expression if she weren't experiencing her own bout of misery.

"Two hundred dollars at Wal-Mart? I'd say you were ripped off," Dean repeated coolly.

Samson looked back at Chyna, ignoring Dean. "Okay, well, sis has my pager number in case you need it. I'll see ya." Samson leaned in again, touching his lips to Chyna's forehead proprietorially before he left.

"Now that he's gone, what do you want to do? Watch *The Young and the Restless*? Want me to get you some lunch?"

"Dean?" Chyna asked skeptically. The day Dean Jameson watched a soap opera would be the day hell had frozen over. "Please tell me you're not into soap operas nowadays."

"Not really. Never been a television person, you know that; but what else is there to do in here? I could get you a Kindle, upload some of your favorite books? It's either that or talk shows," he added with a shrug.

Chyna nodded, not sure what she wanted except to be left alone. She knew attempts to get him to leave wouldn't work and in fact she was secretly somewhat glad for the company. After a beat, she relented. "If you're going to stay for a bit, can you just chill, okay?"

"My pleasure." To her surprise, he pulled up a chair close to her bed and smiled at her.

Only moments later, her fellow nurse, friend and Samson's sister, Charlize Godfrey, waltzed in with her hands on her hips ready to read Chyna the riot act. Chyna braced herself for impact. She huffed a loud audible breath before shaking her head and opening up the curtains.

"What on earth have you done this time, Chyna Lockhart?" Charlize began impatiently. "I can't leave you for five minutes and you're back in here again!"

"Um, hi Charlie," Chyna greeted her. "Uh... you remember Dean?"

"Hi Charlie? *Hi Charlie?* Are you being serious? And of *course* I remember Dean." Charlie shot him a withering glance. "Dean, wish I had nicer words for you, but sorry, I don't."

"I won't take it personally," Dean replied.

Chyna looked at the two, thankful they didn't have more mean-spirited barbs to exchange right now. Samson and Charlie both knew about her checkered history with Dean, and while none of them cared for each other, they had at least been as cordial as could be expected. Now she knew she had just as much culpability in the entire mess as he did, yet she was the one that withheld still more information. Truly, the knowledge of what she did ate away at her moment by moment, especially fearing that at any moment either Charlie or Samson might spill the beans.

"Charlie, just not today, okay?" Chyna said, defeated. "I know I messed up, I'm a klutz. Didn't Samson tell you what happened?"

"No! He just said you'd hurt your leg."

"Well, yeah... that's all, really" Chyna said, wishing that were the extent of the damage she'd done not only to herself, but to her house as well. She dreaded to think what awaited her when she returned home. For now, she hoped her friend wouldn't get any more upset and mad but would instead agree to help her out of the mess.

"Listen, Charlie, my friend. I need help, please. I can't stay here."" Chyna said sweetly. If she could just drag her leg to the floor without banging it, she'd show Charlie she could walk or even hop her way out of there. How difficult could it be?

"Okay," Charlie said dubiously. "But tell me, if you go home, who's going to help you? How will you get around?"

"Well, I could stay with you," Chyna pointed out.

"You could, Chyna, you could, and I would help you if I could, you know that - but guess what? Samson is staying with me, sleeping on my couch, because he's too cheap to pay for a hotel. I live in a one-bedroom apartment, remember? Where is the room in that for you, Chyna?"

Chyna chewed her lip. "My house is such a mess. Truth is, I sent the place crashing about my head. I don't even remember what it looks like. I could manage there, probably. But there's one thing I'm certain of." She looked at her friend again, laughing falsely to keep from crying. "Charlie, I'll die if I have to stay here one more day, one more hour, one more minute! I can't stay in this hospital - I can't!"

Suddenly they heard another voice chip in.

"You can stay at my place, Chyna. I'll take care of you."

9

B oth Chyna and Charlize looked to the door when Dean spoke up. Chyna's nightmare worsened. Despite telling him he could stay if he'd just be quiet and chill, her plea to Charlie had likely come across so desperate that it had spurred Dean to offer to help however he could. More concerning, however, was just how serious he looked about his proposal - and more concerning even that that was the fact she had to bite her tongue before a resounding *yes* leapt off it. She chalked up her almost-response to a moment of insanity and a desire to leave the hospital however she could - but she felt sure Dean's offer was a very bad idea.

Her fight was ebbing fast as Charlie shoved Chyna's good leg back under the covers, her anger at Dean's offer causing Charlie to tuck the covers around Chyna as if that barrier might protect her from him. "You should leave this hospital right now," she snapped at Dean. "And she's not going anywhere with the likes of you!"

Before Charlie could lash out at Dean again, Chyna placed a hand on her stomach. "Dean, I could use something to eat after all... how about – uh - ?" She had to get one of them to leave or they might physically battle it out before her very eyes.

"Lunch will be here in a few minutes," Charlie responded. "And I'll see to it that you have something healthy, not some high-cholesterol, deep-fried, greasy fritter. She doesn't need that junk," Charlize said, looking up at Dean. She wrote furiously on the nurse's tablet, then noisily dragged a slim cart on wheels closer to Chyna's bedside. Once there, Charlie grabbed a thermometer from a plastic sheath and put it into Chyna's mouth. "Why in God's name would she stay with you of all the people in the world? What are you doing here anyway?" she added. "Haven't you done enough?"

"You know, Charlize, this is an A" — Dean pointed to Chyna —"and B" - he hooked two fingers at his own chest – "type of conversation. You can see yourself out. This doesn't concern you."

"The hell it doesn't concern me," Charlie exclaimed. "She won't tell you about your oolfish self, but I can."

When the thermometer's beep thankfully sounded, Chyna took a deep breath. "Please just stop it. You guys, just quit it."

"Don't tell me you'd consider staying at that house, Chyna?" Charlize asked incredulously. "The proximity of where you're living even now is much too close."

"Did I say I would stay there, Charlie?"

"No, but I can tell when a thought of pure nonsense crosses your mind. I can just see the wheels turning in that thick head of yours."

"When can I be released?" Chyna asked tiredly. "I just want to get out of here."

Staying at the Jameson home had crossed her mind before, but the realization that Dean might actually be living there and not just dropping in to do some minor renovations made the offer considerably less appealing. Chyna shook her head, erasing the very idea from her mind. She would manage at her own house. Yes it was a disaster, but so what? She'd stay in the front room while repairs were made. She'd adjust, somehow.

"When can you be released? When can you be released?" Charlize's voice raised to a high pitch with each repeat of the question. "You're asking me when you can be released? You have a temperature, your blood pressure is up, and you're lying on your back with a sprained wrist and a broken leg." Charlize took a deep audible breath and shook her head in disbelief. "I'll see what the doctor can do. I'm not promising anything, and if you come up with another place to stay with someone who'll help you then I'm all for it, but I will not let you stay with him!"

"Please, Charlie, just try," Chyna pleaded. "Just tell them that you'll visit me, like you did when I..." Chyna cursed under her breath and placed her tongue between her teeth. She looked sideways at Dean, who stood casually as if he didn't plan on leaving any time soon.

"You can come see me, check on me, right?" Chyna finished hurriedly. She'd almost let it slip that her friend had come by to check on her during the week following her miscarriage. If Dean found out, she'd never recover. She couldn't bear it.

Chyna watched as her friend rolled her eyes but otherwise didn't say anything. She averted her eyes from Dean's questioning gaze as Charlie hung the chart in its place at the end of the bed and moved to the door. Chyna took a deep breath after her friend left. She settled her back against the pillow and pinched her eyes with her good hand.

"An inspector will be by to check out your place, Chyna," Dean said. "Half the roof is caved in and most of it's flooded. It will likely be condemned: it's barely livable. I'm sorry, Chyna - I'm sorry that I yelled and that we argued. I never meant..."

Dean stopped talking when Chyna waved her hand to request that he be quiet.

"Inspectors are going to come look at my home?" she asked. Dean nodded, and although she didn't want to hear any more, he cleared his throat. "I could get Bubba to do it. He can write it up, make a report to them if you'd like."

She nodded.

"Chyna," Dean whispered.

"What?! What? *What*?" she yelled suddenly.

Placing his hands on the railing of the hospital bed, he scrutinized Chyna. "Why's it so hard for you to ask for help? We're practically family."

She watched Dean take a deep breath and scratch his head, knowing he didn't understand her reasoning for being so distant: to act like she hadn't at some point been an honorary member of his family. She hated acting like a stranger, but at the moment that was completely how she felt.

But they weren't family. They wouldn't ever be family. She looked at him accusingly. "Maybe I don't want your help. Maybe I don't want you to care, or help me, or do anything other than be quiet."

Chyna crossed her arms one over the other, forgetting momentarily about her bandaged wrist, and then unfolded them with a wince.

"Well, I will help you. I *do* care, and I'll do anything - give you anything you need," Dean said firmly. He brushed the hair away from her brow, and Chyna smacked his hand away in annoyance.

"If you're going to stay, at least be *quiet*, please," she said as she turned to look at him. Her eyes drooped with fatigue. Dean nodded and without further comment, he sat down in the metal chair next to her bed. He rested his ankle on the edge of his knee as he crossed his legs and reached to grab a raggedy magazine from the tray table.

"I'll take care of everything," he whispered, just loudly enough for Chyna to hear. "I'll take care of you."

She didn't want to hear him, but she did - and Dean's last statements were exactly what she was truly afraid of.

CHYNA MANAGED to doze off several times throughout the rest of the day and every time she woke, the sameness of the walls and décor greeted her. She felt only moderately comforted by the fact that Dean was still there. When she looked over at him groggily, he stood and placed a drink on her table. "I found you an ice-cold Cola. Don't tell Nurse Ratchet on me, okay?"

Chyna nodded, wiped her eyes and smiled. She didn't drink soda often, but every now and then she did crave it. Another testament to his thoughtfulness and the fact that he knew her all too well only made her more annoyed. Try as she might, she couldn't hate him at all. He was certainly a very good man.

She concentrated on his long fingers as he wiped the top of the can with a tissue and then opened it for her. She took a sip and it was nice and cold, just as he'd said. She smiled despite herself. "Thank you."

"Also, uh, Mom called earlier and she said to call her when you woke up again."

Before Chyna could protest, she heard the faint ringing of the dial tone as Dean handed the phone to her.

"Hello?" Chyna sat up and Dean depressed the button at the side of the bed to bring her head up. She nodded at him.

"Well hi Baby, how's it goin' sweetie ? Dean ain't bullying you is he?"

"It's going, Ms. Alfreah." Chyna smiled at the kind familiar voice. "How are you?"

"You tell me now and then I'm-a straighten him out, he know better. He just like you so much is all. He don't mean no harm."

"Okay, yes." What could she say to that? If Ms. Alfreah only knew that this was so much bigger than the after-school bullies and kid crushes of her childhood. It was way deeper adult problems: lack of communication, trust complexes... Their issues seemed too numerous to name, not to mention the secret she still harbored.

"You don't think I don't know a thing or two about this love sickness you both got, now do you?"

"No Ma'am, I'm sorry, it just seems uh, hopeless, that's all. I..."

"I know it always seems hopeless, sweetie, until it's done. So, I'm not gonna hold you long but you know, I am having a good time down here in Macon with Ms. Tish. I wish you could come and spend time with us. In fact, when you're able to get around better, I want you come down and spend a few days with us here, okay?"

Chyna nodded. "Yes, ma'am," she said, feeling uncertain. Up until then, she'd thought that seeing as she'd been Joe Jameson's caretaker, his death must mean the end of Chyna's time with the family, too. Death usually defined the end of her season with every other family for whole she'd worked as caretaker. Their loved one was dead, thus there was no further call for her role. It was over. There again, she often assumed too much and gave up too easily.

Fine, she admitted to herself: the Jamesons were different. Yes, she was an actual friend of all the siblings, but she'd found with other families that her presence was simply a reminder of the loss they'd suffered. No one seemed to know exactly how to involve her in their lives after losing the person she'd been tasked to care for in life. It was a wonder she could ever get back into caregiving with this constant identity crisis every time a client passed away.

"Deanie told me you done hurt yourself in your momma's house?"

Chyna cringed with the thought. It was *her* house: her mother and father were long dead. Sadly, despite her efforts, it may never be "her house" even though she was trying so hard to put her own stamp on it by renovating it. Oh, she'd put a stamp on it all right: a big orange sign with the words *Hazard, Do Not Enter* would likely greet her whenever she could get back to it.

Chyna took a deep breath and swallowed hard, trying to listen to what Ms. Alfreah said. She fiddled with the fringe of her blanket and stared at the stark walls, with their awful hospital border wallpaper. She loved the Jameson house, despite its age and the inevitable wear and tear from four children growing up here. It was just a great little place. She wondered how Ms. Alfreah managed it: even with everyone gone, the place seemed bigger, well-lit, lived-in and cozy at the same time. They kept it up, which was something Chyna's own parents hadn't done at all. Whatever Dean was doing to it now, she was certain he was making it that much better as well, enhancing everything and making it shine. She would have loved to see it. She always wanted to be there, though she never told a soul how strongly she felt about it, not even her closest friends: Tish, the baby of the Jameson family, and her older sister, Jina.

"So, honey, I'll be here in Macon for at least a year, as I get my grandbabies all settled - so I want you to stay there at the house for as long as you want, you hear me now? Dean is doing some work over there, but I know he can do most of it during the day and get out of your hair in the evening. Please do this for me so you'll be safe, sweetie - I don't want to hear nothing about your moving somewhere else, okay? Our home is your home."

"Yes, Ma'am." The shakiness in her voice could not be helped. Truth be told, she wanted to cry. She managed not to: fortunately, as it turned out, for although Dean had left the room a while ago, he'd just reappeared. She didn't have to tell Dean what his mom had said.

"Let me talk to Dean," Alfreah demanded. *So much for not telling him*, Chyna thought despondently.

"One more thing baby. I can't ever repay you for taking care of my Joe, sweetie: you made the last eighteen months of his life and his final days so wonderful. More than that, you gave me and my whole family a peace of mind. Now, I done looked high and low for peace of mind, and I haven't found any on the shelves, know what that means?" The woman chuckled.

"No Ma'am," Chyna choked out.

"That means it can't be bought. Let us - let Dean and everyone else take care of you for a change."

"It was my pleasure to care of Mr. Joe," Chyna stammered. "I-I miss him... I'm sorry, I know you do too."

"I know, and you have a heart for caregiving," Alfreah said softly. "Not everyone has that, to do it so well, and now it's our pleasure to take care of you, okay? Now, Dean is pretty patient and he's my sweet child, him and Tish - don't tell Jina and Jojo I said that. But my Dean also loves you, I just knows it, and because of that, he'll make the effort to see about you, okay?"

Chyna felt bad. She felt so hesitant about staying at the Jameson house, yet another part of her needed to know: how long would she have to wear this stupid cast? Other than a hotel or an extended-stay place, this was really her only option until that came off. Not to mention, Ms. Alfreah was probably the nicest person in the world and meant so much to Chyna that she'd do whatever the woman asked her.

But you need to get out with your heart intact. This is not a good idea. Chyna listened to the woman on the phone even as her inner monologue increased in volume. Finally they said their goodbyes and she handed the phone back to Dean so he and his mother could continue their conversation. She wished he wouldn't be so open about everything, from staying in the room with her every moment to talking openly to his mother as if he had nothing to hide.

He doesn't have anything to hide. You do.

Dean looked at her and smiled. She could see the old determination written all over his face, hopeful that the deal was done and everything was just peachy. When he told his mother goodbye, he put the phone back in his pocket and smiled down at her as if all was right with his world. He had her cornered.

"Ready to go home?" he said.

She hesitated and swallowed, looking at him. For the first time, she registered a few scratches under and above his eyes, realizing those nicks and cuts hadn't been there the day before her accident. "Dean, this is you helping me as a friend, right? I can't do relationship stuff with you, okay? Not now..." - *not then, maybe never*, she thought to herself but didn't voice anything of the sort.

"I'm here for you no matter what," he said stolidly. "We'll work out our issues and in time, we can see where we messed up - where I messed up and missed the mark. Meantime, my only goal is for you to get better and be at peace, and whatever happens will just have to play out. I have relationship goals, as the young people say, but I'll just have to work on gradually wooing you to my line of thinking."

Whatever she'd been looking for in a response, that wasn't it. It was clear and it was direct, but it was also not what she wanted to hear. He was now the one with too many words and overly sappy expressions. Perhaps the death of his father had made him more conscious of everything. She knew that death and loss - the loss of his business, to boot - did that to many people, but now wasn't the time for Dean to lay on the added caring. It just might drive her nuts.

With nothing resolved, she nodded to his previous question. "I'm as ready as I'll ever be. Thank you."

"You're welcome, sweetie," Dean said, then helped her off the side of the bed. When she tried to use her one good hand, he was in her personal space and all but lifted her to place her into the black leather-backed wheelchair that seemed to magically appear. She didn't want to admit how grateful she was to be leaving.

Charlize stood at the door, her arms folded under her bosom, silently communicating her feeling that this entire farce was a bad idea. She gave Chyna a kiss on the cheek but otherwise didn't say a word. Her stormy eyes were directed solely at Dean. As awful as the situation was, Chyna felt thankful that she was now leaving the place and the disapproving stonefaced glare of her friend's eyes. What lay ahead, however, was now her and Dean's puzzle to complete.

10

D ean helped Chyna through the door of the Jameson home. Smells of paint, sanded wood and primer wafted past her nose, but the comforting smells of home still lingered underneath: baking bread, apple cinnamon, even something fried. Even though Mrs. Jameson wasn't there baking like she used to, Chyna could still smell remnants of all that she might have made if she were.

"I was able to leave Dad's bed down in the room we put together in the den before he... and set things up for you in there," Dean offered.

"I could have made it up the stairs... uh, thank you."

"I got in some of that food I know you like. When your ceiling caved in, water trickled into the kitchen cabinets when it had nowhere else to run, so I had to throw out most of your food."

Chyna nodded, repeating her thanks. She hadn't realized he'd been back but she supposed he would, someone had to help her from damaging herself further. A part of her was relieved, and if truth be told she'd rather not enter the place ever again. Chyna smiled sadly but managed to hop her way into the kitchen with her crutches. They still made her armpits feel weird, but she had to get better at using them or else have Dean lift and cart her everywhere, which, while it should have been romantic, was anything but considering the circumstances. She was not in a romantic mood: despite knowing him so well, so intimately, it felt very odd to be held by him in any capacity now. That said, she was currently at his mercy.

She sat down heavily at the kitchen table, winded from the short walk that seemed to use all of her energy, as well as muscles she didn't know existed.

"How about a sandwich?" Dean offered.

Chyna nodded. Suddenly her hunger had returned full throttle. She couldn't believe she'd agreed to stay at the Jameson home: she began to fret that this might not have been the best decision after all. *But what other choice did I have?*

"I can make it." Chyna broke from her thoughts and stood up determinedly. She washed her one good hand and managed to get the mayonnaise, turkey and cheese from the fridge. Holding the jar against her chest, she somehow managed to twist the top off the jar. Dean just stood back to watch her.

When it was time to cut the sandwich, Chyna realized she had a problem. Searching for a plastic bag to cover her bandaged hand, she found the box, but it was empty. Dean turned toward her and Chyna pretended she was about to do something else. "What?" she huffed irritably as he continued to stare at her.

"Want me to cut that?"

"No! I'm looking for sandwich bags," Chyna replied tersely.

"Planning to wrap everything up and take it on a picnic?" he asked.

"Nope," she said, not bothering to look at him. "If you must know, I want to wrap my stupid bandaged hand in a bag and hold one end of the sandwich while I cut it." She didn't actually know if it would work, but she had to try.

Dean washed his hands and grabbed a larger knife from the drawer. Chyna frowned: she had to admit that it would probably cut better than the butter knife she held. He proceeded to cut her sandwich for her, which only inflamed her irritation.

"Don't you have some place to be?" she asked impatiently - then noticed the clean glass and the juice he'd placed on the table. It was obviously for her.

"Yeah. I've got to meet with the adjuster," Dean said in a low voice.

Chyna immediately winced. She hadn't even asked about his place of business. She knew Dean loved his job, or more specifically, he loved people. He saw many children and elderly folks at his practice, and he was so good with them... She dismissed the feelings that came rushing back, yet chastised herself for acting as if she didn't care when she did. She told herself that staying out of Dean's affairs and that not asking questions, pretending not to care, was for the best. But try as she might, she was still concerned about him.

Like her own life but in a different way, Dean's had seemed to have fallen down around him too, starting with the death of his father. She knew what it felt like when it seemed as if you'd lost it all, but she didn't wish that same despondency on him, or anyone, no matter their history. Not ever. It was the worst feeling in the world. Then again, if she'd been able to share it with someone, it would've been easier to bear.

Chyna wondered if Dean had shared his sorrow with Lisa Stephens. To think about them together hurt. Her sandwich grew cold and thick in her mouth and she worked to keep chewing and keep her thoughts from being displayed all over her face.

"What are you thinking about?"

She looked up to see he'd made some coffee. "Nothing... uh, if I drink coffee at this hour, I'll be up all night."

"Do you want some?"

"Yes," she said, and they laughed.

"I was also thinking about how clueless you are about how people feel," she muttered, trying not to roll her eyes.

"Oh? Well, tell me how you feel, then," he replied. He carried over a little floral tray with small matching porcelain bowls of sugar and creamer alongside their two steaming cups.

She hadn't been expecting that response. She needed to conceal her thoughts around him, considering they only seemed to set her up for emotional entrapment. She didn't want to discuss her feelings: rather, she had been referring to Lisa Stephens. Chyna considered that, like most men, Dean was likely clueless about a woman's advances and thus, in this case, Lisa Stephens' designs on him. Chyna evaded the question.

She finished her sandwich and stood up again, limping to the sink to place her plate in the basin. Despite their new level of communication and cordiality, there was still an invisible wall between them. Chyna had all but convinced herself that the time for them to be together was over and they'd never go back to what they once had. She was truly apologetic for so much more than his place burning down and for whatever hand she played in their relationship's ultimate demise. She had a role, despite statements to the contrary: they both were guilty.

Dean nodded. Snatching a paper towel from the wooden rack, he folded it neatly in half, placing it beside her plate. "I, uh, forgot I bought some grapes. Do you want some?"

"Yes."

"They are seedless just like you like them," he said, fetching a bowl for the fruit. He rinsed the green grapes and set them in front of her.

Dean was thoughtful, and almost too observant. From arranging a room for her so she didn't have to climb the stairs to stocking the refrigerator, he did so much - but he didn't have to. She also knew he had a house of his own in Arlington, so he'd gone out of his way to make the Jameson place comfortable.

"How long has Ms. Alfreah been gone?"

"A couple of months," Dean replied. "It's lonely here without someone to tend to and to look after. It's like... everyone left me." He seemed to look pointedly at her.

"But look," he perked up. "Now I got someone to tend to and fill my days with our antics." He smiled, as if it really were that simple.

Chyna nodded, popping a grape into her mouth. "Your dad always picked out the best fruit," she said, turning around and leaning against the counter, pushing his comments about tending to someone from her brain. "I think you inherited that from him."

"There was always fresh stuff to eat," he agreed. "Mom always liked cooking too. Thankfully, Angie has been teaching me to cook, and she left some frozen meals too, just in case. If there's anything you want, just text me and I'll get it from the store on my way over. I know you're a grazer: you like to snack when you're writing."

Chyna nodded. "What kinds of repairs are you doing to the house?" she asked.

Dean shrugged. "Mostly cosmetic stuff. Painting and repairing, ripping out some old carpet upstairs, lots of sanding and priming. Not major stuff, and not anything noisy to bother you while I'm here."

"It's no bother... in fact," - *bad idea*, her mind screamed - "um, I-I could help paint?" *Oh man.* "I'd like to do that - to do something, to help if I can."

"An artist like you, doing house painting work?" Dean chuckled. "This isn't canvas, mind you: you'd be using straight white general-purpose Interior Latex primer and sealant, courtesy of your local Benjamin Moore." Chyna shrugged.

"I, well, I haven't painted anything in, ah…" *Since before she'd divorced.* "In a long time," she finished.

"Why not? You loved it. And you were good."

She shrugged. "It just sort of left me." It was like that when things didn't work out in your marriage, and in other relationships for that matter: nothing seemed to inspire. She hoped it would come back, but it would probably take some more time. Some of her grief about a number of things would have to ease. Gary had only criticized her work. When she'd put up what she thought was a beautiful flower arrangement in oil over their grand fireplace, he hadn't liked it; so, in time, she'd put it all away, all of her creativity gradually abused and stifled until it was so far down inside that to retrieve it would be like an excavation project.

When she looked up, she found Dean watching her closely and she shoved more grapes into her mouth to keep her from saying all the things that rushed to mind just then.

"Do the authorities have any idea who destroyed your place?" she asked. Dean shook his head as Chyna crunched noisily on the grapes. "I read about it in the paper," she explained. "I'm sorry."

"Thanks," he said. "Will you be all right by yourself for a few hours?"

Chyna nodded without argument. He was leaving. Maybe she'd finally found a subject that sent him packing. She'd tuck that away in the back of her mind. She wondered where he was going but didn't ask: it wasn't like it was any of her business. *Sure would be nice if you'd drop the 'you're such an awful human being' routine,* her mind prodded. *He didn't have to call his mother just to make you felt reassured about staying when in fact you really wanted to anyway. The call just made you feel better, and it was a really nice gesture. Get a grip, Chyna.*

"Yeah, uh, sure. You'll be back later, I mean?"

"Yep, I'm gonna be back later. Try not to miss me. Listen, Chyna, uh, about your house."

"I know, it's a mess..."

"It's condemned."

Chyna set the bowl aside before she ended up dropping it.

"I'm gonna fix it for you."

"Please don't," she pleaded. "I'll just - when I'm better, I'll just pack up and sell it." Never mind that she didn't have the funds for such an endeavor, nor the energy for that matter.

"Would you really move away from here?" he asked. "This is your home." He looked almost stricken and it brought her up short.

"There's nothing really here for me, Dean."

"I'm here."

The words brought tears to her eyes, but she blinked rapidly and managed to hold them in check. She could have a good cry after he was gone, and she had to wait just a few more moments for that. He moved forward but she held up a hand. "Um, I'm all right. It's okay," she rushed out. She couldn't have him comforting her. "Um, thank you, Dean, for inviting me to stay."

"You're always welcome here. You're family," Dean said, and before Chyna could protest, he did move closer - but he didn't touch her except in the most intimate, kind-hearted gesture: he bent to kiss her on the cheek.

"Mama, you covering your smoking again?"

Lisa smiled, knowing the answer before she asked.

"What's it to you?" her mother called back.

"Well, I think considering what the doctor said, you shouldn't do that."

"Come to see about me, did you?" Sheila Stephens said as her daughter entered the room. "What have you been up to?"

Lisa looked away. "Nothing," she said, guiltily.

"Of course, nothing. After all, down at that Hardig building, you're just playing the role of a lawyer. You're what now? A legal assistant? Secretary?"

"I came over here to see about you and this is all you ever give me. You dump on me all the time, Mama. I'm sorry your life is so miserable, but mine ain't a bed of roses either."

"Come to see about me? What'd you bring? See? Not even a pack of smokes."

"Do you think you're lugging around an oxygen tank because you're an Olympic swimmer?" Lisa retorted. She braced herself for a cutting comeback, but the only thing returned was the same incessant wheezing cough her mother would produce whenever she'd gotten herself worked up. Her mean, smart, hurtful responses wouldn't come fast enough these days: they just left her breathless and gasping for air.

Rushing over to her mother, Lisa roughly clapped her hands across her mother's back until the phlegm clogging her airways cleared.

"You trying to kill me?" her mother gasped, when it was evident the patting had worked.

Lisa stood quickly. That line, at least, she had been expecting. A *thank you for your help* would've been nice, but no such luck.

"You still sniffing after that Jameson boy?"

Lisa didn't bother answering. She left the room for the kitchen to fix her mother a plate. After placing a frozen meal in the microwave, she removed a pill from each of the six medicine bottles that lined the counter top and placed the multicolored handful in a small plastic cup while waiting for it to heat. She reached for a large bottle of juice, twisted the top and poured it into a plastic cup.

"You know Jameson?" her mother called through, unde-terred in her line of questioning. "That youngest boy don't pay you no nevermind, huh? Don't play dumb with me, and don't play like you deaf either."

Lisa held the completed tray on one hand, carrying it to the living room where her mother sat for at least ten hours of every day. Without answering, she moved the playing cards, the *Soap Opera Digest,* latest edition of the *Inquirer* and a heap of other magazines and placed the tray where they had been.

Her mother looked up at her, then back disgustedly at the food. "I hate this junk, you know that."

Lisa shrugged, taking a deep breath. "So you tell me all the time," she finished nonchalantly and turned to straighten up the living room, as if the words her mother constantly spewed at her didn't hurt. The truth was, they did: they stung as deep as they always had, but there was nothing she could do. Her mother had turned into a bitter old woman, looking thirty years older than her present age of fifty-two. With a bad heart and failing lungs, Sheila Stephens had nicotined herself as close to death as she could get.

"You need anything else, Mama?" Lisa said as politely as their conversation thus far would allow.

"Anything else? Do I need anything else?" Sheila harrumphed. "How about a grandchild with the last name Jameson? They got more money than the law allows any black man I ever seen. Why didn't nothing happen when you was over there playing financial adviser?" she added incredu-lously. "Two years in accounting school and now you a finan-cial advisor? Lord, if that wasn't funny to me. Girl, you should be in comedy. I should've snagged the elder Joseph Jameson for myself - before he went batty, that is. Look at you. I can't even live vicariously through my daughter. By the way, Chauncey Hardig was over here again looking for you earlier."

Lisa looked over at her mother in alarm. "What'd you say to him?"

"What could I say? You only come over every few days - when you're feeling guilty, no doubt." Sheila shrugged and bit into her food. Transferring a wad of hot lasagna to the corner of her mouth, she looked at her daughter. "Said you was supposed to do something for him. Said Warren ain't been by because he wasn't feeling well." Sheila chewed noisily. "The Hardigs ain't nice," she continued. "They got houses and tons of land, but the cops are probably after them. That young Hardig, he ain't too stable. The Jamesons, see, daughter o' mine, they got a little bit of money, them kids got that. If I was you, I'd bet on Dean Jameson, the doctor. Jojo fine too, but the doctor seems a bit more gullible. Easily duped. That's what you been doing over there, isn't it? Duping them? You know anything about the office burning down? Been all over the news, you know."

Lisa shook her head no. She was shocked that her mother would know so much about a project she had tried to keep secret. Her plan was falling apart at the seams. But ruining the Jamesons wasn't her only aim. She'd somehow gotten herself into a bit of a mess. She needed to talk to Warren, but, like his father, she hadn't seen him in weeks.

Sheila shrugged a shoulder as she let out a snort that suggested she didn't believe her daughter's denial.

"Sure. I tried to dupe a Jameson too, back in my day. Didn't work," she called after her daughter as she hurried from the room.

Back in her car, Lisa pulled the cell phone from her purse and dialed the last number that had called her. "I'm coming to see you now. Now!" she yelled into the phone. "Right now!"

The things her mother had told her were no surprise. She already knew all that stuff about the Hardigs and the Jamesons. She had eyes, so she could clearly see who was the better, more stable and certainly better-looking option: an honest man, with legal investments and above-board dealings. She'd seen all the Jameson finances, and their wealth stood in stark contrast to that of the Hardigs. She couldn't make head nor tail of the latter's line items and spreadsheets: she knew trickery on paper when she saw it. She took a deep, agitated breath.

She had to figure it all out. She tossed her phone back into her purse and pressed the gas harder as she sped away to the Hardig's construction site for their newest building in downtown Alexandria. If they were going to rule the real estate in the area, she was getting a piece of the pie, and Dean was gonna be a wonderful, handsome ornament in her many future plans. He just didn't know it yet. Everything would take a little more time, that's all.

11

"Yep, I'd say she's got some serious water damage up there. See this?" Pulling a piece from what remained of Chyna's roof, Bubba Sparks of Sparks Carpentry held it down for Dean to look closer. He shook it, and Dean had to move back to keep the gross-looking fungus stuff from landing on his head. Bubba brought it closer to his face, turning it in his gloved hand as if it were some type of intricate design he wanted to duplicate.

"Wood's rotten. Cheap roofing don't last long," Bubba mused.

Dean nodded. He always knew there were a host of problems hidden in the Lockharts' home. Feeling somewhat responsible for its present shape, Dean stood in Chyna's now-uninhabitable home to see what his old friend had to say about its repair and reconstruction.

Bubba was thoughtful a moment. He wore waterproof boots: most of the water had dried out, but there were still a few hidden puddles around the soiled carpet. He looked around the place and shook his head in disgust.

"That sorry daddy of hers - musician, wasn't he? Whatever

he was, singing the blues didn't pay no bills, you understand? He didn't keep up the house like a man with a family should."

Dean nodded in agreement. Having met Mr. Lockhart only a few times, he remembered him as a man who stayed out all night in the clubs, barely coming home long enough to rest before he was gone again. Most of the time he started the party with some booze before heading out, and it was then that young Chyna would flee to the Jameson's house as an adolescent, seeking safety from her drunken father. Sometimes the man was gone for weeks, even months at a time. Dean often wondered why Chyna never mentioned him now, and he realized that was because she probably didn't know much about him either.

Bubba took a deep breath. "They weren't nothing like your family, Dean. That daddy of hers was the cheapest man around. If he could get someone to buy air, he'd have it bottled up in a heartbeat and sold it on the corner. Man, this place is a death trap," Bubba said disgustedly. "It's a wonder she wasn't killed. I'll get some folks I know to fix up the place: won't take but a few months. I'll light a fire under some people. Least I can do. She took care of my Georgia before she died, you know. Owe her real good for that." Bubba looked around at the place, then shrugged his shoulders. "Took care of your daddy too, didn't she?"

Dean nodded.

"She didn't ask for nothing much in return," Bubba continued. "My Georgia got that blasted cancer in 'er bones. Chyna would come home from school, give Georgia her bath, kept the house tidy, made dinner. Burnt up my food, though - don't ever let her cook fer ya." He laughed with a saddened air, then coughed a few times to cover the grief. "Yeah, she tried. Did better'n I could. Anyway, don't worry 'bout a thing, son, and tell her not to worry. Just help her to get better. Keep her out of this place for a bit. ain't fit for nobody to live in right now."

Dean watched Bubba move his aging body carefully back down the ladder. Tipping an invisible hat, he gave Dean a courteous nod before he left.

Dean made a mental note to help Bubba with the house. He'd offer physical labor, as well as the finances to see that it was restored. Bubba wasn't the only one indebted to Chyna Lockhart. "Thanks Bubba, I appreciate it."

The older man nodded. Concluding that the place was now mostly dried out but still a disaster, they both moved to the front door and exited. Locking the door behind him, Dean knew he had a lot of work to do. The only comfort was that Chyna was at his home - his mother's home, he amended - and therefore safe.

He checked his watch: he could get to the store and get back before Chyna woke up. He was glad he hadn't taken up the makeshift bedroom on the lower level of his parents' place just yet. There was a lot he hadn't done. Glad to help Chyna, Dean was secretly ecstatic that she had agreed to come to his house at all. It was a welcome sigh of relief. Now, if he could just stay out of her hair, pretend to concentrate on the renovations and slowly win his way back into her heart, or at the very least find out more about what happened with Gary, all would be well. It sounded too easy and he knew it would be anything but; but he was game for trying something, anything. He would make up numerous excuses to hang out at the house and stick around for whatever she needed, hoping beyond hope that she'd eventually open up about the rift between them.

This could go right or completely wrong. He was praying for the more positive outcome. Dean Jameson didn't give up: not without a fight.

CHYNA WAS GETTING BETTER at maneuvering herself about the

house. The pain from her sprained wrist had faded and she had removed the bandage from it just the other day. Using Dean's computer, she could now type at a pretty good speed again to complete her articles and submit bids for more work. Her leg was still in a cast, but at least it didn't feel like a ton of bricks whenever she needed to move. She had even managed a sponge bath, though she longed for a real one, where she could submerge her entire body and let hot, hot water cascade all over her, reaching into every crevice. Until the cast came off, a soapy sponge while standing at the sink would have to do. She counted the days.

Getting the cast taken off, though, was no big deal compared to her anxiety about eventually leaving the Jameson home once her own home was finished. She and Dean had developed an easy camaraderie again, once Chyna had set aside her attitude and allowed his easy-going nature to calm rather than rattle her. She had let down her guard, and if she wasn't careful she'd get her heart into a mess yet again.

"Dinner's almost ready," Dean said, surprising Chyna, who hadn't thought he'd noticed her standing in the doorway. She'd been standing there for some time, lost in her own thoughts.

Limping into the kitchen, she dismissed all thoughts of her life's future direction and took time to notice one of the dishes already on a plate beside a stove. Dean ladled some crimson sauce over it.

"What is that? It looks like something out of a magazine and much too good to eat," remarked Chyna in amazement. "I don't remember your cooking skills being all that great. Angel must have given you some serious lessons."

Dean stood back from the counter, as if he too needed a moment to admire his culinary skills, then shrugged his shoulders.

"I'd reserve the verdict until you taste it," he cautioned. "One thing I've learned about cooking is that it can look good but still taste awful. A couple of failed dishes still linger in my recollections."

Chyna smiled, but she was pretty confident about the taste based on the smells and appearance alone. Her mouth watered.

"Angel has been giving Saturday morning classes for people who want to learn to cook," Dean continued. "Extra money until she starts her catering business, or the restaurant."

"And how about Angel and Jojo?" Chyna asked.

Dean shrugged his shoulders, avoiding her eyes. "They're moving pretty fast. Guess some people just know what they want and go for it."

"Yeah," was all Chyna said. If she counted correctly, it seemed that within less than a year, Dean's older brother Jojo had gotten pretty serious with the type of woman he swore he'd never date. As always, things seemed simple for everyone but her.

Chyna watched Dean as he tossed greens in a wooden bowl. She nodded at the food. "You should take a picture of it. It looks like something out of *Bon Appétit*," she said in awe, all but smacking her lips with want.

"That's a good idea," Dean piped up. "Can you wait while I get the camera?" He hurried out, returning with not just any camera but a sleek black Nikon with an added zoom lens extension.

"Angie mentioned wanting to start a collection of photos to write for some food magazine," he explained. "Accompanying photos help sell articles."

"They do," Chyna agreed. "I occasionally try to get a couple photos to go along with my *General Advocate* articles, but in a food magazine there's no doubt that pictures are the most important thing - more important than the accompanying article, often. I'm afraid photos like that are taken by serious professionals, though."

Dean handed her the camera.

"The photos you've taken look professional to me. You're quite the photographer," he smiled.

"What? Why do you say that?" she asked, shyly taking the machine he held out. Dean cleared his throat. Chyna watched as he attentively removed the salt and pepper shakers from the scene and cleaned up a spill with the dishrag. *If she was a professional, what was he?* she thought, as she watched him essentially styling the shot without even realizing it.

"There are some pictures of us at your house," he explained. "I saw them along with some of your mom's things, while I was packing up your stuff from the house."

He shifted as if he was uncomfortable talking about it. Watching him, Chyna nearly dropped the camera into the pretty pasta dish, but she recovered quickly, maintaining both her composure and her grasp on the camera. She stood up and tried to ignore what he had said. She did love to take pictures, but something else bothered her. What else might Dean have uncovered while he'd been packing up her things? Most everything except clothes and personal items were still packed away in boxes: she hadn't really tackled the task of unpacking them since she'd had them shipped from California.

Startled, she suddenly realized that Dean might've noticed the stack of books she'd once purchased on pregnancy and babies, for example. The explanation she formed quickly on her tongue, that she and Gary were considering having kids, would've been true. But there were some newer books in that selection that she'd purchased much more recently. Books about how to better prepare herself and her body not to meet the same fate she did the first time she'd gotten pregnant. Those books still graced the shelves of her living room bookcase, from back when she'd realized that she was pregnant with Dean's child. She'd meant to pack up those books, donate them to a local birthing center. Now, however, they were lying somewhere in her house: a virtual time bomb waiting to be discovered.

"I see," Chyna said finally, not knowing exactly what Dean had just said as the panicked thoughts raced through her mind. She scratched her head, looking down at the food. Holding the camera to her face, she prayed for steadier hands as she closed one eye and looked through the viewfinder with the other. Leaning closer, she focused the lens and pressed the button.

"I, uh, also saw the books on having a baby," Dean added, as if reading her mind. "I guess you were thinking about starting a family when you were married to Gary?"

"Yes. Yes, we thought about it," Chyna said hurriedly, feeling flustered as she heard her voice go up an entire octave in her response. She rushed through a few more shots, turning the camera and the plate of food, now unsure whether she got a focused shot or not. She just wanted to be done with the entire thing.

"Seems like a lot of books just to be thinking about something you're not actually doing yet," Dean said softly.

"Nothing like pretending you're doing something to get you ready for the reality when or if it should come," she responded briskly.

"How'd Gary feel about kids?" he continued.

"I really don't want to talk about it, okay?"

"Seems like a self-absorbed jerk," Dean remarked conversationally, as if he hadn't heard her. "I couldn't imagine that throwing a kid into the mix would get Mr. Senator to pay attention to someone else's needs. That would mean he'd actually have to care about and nurture someone other than himself."

"He didn't want them," Chyna said shortly. "But I always wanted a family." This line of conversation was bringing her attitude right on back. She looked at Dean, wondering how he could make such a perfect assessment of someone he'd never known or even really met, as far as she could recall.

"You'll have one," Dean said reassuringly.

"One what?" she said testily.

"A child, Chyna. You'll make a great Mom."

"Oh, uh, thanks."

"Should we eat?" Chyna heard Dean say, but before she could nod her head in response, the chime of the doorbell rang and she turned her head from Dean. "I can get it," she said, moving to the door. "Do you have some croutons?" she added, as she passed the salad on the table.

She was pleased when she made it to the door in just a few seconds. Her leg was getting stronger and she was moving faster and more assuredly without the crutches, gradually putting more weight on it every day. What surprised Chyna even more was that Dean hadn't insisted that she sit down while he did everything for her, as usual.

With a smile, Chyna opened the door, prepared to give a hearty greeting to whoever was visiting the Jamesons. They always had visitors and it was always fun to see what old friend was stopping by. Sadly, since everyone knew the family matriarch was out of town, there hadn't been any visitors since Chyna had been staying there.

Opening the door and looking up, though, the welcoming smile and cordial words she had prepared for a familiar face vanished from her mind. She stared into the cold eyes of a man whose presence represented a part of her life she'd rather forget. She didn't have any nice words for her ex-husband's supposed friend, Warren Hardig.

12

"Chyna, what a lovely surprise. I didn't know you were a friend of the Jamesons."

Just then, it seemed the sky beyond Warren's shoulder darkened with the threat of rain. Likewise, Chyna somehow couldn't shake the sense that Warren's visit held impending danger. Nothing good would come of the man standing before her: that much she knew. What was he doing here? Her stomach immediately began to ache with a profound sense of dread and loathing.

"Warren," Chyna managed, as courteously as she could. "I, uh, I - "

"May I come in? Is Dean around?" Warren interrupted.

"Yes, yes, he's just inside..."

Were Dean and Warren Hardig friends? Dismissing such thoughts, she reminded herself that even if they were, it was none of her business. She just hoped the Jamesons never had the unfortunate experience of befriending or doing business with Warren Hardig.

She pointed behind her, but when she moved back from his portly bulk, her good foot caught the edge of the straw welcome mat. Before she could stop herself with her injured leg's waning support, she felt herself falling – before Warren's arms reached out to assist her.

"I'm fine, I'm fine, I... Thanks," she said, once she was standing upright once more. It took sheer force of will not to run screaming from his embrace.

She had plenty of reasons not to like him. She could never forget the night that Warren, in a drunken stupor, had forgotten that she was married to his friend Gary... No: in truth, she never forgot one minute of that awful night.

"You've always had lovely long dancer legs," Warren was leering. "With some practice, I'm sure we could exact the loveliest arabesque."

Chyna couldn't help but wince. His comments, meant to flatter, did nothing but repulse her. Though she didn't know exactly what an arabesque looked like when performed, she was confident it didn't involve a dancer's derriere flat on the floor, and that was the only dance move she'd be able to execute. She nodded, for lack of anything else to say. She kept backing subtly away from him; yet it seemed every inch she moved, he was still right there.

Warren always seemed to open his mouth with something inappropriate to say, reminding her of why she neither liked nor trusted him. Comments like the one he'd just made, not to mention those of a much more intimate and vulgar nature made back in her and Gary's California home, would never be forgotten.

"You okay?" Dean said, exiting the kitchen to see who had arrived at the door. He reached spontaneously for Chyna's hand and, though it felt a little odd to do so, she took it like a lifeline. Willing her nerves to calm down, she used the added balance to gain better footing, took back her hand and moved down the hall. Over her shoulder she said, "I'll leave you two."

She smiled tightly at Dean before hobbling away to another

room as fast as her injured leg would carry her. She didn't bother to acknowledge Warren's courteous goodbye. If Dean had noticed anything odd about the exchange, she could answer his questions later. She'd use the intervening time to prepare her response; but first she wanted to know exactly how and why Dean Jameson and Warren Hardig knew each other.

～

"WHAT'S HAPPENING, MAN?" Warren said as soon as Chyna left, making his way into the kitchen as if he visited often.

Dean shut the door and followed him. He crossed his arms over his chest in a menacing stance. He'd hoped to have a nice quiet dinner with Chyna, and he wasn't about to put off that plan for any Hardig business foolishness – because, with Warren, that's all it ever was.

"Oh, man," Warren said, eyeing the cozy table set for two and giving Dean a big smile. "Sorry, yo, I interrupted. You're making moves here?" With a smirk, Warren gestured at the set table filled with delectable food.

"What can I do for you, Warren?" Dean said, nonplussed, and making a mental note to find out how Chyna and Warren knew each other. After she had turned to leave, Warren's eyes had seemed to linger on her a little too long. That wasn't lost on Dean for a second. Neither was the jerkiness of her movements, nor the rapid nervous pulse that he'd felt pounding in her fingers.

"What can I do for you?" Dean repeated tersely.

"Man, really a bad time, huh? Listen, I just came to talk to you about my struggles with the county zoning ordinances. See if you might be in the market for a new career in the business scene."

"I'm not interested," Dean said flatly.

"You haven't even heard me out, bro," Warren wheedled.

"I'm not your bro, Warren."

"Damn, tough crowd," Warren said, not looking at all abashed. He turned to lean against the refrigerator door and crossed one foot over the other in a casual stance that suggested he planned to stay awhile.

"So what's up?" he continued airily. "Heard about your place burning down. Shame. But now that you know that area is full of crime, seems you'll be looking for some different real estate to work in. Remember I was telling you about my dad and me, our next venture..."

"Yeah, Warren. You asked me about this property stuff before and I told you then I wasn't interested in the construction of a second Hardig empire. I'll tell you again now. Y'all need to stay in DC where you are and be happy," Dean answered firmly.

"Now that don't sound real nice," Warren admonished. "Why people always putting limits on a brother?"

"This isn't about limits," Dean snapped. "You have lots of properties in DC: nothing wrong with growing your bottom line, but you do often face a lot of opposition. Now, I can't imagine that that's because your business acumen is all too hot, now is it? Besides," Dean continued, "even if you seemed above board and the folk welcomed you with open arms, I'm really not looking to rent space a Hardig owns, in any case. I'm a small optometrist - that's it. My parents were into that stuff: they got involved in local and regional politics. Not me. I don't do politics."

"Really?" Warren replied. "So your daddy dies and now you've gone and decided what's important in life."

"Even if he hadn't died, I'd still know what and who I did and didn't want to associate myself with," said Dean hotly. "Now drop the discussion of my father and we won't have any problems. I think our conversation is over."

Thoughtful for a minute, Dean continued: "Come to think

of it, local news been sayin' the majority of county residents don't want another Hardig building in their backyard."

He watched as Warren stiffened and shrugged a shoulder. "County never knows what it wants 'til it comes. Building goes up, people stand in line to shop."

"Probably because other businesses, Mom and Pop type establishments, can no longer afford their livelihood when you take business away from them. You buy up the stuff, you up the rent, they're forced to move out. Sounds like your strategy to me. Isn't that the philosophy of most of the conglomerations you and your dad own? You leave people so little choice, they'll have to come back to buy Hardig products?"

Warren was silent, and Dean saw he'd shut down the man's argument.

Good, Dean thought to himself. Maybe Warren had finally taken the hint and would go to someone else for help. Getting through to the Hardigs wasn't easy, though. They didn't take no for an answer. Dean wondered why they always came to him, of all people. It seemed odd.

"Man, you Jamesons are hard on us. Say," Warren changed the subject, "how's that Gary Williams like his wife over here with the good doctor?"

"They're divorced." Dean's jaw twitched, wondering why the man even cared about Chyna at all. "Do you two know each other?" Dean ventured.

Warren laughed and Dean stiffened.

"We go way back - why don't you ask her? Those parties at Gary's house, off the chain... I miss them. But I miss her most of all." Warren cast his eyes up suggestively, as if recalling a lascivious private thought.

Dean didn't respond in any way. He knew Warren was likely doing whatever he could to push Dean's buttons - and suggesting he knew Chyna in a friendly, even personal capacity was accomplishing just that.

"I think it's time for you to go, Warren," Dean said. The man's lustful glazed-over expression was dancing on his last nerve. He himself didn't like the Hardig's at all - and if his father, Joe Jameson Sr., had had reason to dislike anyone, it must have been a good one. That being said, Joe Senior had never talked about it to anyone, and Dean noted that it was something he should ask his mom about. His curiosity was finally piqued, when he really hadn't thought about it much at all until now.

"Dean look, I like you," Warren began. "Your family is such great people, your Mother a real integral part of the community here. But, listen, um, what if I said I could get you some happening office space in Old Town? Heck, we've got some buildings we're buying in Georgetown, if you want. Get you some clientele to pay the big bucks, put you in a better spot, and cut up some of that rent for ya."

"Why would you do that, Warren?" retorted Dean. "I mean, you can't blame me for being a little suspicious."

"I just need you on my team, Dr. J. You're intelligent, logically minded. People would listen to you..."

Dean took a deep breath, ready to deliver a definitive 'no' one more time; but before he could, Warren interrupted again.

"Look Dean, I've tried to be cordial, to ask, but I'm not really into asking any longer. You make not-nice Warren come out. Now I'm *telling* you to help me. The longer I look, the more I see you don't get it at all. I haven't been asking you to help me all this time because I like hearing the word no. Want to know what else? I think that Chyna Lockhart is the most beautiful, breathtaking woman I've ever seen, and I'd hate to see her run into any kind of trouble... or you. Y'all looking mighty cozy here," Warren continued, looking about the place, "and you know, maybe she left her husband 'cause her heart was always with Dean Jameson. Maybe Gary went easy on her and let her go, but maybe there's more to the story." Warren sniffed. "I'd hate to see her hurt, and you know I'd hate to see your family name tarnished in any way, but uh, this here business negotiation is getting so old. Just bring yourself on around to my way of thinking and things will go so much better for you – you'll see."

Dean listened as the seriousness of what Warren was saying caught hold of his mind. Everything inside him bristled as soon as Chyna's name was uttered. He realized the man was probably just play-acting, but what he said about Chyna and Gary...

"Seems like I lost the thread of what you're saying, Warren. I could have sworn you just, uh, you threatened me - and using Chyna, too? Like, really? You threatened me?" Dean let out a full-throated laugh. "All these years of asking me for stuff over and over again, and then what do you do? Just like that, a threat is supposed to change my mind? You done lost yours. Clearly. You see, Warren, sometimes people mistake my niceness for being soft, but I'm not that guy," Dean continued. "Now, I'm going to let you leave with full use of all your limbs. But if you, or Gary, or anyone sent by you even looks at or speaks about Chyna in any way that brings her any grief whatsoever, you'll wonder whatever happened to your vision and your extremities."

Dean had never threatened anyone before, but then again he'd never had to. He was confused about this unfamiliar hostility he was receiving. Did the man want his help that badly, or was he just playing games? He couldn't figure it out, but the charade was making him angrier by the moment. He'd get to the bottom of it eventually, but in the meantime he believed his own threat had been heeded. Warren carelessly shrugged and shook his head before backing away to the door.

"I thought I did make my business plain but, uh, you know how it goes. These negotiations always take time. Oh, by the way," Warren raised a finger, pointing upward. "Be sure to ask Chyna just how she and I know each other. Man, those parties in California? Let's just say, Gary Williams is a great host. Quite the senator. On second thought, maybe you shouldn't ask. Chyna was something herself! Quite the hostess *she* was." Warren shook his head with a reminiscent leer. "Anyway, I'll be seeing you. Don't have too much fun, you and Chyna, okay? And tell your mother the Hardigs say hello." Warren turned and strutted pompously out of the door.

When Dean turned around, he saw Chyna standing feet from him.

"How in the hell do you know Warren Hardig?" he demanded.

hyna hadn't been prepared for Dean's anger. She registered his expectant gaze, as if she'd done something wrong. She didn't owe anyone any explanation at all, she thought - least of all Dean. This was his house, after all: Warren Hardig obviously knew where to find him and came knocking on *his* door - for him, presumably, not her.

"Excuse me? He and Gary are friends," she replied indignantly. "And I could ask you the same thing! So you're getting into the retail real estate business now, huh?"

"Hell no," Dean returned heatedly.

Chyna took a seat at the table as Dean began slamming pots and pans. He snatched her plate away to shove it into the microwave, punched numbers angrily with his thumb and jabbed the start button.

Chyna hesitated. It was obvious from Dean's behavior that what she said about how she and Warren knew one another wasn't a satisfactory explanation. And, she thought with some annoyance, neither was Dean's response about their business dealings.

"Like I said, uh, he's a friend of Gary's is all," she repeated awkwardly. She did tell part of the truth - though granted, any true friend of another man wouldn't ever have made such an aggressive pass at that man's wife, ex or not. She felt ashamed, but not because of anything she'd done. What caused her the most grief, even in retrospect, was her then-husband's response to her telling him right away that very night that it had happened.

Above all, she was super annoyed that the evening's mood was shot. Right up until Warren's arrival, she'd been looking forward to their dinner. Now all the ambience had been sucked out of the atmosphere. The very residue of his presence seemed to hang in the air.

"Has he ever threatened you, Chyna?"

"What?"

Alarm bells rang in her head. He hadn't threatened her, but that night of his drunken stupor all those months ago kept coming back to mind. He had asked that she not tell her husband... was it a threat that he had made? All she remembered was being so repulsed that she could hardly scramble away from him fast enough and yell for Gary - only he hadn't come. He had been passed out downstairs. His excessive drinking always seemed to put him in a coma. She remembered checking his pulse numerous times just to make sure he hadn't slipped away to alcohol poisoning. That night, with nobody there to stop him, it had taken Warren the longest time to remove himself from...

"I uh, I uh..."

"What, Chyna?"

"He just, uh, came onto me once," she said, averting her eyes.

"He *what*?"

So much for diffusing this situation.

"He'll never come near you again," Dean snarled. "If he

does, I will break his face." Dean set the hot piping food in front of her.

"You will not, Dean. It was a long time ago, okay?"

"What did Gary say?" he persisted.

"Could we please not talk about this?" Chyna stared at the steam rising from her plate.

"He said nothing, right? Because if that's what you're telling me then we got problems. I have two people on my hit list, not just one."

"Don't talk like that, please."

"Tell me everything," Dean demanded.

"I can't."

"Why?"

"I just can't, okay? I'm not ready. I'm just... I'm sorry I said anything."

"Don't be sorry you said something to me, Chyna, please." Dean's tone softened as he saw how upset she was. "Okay? Just never be sorry you shared something hurtful with me. It kills me to think you can't share or talk to me, like we once did."

She nodded slowly. It killed her too, and she was the one holding back. "I'm sorry."

"Don't apologize."

"Okay, fine, what do you want me to do?" she snapped.

Dean sighed. "I'm trying, okay? I'm trying."

Chyna didn't want him to come closer and she really didn't want him kneeling before her, but he did both. She folded her hands in her lap and he took them in his own.

"I love you. I might not have ever said it back then, but I love you and I only want what you want. There is this massive iceberg between us and I'm trying to chip it away, Chyna, I'm really trying, but I've never done anything like this. I never had to work this hard in a relationship before, so I'm inexperienced."

She never realized he felt insecure. They'd had a great relationship once, and while they might not have exactly that ever again, they could at least be friends.

You have to tell the whole truth to be true friends, her mind whispered.

"Could you just -? Oh, I just don't want to see him, ever, okay?" Chyna shuddered. "If he has to come over for business, fine, I'll go for a walk or something, or just go anywhere, at least until I can move back home. If he's a business partner of yours, fine, but - "

"After what you just told me, you really think I'd let him here ever again?" said Dean incredulously. "And no, we don't have any business, Chyna: zilch, none, zero. And remember, I am not Gary, Chyna. I care about you, what you want, your safety - and while you're here, I'm going to continue to show you how much I care. For the record, Warren and I had no appointment today: I did not invite him here. My family, mom and dad have always had beef with them but I've never really known why. Next time I talk to my mom, I'm going to find out once and for all what happened."

Chyna was silent but nodded her understanding. She didn't know anything about Mr. and Mrs. Jameson's past dealings with the Hardigs, but she was curious. She didn't need to know the reason they disliked him; she only considered that it was a good thing they did. Everything about Warren, at least, just seemed underhanded, cutthroat and generally vile. That's what she felt when Warren's wayward hands touched her that awful night. She didn't have a great track record in choosing men. Yes, she had to admit that Dean was completely different, but that night's events had her questioning every decision she'd ever made.

After marrying Gary, she'd gradually realized that he didn't really care about her. Their entire marriage began to seem like just another part of his all-consuming campaign plan and its optics. Married people with children simply did better on the campaign trail than single men, whether black, white or any other race. It had all been about keeping up appearances; thus, to him, her failure to produce a child only meant that part of his picture-perfect photo-op family was lacking. He had begun to hound her: if she didn't produce, the public perception would be that she didn't *want* children. No-one would know she was doing all she could. The night Warren made his 'mistake' was the first time she and Gary hadn't slept in the same bed, and she hadn't returned to their marital bedroom once since. Everything about both the two men repulsed her now, and seeing Warren brought it all crashing back.

"You'll never question how I feel about you."

Chyna brought her thoughts back and faced Dean. He was standing stoically next to her, still holding her hands in his own.

"Whatever thoughts went through your mind just then, I know they were not pleasant," he said. "Someday, I hope you'll feel like you can share them with me: anything good and certainly anything bad. I'm giving you time and space as best I can, but we have to have a conversation at some point about what went wrong so we can see if what we have here is salvageable.

"I don't know, Dean - just let me get through this." She extracted one hand from his grasp, but his own were warm and inviting, just like him. She hated how she could be devastated by the thought of one man one moment and completely enthralled by a different man the very next. The man she'd once thought she'd marry.

"I will be patient, and I promise and I'm going to help you."

With that he kissed her on the forehead and embraced her. She lingered in the crook of his neck and shoulder longer than she meant to; then, all too soon, he was standing and backing away.

"It's getting late - go ahead and eat," Dean said to Chyna,

grabbing his own plate and putting it in the microwave before sitting down. He said a quick grace and they both dug in to the meal at last.

Chyna knew something had changed: the conversation grew a little easier, a little lighter and lengthier. More than that, she now knew his true feelings - and that scared her a little. For a while there, she had truly thought it was over, but obviously they both had erroneous assumptions about the other. Speaking of which, Lisa Stephens hadn't been mentioned once. Chyna might have been alone in her willingness to give up on this relationship so quickly, taking the risk of missing everything and giving up on another dream. But, as ever, she was encouraged by Dean's patience, while also terrified by his candor.

Chyna always believed Dean and his entire family were honest, upstanding, good people: polar opposites of the Hardigs, that was plain to see. Never in trouble, always kind and welcoming to her and to so many other kids. All of those things had caused her to trip and fall in love with Dean in the first place. If she wasn't careful, she could see herself falling all over again.

Haven't you fallen enough?

It didn't count before, she insisted to her inner voice. Stuff had fallen on her in her hazard zone of a house... *It was still your fault*, her mind's devil insisted.

If she was going to fall again, this time she really hoped she knew what was she was doing. Sadly, she also knew that whatever happened next, her heart was in deep trouble.

14

For the first time in several weeks, it was the blaring alarm clock that woke Chyna, but she'd been sound asleep so late this particular morning only because she'd been up almost all the previous night.

The encounter with Warren Hardig had shaken her more than she'd realized. She'd tossed and turned under her covers, thinking back to that awful night years ago. Up until last night, she hadn't really seen Warren since: they may have glimpsed each other at a fundraiser or two, but by that time she'd opted out of most Gary-related appearances.

She and Dean slipped into a comfortable daily routine, and for the most part she loved having him there a little too much. As he worked diligently on something or other each day, his presence just brought her a peace she hadn't ever had while married to Senator Gary Williams, regardless of that big secure house.

"I stayed last night. I slept on the couch," Dean said over his shoulder.

"Oh, I would have slept better knowing you were here," Chyna blurted, relieved. "I, I didn't realize – I mean..."

"It's okay." Though he'd been on the floor fiddling with the door, his eyes scrutinized her closer as he stood up. She was tall but Dean was taller: she had to look up to him.

"Your eyes look really dry," he commented. "Do you use drops?"

"No, I just didn't sleep well," she replied.

Seeing him neatly dressed in fresh jeans and a crisp white short sleeved shirt made her feel self-conscious. He never had a bad hair day, it seemed: he always looked impeccable, well dressed, always crisp. Patting the major bed-head she'd woken up with, she suddenly cared more about her own appearance than she had in a long time. His general composure made her remember everything she hadn't bothered to do for herself over the last months: a testament to how comforting the Jameson family was.

It occurred to her that she hadn't taken her multi-vitamin in a week; she hadn't done much of anything. Day to day, she got up, managed to bathe and brush her teeth, usually donned clean clothes, but mainly just... existed. She went for a walk, she cleaned her makeshift bed and space, she worked on a few articles with minimal progress toward her word count goals and she made a lot of tea, which in turn meant constant trips to the bathroom. She and Dean spoke a little everyday and their conversations, especially after last night's revelations, seemed to grow longer and longer. Now, for the first time in a while, she felt she needed to up her appearance: a welcome sign that she was finally coming out of her fog.

"Do you have to look so put-together and unwrinkled at seven in the morning?" she asked, as she turned to find something to drink to help her wake up.

Dean looked down at what he was wearing. "Well, I am usually at work by now," he reminded her gently.

Chyna hated her words immediately. She offered him a look of apology.

"Hey, I got this alarm-security system thingy," he continued, unruffled. Chyna turned and finally noticed the home improvement project he'd been tackling today. The front door handle had been removed, and while the door was closed, the gaping hole in its place gave her a peephole view to the chunk of sidewalk outside and the street beyond. Set out on a stark white towel by his bare feet were all the brass and metal parts from the door's knob, its many pieces perfectly arranged. Once again, she couldn't believe that she was staying there with him, not a single other Jameson present. It was the oddest thing ever. But he always made her feel safe.

"I'm going to give you the code to it," Dean declared.

"No, uh, why?"

"So you know how to get in here, if you need to. There'll be one alarm to get in, then you enter another code as soon as you get inside."

His instructions felt a little redundant: she knew how alarms worked, of course. Why he felt the need to give her the codes she wasn't sure, but she didn't protest. She wasn't concerned about getting in as much as she was eager to keep Warren Hardig out. "It's amazing you never had this before," she remarked. "Come to think of it, it kind of ruins the whole 'come on in' Jameson vibe."

"People can come in – well, anyone who is welcome here," Dean replied. "We'll just keep the riff-raff out: people like Warren Hardig."

Her sentiments exactly. Chyna could only nod her agreement. It was nice of him to include her, but it still felt odd. She'd be leaving soon, of course: as soon as she was better, and as soon as her house was ready. Today, having putting it off for a while, she'd make a point of going over there to see the progress.

Dean sighed. "Momma is probably going to hate this. You're right, it's a barrier of sorts to our family's open door policy; but it's high time for us to join the twenty-first century. I'll install one at your house, too."

"What?"

Dean raised an eyebrow. "Chyna?"

"I'm not arguing with you Dean, but did you talk to Bubba? I should really get a handle on what the repairs are costing. I can't just bury my head in the sand as if I don't have ultimate responsibility for this entire project. I have to be practical: you know, keep an eye on the bottom line. Please let me know what's happening or ask him to call me."

"There's nothing for you to worry about, a lot is happening but it's all good stuff. It's going to be completely fixed and so much better.

"Dean, please don't let Bubba overdo it," she pleaded. "Just have his guys fix the bare minimum, okay?"

The smile touching his lips told her he had something up his sleeve. She had a feeling that whatever it was, it was either in the works or already done.

"Whatever Bubba does, he has my blessing," Dean said. "He says you took care of Ms. Georgia for almost two years before she died."

Chyna nodded. "She was like a grandmother to me. She baked stuff for school when my mom didn't. I - I felt it was the least I could do, plus it taught me all sorts about caregiving. She was my guinea-pig, so to speak: she taught me a lot, and your Mom and Dad taught me the rest of the stuff I needed in life."

Dean moved closer. "I'm sorry the people closest to you disappointed you."

"It's fine," she answered wearily. "It's hard at first, but then God always sends you the people you need."

"Like God sent you to us."

She hadn't thought about it that way and automatically shook her head no.

"Don't disagree with me - it's true."

"I'm not... it's just not really that way, I guess. I don't see things that way, anyhow. Ms. Alfreah didn't need another child as much as I needed a family. Your family didn't need my services: you could afford anyone, and I offered because I liked," – *loved* - "you guys so much."

"Yes, and we love you. A random stranger doesn't truly care, they're just here for a paycheck. You always told us what was best for dad: therapies, treatment, possible medications and side effects and diet. You went way above the call of duty. And you knew our routines, what my Mom liked, so that made it easier. We trusted you. We could let our guard down."

"There are lots of good caregivers out there," Chyna objected. "You're selling the industry short."

"You know that's not what I mean."

"Of course," she said quickly. "I'm just saying that – well, it's a thankless job for some, if not all, and for very low pay. You have to love it: you have to have a kind of calling on your heart. There are good carers out there, attentive ones, but it is a hard job, especially when some patients get belligerent or plain ornery."

Dean was quiet a moment. "Was my dad ever nasty to you?"

"Of course not," she responded with feeling. "We knew each other, and that familiarity brought about a kindness. To be nasty, you have to have a kind of predisposition for it, I think. You're nasty in the first place, when your mind is all there, then that same nastiness just gets amped up by the disease and medication." She sighed. "That was my Mother for sure. Her existing pain, regret and jilted-lover complex made her pretty horrible in the end. I knew your dad since I was a child. Even if he was ever a little short with me, I knew it was the disease, not him. You have to be able to separate the two."

"He forgot most of us," Dean said, almost to himself. "That was hard."

"I know." She started to reach out, but withdrew her hand

in mid-air. "I'm sorry."

Chyna needed to leave. "I'm gonna go take a shower - or a sponge bath, I guess. That's kind of what I take now." She laughed. "Just a few more weeks and I'll be able to get this cast off: trading it for a boot, I think. At least I'll be able to remove the boot and take a real shower again."

"I just installed a three-way shower head upstairs here," Dean put in. "When you are better you can test it out - see if you want one in your new bathroom."

Chyna nodded but didn't comment. The shower sounded wonderful, but at this point even a bath in the river would be welcome, just so long as she could get her stupid cast off. The fact that he was talking bathroom renovations meant he was thinking in more detail about her home repairs that he should. She needed to check it out, and fast.

DEAN WATCHED HER LIMP AWAY. His mood brightened every time he saw her. Despite her obvious embarrassment at the bed-head and mismatched pajamas, it all made her seem like she was just sixteen again, and just as cute as she'd always been. He moved to the kitchen, filled the tea kettle and turned it on low. Today he'd finish the front door, then do the side and back door before lunch.

Uneasiness still ate at him about what Warren had said. Whether or not the foolish man was serious about any of the gibberish that came out of his mouth, it was enough to propel Dean into action, attempting to control whatever he could. To him, that meant protecting this house, Chyna's house and the people inside each. The alarm system had abruptly moved to the top spot on his long list of home tasks, as well as adding a front and side door camera. Dean's brother-in-law, Chase, had told him which camera to get. It sent an automatic alert when someone came to the door. Thanks to that product, Chase had been able to get to Tish faster that fateful day just a year ago, thereby saving her life. Dean had ordered the device last night online with rush shipping. The renewed urgency he felt was also the reason he had stayed the night.

He hadn't told Chyna about his heightened sense of the threat before because he needed more intelligence around it. Now, knowing that Warren knew her, liked her and had previously given her cause to be afraid of him made him so angry he felt the rage shake his fingers as he tried to place the thin, delicate washers on the small nails securing the new keypad locks in place. Taking a deep breath, he steadied his hands and managed it at last, putting Warren out of his mind for the time being. Now he could screw everything back together.

Also on Dean's agenda for the day was to do some digging around regarding his father's estate. He needed to find those papers that Lisa said she'd given his mother. Understandably, Ms. Alfreah hadn't wanted to deal with many of the practical ramifications when her one and only love had died, so accordingly she'd passed on a lot of correspondence from Lisa directly to Dean, simply forwarding it to his inbox. Truth be told, though, he'd either missed the last few documents or hadn't received them at all. He needed to find them, yet he was also loathe to meet with Lisa again. If Chyna believed something was going on between them, he was sure she wouldn't be visiting his house ever again. Now he had two people to keep out of the Jameson home, he thought glumly. The list was growing.

"Uh, I need food," Chyna announced, turning into the kitchen.

Dean turned, almost done with the door. "I bought some fresh croissants this morning. You can warm those. Oh, and the tea water is on: should be ready by now."

"Wow thank you, that was thoughtful."

He smiled at her as she spotted the items he'd laid out on the counter top next to the brown bag of fresh patisserie - but pretended she didn't. She pulled a pastry apart and popped some into her mouth, studiously avoiding the other items.

Dean got a mug and poured the tea, busying himself while he waited. He handed the steaming cup to her. He watched as she lifted the other bag he set out, with its familiar logo. He'd made sure to take the receipt out and toss it: the stuff was his gift to her, no turning back, no returns. He wanted her to do something that she loved and he really hoped this was a way of persuading her to try her art again. *Or it'll be a disaster and you'll have bombed, yet again,* an inner voice chastised.

"You didn't buy this stuff, did you?" she questioned after a while.

"Yes," he beamed. "Do you like it?

"It's a really expensive brand," she observed carefully. "I only splurge on this kind once in a while. It's, uh, it's nice."

Chyna touched the items reverently and set down the cup of tea he'd handed her moments ago. The collection of gifts were from her favorite arts and crafts store, the white bag emblazoned with their motto: "Everything a canvas in which to dream in color". Inside nestled small tubes of paint in a rainbow of colors, all those she would need to mix whatever color she didn't have, plus a palette for mixing them and six different-sized paintbrushes. She touched the silky bristles, taking in the soft feel of each hand-woven hair. Dean had touched them the same way himself: he wasn't into painting at all, but when he'd been to the store, he'd purchased whatever the eager salesperson had talked him into. He was reassured by the fact that Chyna examined the things as long and hard as she did: her interest as well as her desire and curiosity were hopefully piqued. He cleared his throat.

"Mom always wanted you to paint this picture on the backsplash," he told her, handing her a page torn from a popular home design magazine. "I can install the tile if you think you can do the art." The image showed a large tree: a southern oak, strong at its base, with curving triple-twisted limbs that rose up overhead, with thick moss intricately woven and curling over each branch. At the base of the tree peeped small pink azalea blossoms lining a long gravel road.

Dean was silent as Chyna's fingers followed the lines of the large tree. He didn't know what the picture signified for his mother, but it likely had a lot to do with their family. There were so many symbolic aspects of the picture. It even made him think of himself and Chyna.

When she looked at him, however, the tears he saw made him instantly regretful. "I'm sorry, I'm sorry - I'll return it," he assured her hastily. This was not going the way he intended at all.

"Chyna, it's okay..." He had no idea what to do or say, but he began stuffing the items back into the bag, ready to toss them out the window if he had to - before her hands stopped his and lingered momentarily.

"Thank you," she whispered.

The words seemed to turn his thoughts around. "Okay - I think," he said cautiously. Then she laughed, and he was even more confused. She set down the paper and wiped her tears. "Thank you for encouraging me."

In an instant, Dean moved closer to her and embraced her fully. He hadn't hugged her at all since she'd been there, though he had desperately wanted to many times.

She didn't move from his embrace and he drew her closer, tighter to him. "We all need a little encouragement sometimes."

She looked up at him and he couldn't stop himself. He leaned down and touched his lips to hers: tortuously fleeting at first, as if testing the waters, but in a moment, she leaned into him, returning his kiss fully and unabashedly, and giving him in turn all the encouragement he needed.

15

C hyna touched her lips once again. She couldn't believe what had just happened. Minutes later, she was alone again in the kitchen finishing her tea and croissant, but the memory of Dean's lips on hers would never be forgotten.

She could barely enjoy her breakfast for playing with her new painting stash. Her fingers seemed to itch for the first time in a long time as she stared at the magazine page from Ms. Alfreah. Her eyes traced the lines of the tree – then, picking up a paintless brush, she gently followed the same line again to the edge. She looked up and over at the backsplash above the stove. It was bare, and though she could definitely paint something for it, she'd need to see what she should use to defend against all the build-up and splatter from the delicious food Ms. Alfreah made almost every day.

She wondered why Mrs. Jameson had liked this particular print so much. In the bag of gifts, Dean had also included some plastic stencils. She'd nearly laughed when she found them, and the true painter inside her tried not to feel insulted. *That was for amateurs.* She checked herself, wondering where this newfound confidence came from: so sure of herself, for someone who hadn't been formally trained. She hadn't lifted a brush since her first miscarriage, but something had eased since then, and she slowly felt like she just might be able to revisit her artistic endeavors at last. Maybe. In any case, the fact that this project was for Ms. Alfreah seemed to give her added optimism and purpose. She'd take whatever motivation she could get.

Tearing off a piece of the paper bag, Chyna began to write down a list of additional art supplies to supplement this fine starter kit. She jotted down extra things: acrylic gloss medium, acrylic gel, charcoal pencils, a notebook, and one more particularly fine brush to help her make the finest, spindly lines of the tree's delicate upper branches...

Chyna looked down at the paper again and suddenly crumpled it angrily. With a halfhearted throw, she sent it sailing into the air. It bounced off the wall and back to her.

When the doorbell rang, Chyna jumped. She moved gingerly to the front door to see who it was, but when she heard the jangle of keys, she stopped and backed away in alarm.

Chyna softened immediately when Dean's sister's muffled annoyance could be heard on the other side of the door. Rushing forward smiling, she opened it to her longtime friend, Dean's older sister Jina.

"Hey, what is going on? Who changed the locks?" Jina demanded, breezing into the house.

"Hi," Chyna replied. "Dean changed them when he put on a new alarm system. I'm sure he'll get you a key. I think he just went out to have some made this morning."

"Jeeze Louise, Momma gone a few weeks and he's taken over! Now I can't get into my own house?" Jina exclaimed. "Talk about changes. I can't take no more!"

"Let me take your bag," Chyna offered, reaching for the blue-striped diaper bag Jina carried on the shoulder that didn't support her blanketed bundle of baby. "Is Tony with you?"

Jina shook her head. "We saw Dean at the store. Tony stayed to help him get some stuff - for the deck, I think, or whatever Dean's planning to fix up next. They'll be a while. The only place I could spend an entire day like that would be a shop full of shoes and clothes." Jina smiled. "But enough about them. What's happening here? How are *you*?" Strolling into the kitchen, Jina sat down and gently removed the thin blanket covering the baby to settle him over her lap.

"Oh, I'm great, I guess," Chyna replied. "I feel a little... awkward being here, staying here, without your mom or... any of you, for that matter," she added hurriedly, realizing she had almost mentioned Mr. Jameson.

"And Dad?" Jina finished, reading Chyna's thoughts.

Chyna looked down. "Yes," she whispered. "It's just different, you know? Having been his caretaker and all, at least I had something to do: some way to help."

"Girl, please," Jina cut in. "Before you were his caretaker, you didn't have to do anything or find any way to help. We're practically sisters. What's the matter with you?"

"Nothing." Chyna looked down at her fingers, realizing she'd gotten paint on them. She rubbed them together, the slick, oily texture stirring something inside her. Taking a napkin from the table, she tried in vain to wipe it off.

Jina looked at Chyna's fingers in consternation. "Are you bleeding?"

"Oh no, it's just crimson paint," Chyna assured her with a laugh.

"So you're painting again? That's wonderful," Jina smiled encouragingly.

"No, I... No." Chyna wanted to protest but couldn't find a reason to say otherwise. She did have paint on her hands, after all, not to mention the supplies that littered the counter and a list of yet more supplies to boot. Somewhat abashed, she admitted to herself that she had just been reluctant to believe that she could pick it back up so easily, let alone recreate that beautiful tree. She remembered that anything she was going through always seemed to transmit itself to the canvas. She was afraid, was all. That much she already knew.

She was truly thankful to Dean because he had encouraged her, where Gary had never encouraged her at all. Dean's gifts to her today communicated his firm belief in her abilities. This triggered a need to find something to call her own again. And that kiss - her mind fluttered – well, that had certainly been very encouraging too.

With the renewed goals of the painting project, finishing at least one stupid article and looking for another caregiver job, she felt truly thankful to Dean. His gift was like the most thoughtful, gentle kick in the pants imaginable. While Gary had constantly questioned her painting and all but banished any traces of it from their home, Dean bought her supplies, gave her an idea of what to paint to help her get started, and essentially said it was all right whether she did or didn't. No pressure to move either way: it was just there, waiting for her if and when she was ready. She did get the feeling that he was also waiting for her to make a decision of a different sort: to accept or reject a possible something between the two of them. She loved him for that and so much more. In fact, she hadn't ever stopped.

Chyna took a deep breath and smiled sadly at Jina.

"Is Dean treating you badly?" Jina asked. "You know he's only mean to you because he loves you."

"Ha!" Chyna laughed bitterly and her loud outburst caused the baby to stir briefly. Fresh croissants in the morning, starting renovations projects at a reasonable hour so she could sleep in most days, hot tea or really good fresh coffee waiting for her whenever she got out of the shower, no complaints about how long those showers took, the best free kisses – well, only the one so far, but a very good hug; longing looks, installing an alarm system to protect her... Then there was the very fact that he'd taken her fear of Warren seriously: a response so different from her own former husband to what was basically an assault, not only on her person but on her then-marriage.

She kept forgetting that they now lived in the age of Me Too. All around the world, women were speaking up - and what was she doing? Letting Gary and Warren spew lies and do as they pleased, when all the while she knew and hid the truth about them both. As far as the idea of Dean being at all mean – well, if she were honest, the only jerk she could see in this situation was herself.

"No, J, he's..."

"You know," Jina continued, not listening, "I said that I was going to mind my own business, and you know how hard that is for me, but I cannot stay out of this. Dang it, I really can't, Chyna. That foolish brother of mine needs some help mentally, and probably a whooping too."

Chyna wanted to laugh at the image of petite Jina Jameson whipping the butt of her own much larger brother. "It's so much more than that, J," Chyna whispered, looking out the window. She realized fast that by not voicing all the wonderful things that Dean did, she was indicating to Jina by default that her brother was treating her badly. He wasn't. Chyna held all the cards and kept all the secrets, and now she had no idea how to come clean – or even whether coming clean would ruin whatever they were building together.

"Do tell?"

"Tell what?" Chyna hesitated. She shook her head evasively.

"Let me tell you, then, that one thing is clear: he's a fool," huffed Jina. "My own brother, temporarily insane. Now, Joe and Free Jameson didn't raise any fools. I don't understand any of it.

I don't understand why it's taking almost fifteen years for him to admit what's obvious to everyone else."

"It's not the same as it was then," protested Chyna. "It won't be the same. As soon as my house is built back up, I'm leaving, J. I'm selling the place and I'm moving to another town, another state, as far away from here as I can get. Then he can get on with his life and I can get on with mine."

Chyna hadn't meant to blurt out that she was moving: she had only just recently begun even thinking about that. Moving wasn't exactly what she wanted to do, even; but now it was out there.

"There is a reason all of this hasn't worked out between us in all these years," she continued. *And it's entirely my fault*, she added silently. "I've... I've stopped believing that it will," she continued aloud. "We just... weren't meant to be anything other than friends."

Jina shook her head, confused. "Nonsense!" she said. "I could get JoJo to beat him up for you," she added seriously.

"What?" Chyna smiled and managed a small real laugh this time.

"He'll do it," assured Jina eagerly. "He won't hurt him, just knock some sense into him, maybe bruise that big ol' lip of his. I'll give him a call."

Chyna laughed out loud, covering her mouth. "No, but thanks anyway, J. I'll probably beat him up myself before I move." *I need to beat myself up*, she thought remorsefully.

Jina sighed loudly, throwing up her hands. "So with nothing solved, you'd just leave? Again? Chyna, just like when you went to California? Just like after you quit working with Dad? Where in the world did you go, anyway, and why did you leave so abruptly?"

"Now that, that was different," Chyna began, but realized she couldn't elaborate on the reasons why the situation was so 'different' without explaining what had really happened.

"I had to leave then," she said, when Jina continued to look at her expectantly. "I enjoyed taking care of your father and I'm sorry I left just before he died." Yes, a part of her knew he was going to die, and maybe like a coward she ran - but it wasn't the only reason.

"Tell me why, then?" Jina pleaded. "See, that's the thing no one understands: why did you feel you had to leave? You didn't have to be his caretaker anymore if you didn't want to. Didn't you know that? But to leave altogether? We didn't get it. Still don't. Did it get too hard? Was he too close to home?"

Chyna shook her head. "No, Jina. Most of the people I've taken care of live in this neighborhood. Most of them I've known since I was little." And she could often tell when death was near. She always hated that aspect of her job; but that hadn't been why she'd left for California. Actually, she had thought she might see Gary over the course of a couple of days out there: tell everyone the truth about when their divorce actually occurred, tell Dean they could finally be together without Gary's threats hanging over them, and be Mr. Jameson's caretaker again. Only she had a much larger problem.

"So what was it then?" Jina persisted.

"I was just... I just couldn't, okay? Please, just try to understand. It's not like he missed me anyway, J. Lisa Stephens will conveniently come back around whenever I'm gone, and that will be the end of it. He'll forget about me, he'll go back to her." Chyna felt the old anger returning, thinking of Lisa Stephens. Was the entire family so clueless about Dean's relationship with her?

Jina blinked rapidly. "What did you say?" she said. "Lisa *Stephens*? Don't tell me she's been sniffing around here again?" Jina's eyes grew wide with outrage. "And hello? There is no *go back to her*, Chyna. They were never together: if they ever were, I'd give her a piece of my mind and tell her to stay the hell away from our family."

Chyna looked at her friend, confused but hoping that Jina would go on. Sure enough, taking a deep breath, Jina continued:

"Look, when Daddy got sick, that heifer was around here all the time, poking her nose into our business. She offered to help Mama with Daddy's paperwork and his business - financial advice about what to do with his estate. I didn't say nothing at the time, and Mama was too nice to say anything either. That woman came in here telling everyone what to do like we were a bunch of illiterates. None of us had the word *stupid* stamped on our forehead. We all have advanced college degrees, but she took advantage of Mama and the rest of us when we were grieving and distracted. She used that time to worm her way in here, making it seem as if none of us had time to see to Mama's needs. And that was right around the time Tony and I were having issues..." Jina looked away and then down at the baby. "I never told anyone but T.T. this, Chyna – but when Tony and I had some problems, Lisa Stephens took it upon herself to try to... *console* him."

"What?" Chyna gasped.

Jina nodded in confirmation, her lips pursed. "She didn't get very far. You know, Tony and I had hit a rough patch, but we love each other. We maintained that we would always be able to work things out. That day, it hadn't been twenty-four hours since our fight. Tony was here fixing up something for Mama, and Lisa was over here pretending to do God knows what. I walked in to find her coming on to him. You should have heard the things I heard her say about me. She told him how she could help him 'get over me'. I almost leaped on the counter, I was so furious."

Jina leaned back in her chair. Blowing out a loud sigh, she shifted the baby onto her shoulder. "Don't let her come anywhere near Dean, Chyna. He doesn't like her like that. Mama, me, Jojo, this whole family, we just feel sorry for her.

She tries too hard, and more importantly, Dean does not love her. You hear what I'm saying?"

Chyna nodded.

"Please," Jina snorted, visibly angry. "I thought she and Warren Hardig were an item anyway."

16

Chyna's head was spinning at Jina's new revelations. "Wait, back up. What did you say about Warren Hardig?"

Jina looked up. "Lisa Stephens and Warren Hardig? Well, a couple weeks ago they were on the business page of the paper. She's always dating some high profile something or other. You remember Mark Davies?"

"The basketball player?" Chyna clarified.

"Jenkins and Sapp?"

"Those R'n'B singers? Wow, she does get around," Chyna remarked, completely surprised.

"Yeah and I cannot for the life of me put my finger on why she's been looking Dean's way," his sister mused. "Sure, he's got money, from his investments and all, and maybe that's all it takes; but he's not high profile enough for her usual taste. No parties, no hobnobbing, not into politics even - he's just a regular guy. It's weird for her."

Chyna raised her eyebrows. To her, Dean was not regular. Truth be told, she could see any woman falling in love with him: he was kind and caring and so good looking... but she could understand that his own sister wouldn't see him that way.

"Dean's a good man, I'm not questioning that," Jina said, reading Chyna's mind as ever. "I'm just saying, Lisa likes to move in circles with way more power and money than Dean's got. A party every night wouldn't be too much for her. She probably thought she'd try to get Dean as a placeholder while she geared up for a larger conquest. That girl would run him into the ground, mark my words: it would take her two years, if that. Dean hates politics and doesn't keep up with celebrities. That's why it's just odd her going after him. There must be something else."

Jina paused to adjust the baby's blankets tenderly. "Anyway, Warren keeps bugging Dean, always talking up this new building enterprise scheme of his. Lisa was hanging on Warren's arm in that newspaper picture, and the article implied that the two of them were an item. That particular rag prints lies all the time, though, so who really knows?"

Chyna shook her head, trying to process all this. Jina rattled off information faster than the nightly news and it was often hard to keep up with the many and varied strands of information as well as the vast array of details. "Is it a big deal that she's dating Warren? - aren't they both lawyers?"

"What?" Jina exclaimed incredulously. "Lisa Stephens is no lawyer, girl: she's a legal secretary. Big difference. She's basically a glorified, overpriced receptionist. For real: she answers phones over there at the Hardig building. Not only that, she flat-out lied telling Mama she was a certified public accountant. I did some checking. She went to school for it, but she didn't finish. She told Mama she could invest some of our money - my God, I'm glad Mama didn't give her a dime. I told Lisa to get the heck out of our house and to stop bothering us. She'd probably have taken us for a pretty penny given half a chance."

Reaching across the table, Jina took her friend's hand.

"Hear me, Chyna - please hear me when I say that Dean doesn't love her, he just pacifies her. That's all. You fight for what you want. Do you want Dean?"

Chyna didn't answer, even more confused now than ever. Not to mention she'd just told her friend that she planned to sell her house as soon as Bubba finished putting it back together. It must be clear by now that she had no idea about anything.

"I'm sorry, honey. Just, uh, don't answer that, okay?" Jina shook her head and smiled. "I know you love him."

Chyna kept her head still, her eyes the only thing she let move. She wouldn't answer questions about how she felt about Dean, not even to one of her closest childhood friends. Jina had dropped so much on her that she needed some more time just to sort through it all. As she pondered, she began to wonder if Dean knew as much about Lisa as his sister seemed to.

She managed a smile at her friend and tried to look nonchalant as her mind frantically attempted to flip through, categorize and file all the new information Jina had just thrown her way. After a good few moments of thought, however, things were still quite unclear.

"One more question, Chyna," Jina began again.

"What is it?" Chyna said, though she didn't want 'one more question' posed about issues she was reluctant to address at all, let alone discuss in depth.

"Gary, your ex? He's been in the paper a lot - he's slipping in the polls. The next election doesn't look good for him. Do you think it's anything to do with that interview you gave about the marriage?"

Chyna shrugged, unconcerned. "So what? That doesn't concern me," she said. Gary Williams had nothing to do with her, not anymore. She didn't care one way or the other what became of his political candidacy.

"I see," Jina replied. "I mean, you aren't in contact with him these days, are you?"

Chyna shook her head.

"Now, my brother?" Jina continued. "Chyna, he's stubborn. You should know that when it comes to you, there's one person he feels he can't compete with, and that's your ex-husband. I know you may not believe that. I know it's hard for you to think about Dean having insecurities, as confident as he is, but you're like the only person or thing he has ever been insecure over, okay?"

"When you got married, Chyna, his whole world crashed," Jina went on. "Dean's not poor. If anyone could manage his money, could set away some serious funds and do without, it's my little brother. But a *senator*?" Jina emphasized. "Senator Gary Williams: his title says it all. Not just money, but power, status, access. That man could have given you whatever you wanted. Dean felt as if he could never compete with that. Think about it, okay?"

Jina stood. "Listen, I've got to go potty, then I wanted to go find something in my old stash upstairs. Can you hold the baby for a second?"

Chyna didn't have a moment to adjust her thoughts. Her friend's mouth seemed to run a mile a minute, leaving the listener no time for processing a response. But when she looked up, her eyes widened. *What?* Could she hold him? *No!* her mind screamed in protest. She didn't want to. But now, with her friend standing over her poised to give her the child, she wondered what she could possibly say to get out it. *How about "I'm allergic"?*...

Instead, she stammered: "Uh, why don't you lay him down in the bedroom? I'll keep an eye on him."

"Oh, please, Chyna, you'll be fine," Jina said breezily. "He won't raise a fuss. He hasn't been sleeping long, he's eaten, had his diaper changed, passed gas - he's good for a bit. You take care of frail old people, for goodness' sake! Babies are exactly the same, only cuter."

Jina laughed and, without further comment, leaned down and practically dumped her infant son into Chyna's arms. Instinct kicked in immediately and she automatically opened her arms to support the baby's form. She nudged the child into a more comfortable position, ensuring that she supported his head, while Jina moved to the door, keeping her eyes on them as she backed away. "See, you're a natural," Jina said, before disappearing from the room.

Chyna looked down at the child. "No, not a natural, huh, Robby?" She was thoughtful a minute. "Are they going to call you Robby or Bobby? Robby or Bobby... they're both great," she murmured, half to herself. "I like them both! Robert Joseph, after your grandfather. He loved you, baby. There is so much love here in this house, in this family." Chyna took a deep breath. "Just, uh, don't let them call you Bob. You don't look like a Bob."

Robby's face grew tight, as if he was about to cry. "See?" Chyna breathed loudly. "I'm no natural," she said. "I'm just your regular fool. How does that song go?" Chyna sang an off-key rendition to the child.

Not knowing what to do when Robert began to fuss louder, she stood up and stopped singing, thinking that her cracked rendition would make even a deaf person cry. She began to walk, or rather sway, considering her stupid leg, trying to soothe the baby with gentle motion. "You look a lot like your mama," she whispered, "and you got a little bit of... Dean? I guess. The lips and your nose, and you're bronzy-red like Dean was. How is it that offspring can skip around and miss their parents to look like their aunties and uncles, anyway?"

Chyna looked at the child, his face relaxed and close to sleep once again. "You don't talk much, do you, little man? Well, let me tell you, you got to learn how to talk and fast, because your mama ain't gonna let you get a word in edgeways."

She continued rocking him, examining his cute pie-shaped face, his little pug nose and large eyes. She gasped a little when he opened them briefly to stare at her, then closed them just as quick, as if what he saw wasn't what he wanted.

Chyna continued to drink in his features, knowing that in weeks, even days, he'd grow and change so rapidly. But for now, his breath when he yawned smelled like warm milk and he was perfect for cuddling. In just a matter of months he'd be running around spreading mayhem and destruction. Chyna felt a sting in her eyes and a yearning in her heart.

Taking a deep calming breath, Chyna was determined not to cry. Determined not to get depressed that it was someone else's child she was holding and not her own. "Life is so unfair, but I'm not going to cry - no sirree." She swore under her breath. "I mean, shoot - shoot, sweetheart. Don't ever say bad words like your Momma or me," she cooed. "Oh, man - what do I have to cry about anyway?" Chyna laughed. "I just made a mess, that's all. I made a big boo-boo, all by myself," she said, thinking back to all that Jina had revealed about Lisa Stephens.

"Was there truly nothing between her and Dean?" she asked the baby, wondering if she'd misread everything she thought she had witnessed. If that were the case, she'd shut Dean out when she was hurting most, ultimately unwilling to work hard enough go after the thing she wanted most. "I'm a real fool, Robby, a complete and utter fool."

So lost was she in babbling her musings to the child, Chyna didn't even notice that Dean had returned until she looked up, startled that he'd been able to enter the house and move down the hall as quietly as he did. What on earth had happened to that fancy new security alarm, anyway?

"You're going to be a great mother," Dean said.

That did it. "I've got to go," she said aloud, as she limped her way to the door. Copying Jina's earlier move, Chyna filled Dean's arms with his nephew on her way past. He'd adjust, just as she'd had to a few minutes ago.

Dean expertly supported his nephew's form, but his eyes focused on her, nonplussed. "What did I say, Chyna? Are you tired? Does your leg hurt?" he pressed, when she didn't answer.

Despite the kiss that very morning, Jina's revelations had stirred up the old simmering anger in Chyna once again. Sadly, this time most of it was only directed at herself.

"I am *fine* - please stop asking me that, okay?" she snapped. "And just because I wasn't up and moving around doesn't mean I was asleep, you know."

"I checked on you," Dean said quietly, looking down at his nephew.

Chyna looked away. "Well, I don't need you to check on me."

"No? And what if you break your other damn leg, or need help?" Dean said, his temper rising to meet hers.

"Just like I have found a way to deal with everything else in my life, I'll deal with it," she said, thinking of the recent months. "I won't be in your hair much longer, so there's no need to keep worrying about me."

"But I *will* worry about you, Chyna. Always."

Chyna threw up her hands in frustration. What could she possibly say to that? She turned on her heel to leave, bumping into Jina as she limped to the door. "Sorry," she muttered in her hasty exit.

DEAN WATCHED CHYNA GO. He hated that his sister was there: the more outspoken and sometimes abrasive of his sisters that she was. He loved Jina, of course, but she always had plenty of advice and might unleash it unsolicited at any given moment.

Dean sat down and concentrated on his nephew, amazed at how big he'd grown in just a couple short months.

"Well hello again, dear brother," Jina said as she waltzed back into the kitchen.

Dean rolled his eyes.

"Don't you roll your eyes at me! I was actually going to compliment you on the house, Dean. The improvements you have made look really wonderful."

"Thanks," Dean mumbled.

"But I think what I should really be doing is clocking you over the head with a two-by-four. Got one handy?" Jina quipped as she pretended to search.

"This ain't none of your business," Dean said.

"That may be true, but when has that ever stopped me before?" Jina replied smartly. "I just don't understand you two."

"Welcome to my world," Dean returned.

"A world you made for yourself, big brother."

"I had help, you know."

"Give me a break." Now it was Jina's turn to roll her eyes. "So Chyna helped you make a mess of both your lives. Clean the damn thing up."

"Hey, uh, want me to take him?" Both Jina and Dean looked to the door as Jina's husband Tony entered, indicating his tiny son.

"Yes, honey, thank you. We'll just be a few more minutes," Jina said as she took her child from Dean's arms and placed him in her husband's.

With nothing else to do with his hands, Dean rested an arm on the table where he sat. "Whatever," he said to his sister's expectant gaze. "I suppose Ms. Lockhart talks to you, tells you every cotton-pickin' thing?"

"No Dean, she doesn't tell me everything and she doesn't have to. The tension in here is so super-duper thick, it doesn't take a genius to figure out there's something going on."

Dean lowered his voice and glanced toward the door before returning his eyes to his sister. "I'm trying, alright? I try and I'm not getting a lot of help, okay? But make no mistake: this is both of our faults. And something seems wrong with her," he added in a low tone. "She's usually a go-getter, but right now she just seems stuck – plus, did you notice she's lost a lot of weight?"

Jina simply shrugged. "She's always been skinny, Dean."

"Not that skinny." Dean shook his head. He hadn't voiced his thoughts aloud until now. Come to think of it, Charlie had actively tried to hide the fact that Chyna had been in the hospital recently. Dean had deduced it hadn't been that long ago.

"Oh, Dean, come on now," coaxed his sister. "She's just stressed, probably: her house is a mess, from what Bubba said - her ex-marriage a farce - and now she's just kind of stuck here at your mercy. Frankly, I'd be sick too. I'm fairly sure she's just going through a bit of a rough patch."

"*Fairly* doesn't cut it, Jina. She was in the hospital right around the time she stopped working for Dad. Did she tell you that?" Dean had been thinking about it and was sure he'd finally worked out the order of previous events. Everything from the time Chyna had told his mom she needed some time off was a little sketchy, but he knew for sure that time included a visit to California, a return to Virginia, and a stay at the hospital. What plagued Dean was that whatever issue she was going through might not have been something he could fix. Much like the time his mother had first told him his father had Alzheimer's. Back then, thinking about some life-threatening illness he had no cure for had paralyzed Dean with grief, and this situation felt horribly similar. It brought about a type of panic, and the determination to do anything at all was just zapped from him.

"How do you know? She could've been getting a checkup," Jina countered. "Did you ask her?"

"And you think she's just going to up and tell me?" There was a lot Dean had wanted to ask Chyna, including whether or not they stood a chance at love. Was she sick? Did she love him? Did she carry a torch for her Senator ex-husband?

But memories of their night together before Chyna returned to California, coupled with an all-consuming raging jealousy of her ex-husband, reared up in Dean so strong he had simply left all the matters that needed to be addressed between them unresolved. He settled for their spontaneous conversation, their politeness as if they were strangers. The rogue kiss earlier that morning had had him believing once more that there was something salvageable between them. Every single day, a little progress, followed immediately by twelve steps backward.

"I don't know," Jina replied, "and neither will you unless you try. Stop playing these stupid games and get some answers. She won't just up and volunteer information: you have to dig. Oh, and another thing: she thinks you're seeing Lisa Stephens! Where did she get that idea from, huh?" Jina didn't wait for an answer. "Chyna isn't sick, Dean: she's hurt, and you've got to find out what or who hurt her. Spoiler alert: you are suspect numero uno, Senor Broseph. So make it right. Poke and prod until the truth comes out."

Dean stared at his sister a moment, knowing everything she said was true. He just didn't want to deal with the things she'd rightly told him he needed to confront. He took a deep breath and graced her with a half a smile. "You actually made sense, for once," he admitted begrudgingly.

"Thanks. Having a kid will do that to you. Really gets you down to earth," Jina answered. "If you ever get it together, I guess you and Chyna can have a couple."

Dean sobered at that statement. Realizations slammed into his mind so quick he felt out of breath. Then there was pain. Pain he remembered seeing in Chyna's eyes. The baby books in her home: why keep them if she and Gary hadn't wanted children? And just a few minutes ago, when Dean had told Chyna she'd make a great mother as she had held his nephew, such a look of loneliness and loss had filled her eyes. The final piece fell into place in his head: the last time they'd been together, they'd been... intimate. They'd both wanted to wait, but they had so little restraint. Then he hadn't seen Chyna for a few weeks at all. Now he had it, finally, the answer to this long-held mystery - and he immediately wished he didn't.

Dean felt as if he'd been punched in the chest.

"Hey, hey now." Jina patted her brother on the shoulder and pulled him into her arms in concern. "Don't get winded on me now. What's the matter? Do you feel all right?"

"I'm fine." He'd never be fine until he had the truth, but color came back to his face and he nodded to his sister to let her know he was okay.

"All right," Jina said doubtfully, "but uh, keep taking care of Chyna, OK? If she's sick, as you think, let us know - we're all here for her. She may feel out of place now that she has nothing and no-one to take care of. I tried to assure her that it was fine. She's a part of our family forever."

"Yes, forever," Dean repeated. He'd only been trying to seal their permanence before she'd upped and left town.

Jina stood. "I gotta go, bro. I'll see you soon. Fix this, please. It's gonna be worth it, but like a dislocated shoulder, it's gotta hurt first. You may exchange words you regret, but for the love of God, just get it out there."

Jina and Tony's departure was a blur as Dean stood staring blindly for several minutes. All Chyna's pain and hurt; the real reason she hadn't come back. Now that he had a theory about what had happened, he needed confirmation, however painful that might be. They needed to try to fix their future. It couldn't wait any longer. Resolute, Dean went down the hall to talk to Chyna.

17

Chyna did all she could to keep from crying, but it was no use. Burying her face in the pillow, she sobbed as quietly as she could. When the door swung open, she turned away to hide her tearstained face. She prayed it was Jina. She could handle Jina. What Chyna couldn't handle, however, was Dean. Not now.

"Are you all right?" Dean said as he stepped cautiously into the room and sat at the foot of the bed.

"Fine," Chyna said flatly.

"What's the matter?"

"Nothing."

"Then why are you crying?"

She released a breath, "Because I feel like it."

"Well, I, uh, I figured something out, Chyna. There's really no way to approach this delicately, but I'm not leaving until you tell me what's wrong."

"Suit yourself." Chyna burrowed deeper under the covers. He would get tired of waiting - at least she hoped he would. After what seemed like the longest few minutes of her life, however, she didn't feel the bed release the weight by her feet. He was still there.

When it became apparent he wasn't going to leave, Chyna spoke. "I've made a mess of things, Dean."

"Well, I have some culpability in this too, don't you think?"

Chyna laughed. Leave it to him to be so kind, offering to take responsibility, even though he didn't have that much to do with it at all. It was all her fault: it was what she did and what she'd hidden from him. "Did you hear what I said? I made a mess: an irreparable, messy mess."

"I helped you make the mess," he replied.

The silence grew thick before Dean started talking again. "They say loss comes in threes," he began, and Chyna cringed and felt alarmed at the same time. Perhaps he really had figured it all out. But how?

"First" — Dean cleared his throat — "it was Dad; next, it was my business. I was waiting for one more event to complete the triad. I didn't know what it could be, until Jina mentioned something just now. That something knocked the wind right out of me."

"Loss doesn't always come in threes, Dean - that's just a saying. It doesn't happen like that all the time," Chyna offered weakly, though she knew he was right. The third loss had been their child.

Dean nodded, tears standing in his eyes. "When Mom first told me that something was wrong with Dad, I was like, well, whatever it is, it's fixable. I was certain I could fix it. That no matter what, I could handle it. Not his doctors, not Jojo, Jina, or Tish: just me. Then, over time, I would turn out to be the worst possible person for the job. I could barely handle the news, let alone fix a damn thing." Dean let out a bitter laugh.

"I went to this seminar at GMU one night," he continued. "Just by myself. There was only a handful of people there, mostly older females, wives and daughters; I was the only male brave enough, I suppose. At the door, they give you this little pamphlet, *What to Expect When Your Loved One Has Alzheimer's: A Caregiver's Guide.* The lecturer was up at the front. He starts off with a picture of the brain, a little pointer. 'Alzheimer's is a disease that causes the brain to decline in memory...'"

Chyna lifted her head from the pillow and eventually pushed it aside. She listened quietly as Dean mocked the lecturer, his voice taking on a primly professional and detached tone.

"'This results in dementia, loss of intellectual functions, such as thinking, remembering, and reasoning.' They have a top-ten symptoms list, Web page after Web page link, support groups; one place even had a hotline. Really - what on God's green earth do you say when you call a perfect stranger? Anyway, the whole time I was thinking about everyone: how they handled their grief, how we all coped. Mama got through, and only one other person I can think of was strong enough to cope with whatever happened from the get-go till the end... Only one person had taken care of other people in the same situation, watched them die, and helped them and their family through it. That person served as so much more than just a home health aide, nurse's aid, personal care assistant, whatever the title is these days. That one person was you." Dean looked over at Chyna for just a moment.

"You held it all together and took care of him like you were some kind of super-nurse. You developed a schedule, handled his incontinence, his tantrums... Despite what you said, I know there were days when he was ornery, and no one thanked you or thought you had any other purpose than to do that *duty*." Dean sighed. "You've been there, but I haven't. What I mean is, I wasn't mindfully present for you during what I now know must have been your roughest times. You stayed here when I didn't even want you to, and you've been here for as long as I can remember. When I was sixteen, you were here, calling the ambulance and helping Tish and me, after I nearly burnt this house and myself to a crisp. For the life of me, I couldn't figure out why you left, why you stopped caring for Dad what would be the last few weeks and days of his life. Now that you're back, I... I don't want you to ever leave me again."

Dean took a deep inhale. "Jina told me just in the kitchen there, a few minutes ago, that if you and I ever got it together, maybe we could have a couple of kids. She didn't know it but those few words sent something sharp straight through me. They gave me the key to all my questions and brought about a different kind of pain. Chyna... did you stop taking care of Dad because you were pregnant with our baby?"

Chyna looked away and stifled a sob. If she could have floated away into outer space at that moment, she would have - but no such luck. Instead she sat up, ready to leave the room, when Dean's hand grabbed hers.

"Don't leave."

"Please let me go," she managed, her voice cracking.

"No."

He pulled her back to sit next to him and leaned against her shoulder, turning her into his embrace. "You're going to have to talk to me," he insisted. "It's eating away at me, and you cannot tell me it hasn't been eating at you too, not telling me? And not talking isn't the answer. Where are you going, anyway? Please don't run away, and please look at me, Chyna."

Chyna paused, but slowly her eyes lifted to meet his.

"When were you going to tell me? Didn't you think I had a right to know? I'm sorry, baby, I'm so, so sorry, but I didn't know. I would have helped you, I swear to God, Chyna, I would have been there, if I just knew... if you just told me."

"I didn't mean to hurt you. I made a mistake, okay?" What else could she say? "It's too late for any kind of reasoning behind my decision to matter, okay?"

Dean shook his head as if that wasn't good enough. "When

we made love, I told you that I loved you, and you said you loved me too. Then what? You came to the restaurant and saw me hug Lisa — that's all I did, hug her. She leaned in to kiss me, but I put her off. I've done nothing to encourage her. Did you really think that I could dismiss our love so quickly, so easily?"

"Fine, she kissed you, then you what? You just happened to get into her car and go home with her?" Chyna asked skeptically.

Dean stared. "Did you follow us?"

"No..."

"Exactly," Dean said. "She drove me home, saw me inside, and let me pour my heart out, about *you*. I fell asleep and that was that. I was not so drunk as to fall into another woman's bed, nor did I let another woman in my bed. I wasn't unfaithful to you. I needed you, and I was sad you were gone. By all outward appearances, you left me first. You went to California. You could have taken me with you, you know. Heck, if you were going to tell Gary off, I would gladly have gone with you."

"I didn't tell him off per se. I only went to let him know in person that I wouldn't keep our divorce a secret any longer."

"Why did you keep it a secret at all?" Dean demanded.

"To gain my freedom," Chyna explained. "I gave him my word, before, that I wouldn't say anything other than 'no comment' if reporters asked. For the most part, I could lay low in Virginia and no one in California would even notice I was gone. I just had to wait a few months."

"And then we slept together here and that messed you up?"

"It didn't help, certainly," Chyna said. "Gary threatened to accuse me of infidelity – yes, even though he and I were no longer married. Technically I'm the one who left, so no matter what I said to the contrary, he'd cast himself as the jilted lover. He could mess up my name all he wanted - I have no reputation at all to even care about - but I cared about yours, and your family. I knew all of you didn't need all my drama on top of everything else that was going on, with your father's decline. I didn't want that."

"Do you regret it?" he asked softly.

"No, Dean, I don't regret it, but considering that I lost my baby - "

"*Our* baby," Dean corrected her.

"- our baby, it's hard not to feel as if I was being punished. This... this is my second miscarriage."

"With me?"

"No. I lost a baby while married to Gary, too. Don't you want children, Dean?"

"Of course I do, Chyna."

"Well, I don't know if I can give one to you, okay?"

"So you'd be willing to give up on what we have here just because you can't reproduce?"

"No, but..."

"Sounds like that's what you're saying. Tony and J had three miscarriages before she finally got pregnant."

"It's a hard thing to go through, Dean. I never want to feel any of that again. I just don't."

"I've loved you and only you for a long time. And a child would be icing on the cake, but it's not a necessity," he declared. "Besides, there are other ways to make a family, okay? Natural conception and childbirth isn't the only way to get to the goal."

Chyna shrugged her shoulders. "I wanted my – I mean, our baby more than anything."

"I'm still in love with you. I still love you, Chyna. I had a ring."

"What?"

"To ask you to marry me. You turned your back," Dean said, as if reading her mind and the progression of her thoughts. "I love you, and you turned your back on us. I still love you, Chyna. Instead of coming to me to talk, you didn't even try to ask me what happened. I wanted to be there to help you. I wanted to talk to you about dad, about everything. Now it feels like you cheated me out of even grieving my child." He placed a hand on her stomach. "You are perfect to me. You still are what I want. I don't care about children."

"You do, you just said that..."

"I said there are other ways to have them. But if someone gave me the choice right now: if someone said it's either children and a future with someone else, or a future with Chyna with no children for the rest of your life, I'd choose you everyday."

Chyna took a deep breath and laid her head on Deans' shoulder.

"I'm sorry, I can't just jump back to where we were," she murmured. "I need to take some time."

"Then I'll be here," Dean replied. "But while you're thinking and taking a time-out, I'm going to be planning, because I'm not giving up. Not this time. I won't give up on us. I won't, because I love you."

When Dean stood up to look at her, he was elated they'd finally reached an understanding. His deep sadness over his lost child took him by surprise, and he knew from prior experience with grief that it might even hit him harder later. Right then, though, the air was clear and he had a second chance to get all of this right this time.

"I have a meeting," he said, leaning down to kiss her. She returned his kiss again for the second time that day.

"No more secrets."

She nodded.

"That means I want to hear what Gary said and did and how Warren plays a role. Are you ready for all that?"

She hesitated for only a moment before nodding and Dean stood. He caressed her face and stared loving into her eyes. Chyna took his hand, holding on to it.

"I'm sorry."

"I forgive you. Do you forgive me?"

"There isn't anything - "

"Do you forgive me?" he repeated, interrupting her.

"Yes, of course, Dean."

"Then this is the first day in our new life: of honesty and moving forward. Right?"

She nodded.

As Dean left, he reflected that, right then, everything was perfect as far he was concerned. All they had to do now was look ahead, talking openly and honestly about the future. His tenacious hope was finally rubbing off on her.

18

Their current relationship could only be described as less tense but weird, Chyna thought to herself.

She was leafing through what could only be described as a renovation diary Ms. Alfreah had left. It was where the magazine cut-out picture of the tree had come from. It also contained an abundance of notes about all that needed to be repaired around the Jameson house, right down to what colors to put where. It was a veritable catalog of all the little household things that Ms. Alfreah and Joe Senior had gradually become unable to do as they aged, and thus had been constantly put off.

The more she looked at the book, saw the magazine pages and all the ideas, the more Chyna felt her own creativity returning. She was so grateful Dean had shared the scrapbook with her, as well as furnishing her with all the remaining supplies she had been daydreaming about. Smiling, she reflected that he must have found the crumpled paper from the other day with her abandoned list of crafting supplies.

As Chyna diligently sketched out ideas for the house in her new sketchbook as they came to her, she smiled, thinking how

Dean had encouraged her. Her artistic skill had never left her and once she'd been encouraged to resurrect it, the desire returned as well, almost full throttle. It had just been waiting for her, she supposed: waiting for the vital encouragement.

She and Dean were dealing with everything in their own way. Although she was reluctant to analyze every single part of their newfound even keel when for once she was actually feeling optimistic about their future, the fact remained that she still needed to make peace with their past. Every aspect had to be addressed, she knew: Gary, Warren, both her miscarriages, and thoughts about whether or not she deserved to be happy and pursue that happiness. That's essentially what Jina had been talking about when she'd visited. The revelation that Jina had faced her own loss but had still gone on to have such a beautiful baby gave Chyna renewed hope. The people in this family were unrelenting, but at times she quite liked it. It was a good influence on her.

While providing such considerate help and support, Dean was still careful to give her the time and space she'd requested. In doing so, he subtly pulled her back in love with him. Dean Jameson not only cooked, he also watched the romantic comedies she loved streaming even though he hated them; and, in return, she watched a couple of really bad action and sci-fi flicks. They occasionally ordered take-out and managed a few board games, in between his work on the house and her article writing. Through it all, he charmed her with his gentlemanly kindness, showing her exactly how much he loved her by doing and taking care of everything she needed, true to his word.

Sometimes Chyna woke to the sound of music, and was ecstatic to find Dean playing piano. He'd said before that since his dad's death, his fingers had felt numb and the music just wouldn't come. But these days, his beautiful music drifted against the walls of the house once more, and to Chyna that meant some of the pain had eased, just as it had for her when she'd started painting again. She knew the pain would never go away, but at least it had subsided enough to let those wonderful talents back into their lives. Painting was to her what piano playing was to him, yet in the face of tragedy, they'd each abandoned those things that had always brought them so much joy. Slowly though, they'd both found a way to let the important things come back in; and, more than that, they were finding their way back to one another.

The days began to shorten. Chyna wrote and submitted a couple of ads to promote her services as a skilled private nurse. She was moving on, she thought with some satisfaction, as she stretched her newly cast-less leg. She'd had it removed earlier that week. Although she'd had to replace it with a boot, which was a nuisance, she was nonetheless relieved that now she could at least remove the boot and take showers.

Thanksgiving was less than a month away and Chyna envisioned herself seated with all of the Jamesons, the awkwardness and the tension long gone, as a member of the family she'd always longed to be a real part of. Chyna looked over at the phone, thinking of Bubba. Their longtime friend should be calling any day now with an update on the progress of her house. He'd said it would take a few months and it had been that, though the heavy rains may have set their schedule back a week or two - not to mention the hidden hazards Bubba had unearthed and fixed that would doubtless increase the end cost.

Tossing those worries aside, Chyna concentrated on the present. She was upstairs at the Jamesons' place, searching for the room to which Joseph Jameson Sr.'s things had been moved after his death. Sticking her head into Ms. Alfreah's room, she was greeted by the scent of talcum powder and freesia sachets she'd always kept in her dresser drawers. Underneath Alfreah Jameson's signature scents also lingered the spicy cologne that Mr. Jameson had always worn. It was amazing, Chyna thought, how both their scents had remained despite their absence. Just opening the door seemed to reawaken their memories afresh. It was a comforting and nostalgic smell.

Turning the corner as she left the room, she saw Dean sitting on the floor. She turned, leaving the door ajar as she knelt to join him. "I dumped that last box," she said, wiping her dusty hands on her jeans.

"Oh, good. Thank you," Dean said, glancing at her with gratitude. "I didn't hear you come up."

Chyna shrugged and looked at him with concern: something she'd been doing a lot lately. It was hard going through your parents' personal things, his father's especially.

Dean stood abruptly and Chyna waited patiently for him to talk. He placed what looked like an old watch on his wrist and moved over to the mirror, reaching to grab the numerous Polaroid snapshots that lined the edges of his mother's large dresser-mirror. When one tore he snatched away his hand as if he'd committed a heinous crime.

"I did this," Dean gestured before him at the photo arrangement, "to help him remember us all. I wrote everyone's names on the pictures - not that he could even remember how to read by that stage, let alone remember who we were from our pictures," he added ruefully. "You're here too." Dean pointed to a labeled picture of Chyna. His thumb touched the picture and ran lovingly over her face.

Carefully, he made a small stack of the pictures he'd managed to remove without damaging them. Chyna smiled sadly when he faced her.

"You did everything you could," she said. She knew how frustrating it was when one's best efforts could never be enough, but she also knew that Dean had done so much. Everyone else had their families or budding relationships: Jojo had Angel; Tish had Chase; Jina, Tony; and Dean and his Mom were very close, too. Despite what she'd seen as his tuning out after his dad's initial diagnosis those years ago, Chyna had since come to realize how hands-on Dean had in fact been. Sure, he may have tuned out mentally, as anyone would; but his actions were always loving. He was forever doing or trying something on his father's behalf that just might help, from experimental medications to newly-opened memory care facilities, locally or even across the world: striving to find something, anything, to slow the rapid progression of Joe Senior's symptoms. Although ultimately to no avail, he had tried. It had been the nicest part about working to help his family deal with the issues: she and Dean, working together, like a team.

Dean was at the desk now, riffling through some papers. "There's some final paperwork I gotta go through," he told her. "I've called most of the creditors to tell them, but there might be some places I missed, and I'll have to send them a death certificate."

Chyna only nodded. Taking a seat on the floor, she waited for Dean to roll out a two-drawer metal filing cabinet. Getting on his knees beside her, he began to pull out the numerous file folders containing Joe Jameson's entire life on paper.

AFTER ONLY A COUPLE of hours had passed, it seemed like they'd spent the whole day in that one room on their knees. Chyna shifted and stretched her aching legs out before her. She'd suggested more than once that they should take a break and eat something, but Dean was in no mood to slow his roll. The more the two of them uncovered, the less any of it made any sense.

Dean whizzed through papers like a machine, scrutinizing them and turning them every which way as if that would help him to better understand the information they held. As they searched, Chyna began to realize that the documented numbers didn't add up. The house mortgage was marked 'paid' in one folder, but in the very next one it said it wasn't. There were muddled tax papers, bank account details and hastily scribbled checks. Dean couldn't make head nor tail of it: it seemed impossible to reconcile two piles of similar yet conflicting documentation.

"Dean?" Chyna tried again. She knew that his inability to make sense of everything they were finding was only firing his temper, and she waited nervously for the inevitable frustrated outburst.

"Something is wrong with this." Dean scratched his head and continued to search through the stacks of paper as if he hadn't heard her. "Why the hell is this dated less than a year ago, but this one is dated forever ago?"

"I... I don't know," Chyna said, though she knew he was mostly talking to himself. "What I do know is that we should take a break: take a step back from this and see what's what. I mean, you're getting tired, and when you get tired you get cross-eyed, and the numbers - well, for me, they just blur together. Plus, we should get a hold of some current bank statements and see if we can reconcile those. They of all things should be accurate. Man, I always hated math..."

When Dean looked up, Chyna immediately wished she hadn't attempted a joke.

"I'm not so tired, Chyna, that I can't see two plus two is not six, all right?" Dean snapped, muttering an expletive under his breath. Then he softened. "I'm sorry, Chyna."

"It's all right," she said to reassure him.

"It's not," Dean replied, more calmly this time. "My dad fixed up my building with his own hands. He got it when I was just a teenager: happy to get it for a steal from some rich developer, Mom says. He rehabbed it almost all with his own two hands - only got help with some of the plumbing and electrical. That's how I learned most of the building stuff I know how to do. Then, when I finished medical school and got my practice up and running, he turned the place over to me. He was really proud of me."

"He's still proud of you, Deanie." She felt the pride in Dean's voice over his father, coupled with the pain over losing what his father had given to him at such personal cost. It hadn't just been the material gift, but the deeper and more emotionally significant gift of a place and a space in the family's community. It must have been quite something, especially back then. It hurt her to see so clearly that Dean was still hurting.

"The problem with this" — Dean waved his hand over the erroneous stack of papers — "is that it makes it seem like he, and now I, still have a large amount of debt: for materials, services, electricians, plumbing, you name it. There's all kinds of crap listed here that he already had the know-how for, or knew someone who knew how to do it, so I know he would never have paid for it. Now, on the other hand, this over here" — Dean picked up a sheaf of the papers — "makes it seem like everything is legit and that we're in the black."

"Right," Chyna agreed, "but we can't figure it out for sure if we have two different data sets. We need to see the bank manager, an accounts specialist, even see what the IRS has to say." Chyna paused and thought for a moment. "You should talk to Jina, too," she added carefully. "She said that Lisa Stephens might have something to do this."

"What?" Dean said abruptly, nonplussed - but before he could question her further, the ringing phone stole his attention. "You want me to get that?" Chyna offered, but he shook his head as he reached for the receiver on his mother's nightstand.

"Hello?... Hello?" he repeated. He heard someone breathing, but no voice answered. "Hello?" he said again, but the line clicked. Dean hung up, shrugging his shoulders at Chyna's questioning gaze. "Probably a wrong number. Only a handful of people called my mom's landline anyway. Hey, what else did Jina say about Lisa Stephens?"

"Well, so Dean, we can talk about that in a minute, but right now I'm so hungry I can't focus," Chyna finally had the chance to explain. "I'm going to go make us something to eat before anything else happens. Then we can call your sister and talk about it, if you want." She knew that if she attempted to cook, Dean would pretend to eat her creation out of sheer politeness. It was the only way she could think of to get him out of that room. Now, as much as Chyna dreaded the conversation, they'd have to talk about Lisa and what she might have done, whether either party wanted to or not.

More significant than whatever Lisa had or hadn't done, Chyna thought, was the fact that Dean had been putting off coming up to his father's room to go through his personal affairs for so long. Chyna knew from many years of helping others in the same situation that one shouldn't immerse oneself in such a project for entire days at once, but rather tackle it in stages at various intervals. It was also advisable to have some help on hand for those times when it all became a little overwhelming: kind of like it was now. Whether Dean admitted it or not, she knew he needed a break. "I'm going to make something in the kitchen and you're going to eat it," she reasserted firmly.

"Will it kill me?" Dean asked with a grin.

Chyna sighed and rolled her eyes in mock offense. That he was making a joke was a good sign, though, and right now she'd settle for anything to ease the tension. Shaking her head, she returned his smile. "How about, if I burn it, I'll order pizza; but if I don't burn it, which means it's edible, you'll eat it?"

Dean nodded. "Fair enough." He grabbed her hand, pulling her toward him. "I'm sorry for snapping at you... oh, and Chyna?" — he looked away from her piercing eyes — "I really appreciate your being here. I need you to... to help me. Can I kiss you?"

Chyna nodded, and his lips met hers. She wanted to tell

him that everything would be all right: that she would be there, always, to help him... but she didn't. Not just yet.

Despite what she'd been expecting, his kiss was brief and cordial, a very sweet thank-you kiss. She looked at him, longing for more. But she'd started this I-need-time bit, so until she told him she was ready to move a little faster, he would always respect her wishes. *It won't be long,* Chyna thought as she moved to the stairs, a bit of pep in her step at the very thought.

Down in the kitchen, she washed her hands and searched the fridge for something she knew how to make without burning it. When the phone rang, she absently picked it up, forgetting that Dean would answer it upstairs. "Hello, Jameson residence?" she said.

"Hello, Chyna, it's Gary. Remember me?"

19

"You can't seem to do anything right, can you, Ms. Stephens? Once you altered the records, you were to take them to the bank, speak with the man I personally put in place, and he would do the rest. How hard was that? Tell me. What my son sees in you is quite beyond me."

"Your son doesn't 'see' anything in me, Mr. Hardig," returned Lisa coolly. "We're mere conveniences to one another. Isn't that what you wanted? Warren and I have... different goals. He wants Chyna Lockhart, and I certainly don't want him."

Chauncey Hardig nodded. "My son thinks he wants Chyna Lockhart, but he'll get that notion out of his head soon enough."

"Where the heck is he, anyway? I want to deal with him, not you," Lisa shot back.

"He's not feeling well. He will be available in a few days."

"What the hell is the matter with him? Did you have him committed or something?" asked Lisa suspiciously.

"Of course not. I just said he'll be along, and he will." Mr. Hardig stood to return to his office just down the hall.

Lisa stood too, a stack of papers in hand. She hated working here, but she just needed to finish their little project and then she could leave. "You're a real pig, Mr. Hardig!" she muttered under her breath as she turned toward the filing cabinet.

"Be careful what you say," snarled a voice at her back. "I sign your paychecks, and don't you forget it."

Lisa nearly dropped the stack of papers as she flushed crimson. The man had crept up on her again and heard her muttered comment. She hastily stuffed the items into a drawer and went back to her desk.

She was annoyed at what Warren had called to tell her earlier. Chyna and Dean were practically living together! Well, so much for her plans. She hadn't done what she needed to at the bank, either: well, she hadn't finished, but then again she also hadn't had an opportunity to catch Dean Jameson without Ms. Lockhart present. She hunkered down, conjuring a new plan that didn't feature Ms. Lockhart in the picture at all. This was just a temporary set back. Lisa Stephens always met her goals, one way or another.

ALFREAH JAMESON KNEW she'd left something of a financial mess back home in Virginia. Worse, though, was having left the place she called home - and as a widow, too, after forty-six years of wonderful and loving marriage spent there. To put it mildly, the last two years hadn't been the best. To be more realistic, they'd been filled with downright pain, as well as loathing for a devastating and rapidly-progressing disease that had snatched away her husband's mind and all of their shared memories before taking him from her in the flesh. That was why she had left Virginia. Her sons would tackle the finances, and she was confident that it would work out. Meanwhile, she'd had to leave to save her own sanity.

After the funeral was over, after thank-you cards had been

sent and calls made, she'd packed up what few pieces of luggage her baggage allowance permitted and moved to be with her youngest daughter, who now resided in Macon, Georgia. Alfreah kept using the word *temporarily*, but the longer she stayed, the longer *temporarily* lost its appropriateness for the situation. She could make Macon permanent, sure, but for her other children's sake Alfreah maintained that she would, one day, return to Virginia. She had to. She was concerned about Dean - but thank God Chyna was there in the meantime. That girl had been a godsend during her husband's illness and had come to mean so much more to Alfreah: like a third daughter, whom she trusted with everything.

She could just hear the collective gasp of her Virginia children if she were ever to mention her desire to stay right there in Macon, indefinitely avoiding everything back at her longtime home. Any kind of change, especially one so drastic, would spark a great debate among all of them. After Jina voiced her initial complaints, Alfreah pictured with a smile, Jojo would take the floor: always the director. Dean and Tish, her quieter ones, would opt to visit with their mother individually, poking and prodding her with endless questions: *Mama, are you sure? Mama, you could move in with me... Mama, Mama, Mama...*

Nope. For the time being, Alfreah kept reviewing her options and reliving her treasured memories. Asking her youngest son to do some renovations back home had had an underlying purpose. Sure, the house needed fixing up, but Dean also needed something to do with his time. It was evident in the way he bumped around the house after Joe had died, even when Dean had a perfectly good home of his own in Arlington. He'd stuck around to see about her, or so he said, but although she was so thankful he'd moved in and was there for her - especially at night when it was the most lonely – she had to admit it drove her a little crazy.

The way the house was now, coupled with all the memories

that lingered there, made it unconscionable for her to return alone. She'd had a man in the house for most of her life, then suddenly she'd been alone. Additionally, most of the things featured in the stack of magazines she'd been perusing - *House Beautiful, Better Homes and Gardens, Homes of Color* - were so different from what she truly liked. Modern, upscale and elegant was the flavor of the day, while she and her husband had always gone more for the country, traditional and rustic aesthetics.

No matter what, Alfreah Jameson still had her memories in her heart and in the journals she still kept. No matter where she was, she could read back over her passages and be transported once more to that time whenever she needed to escape the more painful present. Right then, though, she had grandchildren on the way and that was what she chose to focus on.

Alfreah shook her head as one last thought of Virginia and all that it stood for came unbidden to her mind. The distant time in her life way back before she'd married her husband: that one-time mistake that had left her forever shackled to Chauncey Hardig.

Hardig was an unscrupulous man. In his pursuit of her over all these years, he had completely disregarded the word "no". Even when her beloved Joe had been diagnosed with Alzheimer's not many years ago, the indomitable Chauncey Hardig took it upon himself once again to visit her, to ask if she needed anything, to try to console her; then he'd redoubled his efforts after Joe had died. There was only one man for her, and he was gone. Alfreah resolved that she would forever respect his memory, and never would she take up with his nemesis.

Her blunt refusal of Chauncey's advances hadn't gotten through the man's head in all these years. In other ways, though, he was smart - too smart. He always 'happened' to stop by for a visit whenever she was alone: when her children had left for the day, or when Chyna took Joe for a walk, or when

Dean was helping him dress. Now, far away in Macon, Georgia, Alfreah believed she'd finally be free of him. Hardig would never leave Virginia: of that, at least, Alfreah had been comfortably certain. He would never, *could* never, leave the sprawling business empire that he'd established up there; which meant that if Alfreah stayed in Macon, he wouldn't ever have cause to 'stop by' her home again. She hoped that her latest move would finally put to rest his insatiable greedy desire to have her now that Joe had died.

She really should tell her children why the man was so incessant, tell them all the true reason for the rift between the two families and why Joe Senior had every right to dislike the Hardigs so passionately. It must have looked odd to them, after all. Two prominent Black families in the historical Alexandria area might well have been friends: their children might have played together... Alfreah shuddered. Discussing it with them even now would bring up too much pain for her. She couldn't. She simply prayed that her absence would shake Chauncey Hardig loose from her life once and for all.

THE HANG-UP CALLS to the Jameson house had become more frequent - only they weren't for Dean, or any of the Jamesons. At last, whenever Gary Williams was able to reach the person he was looking for, he decided to speak, and unfortunately Chyna listened.

For an entire week, she was at a loss about what to do with her ex-husband's requests to see her. Finally, as she knew her continued refusals would only spark more phone calls, she had agreed to meet with him simply to find out what he wanted. This time, though, she'd be truthful with Dean. Things were completely different between them now: open, honest, the truth always. She told Dean everything.

"No way in hell." That's what he said for the umpteenth time when Chyna had suggested that she meet with Gary. His usually kind eyes always turned a darker shade when it came to her ex. She smiled at him just across the table from where they sat and took a heaping forkful of noodles, yellow squash and zucchini, with plenty of the brown spicy peanut sauce that made the Asian-style fusion dish taste so heavenly.

"This is really good, Dean," she mumbled approvingly around her mouthful.

"Don't try to change the subject," he said.

"I'm not," she shrugged, covering her mouth as she crunched.

Dean set down his own fork. "You go, I go," he announced decisively.

"He likely won't tell me anything with you present," Chyna reminded him.

"Ask me if I care about anything he is or isn't planning to do," Dean snapped. "I don't appreciate him calling this house, come to that."

"I know, but I haven't answered my phone in forever," Chyna reasoned. "He probably felt he had no other way to get to me."

"And how did he know you were here?" Dean pressed.

"He knew I worked here before," she replied simply. "I doubt he heard about your father's passing."

"Still, it's suspect, and I still say he shouldn't be calling here," Dean grumbled.

"You're right. I'm sorry."

"What are you sorry for, Chyna? He's calling, not you," Dean reminded her. "You should not be sorry."

"I know... I just didn't think about how it looks," Chyna confessed. She could see Dean's jealousy welling up once more. There was no reason for him to be jealous, of course, but Jina's words about insecurities came back to her. "I should look to see if he left any messages on my phone. But you're right: he shouldn't be calling me at all. Obviously it's over, Dean: I promise."

"It's all a ruse anyway, just to get you away from me," Dean continued. "Get you into his snares, then persuade you to do some underhanded thing that in the end only helps him."

"There's no place I'd rather be than here with you," Chyna said firmly. Although she truly meant that, she reflected that she hadn't really been that generous with her verbal affirmations since her acknowledgement of her feelings for him. Her affections came slowly, that much was true, and Dean respected her space. Every time he gave her only small and hesitant kisses, though she found herself wishing they were so much longer.

She smiled, setting down her fork. She was thrilled that Dean had been listening to what she'd shared about Gary and their marriage and how it had always gone with him in the past, and Dean's take on the current situation was absolutely accurate. The only problem was, she kept having salacious thoughts about Dean, but he continued to talk about her ex, ruining the mood and the moment. He had no idea how much she was over Gary...

She stood from the table and moved over to his side. Dean scooted his chair away from the table to make room for her on his lap. Her arms came around his neck and she hugged him close.

"I love you so much," she whispered. "I want you to know that I have never stopped loving you. I trust you with everything I have and you're the only person I want and need. You have to believe me. I'm communicating with you about Gary because I want you to know everything, because I want you by my side. A part of me, though, wants to go just to show him I'm all right: that I've moved on."

"And I appreciate that, thank you, but you don't owe him a single thing," Dean reminded her. "Know what else?"

"What?"

"I love you too. I have never, ever stopped loving you, and I never will."

Chyna had thought she was done crying, but happy tears now pinched at her eyes. She laughed.

"Know what else?" Dean continued.

"What?" she said.

"I will accompany you to see Gary, if that's what you want. I'll behave and I'll be calm and I won't say a word. We'll see what he has to say."

She raised a skeptical eyebrow at him, leaning away to see his face fully. "You promise you'll be calm?" she tested.

"Yes... but one cross word and I will calmly punch him in the face," Dean said with a grim smile. "Perhaps I can even wring an apology from his turkey neck."

"Oh boy," she said, and they both laughed. She tried to return to her seat, but he held her there on his lap for just a little longer, feeding her the remainder of the delicious meal he'd made for them. She was perfectly content: in his arms, on his lap. She could get used to being there all the time, and a brave little part of her heart was starting to believe that she eventually would. She kissed him with all the hope she could muster.

They finished their food and enjoyed the rest of their evening, decidedly in love, ready to put the past behind them and move forward. They had to confront some demons first; but honestly, Chyna felt she could do anything as long as this man was beside her.

20

W hen she stood at the door of Senator Gary Williams' upscale office in the heart of DC, Dean's words about her not having anything to prove came flooding back. Suddenly, she felt that perhaps being here was indeed the dumbest thing she'd ever decided to do. She looked over anxiously at him. "Let's just leave - forget about it."

Dean's comforting hand touched her back. "No, we're good, you can do it," he said reassuringly. "Show him you're not afraid, that you moved on. Want me to knock?"

She hesitated, then nodded, apprehension filling her bones. She'd have preferred to come at an earlier hour: now, at five o'clock, the cavernous corridor was eerily quiet. No secretary was there, no interns, no hum of all the players who'd usually buzzed around Gary during his work days when they were married. Not knowing about Dean's presence, Gary had prob-ably intended to corner her somehow and bully her into submission, about whatever he needed. Gary Williams took up more than five years of her life, because she'd let him: because he was unhappy with himself. His only coping mechanism for the frustrations of a job his deceased father had thrust upon him had been to use her as a verbal and emotional punching bag for all that time. Despite having once thought otherwise, she knew now that they couldn't ever be just friends.

Maybe that's what had brought her here, she reflected: was she holding out for an apology that Dean had even mentioned wringing Gary's neck to get? She daydreamed for a moment that Gary might even ask outright for her forgiveness. In any case, she was going to find out in just a few moments whether or not her ex had truly changed.

"Chyna?" He appeared at the door.

"Yes, hello, Gary."

The senator regarded the two of them shrewdly. "Oh look at that, you're finally together. Headed for wedded bliss, no doubt, just as I suspected," he sneered. "Like the song says, you held out for a hero, huh Chyna?"

Dean glowered at him. "You've been calling Chyna, so now tell us what you wanted or quit talking," he growled.

"Oh, he speaks!" Gary threw up his hands in mock amazement. "Please go on. I've always wanted to meet the man that defiled my marriage bed."

"*Gary.*" The voice that came out was of a much sterner tone than Chyna had intended. She stood a little straighter, strode into the office and took a seat without his invitation, waiting for them to join her. Dean took a seat beside her and Gary came to stare at the two of them from behind his massive desk.

"I'm sorry, Chyna, I'm sorry," he wheedled. "Just knowing you left me for, uh, for a... never mind. Look, uh, I have a few things to tell you. There's no sense beating around the bush. I'm announcing my candidacy for president."

"Wow. From what I hear, you're having a hard enough time keeping your senate seat," Dean put in harshly. "A little presumptuous there, Gary?"

"I didn't ask you anything," Gary retorted.

"And yet I asked a very good question you should consider, free of charge."

"Dean?" Chyna touched his arm, willing him to hit the brakes, before returning her gaze to her ex. "What does this have to do with me, Gary?"

Gary leaned back in his vast desk chair. "I've written a book, Chyna. Well, two, actually. The first is personal, the other is on leadership."

Chyna blinked again. Why tell her this now? She told herself she didn't care: that whatever details of their marriage as he remembered it were his to tell, accurate or not. She couldn't stop him. Whatever lies he wanted to spew, at least she had no living family to be concerned about. Then, with a sinking feeling, she remembered Dean and the rest of the Jamesons. She wouldn't want to cause them any grief, and Gary knew it.

Gary regarded her, tenting his fingers under... was that a smirk? "I just want you to be prepared, is all."

"Prepared for what?"

"I talk about our miscarriage," he replied.

Chyna gut crashed. "Why? You didn't care, you didn't want children," she blurted out. "But you wouldn't necessarily tell the truth in this stupid book, would you? You probably make it seem like you did want children - that's the spin, right? Build your campaign on lies, like everything else." She felt sick.

"It's my truth, whether you believe it is or not," Gary said smugly. "It's my account and I certainly didn't want you to lose our child just so you could..."

"And you'll drag her through the mud, just to make yourself look good and seal a farce?" Dean interrupted

Gary glared. "Look, I asked her here, not you. I'm trying to be nice, that is all. Give you time to see what I've said and move forward. Here."

He extended the book toward her. Chyna snatched it from his hands and threw it back at him, narrowly missing his head.

"You think you're president Obama now?" she demanded, aware that her voice had become a shout. "You think a tell-all is going to solve all your problems for you, make the world like you? Understand you? What press nut gave you this idea? No, don't tell me, I don't care," Chyna snorted. "Did you write in there about what you did, Gary? Or rather, what you didn't do? About Warren?"

"That is not true," said Gary smoothly. "It's a lie, Chyna."

"It's not a lie! Any real man would have believed me; any real man would have protected me and taken his wife's word over some deranged, disgusting, drunken animal. I already knew you wouldn't admit anything," Chyna fumed. "I just wanted to see if you remembered, and it's clear you do. You weren't as drunk as you claimed to be. Anything could have happened to me. I could have been raped."

Dean had moved from his chair so lightning fast that Chyna's head spun. Gary scrambled up but was snatched up in a chokehold before he could scramble away. "Chyna, Chyna, please don't let him hurt me," Gary yelped pathetically. "Stop it, stop it!"

"Dean, please?" Chyna hurried to the other side of Gary's desk and extended her hands beseechingly. She didn't think Dean would hurt him, but she had to admit she also quite enjoyed seeing Gary squirm, if only for a few moments. She was in a daze, triggered by her pain from the past but able to dismiss it enough to focus on getting Dean off of him.

"What did you do, punk?" Dean snarled.

"Nothing," Gary sputtered. He looked up at Chyna, pleading for his life. "Chyna, I did not offer you up to Warren for a campaign donation."

"You did too," she said. "You did do it. You absolutely did. I saw the check myself." She paused. "Dean honey, please: he's not worth it."

"Okay, okay." Dean seemed to relax a little.

Gary saw his chance and worked the angle. "Chyna, he's crazy, he's - Warren always liked you and I-I... I didn't take the money." He tried to make his face look ingratiating, which was difficult to accomplish in a chokehold.

"Dean, let's go, please just let's go - I gotta get out of here," Chyna pleaded. Relieved, she saw Dean relax his hold, but only slightly. After a few moments, Dean pushed Gary forcefully into the tall bookcases flanking his desk. A few of the books fell around his feet as he stumbled forward trying to right himself, clutching his chest and neck with both hands and gasping and coughing for air. Overcoming her distaste for even touching it, she grabbed the book and left. She'd have to close this chapter on her life if she was going to remain sane.

In the elevator, Dean consoled her, holding her tight as she once again tried to let go of a time she often grew sick just thinking about. She realized this was the first Dean had heard about the full truth of Warren's involvement. She'd told him almost everything but the fact that Warren had tried to pay Gary for her, for sex, as if the decision was his alone to make about her body. Back then, she'd truly thought she'd either lose her mind or kill her then-husband.

"I promise there aren't any more secrets, okay - I promise."

"I got it, it's all right." She grew quiet. She knew he understood and he was okay with it.

When the elevator opened, they moved quickly to the car and sped back to Virginia, away from a complete mess of stuff made for television dramas. Thankfully, she no longer had a starring role in any of it.

～

GARY WILLIAMS LOCKED his office door and closed all the curtains, obscuring the lights of the city as they came on. The approaching fall brought darker afternoons, and the only illumination in the room came from his computer screen, the lights of his desktop phone and a candle he'd lit. He returned to his desk a little unsteadily and sat down heavily, barely able to take a deep breath without coughing, and pulled an untraceable prepaid phone from his top drawer.

He put on a hauntingly sad song and reached for a flask. After a hasty sip which burned his throat further, he called a number he hadn't called in a while and spoke without preamble: "Do whatever you want to her. I no longer care."

"Nice to hear from you too, but you know I don't need your permission to go after her," came the tinny reply. "I only needed permission when the two of you were married. Now that she's available, no permission slip required."

"Well, I'd have thought you'd already have made a move by now. What have you been waiting for?"

"Oh, handling the Hardig business stuff. You know I'm going to take it over soon. I need to get those ducks in a row before I get to capturing her affections."

"Ha, she'll never have affections for the likes of you," sneered Gary.

"Well, you didn't have much luck either now, did you? I certainly can't do any worse than you did. It's a slow process."

"You think she'll come around?"

"She won't have much choice once I threaten her precious boyfriend."

Gary rubbed his neck. Considering Jameson's strength, he'd pay to see a fight between those two. Warren Hardig wasn't necessarily athletic or strong, just deranged enough not to hold back. Not to mention the fact that he'd been known to dabble in various drugs. Dean Jameson might have been smart and quick, but Hardig had a certain type of brute strength. The

Jamesons seemed a working-class sort, though, unlike Warren. Born into wealth, Warren had never been anything more than a brat taking things from others as he pleased. His father had made a living bullying people out of their livelihood and properties. The empire was sealed by the time Warren came around, thus he'd never had to lift so much as a pinky finger to earn any of it. It was just... *there.*

"Would you like to watch when I finally capture her?" Warren offered. "I could invite you over, get you set up with a two-way mirror. She wouldn't even know you were there."

"You're a real sicko, Hardig." Gary laughed: a hollow sound. He wheezed a bit, hoping it wasn't heard. It was more of a panicked chuckle.

"That's what they keep telling me. But hey, you knew that already," came the reply. "I'll send a check for that campaign stuff, then we can see about ruling the world and having whatever we want at your inauguration."

"If I win," amended the senator.

"Well, that's no real sign of confidence. Everything can be bought, Gary. Cheer up: your younger, richer and better-looking friend is here for you."

"Right, well uh, catch up with you later." Gary wanted to end the conversation, feeling a little sorry that he'd dialed the number in the first place. Knowing someone planned Chyna's demise did make him feel better, though. Bringing her bodyguard and lover in here with her: what an insult. That said, whatever Warren was planning, the gory details of how it might happen made Gary nervous. He could do without that part. He'd always had a sensitive stomach.

Gary hung up the phone. He could win the nomination, of that he was sure: he had a Hardig in his corner, he had wealthy friends and influence and status; and if that wasn't enough, the bribes and ugliness of a cutthroat campaign would turn him out looking like a saint. Everyone in politics had problematic marriages and torrid relationships - so what? His marriage had been less than perfect, but so was everyone's.

Working to his advantage was the fact that Chyna had left him, not the other way around – as well as the fact that she was now with Mr. Jameson and he, Senator Williams, was alone. He hadn't been seen with anyone, at least not in public. In fact, he should set about grooming a nice homely young lady as wife number two. Give her everything she needs, and this time ensure she's not lusting after some childhood sweetheart. A romantic but lengthy courtship could be fabricated, and the public would eat it up, eventually rooting for him to marry again. It could all be attained in due time. He knew from experience that people could be lured to his side just for the kind of story they loved to see depicted each night in their evening news feed.

All he needed was patience. The rest, as they say, was about to be history.

21

S omething about her meeting with Gary lit a fire under Chyna that she hadn't ever experienced before. She was so angry that she'd been duped, not to mention that his antics had brought up issues she'd thought she'd dealt with and let go of long ago.

Dean was everything to her. He consoled her, he pushed her, he protected her. He even mentioned filing a protective order, which she didn't want to hear anything about. At the same time, she didn't yet know what Gary had written about her. Dean had taken the book, insisting that he'd read it first, only she knew he hadn't started it yet. While a part of her was undeniably curious, and she knew she needed to prepare for whatever Gary had said, another part of her wanted to go on pretending that it didn't exist. Another lie, she knew; but she had to get a handle on her thoughts and feelings about the entire thing or risk losing a wonderful future with Dean.

Earlier that day, she'd done an interview with a new family for an article she was working on, and now she was attempting to review her notes while sitting in traffic on her way home from an appointment where she'd finally got the green light to remove her boot.

She hoped she'd captured something worthwhile at the interview, not just the lofty daydreams that sometimes worked their way into her shorthand. She'd been attentive to the little boy with Down Syndrome and engaged well with his family. They'd seemed to like her immediately, even asking if she wanted to stay for dinner, but she had declined. She knew she'd be able to sell her written work again eventually, but a part of her just wasn't ready, so it felt insincere to let them think of her as a fully-fledged journalist worthy of being invited to a meal as guest of honor. Toward the end of the interview, she had almost apologized for wasting their time.

Pulling into the gas station, Chyna was almost home: almost back to Dean. Rather than drive her old clunker on today's errands, Chyna had taken Ms. Alfreah's Honda SUV. It wasn't full of gas as they'd usually kept it, probably because Ms. Alfreah hadn't been in Virginia in weeks. If she were there, one of her four children would've made sure to fill it for her. Chyna herself had only taken it at Dean's insistence: he said she would be safer in the larger vehicle than in her compact car. Plus, she knew this car well. She had fond memories of using it to chauffeur both Ms. Alfreah and Joe Jameson to church.

That time seemed so long ago, she couldn't believe it. She found herself looking in the rearview mirror, where she used to peek back at Mr. Jameson. He was always back there: somewhat slumped and usually silent, but there nonetheless. Today, all the passenger seats were empty. Maybe she'd get a couple of car seats, or a car seat and a booster seat perhaps. One a little older than the other - maybe two years apart or a little more. One day. Chyna allowed herself a private smile, but brought her thoughts back to the Jamesons of the present. They were always the family she didn't have, so woven into their lives was she; and she'd left all this for what - for a misunderstanding? She

winced at how easily she'd given up, mad at herself now for
thinking she was somehow undeserving of a happy ending.

Chyna pumped her gas and had just secured the gas nozzle
when the roar of a truck pulled up at the terminal just on the
other side of hers. The door flew open and strappy heels
emerged, seconds before a woman ran up to her.

"Chyna Williams?"

Chyna looked over and hesitated. "Yes – well, Lockhart,
Chyna Lockhart." The woman didn't look as if she much cared
what her name was.

"Lisa Stephens," she replied. "Nice to meet you again."

"Oh okay, hello." Now she saw Lisa's face up close, she'd
never forget the woman that had sent her packing away from
Dean. She no longer saw Lisa as a threat, although she did
wonder somewhat uneasily why on earth Lisa had given up so
easily. "Uh, well, how are you?"

"Must be really nice staying with the Jamesons and such,"
said Lisa sunnily. "I heard you're living there now. You and
Dean shacking up, while Ms. Alfreah's gone... well, I don't
mean to intrude, but that's a bit disrespectful, isn't it?

"I'm not living there," Chyna explained hurriedly. "I injured
my leg and my house was in a bit of rough shape so Ms. Alfreah
graciously offered to let me stay there for just a little while."

She was immediately unsure why exactly she felt the need
to explain herself. She and Dean had done nothing scandalous
or improper. She knew Ms. Alfreah was very conservative, and
it just wouldn't feel right anyway.

"Look, don't you think it's time to move on from your little
fantasy with Dean Jameson?" Lisa continued.

Chyna raised her eyebrows in surprise. Arguing over a man,
at your local gas station no less, was really weird, but at least
she was finally getting to meet Lisa Stephens up close and
personal. Now she was actually confronted with the reality of
her, though, it wasn't at all pleasant. The woman looked like

she was straight out of a magazine: short tight black skirt, pretty silky purple blouse and black blazer, lots of make-up, glistening glossy lips and lots of reddish-brown hair extensions. Is this what people meant by 'high profile', Chyna mused: always dressed up in case of an impromptu meeting, or perhaps a late-night outing?

She herself had never had any idea what to wear to an event taking place after five. As Senator Williams' wife, she'd had to maintain a full wardrobe, plentiful accessories and a fully-stocked fridge, to be ready to accompany Gary at a moment's notice to anything from a dinner party to a golf tournament. Fundraisers, galas, hosting tapas parties at their house...

Focusing, Chyna deduced that this woman was awfully bold - *or rude, rather*, her mind interjected - to start such a personal conversation right off the bat. They barely knew each other. Since her unfortunate visit with Gary Williams, Chyna actually begin to feel her own resolve flare inside of her to shut the woman down. This is what Jina had been saying. Now, presented with such a confrontation, she should have been ready for a fight, considering all the time she and Dean lost. But she wasn't used to confrontation. A part of her would rather let their relationship and their reconnection speak for itself.

"Listen," Chyna began.

"No, you listen." Lisa cut her off. "If Dean were serious about you, you'd be married by now. As it stands, I really think it's time for you to move on. He's just much too polite to tell you."

"Is that right?"

"Are you challenging me, you bi---?"

"No Lisa, I just think you just have your facts all wrong." Why Chyna was wasting her time she didn't know. She made a move to get back into her car, checking to ensure she'd secured the pump and that she hadn't forgotten anything. With relief, she saw Lisa open the door to her own truck. She prayed that the woman would take a hint at last: that Chyna wasn't about to spend any more time discussing Dean, or anything for that matter, with such an unreasonable person.

There was a sudden movement in her peripheral version, and Chyna instinctively covered her face - just a split second before a long black crowbar smashed through her window. Glass exploded across her hands, face, lap and legs.

Chyna screamed, but Lisa was already gone, engine roaring and tires screaming.

"Oh God, Ma'am, you okay, Ma'am?"

"Yes, yes, I'm fine," Chyna gasped. She attempted a look in the mirror at her face, but every tiny movement yielded the crunch of the glass strewn all about her. First things first, she had to get out of the vehicle. She reached for the door but winced as more shards attacked her. Jagged edges of the window bit into the palm of her hand and she snatched her hand away in pain.

"Hey, hey, please don't move," the older woman insisted.

"Okay, but I think I need to get out of the car..."

"Okay but keep your hands up, don't touch anything," the woman instructed. "I'll open the door for you, dear." The lady brushed away more glass carefully with her bare hands, giving scant regard to the nicks she was incurring herself. She pulled the door handle gingerly, and yet more glass spilled out as it slowly creaked ajar and Chyna's rescuer helped guide her out of the car.

Chyna was thankful to the older woman, whom she assumed had seen what happened. Chyna moved slowly, trying not to lean on anything, and eventually managed to stand. More glass pieces fell from her lap onto the ground and sparkled like diamonds at her feet. She thanked God she'd been wearing professional shoes and knee-highs for her interview, rather than her regulation comfy sandals and bare legs.

"Be careful, honey!"

Chyna smiled tightly. "Yes, yes, thanks so much. I was just looking for my cell phone. I-I wanted to call my boyfriend."

She needed to call Dean and fast, but she couldn't find her phone anywhere. The woman remained, chattering on and on about the awfulness of what had just happened. Any other time Chyna would have had a very patient and kind ear to listen at length, but right then, she interrupted the woman and asked to use her cell phone. She could not for the life of her remember Dean's cell number, though, and she dialed erroneously several times until she remembered that the Jamesons still had their old landline. That number hadn't changed in all the years she'd known them.

She surveyed the damage to Ms. Alfreah's car as she listened to the phone ring, making a mental list of next steps starting with having it towed. The fact that it wasn't even her own car was all the more galling. She looked into the various windows to ensure nothing of value was missing. She would ask the gas station staff if they could at least vacuum the car for her. After her recent broken leg, she had no desire to sustain any more injuries doing it herself.

The phone rang and rang, and eventually she hung up in disappointment. She'd call the police next, she supposed: get some help, file a complaint and try Dean again after a bit. She handed the woman back her phone and glumly thanked her again for her assistance.

Chyna hated what had happened, but she was thankful she didn't have more than a few scrapes and for the most part was all right. She worried, however, how Dean would react once he heard.

22

D ean was annoyed he hadn't heard from Chyna for the better part of the day. She'd sent him a text early that morning about the interview she was doing for work and he'd said great, truly happy about her moving forward and letting nothing, certainly not Gary Williams nor the pain of the past, keep her from living her life. If they were ever to be married, though, he made a mental note that he should tell her he didn't care if she worked or not. He needed to consult his sister about that particular idea: test it out to see if it was as romantic as he thought or just a more archaic way of thinking.

Now it was almost dinner time: Dean and Chyna had fallen into a routine of eating together. The place settings were laid out with plates, water glasses, forks, napkins and silverware. There was also a huge bouquet of fresh flowers on Chyna's side of the table. That evening he was especially excited to see her: he had something special to show her at her brand-new house. Even Dean couldn't believe the progress that had been made on it. The results were way beyond his expectations.

He and Chyna ate there almost every night: like a real

couple. He knew that's what it was, yet it was still hard to think about it in that way. It was what he wanted more than anything; it was also just completely routine, even from their childhood. Back then, there were certainly many more mouths at the table, much more chatter, with his mother cooking for everyone. Chyna was such an integral part of his life, it was a wonder either them could ever have moved on. Now, he knew for sure that neither of them had ever wanted to. Unhealthy as it might have looked to others outside his family, it really didn't matter what outsiders thought. He knew what he wanted. They were friends first and forever.

Dean took a deep, tired breath. He now viewed all these outside people as roadblocks. His brain grew tired thinking about it all. It was now clearer to him how three separate people had set out in their own way to sabotage his and Chyna's relationship. Come to think of it, the stress of it all had likely played at least some role in the miscarriage, too. He hadn't really taken a lot of time out to think about the enormity of that loss. He'd just tried to keep going so they could see about marriage and, some day, maybe have another try.

Concerned at Chyna's tardiness, Dean was toying with the idea of using the GPS to find out where his mother's car was located when his attention was diverted by a knock on the front door. Before could get there, the knob rattled roughly and the door banged harder still. Dean checked his phone and frowned at the picture that flashed up on the doorbell app. Considering he was thinking of proposing to Chyna that very night, he supposed that right then was as good a time as any to tell the woman on the other side of the door that he wasn't ever going to be, nor had he ever been, interested in her.

"Hey, there you are!" Lisa greeted him brightly, as if she hadn't been attacking his front door like a wild cat just seconds before. "You were serious about the security, huh? Seems that Ms. Alfreah's open-door policy's gone and left town with her,

Stranger danger be gone!" Lisa chuckled at her own comments as she moved toward Dean.

"Sometimes wolves come in sheep's clothing," Dean observed, regarding her seriously.

"Yeah, I guess," Lisa said airily, continuing to move forward. Dean kept ahead of her, blocking the entrance to the kitchen to thwart her attempts to move any further into the house. *Now was a good time*, he thought. *Just tell her.* Like pulling off a band aid, it would be best done all at once, and fast. Now that the air was clear between he and Chyna, especially now that their feelings for one another were out in the open, he needed to actively remove people that weren't a part of their relationship goals: Warren Hardig, Gary Williams, and of course Lisa Stephens. The day prior, he'd witnessed Chyna make as clean a break as she could from Senator Gary Williams. Now it was Dean's turn to say a clear goodbye to Lisa.

Absentmindedly, he lifted the lid from a large red roasting pan simmering on the back burner and turned the flame off. Time was up. He needed to stop trying to pacify Lisa. He saw her noticing the dinner arrangement before her gaze gradually rose to meet his. Hopefully, seeing the set table and hearing his words would make her realize he was serious with Chyna, not at all with her. He realized belatedly that Chyna and his sister had been right: the way Lisa was looking at him now was unmistakable. Dean hadn't wanted to hurt her, but really hadn't had a clue that she liked him in that way.

"Whatever is in that pot, Dean, smells heavenly. Can I see?" Lisa wheedled. "What is it?"

"It's just, uh, nothing much really Lisa. What's going on? Why are you here?"

"Oh, so you cook for her?" Lisa asked. "I didn't know you could cook at all!"

Dean didn't know what to say. "You, um, you never asked."

Lisa looked like she'd swallowed a canary. Dean noticed all of the emotions flitter across her face.

"Listen, Lisa..." Dean attempted patiently.

"You love her – you're back together?" she sniffed.

"Lisa – "

"You love her?!" Dean's eyes grew wide as Lisa almost screamed at him. It had him looking at her as if he didn't really know her at all – and, he reminded himself, he really didn't.

"Lisa, do not make this out to be more than it is, okay? You're a friend: you've always been just a friend, and I don't think I have encouraged you."

"You kissed me!" she screamed again.

"No I didn't," Dean replied emphatically. "*You* kissed *me* - and anyway, I thought..." It didn't matter what he'd thought. It was fast becoming clear that she read too much into everything he did, or even whether he did anything or not. She had something in her mind that he didn't, making the relationship exist more for her than it did for him. All this time, he hadn't been looking closely enough at her actions, misguided as they were.

For the first time, Dean noticed something familiar clutched in her hand. His vision blurred, then corrected.

"What - what are you doing with that?" he asked, alarmed. "You've seen Chyna? Where is she, Lisa?" Horrified, he snatched Chyna's cell phone from her grasp, feeling a slick red substance coating his fingers from the screen. *Blood.*

His panic escalated into a cacophony of questions: exactly why Chyna wasn't here, why Lisa was, and how she'd gotten hold of the phone. He grabbed her shoulders roughly and gave her a little shake, not hard but enough, as he clutched the phone. Pulling his own car keys and phone from his pocket, he addressed her sharply:

"You better answer me. Is Chyna hurt? Did you do something?"

"No, Dean. I love you; I..."

"I *said*, where is Chyna?"

"Dean, I-I didn't tell anyone that you wanted to be done with your medical practice, but Chyna - " Lisa babbled. "She - she thinks *you* burned it down, and y-you said you wished it would burn down that night we met! Remember? You said you just wanted to be done with the practice - but I wouldn't tell, Deanie, I promise, I wouldn't ever tell anyone. I kept all your secrets. I had to stop *her* from telling anyone, I had to - "

Dean paused to look at her, not understanding what she said. Her mind was completely off: he felt like he was going batty himself just listening to her insanity. The rage he felt grew inch by inch. When he spoke, his tone was low.

"If something has happened to Chyna, you're going to lose way more blood than is on this phone."

23

Once Dean had used the onboard navigation system to locate his Mom's car, he texted Jojo to ask if he could go to the gas station. He didn't add that he couldn't go himself because he was about to choke out the woman in front of him.

He took several breaths as he thought about what to say, how to respond and get her the heck away from him without doing her harm - but at this moment, he knew that he could seriously hurt her. He had a lot of anger still bottled up that was meant for Gary Williams, and unfortunately Lisa Stephens might receive the punishment in the Senator's place. Dean realized he'd have to try a different approach.

"I appreciate your concern for me, Lisa," he began. "Look, I'm sorry - I am a bit crazed..."

"You should dump her," Lisa urged. "I could help you get rid of her. I could."

Dean nodded. *Oh man.* "I, uh, I thought you said you already did something to her?" he inquired, trying hard to keep his tone conversational.

"Well not really," Lisa admitted, casually patting her hair. "I just broke the glass on your Mom's car window. Chyna's fine, for now anyways."

Dean's mind whirled with the new information. Did she even know what she'd said?

"Dean, honey, I know someone who really likes her," Lisa continued conspiratorially. "They used to date. I hate to tell you this honey, but did you know she cheated on Gary? Isn't that horrible? She cheated on him, and I knew all this time - I just didn't want to taint the image you had of her." Lisa pursed her lips piously. "Oh honey, I'm sorry."

He would have laughed if he hadn't felt so sick. He moved away from her to think, realizing that all his sister had said was true. The only problem was that Jina had no idea just how crazy Lisa Stephens really was.

"I guess, uh, you're always coming to my rescue huh?" he offered. "Always popping up at my lowest points."

Lisa glowed.

"Oh no, I just feel like you need someone - someone to help you and your family and your mother with your dad's estate," she purred. "It was my pleasure to help out, really. Now, wait here just a minute, honey – I have to go potty."

She left the room, ruffling his hair on her way past. Dean glanced at his phone. His brother had texted him that he had Chyna and that she was alright, if a little shaken. The relief that Chyna was safe made Dean feel dizzy. He texted back as quickly as his shaking thumbs would allow, telling his brother that Lisa was with him and instructing Jojo to take Chyna back to her own house, that he'd meet them over there, and to call the police. He set the phone face down just as Lisa emerged from the bathroom. Jojo would likely respond with a thousand other texts that she shouldn't be allowed to see.

"Lisa, like I said, I appreciate your help," Dean said carefully. Dean remembered that night more vividly now. Yes, he'd said offhandedly that he wished he could somehow get rid of the place where he went to work every day because it was a nuisance, or something; but he'd never once suggested an urge to torch it. For one, that was illegal, and for two there were so many people that could have been hurt. How stupid did she think he was? Truth was, even if he didn't already love Chyna, there was still no way on earth that he'd be after someone like Lisa: gold digger that she was, liar that she was, deranged and desperate that she was.

When he felt her arms come around him, he did everything he could to keep his hands away from the base of her neck. He didn't even desire her. He'd never desired her. Her light-colored contacts, far from rendering her more attractive as intended, made her look to Dean as if she belonged on the set of some vampire movie. Her acrylic nails were much too long and pointy, going along with the vampire theme, and he guessed she'd picked out their color to match her hair streaks. Everything about her was fake. Her skirt was too short, her pneumatic bosom in his face all the time. For once he looked at her, really looked at her, and wondered what in the world he had ever said or done to make her think he'd ever wanted something more than friendship from her.

"Oh, Dean, I'm so sorry about all that's been happening," Lisa sighed melodramatically. "I know that Gary is releasing that tell-all book next month, and I know that he'll likely tell the truth about Chyna and... what she did to him."

"Stop it."

"Oh Dean. That greedy woman didn't deserve you. I had a hunch you'd be over here sulking." She laughed lightly. "I don't mean to make a joke out of this, I'm sorry - but I think this time you'll realize what I've been trying to tell you all along. I know it seems like I'm always around, but I just truly care about you and your family so much."

Dean stopped her hands from moving up his neck. This was ridiculous. He had to drop the façade.

"I think it's time for you to go, and to take your lies with you," he said coldly. He pushed her to the door. "I don't ever want you to come around here again. Leave me and my family alone - never come back here. I'm going to press charges against you for stealing Chyna's phone and for assaulting her, so I think this is over. Every word you say is a lie. You really think I wouldn't believe and trust someone I've known my entire life over your lying, conniving ass? And I know about the papers you tried to switch up at the bank," he added hotly. "I have corrected the issue and you should be served some papers any day now. There'll be a warrant out for your arrest, and perhaps you'll even be denied bail after what you did today. If you come near Chyna again, I will seriously hurt you."

Lisa gaped, tears in her eyes. "I didn't, honey," she gasped. "I-I invested your Mom and Dad's money, I have the papers, I..."

Dean cut her off. "You lie, that's what you do. You invested in what: a Hardig building, or maybe some offshore accounts?" He snorted derisively. "There is no investment. No matter, anyway: all that stolen money will be found, and anything that isn't found, you'll be fully responsible for."

"Oh, Dean," Lisa said, turning to touch his face.

He smacked her hand away. "Do not touch me. I asked you leave; do you need some help? Let me escort you." He grabbed her arm, steered her closer to the door and opened it.

"Dean, stop, please - you're hurting me," Lisa whimpered.

"That's the least of your worries." Dean got her out of the door at last, pushing her away from him.

"You'll regret this Dean - please don't," she implored.

"I already regret knowing you."

"No, that's not true! You'll regret turning me away! The Hardigs have it in for you – Dean, Warren wants Chyna, Dean. He wants her, he'll stop at nothing to get her, okay?" She was all but clinging to the doorframe to avoid leaving.

Dean paused. "And you know this how?"

"Because I was sleeping with him," Lisa blurted. "I just needed someone Dean, that's all. But I don't love him, I love you."

"I hope you know what you're doing, Lisa," Dean said slowly. "This isn't the way, okay? I do not like you, but I don't want you to get mixed up with them. Seriously, just give up these stupid games..."

"What game? It's not a game. I could hurt Chyna, you know that," said Lisa defensively. "I could hurt her, worse than I did today. Today was just a warning."

Dean had had enough. At that moment, the cops rolled up to the house, and the next moment an officer was approaching them.

"Lisa Stephens? Ma'am, you're under arrest on suspicion of assault," the officer declared. "Mr. Jameson, Cody here will take your statement."

"Dean, please don't do this, please!" Lisa yelled as she was dragged away. Under her breath, she added: "I - I will hurt your precious girlfriend."

The officer looked at her sharply. "Would you like to add threatening with intent to do harm to your list of offenses, Ma'am?"

Lisa shook her head and remained meekly quiet as the cop cuffed her and read her her rights. It was not until he placed her in the backseat of the cruiser and closed the door that she began to scream.

Dean wasn't sad it had come to this. He hoped that the threat of jail time might make her come to senses and stop her crazy scheming. He could only hope it settled her down, and he could only pray that the woman's deranged warnings about Warren's intentions were yet more lies intended to keep him and Chyna apart. Nonetheless, his mind worked quickly to come up with other precautions he could take to ensure Chyna's safety.

The officer taking Dean's statement happened to be one who had known the Jameson family for almost ten years. As luck would have it, it was the very same officer who had helped Tisha uncover a devastating incident involving a child at the school she was teaching at, years ago. If there was anything that Dean was thankful for, it was that he had lived there long enough for his entire family to be truly embedded in the community. Surely no one would ever believe he'd burned down his own practice. He was sickened that any such thing might have left his mouth at all, however inebriated he was.

"Thanks so much, man, for everything," Dean said, walking the man back to his police car

The officer nodded. "So, I'll call you if we need anything," he concluded. "We already got the surveillance footage from the store before we talked to Ms. Lockhart."

"Wow, that was fast," Dean commented.

"Actually, that particular store is connected to one of our police feeds. We're encouraging all local businesses to get them, sort of like Neighborhood Watch. I would credit that technology with our being able to arrest Ms. Stephens so fast."

The program sounded interesting, and he was indeed thankful for the speedy arrest, but at that moment Dean didn't really care how it was all managed. His mind was already down the street, itching to get to Chyna's house and see her. "It sounds really great."

"Yeah, thanks Mr. Jameson. Oh, and sorry to hear about your old man."

"Yeah, appreciate it. Now I gotta run, okay?"

Once the car was around the corner, he raced off on foot to Chyna's house, to hear first-hand what Lisa had done to her.

Jojo met Dean halfway, and as they ran Dean quickly gave him the lowdown of all that Lisa said. He told his brother the lies Lisa might put forth about how his practice had burned down. Jojo whistled his surprise. "Wow, always the ladies man, huh, bro?"

Dean cut his eyes at his brother. "That's not funny," he huffed. "If that's what being a ladies man is, I'll let you keep your title."

"Not anymore bro, not any more."

Dean smiled. All joking aside, he was genuinely glad his brother seemed to have connected with someone. Jojo and Dean had always been as close as brothers should be, and the fact that they'd gotten more distant in the last year was only because Jojo now had a long-term relationship. For once, Dean actually liked the woman his brother had chosen.

"Enough about you - how did Chyna seem?" he panted.

"She's all right," replied Jojo, keeping pace without breaking a sweat. "She was concerned when you didn't come to get her, but I told her you were tied up – also, that you'd had the brainwave to use the GPS on Mom's car to find her. She's all right, Deanie," he repeated.

"Yeah, thanks."

"No problem."

They had reached the Lockhart house. The door swung open as they walked up the driveway and Chyna and Bubba stood in the frame. All thoughts of his brother's love life forgotten, Dean bounded to Chyna, looking her up and down like he hadn't laid eyes on her in the longest time.

"If I wasn't retiring son, you could come work for me," chuckled Bubba. "I had no idea the work you put in there before I even came on the scene. Looks real good, son."

"Thanks, Bubba." Dean reached out to shake the older man's hand.

Chyna moved closer, linking arms with Dean and laying her head on his shoulder.

"You treat this guy right, now, Chyna," said Bubba with a twinkle. "He done more'n made up for his former slothfulness, okay? I know he don't always act right, but you gotta forgive stubborn men like us."

"I will," Chyna smiled, looking back at Dean. "I can't believe it," she breathed.

"Me neither. Hey, how ya doing boy?" Bubba turned to Jojo.

"I'm good Mr. John, how are you?

Bubba chortled. "You kids funny: so mature, taller-n me, now calling me by my first name." He tutted playfully. "Just like your daddy. Hey, I gotta go. Seein' ya all grown up make me sick. Tell your Momma hey fer me."

He moved off, mumbling to himself as he shambled his aging body back to his truck, hauled himself inside and waved as he drove off.

Jojo also said his goodbyes and gave Chyna a hug and kiss before leaving. As Dean pulled her inside, she admired the new brick-colored door in front of her, reaching out almost reverently to touch its perfect stain.

He tugged on her hand and she followed him, her deep brown eyes on his the entire time. Once they stood inside, Dean shut the door on the world and its mess of others' lives trying to trip them up. Without hesitation, Chyna leaped into his arms, planting kisses all over his face.

24

Chyna felt as if she'd been through the wringer, but as soon as she set foot in her newly renovated house, all her dealings with Lisa Stephens seemed to evaporate. She had never been so glad to see Dean, so much so that she felt as if she would squeeze him to death.

"Sorry," she said, wiping her eyes and giving him another kiss. He kept his arm around her, looking deeply into her eyes.

"Don't ever apologize."

She nodded. "Dean, this place is the most beautiful thing I've ever seen. When on earth did you have time?"

"Wait until you see the upstairs. You haven't yet, have you?" Dean said, a prideful grin on this face.

"There's so much to see here, I haven't even scratched the surface just yet," she said in wonder.

The place had been truly gutted. Her feet stood on plush beige carpet, where she'd stopped when she'd first arrived for fear of her shoes getting it dirty. She'd quickly removed them as Bubba had placed the shiny new set of keys in her hand. Taking it all in, she'd wondered for a moment if she'd been let into the wrong house. She went to the sofa and sat down for fear she'd fall down.

"Well," Dean said, coming and sitting beside her, "honestly, seeing Bubba in action here, I felt sorry for him. He wanted to do so much for you, but as we got to working, it was clear that his physical ability has really waned now that he's older, you know? He has a lot of contacts in the biz, though, so without trying to be insulting, I gradually asked him to see who he could get for various smaller parts of the job. Most of the rest he walked me through doing myself." Dean paused. "Don't tell him I told you: he's real proud and he did do a lot of it, he just needed a little muscle to help. I really liked working with him."

"Dean, you're so handy."

"Enough about that, though. Tell me everything that Lisa did and said to you."

"Well, firstly I'm sorry about your mother's car," she began ruefully.

"It's fine," Dean assured her. "I'm so glad you had it because of that GPS we got back when Dad was still driving. I'm glad I insisted you take it: that was the only way I could find you. Now, tell me," Dean urged.

Chyna nodded, although she hated to leave her current blissful state in order to think about something so unfortunate. She took a deep breath. "Where is she?"

"Are you serious, Chyna? Getting her stupid mug shot, that's what; then she'll be off to jail and hearing for her bond. Where else did you think she might be?"

"Dean -"

"Quit stalling and just tell me what happened, please."

Chyna bridled at his insistence. "Okay, well, I just pulled into the gas station, then Lisa came roaring up in her truck... hey, also, I don't know where my phone is."

"She had it when she came to my house," Dean assured her.

"Ah, OK – good. Maybe I left it on the top of the car," Chyna reflected. "I remember putting it down to put in the gas nozzle – anyway, I had no idea what was happening when she rolled up. She was yelling something about you being her man. I was just caught off-guard. Then suddenly she got a crowbar out of her truck and struck my window. Glass was everywhere. Thank goodness I covered my face in time."

"How do you feel right this minute? Are you all right?" Dean pressed.

Chyna nodded distractedly. Honestly, right then when she focused on her surroundings she didn't care what else had ever happened. Now she was back in her very own house and fast noticing that every single item was new, from the velvety blue sofa and a set of wingbacked chairs in the living room to the new curtains and even a gas fireplace. Hardly daring to believe how beautiful everything was, she looked up and noticed the exposed beams of the ceiling, looking just like she'd always wanted. She looked over at Dean, astonished.

"Why did you do all this for me? I might not even live here!" Dean shrugged.

"I suppose I can't let go of us, Chyna. This is... *us*."

Chyna watched as he got up from the sofa and moved across to a wall of bookcases flanking the fireplace, above which a flat-screen TV was already mounted. He flipped several switches and golden-blue flames leapt instantly to life in the fireplace. Her mouth hung open at the sight.

Dean bent down before her. "I realize this is partly to protect you, but I want you to know that besides that, I still want to marry you. You belong with me, and if you want to leave here, I want us to leave together."

"I didn't really mean it about moving. I can't leave now," she admitted. She had no idea where or what she would do or where she'd go, anyway. Virginia was her home.

"I will take care of you for the rest of my life, okay?" he said softly. When he pulled something out of his back pocket, her breath left her lungs.

"I have had this for almost a year, but there never seemed to be an opportunity," he said. "For a minute there today, it felt like I wouldn't ever get that opportunity, and I was so scared. Now I see hope again, so I just can't wait another day. I'm giving you this because I want you be my wife, forever." Dean drew a deep breath. "If you don't want to give me an answer now, it's going to kill me, but I'll accept it, and keep waiting as I have been for the last couple of months. I'll wait for you forever if I have to."

Chyna laughed. "I always wanted you, Dean, since I was too young to know what real love is. It has always been you."

Chyna's face felt the tears first. She stuck out her hand and he was surprised at her quick acceptance, she could tell, but she didn't want to wait either. She knew she would not lose out on this deal. She'd seen what a bad marriage looked like, but she wanted Dean every single day.

She had a second chance and now she could see everything in their future unfold all at once before her. She hated the way her hands looked, but she stuck them out to him anyway.

Dean looked down, distracted by all the lacerations on her delicate fingers, all the blood now dried to brown. He turned her hand over, looking at the larger wound in the center of her palm. He touched it gingerly with his thumb. "Does this hurt?"

"No, it's fine - it's not deep," she said.

"Still, let's clean it and put some cream on it." Ready to get up, Dean was about to stand when her hand tugged on his arm.

"Dean, you're in the middle of something here," she reminded him. She grabbed the box he hastily set on the edge of the coffee table and put it back in his hands. "You really know how to kill the moment - jeez." She laughed.

"Chyna Lockhart, will you marry me?"

"Yes and yes!" she almost screamed.

Dean slipped the ring on her finger and she put her hand up, admiring the beautiful heart-shaped diamond stone with a center featuring her birthstone.

"It's so beautiful," she breathed.

Dean moved to the kitchen and returned with another, larger box: a first aid kit. Kneeling before her, he took her hand again and dressed her wound, gently cleaning it and using a large square bandage to cover it. He pressed it gently into her palm, pressing the sticky edges to her skin.

"Today is our beginning. We let go of the past and move forward" he said. "When the investigation is solved, we'll go away for a bit to let things with Gary's book die down."

"I'm ready to tell what really happened," Chyna added. "That way, everyone will know the truth - and it'll maybe tank his book sales, too."

Dean shook his head doubtfully. "Only if you're sure. You know you don't have to go through that. We can go away and..."

Chyna cut him off. "I should tell what happened, and I want to. I need to make sure he cannot lie: to ensure he doesn't make out that what you and I have is some sort of scandalous affair. My silence is my continued protection of him, or at least will be seen as a kind of endorsement - or, worse, that I'm guilty."

Reluctantly, Dean nodded his understanding.

"Promise me, Dean?"

"What?"

"That anything that happens going forward you will tell me. You won't keep any stuff away from me to protect me? In a minute, you're going to tell me everything that Lisa said to you. We will not keep anything else from each other. Deal?"

Dean hesitated. "I won't keep anything from you, but some of the things Lisa said scared me," he said, leaning in to kiss her. Chyna was about to kiss him back, but, undeterred, she grabbed the lapels of his crisp blue shirt. "What did she say?"

"Oh, plenty," he replied. "Enough to let me know that she is all kinds of crazy. Like, *deranged.* So, I've been thinking that now is a perfect time for you to go down south and, say, visit my sister and Mom."

25

"You know what, they'll probably be married by the time you even get your act together." Lisa sniffed. "While I've been telling you all that's been happening since you've been God knows where, you continue to do nothing. I hate dealing with your father, too, and I'm sick and tired of dealing with him every time you decide to go on vacation."

"Is that what my father told you?" Warren asked testily.

"Yes, that's what he told me!"

Warren silently shook his head.

"Well, where the heck *have* you been?" Lisa threw up her hands in exasperation. "And what the heck is wrong with your face?"

Warren looked up in confusion.

"Your face," she repeated, gesturing. "You're breaking out or something."

Warren swiveled in his chair and pulled a small mirror from a drawer. Holding it up to his face, he scrutinized the tiny bumps. "Ah, that. It's probably the medication."

"What?" she snapped.

"Nothing," he said hastily. "I mean – I'm having an allergic reaction to something I ate."

"Well, find out whatever it is, so you can stop eating it. You look psycho."

"Don't call me that."

"I wasn't calling you that, I just said you *looked* — " Lisa ducked, and a split second later the small mirror smashed on the wall behind her.

"I *said* don't call me that!"

He'd almost hit her dead in her face. Somewhat taken aback, she stood up. He looked crazy. She backed away carefully to the door, the shards of the broken mirror cracking under her heels.

"If that's the way you're going to treat me, I'm out of this deal. It's not worth it. All I wanted was Dean Jameson, but it's not going to work."

"I'm not psycho," Warren yelled at her.

"You're right, you're not," she soothed, and he visibly relaxed. "I'm sorry Warren, and thanks - thanks so much for bailing me out of jail."

Warren was silent. Lisa paced in front of his desk. She wanted badly to leave, but it felt like she couldn't get out of the mess she'd gotten herself into. She had her own problems. Dean would have helped her, she knew; but she was in her own way.

She looked over at Warren, who acted as if she'd left already. He didn't say a word as he pulled open another drawer. She braced herself, ready to bolt if he found anything else to throw. Instead, he located a thick white envelope and retrieved what looked like a heap of photographs. Lisa moved closer as he ran his fingers over the pictures, spreading them out on his desk before him: hundreds of still, candid shots of Chyna Lockhart, at various time throughout the day.

"Your services are no longer needed, Ms. Stephens."

"You will not - !" she exclaimed in disbelief. "I know you are not firing me. The hell you are! I will rat all of you out, I will tell the world what you did... I - "

The door opened at her back, Warren's father Chauncey Hardig walked in and Lisa's bluster died on her lips.

"My son said your services are no longer needed, so please leave this office and never come back," Chauncey said crisply, as if he'd been there the whole time. "If you think we will be threatened, Ms. Stephens, you need to think again."

"I just, I just thought - " she stammered.

"You won't have to do that any longer."

"What?" she questioned warily.

"Think, Ms. Stephens." Chauncey clarified. "You won't have to think any longer, about anything. You see, we've left you a nice severance package in exchange for your cooperation and your silence. Now, if that is not sufficient for you, we know plenty of people who would rather take it and stay alive than argue the alternative. Do you understand?"

Lisa nodded. She understood. "It had better be enough, too," she spat, as she grabbed her purse and stalked out.

"Well, Warren, I'd hope you'd know better anyway, but I'm assuming you weren't in love with the likes of Ms. Stephens," his father said. "She's cost us enough time, doing absolutely nothing. She didn't plant the right items at the fire, and she didn't get Jameson to sleep with her. I've never seen anyone so piss-poor at executing a simple mission. By the way, I'm aborting the Jameson project. We'll get the property some other way."

"What about Ms. Lockhart?"

His father snorted. "Are you stupid, son? She is not interested in you, psycho, and frankly I don't want her in this family. Is that what you want, anyway: Gary Williams' slutty reject?"

Warren bridled. "She's a wonderful, caring woman, not a slut," he retorted quietly.

"Who isn't interested in you, mind you," his father reminded him.

"She could be... persuaded," Warren protested.

"By what means, son? Oh, you're going to kidnap her now? You going to drag her off to your little lair and keep her bound and hidden forever?" Chauncey laughed.

Warren shrugged. His father's face darkened.

"Please tell me you're not serious?"

There was continuous silence. Warren knew his father hated his evasion tactics. He sulkily moved more photos around his desk until he found an unfortunate picture that needed altering. He gripped it tightly in his hand and searched through another drawer until he found a pair of scissors. Ensuring that her perfect face remained unscathed, he carefully cut out the smiling man beside her. His father was right about that much: it was time to abort the project.

WHEN CHYNA AWOKE the next day, it seemed she was in a foreign place.

She sat up in bed: a bed she'd seen for the very first time only the previous night. White and lace enveloped her like a beautiful cloud. Part frightened, part delighted, she rubbed the sleep-induced grogginess from her eyes, still not quite believing that this was her house.

She smelled coffee and some type of food and called for Dean.

"Making coffee - don't tease. I'm not coming up there," he yelled back.

Chyna fell back, giddy with joy, knowing this would be her marriage in due time. She was still in shock that Dean had proposed to her. After practically carrying her upstairs last night, he'd shown her everything, from the new flooring throughout her second floor to the two newly-renovated bathrooms.

He wasn't coming up there, she knew that. The elation they both felt over moving forward to a wedding in the near future meant they'd committed to staying out of one another's bedrooms. Dean had been there just momentarily last night, but after several kisses born of the ultimate relief of being safe in each other's arms once more, they'd managed to restrain themselves and he'd said goodnight.

Granted, the new place had felt undeniably lonely as she'd moved about her house, learning all the newness and making mental notes about any things she needed. Even when she finally went to bed, though, she and Dean had texted back and forth for the majority of the night.

"Well, good morning, finally," Dean said when she placed her arms around him down in the kitchen. Chyna held him loosely as he turned in her arms and embraced her, kissing her lips while also managing to punch the coffeemaker button.

"Good morning to you," she smiled back. "I just wanted to tell you how awesome that bed is. The bed, the shower, the beautiful claw-footed tub... everything is ridiculously heavenly."

"Um, that sounds like a trap. I'm on bed restriction, remember? I cannot visit yours until our wedding night."

"I think another Chyna Lockhart must've made that decision," Chyna grinned. "What a dummy, why'd you listen to her? She's nuts."

Dean laughed. "Sorry, but whomever this Lockhart person is, only and I do mean *only* Mrs. Chyna *Jameson* can grant me access."

Chyna looked at him, mock surprise on her face. "I always wanted to be her: is it silly?"

"Yes, you're just obsessed, you crazy woman you: in love

with a complete idiot." Dean played along. "What's the matter with you?"

"Well, he learns really fast, he's rather handy and he sure can cook."

Dean laughed. "He's also unemployed."

"He has skills and can be whatever he wants," she amended.

"I'll try to keep that in mind; but to your other question: no, I don't think it's silly. Truly, it might be silly if you weren't the woman for me, but you are."

"And you're the man for me," she answered.

"I want to give you everything, Chyna," Dean said, breaking into her thoughts. He kissed the side of her mouth.

"You gave me you," she replied. "God gave me you. I won't deny His gift any longer."

"Did you like your bathroom?"

"It looks heavenly, but I had to see you first, so I haven't taken a shower yet."

"Okay, but listen, about what we talked about last night?"

"Nope, Dean, for the hundredth time, I'm not leaving you. I'm not even sure why you're bringing it up. The last time I left, Lisa came over here, to your Mom's house and had you doubting me and what I felt for you. I'm not having it again."

She broke her hold of him to make herself a cup of coffee; he retrieved a mug and rinsed it before handing it to her, then pushed the cream and sugar closer. She added lots, despite his disapproving look. She was only giving herself added fortification, she told herself, to win this particular battle with him over the suggested trip. The Battle of Macon, she thought with a grin. She wasn't exactly sure that she could win, but she would give it her old college try. She knew each one of his brooding features, and his dark concerned eyes presently wore a look that said 'you're getting out of this town, end of story.'

"Tish wants to see you," Dean began.

"Um, I think she can wait," Chyna replied. "Isn't she kind of busy?"

"Momma wants to see you," Dean persisted. "Plus, I was thinking you could show her your first few trees."

"I don't show anyone my work until I'm closer to the final rendering. Dean, look: I want to see both of them, but... hey, you didn't already tell them I was coming, did you?" She frowned suspiciously. Because it was hard to deal with Tish being blooming and pregnant after her own miscarriages, Chyna had deliberately stayed away from Georgia. That was wrong, yes, but she didn't want to kid herself that seeing Tisha in person wouldn't bring up terrible thoughts. She wanted nothing but the best for her friend and her unborn babies, of course.

Tish was her closest friend, and of all the people to share her own tragic ordeal with, Tish had come to mind first. Granted, telling Jina had meant risking the whole family finding out as well, and Chyna knew anyone who found out secondhand would be angry and sad that she'd kept such news from them. So Chyna hadn't reached out to share in the first few weeks of Tish's joyous news. She felt really bad about that. Between Chyna's own issues with Dean and Tisha's new family, the two friends had been just a little more distant of late - but when they did connect, Chyna knew it would be like no time had passed. They were truly like sisters.

Plus, she thought excitedly, if she did visit, she could get to know Thomas better. She'd loved the boy instantly but had only spent a little time with him back at the wedding. She hadn't stayed long at the reception, as the tension between her and Dean had already been thick and increasing every moment, known to no-one but the two of them.

"Chyna?"

"Ye-yeah?" Chyna said, looking up belatedly.

"Um, honey, where were you just then?" Dean asked, concerned.

She hated to ruin the moment, but all the thoughts came rushing back to her. "I don't want to see your sister, Dean, because seeing her reminds me of our loss," she said in a rush.

Dean's face fell. "I'm sorry. I should have thought of that, Chyna. I thought it would be good - "

"Stop. It is good. It's a great idea," she assured him. "I do miss her since she moved away."

"Maybe she could rub her belly on you or something, give you some good pregnancy ju-ju?" he suggested.

"Seriously? That's the stupidest thing I've ever heard. Pregnancy is not a virus," she laughed, forgetting all about his silliness when he kissed her again and again.

Dean lifted her chin and set her coffee aside, her warm fingers coming up to touch his face. He leaned forward, whispering in her ear as if he had a secret to tell her. It tickled, but she drew closer to hear what he said.

"I love you. Please just trust me."

"I do, you know I do," Chyna murmured, rising up on the tips of her toes to get closer.

"Then know that I'm only thinking of you: that I always think only of you."

Chyna was thoughtful a moment. She took a deep breath and relented to a negotiation. "Three days, two nights?"

"Four nights, five days" Dean countered.

"Sounds like a cruise, and it's no cruise without you," she parried.

"But you'll be smooth sailing."

Chyna shook her head, ready to counter with her original offer when Dean's cell phone rang. He didn't let her go of her but reached inside his pocket with one hand to retrieve it.

"Oh, hey there," he said, placing the phone to his ear. "You have the most perfect timing, you know that? She's right here."

Chyna heard laughter on the other end and, recognizing the familiar sound, seized the phone from Dean's hand.

"Hello," Chyna said and that single word launched her into a long discussion with Tisha: how excited she was that her best friend would be visiting and how she couldn't wait to see her. Chyna looked at Dean, annoyed, but he pretended to do something else in the kitchen as Chyna tried to make peace with leaving him for as little time as she could get away with.

26

Chyna couldn't help feeling apprehensive over the next couple of days as she packed up her clothes for the trip. Every moment she thought about Dean, though, she stopped whatever she was working on at the time and just smiled into space.

She glanced disapprovingly at the small luggage set with tags still on: just another mark of her defeat in the Battle of Macon. What with Dean, Ms. Alfreah and Tisha herself all ganging up on her, she hadn't stood a chance. She couldn't shake the nagging worry: *What if Dean got into trouble?*

"Did you test out the alarm?"

Chyna set down her paint brush. They'd been working on painting the small dining nook, now that it was no longer used as her art space. She'd relocated her art supplies up to the second floor, where natural sunlight was more plentiful in the evenings. That was her favorite time to paint. The light of the fading sun was ideal for her favorite scenes of country fields.

"No, I haven't learned how to work it, yet," she answered. "I - I don't want to."

"One more time, let's learn this," he said firmly. "Then I

gotta go to the store, but I'll be right back to take you to the airport. Oh, and I'm having dinner with Jojo and Angel tonight."

"No fair, I want dinner with Jojo and Angel," she protested as Dean laughed at her. She was being a brat, she knew, but she meant it. They'd had dinner with Jojo and Angel once before, and it had been absolutely unbelievable. Describing Angel as a cook was like saying Anne Geddes worked at JCPenney's baby portrait studio. Chyna's palate had never encountered anything so good: a whole fish, crisped to perfection, the meaty flesh just falling off the bone.

"Do you think Angel could teach me to cook?" she mused.

"Let's not ask her to work miracles until she marries my brother first, okay?" Dean laughed as Chyna feigned deep offense. "OK, now," Dean snapped his fingers. "Pay attention, here's the security code."

Chyna watched him enter a series of codes. She knew how to use an alarm system, but at Gary's house she'd mostly made him deal with it. Her only gripe was how loud it always seemed to be, alerting her to every single entry even if someone was only working outside but kept coming in to get things.

Chyna entered the number, Dean opened and closed the door, and this time she was pretty sure she had it. She hoped she never had cause to use it, though.

"I'm going to take a bath," she announced.

"Okay. I'll be right back: about thirty minutes."

Chyna nodded, and he kissed her before she headed upstairs.

Before she even got to the bathroom, she smelled the gorgeous fragrance of burning candles. She looked at the bathtub and was sad time didn't permit her to lounge there for an extended period of time today. She wondered if Tisha and Chase had such a spacious guest bedroom en-suite... *Hey now: your house was just fixed up after you almost single-handedly demolished it - don't be getting all snobby.* Chyna laughed at her wayward thoughts. An ex-NFL football player likely had just as nice a bathtub as hers, of course, if not better. Heck, they could probably accommodate the whole darn family in luxurious comfort at their home, even if all the Jamesons just happened to descend on them at the same time.

Almost undressed and ready for a quick shower, she heard the doorbell ring: momentarily as foreign a sound as some tribal drumbeat. It rang again and, returning to Earth, she turned off the water, zipped her pants back up and threw her shirt on, hastily buttoning it with some irritation as she went down to answer it.

She looked down at the alarm and hesitated. The word 'stay' was highlighted with a red light, and she frowned. Dean had probably done that just so she'd be forced to test her learning of disabling the alarm, but she had no clue what it meant. He'd also forgotten that she hadn't yet learned to use the camera. She gingerly pushed a button on the back of the door. She was pretty sure the screen was supposed to light up and show her whomever was there, only it looked black. Did she even have a porch lamp?

When the knocking came again, along with the doorbell, Chyna gave up and pressed the code on the alarm, hitting off. "Off", the alarm's automated voice agreed, and she thanked it reflexively, trying not to laugh. Who recorded these things, anyway?

Cracking the door, her eyes traveled quickly up the suit to the cold eyes of Warren Hardig staring back at her.

Catching her off guard, he seemed to push on the door with superhuman strength, pushing her to the floor.

"Hey honey, I'm home."

In horror, Chyna scrambled up as Warren's imposing height loomed over her. "What are you doing here, Warren?" she gasped, "I suggest you leave right this minute. Dean w-will be back any moment."

"Really? I just saw him leave," replied Warren calmly. "Did you tell him about us yet?" He looked crazier than she could ever have imagined.

"There is no *us*," said Chyna, trying to keep the shake from her voice. "Does he know you crawled into the bed of your supposed friend's then-wife? Then yes, I told him that. You always blamed it on your state of drunkenness, but I'm beginning to wonder if that's what it was. Does he know you paid Gary to have me? Well, then yes, he knows everything. I think you're actually very sick, Warren. Your actions can't be blamed on alcohol." While she spoke, Chyna moved to the kitchen, trying not to make it too obvious. There was a phone there, as well as an array of knives. She regretted not bolting for the door when she'd had the chance.

"It's not nice to call people names, Chyna. I'd have thought better of you."

Reaching the kitchen at last, she grabbed the phone and opened the drawer at the same time, reaching for a large knife, thanking God they were in the same place.

"Oh my, such a big knife you have," Warren intoned, moving toward her.

"Do not come closer to me, Warren," she warned. "I will use it."

"Really, darling, when did you become so violent?"

"Being married to a monster and meeting his monster friends will make you more cautious," she shot back. "Your girlfriend Lisa attacked me, too. Know what else? I'm thinking about buying a gun, and it has your name written all over it."

"Wow, honey, I'm so sorry Gary was nasty to you. I would never let Lisa hurt you," Warren said, suddenly gentle. "Are you okay?"

"I'm not your honey, I am fine, and 'nasty' is an under-statement."

Chyna couldn't figure out why the phone had no dial tone, but she still brandished the knife, holding it out steady in front of her. She kept her eyes on Warren as she set the phone aside.

Chyna heard the door click and the alarm beep, announcing uselessly that a door was opening. She yelled for Dean – but in a moment Gary entered the room. He lunged for her and pinned her down, the knife between them unusable. She struggled, but he put a hand over her mouth. She bit it and he recoiled.

Suddenly, blessedly, there was Dean.

"Dean!" she yelled, even though there was no need to yell: his very presence had halted whatever Warren was trying to do.

Wriggling free, Chyna grabbed for the knife but saw with relief that Dean already had it.

"Call the police – outside - now." He gripped the knife more tightly.

"Dean, Dean, come with me, please - just come outside too," Chyna pleaded.

"I have a pig I have to carve. Go. Do it now, Chyna," he repeated. He practically pushed her from the kitchen, his eyes never leaving Warren's face.

"Hey, man," Warren said as he stood up, casually brushing off his suit as if he'd just been planting roses in a flower garden.

"You got a death wish?" Dean asked him coldly.

"No, man, Chyna invited me over..."

Before Warren could finish his statement, Dean kicked his legs out from under him. As Warren got back up, Dean used his fist to knock him down again and threw the knife aside. "I'd rather kill you with my bare hands, but I just redid this kitchen and I'd really hate to mess it up with pig guts all over the floor."

Chyna didn't leave the house. She leapt up the stairs three

at a time, feeling as if her leg had never been injured, and finally retrieved her cell phone to dial 9-1-1.

Dean and Warren struggled, but eventually Dean had Warren by the arm, twisting it painfully behind his back until he seemed to relent and eventually went down on his knees. In seconds, however, he wrestled free and headed straight for the knife. Returning to the kitchen, Chyna rushed forward to get it before he did as Dean pushed Warren to the ground and rested his weight in the center of Warren's back, pinning him to the floor.

"You're big but dumb Mr. Hardig - not only that, you also underestimate me," Dean hissed. "You so much as call here again and things'll be much worse than this little skirmish we've had today. Get it through your thick head that Chyna Lockhart is off limits and stop coming in here with your little punk games."

Chyna continued to breathe deeply in and out. She was as winded as Dean and Warren put together, as if she'd done the wrestling herself. Dean even took a moment to wink at her, which let her know that everything was okay. She scowled back, unimpressed at his show of playfulness while such a sinister, seemingly unstoppable man lay face down on her kitchen floor. Dean perspired yet looked unhurt, while by contrast she felt as if she'd been through the wringer just having watched.

When a loud knock came on the door, Chyna turned, remembering just in time to put the knife down on the coffee table. She flexed her fingers, thinking it was best not to bring a knife to the door when greeting the helpful people who carried guns.

The officers asked if she was okay and before she could speak, Dean had dragged Warren to his feet, bringing him to where they all stood. Chyna rattled off details of the day's events to one officer, while another snapped Warren into a pair of cuffs. Keeping her eyes on Dean, she tried to answer their many questions.

As soon as Dean could see straight and was calm enough to talk once again, he took over from Chyna, telling the officers his own more heated version of what happened. "You get him out of here," he demanded. "You just tell me what I need to do to get a restraining order."

"Yes, Mr. Jameson," the police officer said, taking notes. "You might have to come to the station to sign the charge, Ms. Lockhart."

"Fine, fine, whatever you need," Chyna said, her focus on Dean and his state of mind, not to mention his torn shirt. His hands were tight fists, balling and releasing again and again. She didn't register what the officer said, but whatever it was it must have had the word 'goodbye' on the end, because he got into his car and left, taking Warren with him.

27

"L et's go."

"What?"

"I said let's go," Dean repeated.

"Go where?"

"To the airport."

"No, I'm not leaving you Dean."

"You are," he said firmly. "It's not safe for you here: we know that now. Are you all right?" he added, and kissed her cheek. Chyna nodded.

"Are you sure?"

Chyna nodded again. "Dean, sit down."

Without protest, Dean took a seat at the small kitchen table.

"I'm fine, okay? I'm all right." She tried to reassure him though she knew it was futile. He was too concerned about her safety and she both knew and appreciated that, but running away to Macon wasn't the answer. There was safety in numbers, even if it was just the two of them.

"And if I hadn't come? Who knows what the hell would've happened? He's got problems, Chyna. Serious, like mental, you know? He thinks he can go wherever he pleases, do and take whatever he wants. He's got to be crazy."

"I know, I know, but I'm all right. I am," she reassured him when he looked at her.

"We're going to the airport," Dean started again.

"No!"

"Can you handle Warren, Chyna? Did he force his way in here? You could have hit the panic button, or..."

"No, he didn't force his way in: I opened the door. I thought you might have forgotten something."

"This isn't a game, this is serious," Dean said, clapping his hands as if the loud sound would knock some sense into her. "You've got a delusional, violent woman who will hurt you all because I'm not her man, and you've got an obsessed man who almost... well, anything could have happened all those years ago, and today too, Chyna. Obviously your absence has made the nutzos multiply..."

"I know that," she protested. She didn't want to think about what had almost happened yet again. What if Dean hadn't returned so soon? "I know him," she went on, "but..."

She had no more excuses. It was a good idea to leave, she knew that really; but she'd file a restraining order first. Surely she could convince Dean of that, to buy her a few more days. Furthermore, she had to find a way to get Dean to come with her. She blew out a frustrated breath.

"If they know you're still here in town, they'll continue to try to get to you any way they can. This is all a game to them, but games can turn dangerous - it's sick and twisted. I need to have you close. Your safety, above all, is the most important thing to me. You are a pawn."

"So you just want to remove the pawn from the board?" returned Chyna. "It won't disappear, you know: your opponent just can't see it. My leaving doesn't solve anything for good: what happens when I return? Same problems. You are a pawn too – don't you see? They are doing all of this to get to you, too." Chyna flopped onto the sofa.

"But it does change things," Dean said.

Chyna grabbed his hand when he stopped pacing long enough and took a seat next to her on the sofa. Her eyes followed his to the large knife nestled between a stack of antique books and a silver vase of fresh roses on her coffee table: completely out of place. Such a stark contrast with those lovely things that made her happy and calm. Dean pulled her closer to him and she placed her hand on his chest. It was warm and inviting in his arms, but his heart beat fast under her palm. He was anxious over her safety and, truth be told, she was anxious over his.

"Tish will be happy to see you," he concluded, undeterred and silently daring her to stage any more protests. "I'll make one concession. I'll come up this weekend."

She was silent as she thought about Tisha, her family and Ms. Alfreah. However, she thought ruefully, she and Dean had only just gotten together. The last few months had been everything she ever wanted, and they'd just decided to commit to one another for the long haul, and now he was asking her to leave him for what could be a much larger mess if they couldn't face it together. Frustrated yet resigned, she nodded, knowing there was nothing that could be done or said to change his made-up mind.

TISH JAMESON-ALTON MADE her way to the door with just a twinge of apprehension in her gut. When the door opened and her friend walked in with a huge smile on her face, some of that tension left immediately. "Hi," she said and returned her friend's smile with one of her own.

"Hey," Chyna replied. "You have a sweet husband. He

chatted the whole way here with endless stories about you and Thomas. I'm so glad you're so happy."

"He's had that effect on me, yes," Tish smiled. "He gives me everything I want and if he doesn't, my little boy does." Right on cue, her husband, Chase, walked in. He bent to kiss her cheek before turning to Chyna. "I'll put your bag in the guest room. It's upstairs and to the right." In a matter of moments, he returned. "Would you like something to drink, Chyna?"

"Well, got anything super-caffeinated? But you gotta promise not to tell Dean, okay?" Chyna laughed at the raised eyebrow and puzzled face Chase made as he glanced at his wife.

"I think that can be arranged. We won't tell, will we, honey?" Tish said.

"If you asked me to keep it from Jojo, I would've said no way," Chase said seriously. Chyna looked back and forth between the two of them, a tad confused.

Tish hugged her friend and stood back. "Chase means that he is scared of Jojo," she said in a stage whisper. Both of the women laughed, and Chase's face remained serious as if there was nothing at all funny about the issue before he disappeared into the kitchen.

"Thank you so much - and, you guys, I could've gotten a ride from the airport, you know..."

"I didn't mind," Chase said from the hall.

"Nonsense," Tish amended. "Come into the den, we'll talk." She led her friend to the end of the hallway and around the corner.

"This is a beautiful home," Chyna commented as she followed slowly behind Tish, taking time to look at the pictures on the wall, the structural ornaments, and all manner of other things that piqued her interest. She realized for the first time how design-conscious she'd become since her renovation, as well as witnessing the many updates Dean had also made to the Jameson family home. For the first time, she also realized that everything he'd asked her about adding to and changing Ms. Alfreah's home had been a subtle way of finding out the things she liked and disliked. She missed him terribly, and she had only just arrived here.

"Thank you," Tish said. Upon entering the den, she flipped a switch and a light blinked on, bathing the room in a soft glow.

Chyna took a seat, trying to keep up her show of looking and sounding relaxed and happy. Sure, she was happy, but 'relaxed' was a bit of an overstatement. In the background, her thoughts of Dean continued to fuel a sense of impending danger. She'd have to keep that hidden from Tish and Ms. Alfreah — which, now that she had arrived and seen Tish face-to-face, she no longer believed she could do. She stared at Tisha's protruding belly. She'd try as hard as she could, knowing the stress would not be good for her unborn twins.

Surprisingly, as she thought about her best friend's current pregnant state, the sadness she felt at losing her own children didn't come on as strong as she'd feared it might. She knew one reason was that she was focused on moving forward and secondly, she was truly happy for her friend. Tisha deserved all this happiness - and of course Chyna was going to be the first person signing up to babysit whenever she could. It was impossible to harbor any animosity toward her friend. "I can't wait to spoil those two little ones you're carrying. How exciting, TT," she said aloud, in quiet awe.

The resistance to caffeine she'd maintained for the duration of her journey had snapped as soon as she'd landed safely. She hoped the cup of calming java would work to soothe her jitters whenever Chase brought it out. She concentrated on the decor Chase and Tish had chosen for their home, looking around and noticing some of the intricate patterns.

"Thank you Chyna, but are you happy?" Tish asked, patting her rounded stomach. "I just feel so bad about, you know... I'm so glad you're here, but I want you to be all right with this. I worried about it. When Dean said you were coming, or suggested that you come, I wondered if he knew how you would handle that, how you would feel about me. Men are so clueless sometimes. I didn't want you to say you were all right just to pacify him, or me - just to avoid either of us being worried about you. Are you okay with... with this? With being around me?"

Chyna waved a hand dismissively. "I wouldn't have come if I wasn't going to be okay. More importantly, I would never have come if I thought I'd be bringing any negative energy to your home and to those unborn babies. I think... I think I'm fine."

But Dean's in trouble and he's taking on this man that hates his guts because of me, and my ex-husband has it in for me and he might get hurt!

Chyna took a deep breath and closed her mind to the encroaching thoughts so she wouldn't say them out loud, but not without a colossal effort.

"I'm fine now, but I probably couldn't - well, I *know* I wouldn't have said that a couple of months ago," she admitted. "But I'm so happy for you, Tish: much too happy to focus on my own loss. That would be utterly selfish."

She was a selfless person, she knew, and that's how she was able to cope so well. Not to mention that maybe she could help Tish prepare for the babies. She and Dean were going to be together, that was what mattered; and she'd bring a child into the world at the right time, in their own time, which had to be God's time. As hard as it was to accept that His time wasn't theirs, she was slowly making peace with that concept. "Our time is not God's time," Chyna whispered, smiling at her friend.

"Well, all right then!" Tish exclaimed, smiling. "That's wonderful: I'm happy to hear you talk like that at last. I'm just sorry I couldn't be there for you. I wish you had told me about being pregnant, but I know you couldn't have: you'd've known I would have advised you to tell Dean. He is my brother, after all."

"Yes, I know, and it would've killed him and you if you'd known and kept it from him," agreed Chyna. "I know how close you two are. I'd never put you in that position."

"Yes. Thank you for thinking of that. I just wish..." Tisha hesitated. "Well, it's the past, anyway, and I'm so glad you are finally together." Tish moved her hand as if shooing the past away. "I'm so happy for you guys."

"And my ring! I didn't show you." Chyna pulled out her hand from her pocket and waved it before Tish's eyes.

"Well, keep still, would ya? Let me get a look without getting cross-eyed," laughed her friend, grabbing Chyna's hand for inspection. Her eyes grew wide. "Oh my, this - I think this is our great-grandmother's ring. Oh, it looks so new, but it still has the antique finish."

"Yes," said Chyna proudly. "He told me he had it reset and cleaned. I used to see it in your mom's jewelry box and secretly wish it was mine, from him," Chyna said.

"You got your dream," Tish said in wonderment.

"I did," Chyna replied, looking up toward the ceiling, her eyes blurred by tears. "I got it. Do you think it's silly - my dream, I mean?" she said, looking at her best friend.

"I think it's silly your wanting my big old, dumb brother," Tish quipped. Then she sobered. "But seriously, Chyna, without dreams, we have nothing to attain, nothing to desire, and then we have nothing to pursue and hope for. What have we? What are we doing? If we don't go after what we truly want, we're just beings floating blindly along, existing in a space, with no drive, determination or aspirations. So, no, I don't find it silly. You're strong, you're so strong, and you've held on and fought for what you wanted, even with all these monkey wrenches thrown into the works along the way. It's easy to give up, it's easy to let go, but it takes someone real to hold on and fight."

"Thank you so much, T.T.," Chyna said earnestly, calling her friend by her childhood nickname. She blinked rapidly to banish her tears. "So! What are you going to name these beautiful babies?"

Before she could respond, Ms. Alfreah walked in. Tish looked up: "Oh, hi mom."

"Oh, Mrs. J.! How are you?" Chyna stood to greet the woman that had taken her in as if Chyna were one of her own, and taught her so much in her own mother's absence. The two women embraced each other, holding hands until they moved to sit down together on the sofa.

"I'm doing quite well, now that my third daughter and my silly son are acting like they have some sense," Alfreah said matter-of-factly, wasting no time in cutting to the subject on the tip of everyone's tongue.

"Be nice now, Mama," Tish warned. Chyna looked at Alfreah, waiting with bated breath. But Mrs. Jameson merely looked over at her daughter and without missing a beat said, "Excuse me, did I ring your number?"

Seconds passed, silence swelled, and Chyna bit her tongue to keep from laughing, until finally all three women in the room dissolved into a fit of giggles.

28

"Good night you guys," Chyna said to Tish, who moved slowly and tiredly up the stairs. Chase was behind his wife, half-carrying her, having been the one to urge her to turn in for the night.

Chyna turned once Tish and Chase had left the living room, Chyna regarded Alfreah. "He's so protective of her: it's so wonderful."

"Yes, he's a good match for her."

"How are you, Ms. Alfreah, since... uh...?" Chyna struggled to find the words.

"Since Joe died?" Alfreah finished, and continued when Chyna nodded her head. "I'm all right..." Taking a deep breath, Alfreah nodded. "I'm all right," she said again. "How's everything in Virginia?"

Chyna bit her lip, wondering just how much she should relay. She didn't know whether Dean had planned on telling his mother anything about the Hardigs' antics, or about Chyna's ex. "Things are good," she said carefully, after a beat. "The house is looking very beautiful - you should see the work Dean's done. We've referred many times to the idea journal you left, and he's implemented a lot of them. You had a wonderful vision for the place." Chyna smiled. "I hope you'll like it. I know much of it was just repairs, but..."

From the way Alfreah looked away, Chyna could tell she wasn't as excited as one might have expected. It must've been hard.

Alfreah looked at her hands. She worried the wedding ring on her left hand, twisting it around her finger. "I'm sure it looks nice," she said at last. She stood abruptly. "I'm going to go to bed now."

Chyna touched the older woman's shoulder. "It will get easier. It just takes time."

"I know, sweetie pie," Alfreah said tiredly, patting Chyna's hand and turning to leave. Chyna knew then that it wasn't the time to let her know about the near-disaster of the finances, nor the situation with the Hardigs. Dean would handle it, she told herself, and she'd help him clear up the rest when she got back to Virginia. Here and now, however, she remained, staring at the kitchen's dirty dishes. For lack of something to do, she wiped down the counters, cleaned off the table and loaded the dishwasher before heading up to bed herself. She resisted the urge to make another cup of coffee, considering she likely wouldn't sleep anyway. Chyna hated to admit that all the activity still didn't keep her mind off Dean. She missed him desperately, especially at night when there was no-one to talk to.

Tish and Alfreah had visitor after visitor during the day - teachers from the school where Tisha taught, and ladies that Tisha's natural warmth had made quick friends at the local church - and that helped make the time go faster. Chyna was pleased to see her second mother and best friend each integrating into their new lives in Georgia, while creating for Thomas the same kind of idyllic childhood that Tish had had and that Chyna remembered. Thomas and the many friends he had over loved the "cool" house. They blasted music and pretended they were up-and-coming rappers, hip-hop or pop stars or whatever the cool thing of the moment was, down in the basement surrounded by snacks and video games. It was just like Chyna remembered the Jameson house being. It was nice to see Tisha replicating what she'd grown up with.

To her surprise, Chyna had also enjoyed helping ready the baby room for the arrival of the twins. Per Tish's request, she painted a few little flowers and butterflies around the light switches, wall sconces and windows, plus a delicate border pattern around the wall: little girly things, since they already knew the twins' genders. Besides Ms. Alfreah's ever-evolving tree, which was nowhere near completion, it was the only thing Chyna had painted in years. She felt more confident in decorating the babies' room having recently done so many practice versions of Ms. Alfreah's drawing. Both Ms. Alfreah and Tish raved over what were essentially basic lines, brush strokes and antennae. Chyna smiled at the memory of Dean gifting her all those supplies: material things representing those intangibles that no sum of money could ever obtain. Those things supplied her with a deep-driving purpose, encouragement in her darkest hours, and the love she longed for.

Chyna also spent some time with Thomas, but he had seemingly boundless energy and not much time for older folks. He had lots of friends, just like his new mother, Tish, had as a child. They were so close now that it almost seemed like Tish had birthed the boy herself. Watching them, Chyna saw how adoption could work. Thomas wasn't adopted, but he just fit with Tish like he'd somehow been waiting for her. Though Chyna's deepest desire was to give Dean a child made from the both of them, she wasn't averse to adoption, although it wasn't something she'd considered that deeply. She supposed that's what happened when you assumed you would just do everything in the "normal" order you thought things followed, and then God said otherwise.

As she tossed and turned, unable to fall asleep, she thought she heard some male voices downstairs, but shrugged off the thought and tried again to rest. When she'd spoken to Dean earlier that day, she had somehow suspected that something had happened, although he hadn't mentioned anything specific. She was perturbed, but the fact that he had been alive and talking to her on the phone was the only thing short of seeing him with her own eyes that could give her comfort.

Chyna felt as if time may have lapsed and maybe she did manage to drift off... but then she heard the deep voices downstairs once again and sat up, silencing her movements to listen intently as the voices quickly died down. Maybe Chase was on the phone or something.

Turning onto her back, Chyna looked over at the clock. Almost one AM. Giving up on getting back to sleep, she put on a robe, quickly finger-combed her hair and started downstairs. When she got to the second landing, she saw Dean, with a large bag over his shoulder and tiredness in his eyes. She ran downstairs, nearly breaking her neck, jumping from the last step and leaping into his arms. "Oh Dean!"

"You were expecting the tooth fairy?" he grinned. He released the sport bag he carried, dropping it to the floor, and carried Chyna over to the living room. It was still late, so rather than wake everyone up, he set her down and then joined her on the couch. He kissed her soundly and she hugged him tight, thrilled at the sight of him, even days later than he said he'd come.

"Why couldn't you come up yesterday?" Chyna asked, moving to get comfortable in his arms. She helped him out of his jacket and laid it on the back of the couch.

He looked away. "I told you on the phone... I got tied up."

Chyna nodded. "Any news?"

Dean merely shook his head.

She was ecstatic that he was there, but something was on his mind: that she was sure of. "I can tell there's been some sort of development, Dean, so spill it. Is Warren out of jail?"

"Man, I missed you, and this mouth." He kissed her lips and smiled, satisfied, when she kissed him back. "I missed that the most."

"Don't you change the subject," Chyna moved out of the range of his eager lips and searched his face. Her instincts honed by their new honesty policy, she now knew instantly when he was keeping something from her. "Stop it," she said firmly when his hands got a little bolder. "We are not gonna grope each other in your sister's living room like we're teenagers."

"Please?"

Chyna laughed and continued to halt his hands. "You have to answer my question first, and we're guests here! What if your mother comes in?"

"You really know how to douse a fire," Dean said incredulously.

"Dean, what happened?" she asked mustering up a serious tone and folding her arms, unrelenting to his advances.

Dean sighed. "Did you miss me?" he said, ignoring her questions and kissing her lips again.

"Yes," Chyna said, turning to lean into him. She tucked her feet under her and continued to stare at him expectantly, somehow knowing he was about to say something serious.

"Someone wrecked my car."

Chyna was silent for a moment, then she leapt up to face him. "What did you say?"

"The car, someone smashed it up. Lisa, probably." Dean rolled his eyes. "She's obviously got a thing for smashing cars. Gonna cost me an arm and two legs to fix it. They have it at the shop, but it's being investigated for prints, and whatever else they can find." Shaking his head, Dean went on. "My beautiful car. I loved that car," he said dreamily. "Oh well. Maybe I can get me a truck. What do you think? Chevrolet? Or maybe get me an SUV, four-by-four, a man's truck. I should ask Chase about his Navigator..."

"You. Would you stop it, please? You are asking me about my preferences for a stupid piece of machinery at a time like this? Are you all right?" Chyna asked, sitting down again. Her hands ran over his before touching his brow, relieved beyond words that he hadn't been hurt. "Doesn't this make you see why I should be home in Virginia rather than down here? And stop going on about some stupid truck. Can we rewind to the part about someone smashing up your car? It was probably Lisa, like you say. Where were you when it happened? What exactly happened?"

"Shh, I wasn't in it," Dean reassured her. "I was visiting Jina and Anthony in D.C., so I parked the car and took the Metro in. And you're getting all in a huff. You know I don't want Tish or Mama to be worried, so keep your voice down. I'm handling it."

"Dean," Chyna replied, whispering this time, "tell me this: when you booked your flight home, did you get two tickets?"

"No, I didn't. I only got one, because you're staying here. Just a few more days."

"The hell I am, Dean!"

"Can you come closer, please? I came a long ways to be here, and now you're all in a huff. Didn't you miss me?" he wheedled.

"Of course I did, but I will miss you even more if something happens to you. Do you understand?"

Dean nodded and Chyna settled into his arms again. "Can we not talk, not right now?" he murmured.

"Well, we can just relax here, if you like, but we're not going to visit someone else's home and be inappropriate."

Dean rolled his eyes. "Like they aren't most probably being... *inappropriate* up there right now."

Chyna laughed at the thought. "Dean, shut up. That's your sister, for goodness' sake!"

"You're right, that's disgusting. I feel nauseated."

Chyna chuckled and tried to keep her laughter down when Dean tickled her ribs with his fingers.

For the better part of the night, they talked and laughed, enjoying each other after missing each other for the last several days. While Chyna was so happy he was there, safe and sound, she resolved that he wasn't going home without her, even if she had to stuff herself into the largest shipping container she could find. She was getting herself back to Virginia to face those that meant to harm them, and maybe even help fight them. The more she thought about Warren, Gary and even Lisa, the more she began to see how they could all decide to converge and conspire against her and Dean, each with their own, crazy agenda. She hated to think it, but deep down, she felt as if she had figured it out. Gary wanted her life to be a disaster, just to show the media and his campaign that he was the jilted husband. Warren wanted to bed her as crazy as it sounded to her own ears, hating to believe or utter a word about that to Dean. Lisa's part in this, wasn't about neither Gary nor Warren but all about Dean. She didn't ever want to come to the conclusions that she had, but what else could it possibly have been? Gary would do anything if it meant more money in his coffers to win his bid for reelection. He had no idea about the dangerous game he played.

She and Dean would tackle things together this time, confronting whatever lay ahead of them. She may have drifted off to a semi-peaceful sleep in his arms after the shock and worry of his revelations, coupled by her own thoughts as they came and went. Even as she drifted, however, one thing was clear: whatever protests he had come morning, her mind was well and truly made up.

$$\sim$$

THE TWO DAYS of Dean's visit went by unbelievably fast. The family was caught up in discussing the twins, Thomas's little League game and Chyna and Dean's plans for their nuptials. Dean hadn't given the latter much thought yet, but to see her excited about moving forward buoyed his own spirits.

Already they'd eaten dinner on the second day. Dean would be leaving in a matter of hours. Chyna had no idea that he was just as sad to leave her side now as she had been to leave him, but it had to be done. First, he had to wrap things up in Virginia, and he needed to talk to his sister about possible recourse against Gary's book release. That plan was in motion already. Plus, Dean had heard that the FBI were already onto Warren and Lisa for illegal activity in their business dealings, so Dean was just trying to keep Chyna away until the case progressed a little further. He couldn't stand to stay away, but if it meant she was out of Warren's reach, he'd make that sacrifice. Of course, he knew the man could find her if he had his unstable mind set on it: Warren had money and means, and although it wasn't a real secret where she was, at least he couldn't just pop up quite so easily at her house.

In any case, Chase's security system was solid by now. He'd had ample chance to develop it during the saga with Tisha's principal a year ago, as well as that of Chase's ex-wife. With so many people involved over the years, he reflected happily that the people he loved most were all together now, and that meant they would fare better even when he wasn't around.

"I know your flight is departing soon." Chyna's words broke into his reverie. Dean stared up at Chyna as she held a mug out to him. Her cut-off jeans came to her knee, the edges frayed, a stark contrast with her sunned skin, and a simple loose-fitting pink top. It was still warm in Georgia at this time of year, and she looked like a summer dream in front of him. She wore minimal make up: just some sheer gloss on her lips, flower earrings in her ears and eyes that mesmerized him. She tucked her long elegant legs under her as she sat down next to him.

He took a sip of his coffee. She always doctored up perfect coffee, just the way he liked it, with a little sugar but otherwise completely black. He set it aside when she held her own and snuggled closer to him.

"How much of that have you had?" he said to her, wrapping his arm around her waist and pulling her closer.

"Not that much, but anyway I'll never tell," Chyna grinned. "Chase has been sworn to secrecy, too."

"I'll find out from Thomas," Dean teased.

Chyna laughed. "Mr. Thomas's calendar is booked solid from a parade of friends and constant video gaming activity. I assure you, he does not have any interest nor time to monitor my caffeine intake, nor to report it to you."

Dean laughed. "That so?"

Chyna nodded. "Dean, there is something serious I want to tell you though." She set her coffee aside and reached for some papers on the coffee table.

"Um, okay. What is that?" Dean said warily, as he moved to lean on Chyna's shoulder. He rubbed his belly in satisfaction, thinking of the changes to the Alton family. For one, Chase had a new cook, but his mother has also contributed to the meal, reminding him how much he'd missed his mother's cooking. He couldn't wait until everyone was back together in Virginia again, including the woman before him.

Looking back down at Chyna's notepad, he registered some light pencil drawings next to another list of craft supply items. Intrigued, Dean sat up a little straighter. "What are you doing?" he asked, raising a skeptical eyebrow.

"Tish asked me to paint some butterflies in the baby's room - I thought I showed you. Now I need to put a glaze over them," she replied, tapping the picture. "I finished them the other day but I should get something to protect them, so they'll last longer. I forget which kind..." She stopped as she noted his expression. "What?"

Dean closed his gaping mouth. "You agreed?"

Chyna smiled and nodded. She put down the notes and the sales circular, after highlighting one last item in neon pink. She turned to face Dean and gave him a long leisurely kiss. "I love you, Dean, and I thank you."

"I like that, I love you too, but what are you thanking me for? Tell me so I can do more of whatever it is and get more of those kisses."

"For giving back to me something that I thought I'd hate forever," Chyna smiled. "I'd associated all my art with tragedy when in fact it always brought me so much joy. When I get back home, I'll finish Ms. Alfreah's backsplash. Perhaps I could give it to her for Christmas?" Dean nodded. He didn't see why not.

"I've known for a while that I would paint it for her," Chyna continued. "I'm enjoying contributing something to the house."

"You are a part of our family and consequently our house, Chyna. Forever."

"I know, but really, something special just needs to go in that blank space. I looked online and found what I needed to keep it from getting ruined by Ms. Alfreah's awesome cooking. It has to withstand the heat, splatters and moisture of a well-used kitchen, so I was thinking about painting it on tile."

Dean nodded, listening intently as she talked about her craft lovingly for the first time in a long time.

"See, I had associated my painting with my time with Gary and my miscarriage when the one had nothing to do with the other, and now I feel ashamed for abandoning what most see as my God-given talent."

"It is a God-given talent," Dean agreed. "Your art is special." He hated what Gary had done to her morale over the years. There was anger every time he thought about it.

"I want to give you everything, make you so happy," she told him. "Another thing: as soon as we're married, I'd like to pursue adoption right away. I'd like to start our family as soon as possible. Thomas and Tisha have something so special. I know she loves his father, of course, but the relationship between her and Thomas especially has worked out so beautifully, it gives me hope."

"Um, we could get started right now though, on making our family," Dean suggested slyly.

"Technically we could, but we already made a commitment to wait," Chyna reminded him. "A commitment that you have absolutely no willpower for, I see," she added with a laugh.

"Well you make me so weak and forgetful, what can I say? I've been waiting a long time for you."

"I'm here now, and we have so much time."

Dean nodded, thinking about all the many possibilities both now and in their future, including children. He thought about his own parents' almost forty-five year marriage, in contrast with the comparatively short time he and Chyna had lost on what felt like hurdle after hurdle. Time was so short, he knew that, but only in the last few months did it really sink in, when he'd lost his father. He had no plans to waste any more precious time.

"Listen, Dean, I had another thought." Chyna sat up, crossed her legs one over the other and looked seriously at Dean before continuing.

"Hmm, what is it?"

She took a deep breath. "I wanted to tell you that I noticed how we have reconnected and it's wonderful, so much more than I'd hoped. Dean, look at me." When Dean looked back at her she continued, "I'm not the only one you pushed away. You pushed away your family by staying in Virginia by yourself, while everyone but you seemed to move on with their lives. I know you didn't think I noticed, but I did, the last few months. We worked on us and that was important, but now you need to work on you, and your mom, and everyone else. Have you talked to her? I mean, really talked to her? I know you're set on cleaning up this mess with your father's finances by yourself after Lisa's involvement, but you've also been pouring your energies into the house repairs and your office with little help. Now you're getting involved with my messes of Gary and Warren, even though you won't tell me what that entails, so you're pushing me away, too. You can't do all this alone."

Before he protested, she put a finger on his lips. "Yes, I know the Warren and Gary stuff is for my safety, so I went along willingly and I'm safe here, but talk to your mom, okay? Don't just handle things and clean it all up: include her. I know you don't want to bother her with this, but just give her a small dose at a time. Also, Dean, I told her about the renovations that have been done to the house, but I was surprised when she didn't seem all that excited. I don't know exactly what that means, but it can't be good."

When Dean took on a serious worried look, Chyna reassured him. "I'm not sure, I just think it would help if you're talking about things. You should see where she's at, see how she feels. None of the changes are that drastic, I know, but any change to a home she lived in your whole life is a change nonetheless. Make sure she's all right with the changes. It's one thing to request some minor renovations, but quite another to return home and find things completely different." She paused. "I don't know, just a hunch. She shared so much time in that house with your dad and all of her wonderful children, Dean. There is love there, I feel it, so even little changes must seem huge to her."

She rose. "I'm gonna go help Chase and Tish clean up now.

I'll see ya." She kissed him and he held on to her hand, preventing her from leaving right away. When she turned, he brought her hand to his lips, kissing each of her fingers. "Looks like I'm the one who needs to thank you."

She smiled. "We've got the rest of our lives to thank each other." With a final squeeze, she left him alone with a lot to ponder.

29

C hyna was right: Dean knew that as he moved down the steps and into the basement. To his surprise, it was like a second house floor plan unfolded before him on this level. It didn't have the dark, dank dungeon feel of most basements. The light-colored carpeting emphasized the high ceilings, with plenty of clearance for his six foot frame: his fingers could only just graze them. It was cozy with soft lighting, all warm, airy and inviting, fully furnished and segmented into clearly defined spaces. The basement's living area featured a large television screen, a sectional sofa, chairs and another area with a small bar, refrigerator and sink.

Further in, Dean saw the door leading to his mother's bedroom – and there, beside a small coffee table, he saw his mother seated in the corner of the long tufted couch, looking smaller and more timid than he'd ever seen her. Her capable hands worked carefully yet quickly with a long line of string across her lap, issuing from a large tote bag full of other balls of yarn: fluffy yellow and green and gray. She spotted him and stopped.

Given Dean's nature, it was much easier for him just to work these things out independently than to ask for help: work hard, take care of it, smooth it all out, clean up the messes regardless of who made them, resolving issues for the people he loved. What annoyed him right then, however, was that he didn't quite know how to fix the problem that presented itself: a rich, powerful and entitled man, bent on enacting some sort of perceived revenge on Dean's family. He wasn't out of options yet, Dean reminded himself. After all, that is what his father would have wanted him to do. *Figure it out, son,* Joe Senior had often said.

Dean felt capable and was glad to have both the knowledge and the tools to pay his parents back, to take care of them as best he knew how, repaying all their years of sacrifices, care and patching up of the various boo-boos he and his siblings incurred even as adolescents and young adults.

Top of mind today was the thought that none of them, himself nor his siblings, should ever have let Lisa Stephens step in to 'help'. With the four of them around, there should have been no need and no room for her to worm herself into the house and their family life, only to dupe them when they were at their most vulnerable.

It was hard to see how this could have happened when his mother had four perfectly competent children; yet at that time, Jina had been pregnant and having marital issues, and Jojo had been away off and on, serving numerous tours of duty. Dean should have been there, but he too had run away for various chunks of time, to figure out how to deal with his father's new way of life. He was so angry back then, and that anger had not only pushed him and Chyna apart but had eventually led to him tuning out, leaving his mother susceptible to all kinds of scammers. Yes, he admitted to himself, he should have been paying closer attention.

His mother was scrutinizing him when he finally looked up.

She never rushed any of her kids; she just always seemed able to tell when something occupied his mind.

Taking a seat on the floor like he used to do as a child, Dean looked up, stretching his legs out in front of him and resting his arms on each side, his shoulder leaning against her gently. "Mama," he said, gently touching her knee.

"Yes baby. I'm always listening."

Dean chuckled. "How are you doing?" he asked, not quite sure how to broach the many subjects on his mind. He wished his mother was in a cut-to-the-chase mood, as she often was.

"I'm doing all right."

"Are you?" Dean wondered aloud.

"Well, I'm sorry I ran away from a mess," Alfreah said.

"What mess?" Dean said, thinking his mother not only cut to the chase, she'd picked up telepathy. He looked up abruptly, ready to deny that anything was wrong, but even as quickly as she had switched subjects, he could tell she knew something was going on back home.

"I didn't think that you knew... anything about the financial situation, son."

"I can handle it, Mama," Dean finished firmly.

"You shouldn't've had to," his mother insisted. "I knew your father had bills, but he never told me about them. I guess I just turned a blind eye."

"That's just it, Mama. Everything is paid off. There aren't any outstanding debts. There's a larger problem, but none of it has anything to do with missteps by you, or by dad."

"What?" Alfreah leaned forward and set aside the knitting needles she had been holding so tightly. Before they could roll to the floor, Dean picked them up, stuck them through the ball of yarn as he'd seen her do and placed them neatly on top of the patterned tote bag. The blanket was a pretty peach color, so soft to the touch: no doubt destined for one of his future nieces, due so soon. Perhaps she'd make he and Chyna blankets for their child one day. The thought made his heart beat faster... yet worry still consumed him.

"It's the Hardigs and Lisa Stephens," Dean told his mother, unsure at this point what he should hold back and what he should reveal. "They've conspired to do us in – our family."

"Is this about that property?"

Dean nodded and watched his mother close her eyes. She smiled almost wistfully for a moment, then her look saddened.

"I had told your father that building was... well, I just couldn't see any use in having it. We as Black folks owning a nice three-story brick building in a popular plaza strip was just unheard of in the sixties and seventies - I mean, unless you had a church or a soul café or a little dry cleaning outfit, something like that. But my Joe roughed his hands building the place that he always intended would go to his youngest son. A man gave him that place for nothing: Elliot Poynter, a Caucasian man that had too much money. He and your father, they were friends. And then there was old Chauncey Hardig..."

Alfreah paused, then tried to stand, but the sofa's soft cushions seemed to work against her efforts. Dean was instantly on his feet to help her up. Alfreah looked up at her son.

"Hardig was a man who... took things. He created his destiny by undercutting, wheeling and dealing: cheating people to build his empire. Your father, the man I loved, was a kind man, honest, and sometimes people just gave him things out of esteem - although Mr. Poynter giving him that new brick building was an extreme and unprecedented example. See, Chauncey Hardig always wanted whatever a Jameson had..."

"He wanted you, too, didn't he?" pressed Dean.

His mother blushed. "That's not... that's not what we're talking about here, sweetie. I never entertained him."

"It just came to me, Momma. I'm sorry," said Dean, embarrassed. Rather than denying it, though, Mrs. Jameson looked down. "I thought leaving would let it die," she said softly. "I didn't want him to start coming around now that your father had passed, so I left. He wouldn't be bold enough to come looking for me across state lines, I hoped."

"Has he?"

"No honey, thankfully. The Hardigs have no regard for what is or isn't theirs, though, and they certainly don't care whether or not their affections are reciprocated. Sadly, baby, I think that Mr. Hardig has instilled that same take-all attitude and drive in his own son."

It was sad to imagine that Chauncey Hardig would harbor something so long, but the part of Alfreah that was so reluctant to return to Virginia knew without doubt that he would.

Dean looked down at her, scrutinizing and assessing. "The office - do you think the Hardigs burned it down?"

"I don't know, honey, but uh... well, I don't want this repeated, but Warren's been rumored to have some mental illness."

"What?" Alarm bells went of in Dean's head. "Momma, he's had his eye on Chyna. He's made... inappropriate advances to her."

"My goodness. Dear Lord," she exclaimed.

Dean nodded. "I sent her down here to Georgia because the other day he forced his way into Chyna's house."

"Oh goodness, honey she didn't say anything," gasped Mrs Jameson. "What in the world is going on?"

"Momma, I need to know if you think Warren would do something really awful?"

Dean didn't want to scare his mother, but now that he knew Warren had mental issues, whatever the official diagnosis was, it certainly explained a lot. He realized now that the look he'd seen twice in Warren's eyes wasn't just a lust-filled gleam for Chyna but potentially something much more deadly.

"I didn't think Chauncey Hardig and his son would kick us when we're already down with Dad passing away, but that makes a lot of sense," Dean said slowly, trying to fit all the pieces together. "I can't keep Chyna here forever, though: she's probably already bought a ticket home."

"Well now, she's concerned about you too," his mother pointed out. "Oh honey, I feel awful. I should have nipped this in the bud many years ago."

"How, Momma? You just need to stay away from him, is all."

Alfreah shrugged. "He's smart, honey. He would see how this can only lead to something awful for Warren. Perhaps I should reach out to him, I just... I don't know, perhaps I could just go in person and beg him to leave us be once and for all: ask him to stop their family's reign of terror."

"You will not go to him for anything, Momma," Dean insisted. "Dad would forbid it."

"I want to keep my children safe."

"We're fine. I'll handle it," Dean assured her.

"Okay but, uh, please just work with the police honey. I could make a statement about all the years he's - "

"You don't really have any proof against Chauncey though, Mom. But uh, I'll let you know if I need that," added Dean, not wanting to dismiss his mother completely. "Let me keep working on it. In the meantime, Momma, please do not have any contact with him, okay? You don't need to fight this battle."

Alfreah smiled sadly but nodded her agreement. "I'm so proud of you, son. You've been waiting on that girl of yours for twenty years, and she's been waiting on you. It seems you've finally been patient with each other. A long marriage takes patience and forgiveness, do you understand?" Alfreah patted his hand.

"I love her, but you knew that."

"Did I? Well, of course I did; but I like to think it was the work on my house that finally got you two together, don't you?" Dean laughed as his Mother brushed at her shoulders. "Oh really, Momma? Are you taking credit for this?"

"Well, let me take credit for at least *something* positive. Goodness." Alfreah gave a chuckle. " And one more thing, Dean honey. I know that you enjoyed your practice, but I also know that in the last few years you had sorta lost your passion for it. Totally up to you, but perhaps it's time for you to sell the property. Stop resisting Warren's greed and just get yourself out of his way. There is really no need to quarrel over this with him. Your father wouldn't want you to hold onto something – something he got for free, mind - just because he was so proud to work on it and to give it to you. All that's over now. You don't have to do anything with it, you don't have to hold onto it, okay? And that wouldn't count as giving in to those Hardigs. I know change is hard, but you have my permission just to part with it already, honey." Alfreah nodded knowingly. "You could do some consulting."

Dean raised his eyebrows. His mother never failed to surprise him with what she intuited or knew, and also what she'd kept to herself all this time. So much for his attempts at hiding things from her. He should know by now that he couldn't hide anything from this woman.

In fact, he'd thought a million times about what he could do with his life, what he should do next. Thing was, part of letting go seemed to involve uncertainty, and who'd want that? Especially now that he had Chyna and wanted to provide for her - not to mention that he'd worked all his life. He couldn't remember being jobless, ever. Even as a child, he cut grass in the spring and summer, raked leaves in the fall and shoveled snow in the winter. He was getting ready to have a family, and leaving your job wasn't exactly the way he'd envisaged prepping for a married future with kids. He was excited about that. He couldn't believe how things had changed so drastically just in the last few months. He had money for sure, he wasn't a big spender; but he wanted the stability provided by a steady job. He would have to find something else. He wasn't the type to sit around and do nothing.

A part of him wanted to stick it to Chauncey Hardig, to play out this scheme just to make it difficult for him. A part of Dean might have taken the risk, if not for Chyna. To be feasible, it would have to be a clean fight, not something that could get him killed. It was one thing to play these sick possession games just to be spiteful, but it'd be another thing entirely to make a dangerous, powerful man and his mentally unstable son angry enough to hurt the people he loved. His current and future family members were off the table. He knew the crooked and corrupt wouldn't ever play fair, however, so in order to fight back he'd have to adopt a different kind of character: become as awful and crooked as they were, and he would have none of that.

Dean was simple and decent at heart; and Chyna had already been married to one greedy, conniving fool. He hoped it was his own fundamental decency that made her choose him in the first place. Once he started playing on the corruption field, he would likely be down a road so far he could not return, not to mention he could lose all the people he cared about if he were so blinded by revenge. Even back in Gary's office, he'd felt so much anger, it was a wonder Chyna had been able to talk him off the ledge. That sort of instinct was simply evil: it was blind rage, and he could sense it would end up hurting people. It was a powerful feeling that had the capacity to overpower him beyond all reason.

Taking a deep cleansing breath, Dean closed his eyes to clear his mind. It didn't take a genius to see the costly dangers of getting on the same path as Chauncey, Warren and Gary. He returned to his mother's suggestions. Consulting, yes, but what about teaching? Thoughts of teaching seemed to stir something in him.

"Teaching," his mother said as if reading his thoughts. Dean nodded and looked at her, feeling not one shred of surprise at this point that his mother knew him so well.

"And maybe missions, baby," she added. "Maybe outfitting children for glasses in Africa or something, honey. You and Nurse Chyna, correcting the vision of thousands of children, helping ensure their future with something we take for granted, so people could see, and have a future and a childhood as good as your own... Oh yes, I could see it. Think about it, son. And you know what, sometimes the very environment we live in stresses our bodies. This Gary and Warren situation ain't nothing but stress. It's time to leave all of that behind."

Alfreah reached out to hug her son tight, her tiny frame barely reaching the middle of his chest. Dean wrapped his arms around his mother's shoulder and placed a kiss atop her graying hair.

"You'll fix it, sweetheart," she soothed. "If I thought you weren't capable of doing so, I would have stayed up in Virginia. You'll handle it. But please, let these hindrances go to focus on your family. Always remember what's important, baby."

Dean nodded and smiled. He felt a certain inner hesitation lifting. He wasn't sure what it was: almost as if he had needed his mom's permission all along. That building had been such a source of pride to his parents, it seemed such a shame to just sell it off; but thinking about service in Africa really did pique his interest.

"I'm glad to see Chyna so happy," Alfreah said, changing the subject again.

"I'd do anything for her," Dean replied.

"I know, honey. Now, I've been thinking about the house."

"She mentioned that you didn't seem enthused about the changes happening."

Alfreah nodded. "Your father and I used to joke that when you all left, we'd up and move into a small apartment straight away just so none of our kids would have room to move back."

Dean felt wounded and it must've showed, for his mother rolled her eyes. "And did we move?" she added.

"No," Dean said.

"No, of course not. Therefore, it has to be obvious that we didn't mean a single word of it. We loved all of you so much. But being there without him now, every nook and cranny has some memory of him, and that makes me sad. I often think I'd still like that small apartment somewhere, a slower pace and all. The Metro area is a bit too... *fast* for me."

"You wanna sell the house?"

Alfreah shook her head. "No – but I was thinking I'd give the deed to someone who could really use it. Someone who used to wish she lived there, as a little girl..."

Dean's eyes went narrow for a minute, unsure of how he felt about that. With Chyna, he knew he could live anywhere... but would his mother really do that, or was she temporarily forgetting her long-term feelings about the house she and his father had shared for such a long time?

"Are you sure, Mama?" he asked dubiously.

Alfreah nodded. He had no doubt about the solidity of his mother's decision-making. She'd had the time to think about all this while staying with Tisha for the past few weeks, and, knowing Alfreah Jameson, maybe she'd had the notions for far longer than anyone realized. Either way, Dean knew he couldn't make any calls about anything. For now, the house would remain in the family, and it would always be his mother's house. He felt bad enough for debating selling the property that his father had labored so hard to make into an office for him.

"We'll talk about it another time," Alfreah said as they both looked toward the door when Chyna entered. Dean glanced at his watch, remembering he had to catch a flight soon. He needed to repack and say his good-byes before he left for the airport.

Letting his mother go, Dean waved Chyna inside. Taking her hand, he pulled her close to him, kissing her temple.

"Is everything all right?" Chyna asked, looking back and forth between mother and son.

"Yes, yes. Excuse me - I'm going to go see what my one and only grandson is up to." Before Alfreah left, she kissed Dean on the cheek and, to Chyna's surprise, kissed her as well. "The ring looks beautiful on you," Alfreah said quietly before she left the room.

Chyna looked toward the door, tears in her eyes, and then tried to blink them away before she looked back at Dean.

"Hey, quit that," Dean said, lifting her face to meet his.

"Shut up," Chyna replied, using her fingers to rub her eyes.

Dean sat down, pulling her gently onto his lap. As she wiggled around, she pulled his phone from her pocket. "Here, you'll need this, so when I text you when you get home you can text me right back to let me know you made it. Deal?"

"Yes ma'am. Jeez, I haven't even left yet," Dean said, smiling at her pouty lips. His mind quickly wandered back to the conversation with his mother about Warren Hardig, then to his mother's suggestion of gifting her house to Chyna for the two of them. Whatever the outcome, whatever his mother decided to do, he realized that letting go of the house would be a huge deal and that of course it wasn't up to him and his mother alone. He was working on the renovations, yes; but he had two sisters and a brother to contend with, no matter what his mother said. In any case, he had to make sure it wasn't just the burden of grief talking.

"Hey Chyna, what do you think about a longer-term missions trip to Africa?" he began.

"Wherever you are, I am - the end." Chyna laid her head contentedly back down on his shoulder. Dean kissed her again. He was happy to hear that she was game for anything so long as they were together.

"I want to tell you that I love you so much and that'd I'd lay down my life for you," he said softly.

Chyna popped her head back up, her brow furrowed, her look serious. "Why would you say something like that? Did you not tell me everything that happened to you since I left? What on earth did you leave out, Dean?"

"I told you everything," Dean spluttered, nonplussed. "I have no secrets," he tried to reassure her.

"Then would you please not say such alarming things to me? No one is laying down their life, no one is going to get hurt," she replied, the alarm still written on her face. "We can get married, we can have a wonderful wedding, then maybe we can honeymoon in Africa to see if we'd like to stay there for a bit. I don't care, as long as you are by my side."

Dean nodded as she settled back down in his arms. He loved listening to all her ideas and contemplating the future with her. They continued to discuss those plans while he waited to leave for the airport: he'd scheduled a rideshare from his phone rather than bug any family. He hoped beyond hope that Chyna's vision of their next few months and their eventual nuptials were really going to be so smooth and simple. He hoped and he prayed.

30

With the airline's new flight alert system, Chyna received a call that her flight had been delayed.

While it had been true that Dean needed time to chat with his mother about the house, about the finances and so much more, Chyna had had her own motives for pushing him to talk. Little did he know that exactly five hours after he'd arrived in Virginia, Chyna's own flight was scheduled to be descending into Dulles International Airport. She'd timed it perfectly. It had been easy to get his flight information and book hers accordingly: she knew he'd be savvy enough to keep ticket information on his phone, and he'd left that in the den upstairs.

She wasn't duping him, she wasn't being secretive: she was returning to her home, a home with Dean there. She loved Tisha and Thomas and Chase of course, and she certainly cared for Ms. Alfreah like her own mother, but this little visit was soon going to be over. Whomever they had to face, they had to do it together. Back home alone, Dean was a sitting duck.

Much to her dismay, however, the current situation had her stuck at the Alton house for a few more hours than planned. She looked up from sipping her tea. She was agitated over Dean's return to Virginia, and all because of that stupid, worrisome, maddening comment he'd made in their last few hours together. A simple comment, which likely meant 'in love' in most people's understanding, pushed Chyna to conjure all kinds of horrible thoughts. With that in mind, she started counting the people that had it in for him. There was Chauncey, who wanted that stupid land; Lisa, who'd keyed Dean's car because she obviously had some sort of car fetish; Gary, whose book was now halted; and Warren, who still held unreciprocated affections for her.

It bothered Chyna being uncertain just how embedded Senator Gary Williams' was with the Hardig's evil doings. She really had no idea, and she couldn't find out a single thing of any import sitting there sipping tepid tea with Tish - and piling on nearly as many pounds as pregnant Tish, for that matter, she considered moodily. Chyna had nothing but drama to blame for her own stress-eating-related disorder.

Chyna and Tish sat together in the living room, almost a nightly ritual in the Jameson house. Music played, or the television was kept low as they discussed the news of the day. Normally it had been a fun ritual, only this time Dean wasn't there, and her consequent worry meant that it wasn't much fun. In fact, it was pure torture. She took a deep breath, so frustrated she felt like screaming.

"Have any of your coworkers thrown you a shower? I'd love to throw you one," Chyna said, startling them both initially until her voice found a less frantic tone. She hid her mouth behind her mug for another sip. Lowering the cup again, she tried a fake smile.

"There's been some talk of it. I think it's supposed to be a surprise," replied Tish, a little confused.

"I suppose you could have two, one from them and a smaller one given by your family," Chyna supplied brightly.

"I suppose," Tish nodded, giving Chyna a funny look. Chyna looked at the door. It was only the umpteenth time she'd looked over there, but who was counting? She rubbed her stomach, as a new kind of pain seemed to eat at her gut. It had started when she first arrived in Macon, when she'd left Dean, and now that Dean was gone again she felt it creep back little by little. Chyna knew it was her own signal that danger was approaching.

She set the tea down hurriedly, splashing some onto the table and droplets on the rug. She looked down and then at Tish.

"I'm sorry. Let me get something to wipe that—"

The phone's piercing trill nearly made Chyna jump from her skin. "Who's that?" she said, as if her friend could somehow know who was calling without answering it to find out.

"Chyna? I don't know. Someone else must have picked up. What's the matter?"

Something was wrong: terribly, terribly wrong.

"You're so nervous!" Tish said.

Chyna dismissed her friend's correct assessment. "Can I use your computer?" she asked quickly. A sense of urgency so strong it nearly stifled her had arisen with the ringing of the phone. Already it had abated slightly, but still she felt a sudden need to be somewhere else: home in Virginia, to be exact.

"Sure," Tish said, standing. "You can use the one right here. Just—"

"Thank you."

"Chyna, what's the matter? You're shaking."

"Nothing," Chyna said. She counted to ten, then to twenty and thirty when that didn't seem to work, to calm her suddenly jittery nerves. She then used that nervous energy on the computer keyboard. In a matter of moments, she was watching the small buffering circle work itself maddeningly around and around as it tried to connect with the website she wanted.

"You think something's wrong at home?"

"Nah," Chyna said with exaggerated an air of nonchalance. She waved a hand airily and smiled, though she didn't dare look at her friend.

"Are you lying?" Tish said, placing her hands on her hips.

"Of course I am," Chyna said. She folded her hands between her legs while the windows painstakingly revealed the website. "Seriously TT, you need Fios or something," Chyna said with a nervous laugh. "Listen to me, the computer techie... I don't even think that's the fastest one available nowadays," she babbled.

"Yeah, Chase mentioned upgrading to something," Tish agreed, looking carefully at her friend.

"Huh?"

"What's the matter, Chyna?"

"Dean," she whispered.

"Something's the matter with Dean?" Tish pressed.

"No..."

"Chyna!" Tish said again, this time taking Chyna's hands in her own. She looked down at them, noticing how they trembled in her own hands. "Talk to me. Are you having some kind of premonition or something? I've never known you to do that."

"I've never had them, not really, I just know when something was wrong: it is kinda like a sixth sense, I guess."

"Okay, what does it feel like?"

"I have to go home - like now, Tish. It feels... like I can't stay here - Dean... fire..."

Chyna looked back desperately toward the computer. "There's gotta be a way back home." Chyna tugged one of her hands out of Tish's grasp to open another site. "Tomorrow? Tomorrow night? Oh, geez," Chyna wailed. "But... I could drive. I could rent a car. What's the name of that place?"

Chyna extricated her other hand and began typing feverishly. "Oh, look," she said, scrutinizing the computer monitor. "There's another airline I've never heard of, it's—"

"Chyna, please, take a moment to sit down - over here," Tish implored.

Reluctantly, Chyna moved to the chair at Tish's coaxing and sat down.

"Now, just start from the beginning," Tish instructed, gently but firmly. "Tell me what's going through that mind of yours. When's the first time you've had something that came true?"

"Just once. I had a feeling - that time..."

"What time?" Tish pleaded.

"I was doing my chores, Tish. I was coming, but I didn't get there fast enough. I tried, but I couldn't..."

"When?" Tish took her friend's hands again, shaking them slightly to get her to focus and explain all that ran through her mind.

"The fire," Chyna wailed. "I was too late, and you got hurt too... I'm so sorry."

"That wasn't your fault." Tish shook her head frantically.

"But if I tune into things, if I could just sit still for a moment, I'd just pay attention to my gut - oh God, I never should have left Virginia." Her tone grew angry. "This is Dean's fault, his stupid ideas..."

"I thought you wanted to come here?" Tish asked quietly.

"I... I did, but..." Chyna couldn't explain further without more questions, so she stopped talking completely.

"Chyna, listen. I am sure Dean is fine."

"What if he's not?"

"Then Jojo will call us," Tish assured her.

"Not if they don't want me – I mean, us to be concerned. They won't call."

"What exactly is going on that is to be so concerned about?"

Tish asked, with a note of impatience. Chyna didn't answer. "Well, then, let's call them," Tish went on.

"Good, good, yes, you call them, let me talk to Dean. Don't tell him I'm coming home, though," Chyna said as she stood up again, took two steps back to the desk where the computer was situated, and sat down, commencing clicking over the keys again.

Tish moved to the phone, where she dialed Dean's telephone number. When there was no answer, Chyna continued to listen and noted that Tish left a nice, casual message for Jojo.

"Tonight? Look!" Chyna squealed, taking a deep shaky breath. "I found a flight tonight! The red-eye, that's all there is," she said, frowning. "Well, I'm taking it," she informed the computer, hitting the enter button decisively. "Did you get Dean?" she added over her shoulder, without relaxing her fingers on the keys or even looking up. She knew the answer: she had been listening, and she knew it would only confirm the terrible thoughts her mind conjured.

"No, I left a message for Jojo. Uh, he always calls me back right away," Tish replied encouragingly.

Chyna nodded, feeling only slightly better: as if some of the danger had passed, but not enough that she would cancel her flight.

When the phone rang, Chyna jumped again as Tish answered. Chyna was sure that it was Jojo. She wasn't prepared when Tish looked at her, still holding the phone, and said, "Yeah, she's right here, okay-" Tish turned and handed the phone to Chyna.

Chyna took it. "Hello?" she said shakily.

"Hey," Dean's voice sounded strained as he spoke, more of a labored puff of breath, barely above a whisper: ample confirmation that her fears had been warranted.

31

"Y ou are not good for one single damn thing!" Dean exclaimed as Jojo replaced the phone in its cradle.

"I'm in better shape than you, little bro," Jojo replied. "Got some facts on these people?"

Dean tried to shift himself higher on the hospital bed. Looking up at Jojo, he rolled his eyes in exasperation, recognizing the *you're pathetic* look from his brother as he stood over him holding the phone.

"Yeah," Dean muttered between clenched teeth, still trying to adjust himself but failing agonizingly. "They carry knives!" was all he offered. "And they're big, and they wear masks. Is that enough information for you?" he added drily.

Dean was annoyed. He hoped he'd sounded stronger than he felt when talking to Chyna, but he knew deep down that he'd fallen short in the task of reducing her anxiety levels. Now he was consumed with worry for her safety on the journey home alone. He knew he was powerless to stop her and that she would soon arrive back in Virginia, no matter how she had to get there and no matter what anyone said to deter her. That worried him more than the crooks that had stabbed him twice in his torso.

The pain had been the worst, and he'd lost a lot of blood. The lower stab wound left him feeling weak, almost immobilized. Thankfully there were no signs of paralysis, though he noted with dread that his body felt numb from his belly button down. Plus, the medication made him feel dazed, almost comatose. Everything was fuzzy and he was growing increasingly frustrated.

"And why the hell didn't you tell me what was up?" Jojo continued. "My brother, handle everything solo? You best believe it's a family affair now, at any rate" Jojo said, looking at Dean with mingled love and irritation. "I'll go down to the station, check with the police and see about the house, and get back in time to meet Chyna."

Dean could only nod in return. He didn't want Chyna anywhere near the hospital - or within a mile of the state line, come to that - but considering that simply inhaling and exhaling hurt like hell, he knew bitterly that he was in no position to do anything at present. He nodded to Jojo, who quickly left the room.

CHYNA NEARLY COLLIDED with the automatic doors of the Inova Alexandria Hospital as she rushed through them. Her legs felt like wooden stilts as they ate up the ground before her, still not moving her body fast enough. She was on the verge of tears when she finally saw Jojo's head, high above others. He smiled reassuringly when he spotted her.

She believed she would have been all right, even considering the news, if her plane ride had been a bit more pleasant. The airline no-one had heard of was, she now knew, a kid-friendly company. The only other adults on board were parents of toddlers: the rest of the passengers a bunch of babies who seemed to have all just been woken from their naps and pinched in unison as they boarded. Chyna winced as she remembered the only other non-parent on the noisy plane, her elderly seatmate who, upon plopping down beside Chyna, had downed two pills and was immediately out cold: mouth twisted, head practically on Chyna's shoulder and snoring in her ear to boot. If Chyna had been a meaner person, she'd have woken the old hag back up and asked her to regurgitate one of those magic pills so Chyna could join her - but no such luck. Chyna had sat wide awake for the entire flight listening to the chorus of wailing infants, worried sick, with nothing but strong coffee to keep her company as her thoughts ran rampant from the moment she sat down until the very bumpy landing. But she hadn't gotten sick, not yet. The contents of her stomach remained, thankfully, below deck.

This entire mess was what Dean had deemed necessary to keep her safe, she fumed: nothing more. He would stop protecting her at this very moment. *When I get my hands on him,* she thought to herself, *I'll tell him how much I love him... and then I'll beat him up.* The thought cheered her only slightly.

Chyna stood before Jojo as he finished talking with a nurse, sporting a guarded stance and his army fatigues. Unfortunately, she'd only been able to catch the tail end of their conversation and nothing offered had been any kind of help. Chyna focused on Dean's no-nonsense, facts-only brother, trying not to view him as yet another nuisance delaying her from reaching her destination.

"Where?" she said without greeting. Considering the circumstances, she knew that Jojo of all people wouldn't care, wouldn't take it personally. When she noticed his eyes, though – stormy, as if he were ready to enact the very combat he'd been trained for at a moment's notice - her mind began to dread that there might still be a threat, and it might be closer than they'd been telling her.

Endless guilt consumed her. A gnawing thought entered her mind: that Dean's current status was all her fault, that perhaps even Jojo and the rest of his family would find her culpable in the mess. After all, Dean wouldn't be in this situation at all if not for the deranged criminal she'd married all those years ago. If only she'd pressed charges against Warren, too, Dean would've been fine. Chyna couldn't fault Jojo or Dean if either did blame her. In fact, over the course of the plane ride, she'd crafted several compelling reasons why her future husband's entire family should blame her. Everything was totally her fault, she'd concluded.

Telling Tish and Ms. Alfreah about Warren and Gary hadn't been easy when she was trying not to upset them. While Ms. Alfreah had assured her that things went farther back with the Hardigs, before her time even, Chyna still felt that Gary's anger over his halted book and its possible ruin of his bid for the Presidency had angered him enough to pile on and play a role in this too. She wasn't sure of everything except that she loved Dean deeply. Once again, she resolved that together they would finally put an end to the interference Warren Hardig, Gary Williams and Lisa Stephens kept injecting into their lives.

"Are you done overthinking everything?" Jojo's deep voice broke through her reveries. Chyna looked up, surprised at his accurate assessment of her mental musings.

"Next, can you just calm down and wipe those crocodile tears?" Jojo said, standing stiffly.

"Sorry, Jojo." Chyna took a deep breath. "Uh, how bad is it?" she ventured, walking quickly beside him.

"He's all right, really. Someone did a little job on him, but he's cool," Jojo said slowly.

"When was the doctor's last visit? Did he need surgery? When is the last time he ate?" Chyna rushed on.

"Hey, I said he's okay. What's the matter, you don't trust me, girl?"

"No, actually, about this, I don't trust anyone!" Chyna returned matter-of-factly. More calmly, she continued: "Sorry. I know you're trying to make me feel better."

"That's what family's for."

"Well, you can just cut the crap because it's not working!" Chyna yelled harshly, belatedly looking around and realizing that not only were people looking at her but that she had alarmed Jojo. Her nerves were bad and she was beyond stressed.

"I want to see Dean right this minute, and I want you to get the doctor to come again and tell me what's going on. I don't care if he just left, I want to see him again. I will hear information from *his* mouth, not some surrogate meant to give me the b-s-rated version in order to protect me. Understood? I want to know what the police know, and you're going to tell me, and then I'm going to call Gary and somehow I'm going to make him give up what he knows... and to tell the police."

Jojo gaped. "You're kidding, right? If Dean knows you went to Gary for anything, even so much as a teaspoon of sugar, he'd kill the man the moment he is able to stand up. And what makes you think Gary can tell anything without incriminating himself in some bad deal, Chyna? Seriously."

"If Gary is as half as guilty as the Hardigs, he'll be arrested too," she said smoothly. "Then Dean and I won't have to worry any more."

"The police and the FBI are onto Warren," Jojo reminded her. "There really isn't a need to involve your ex."

Chyna cleared her throat, eyeing Jojo as he raised an eyebrow and crossed his arms over his broad chest. His entire stance said that he was concerned about just how far she'd go to avenge herself on whomever had tried to hurt, even kill, Dean. Her heart stumbled at that thought.

Truth be told, her plan had spilled off her tongue on the fly, making her brain work so hard it gave her a headache. She had too much on her mind, and the caffeine mixed with the worry over Dean's condition wasn't helping matters. She just needed time to formulate a solid idea... but yes, it was true that she would unhesitatingly threaten whomever she had to, even involving Gary if it would help resolve this issue. Right then, it was as good an idea as any of the others she didn't quite have yet. So much in fact that she now wished she had thought of it on the plane and then again on the car ride over. She could have sent him a message then, while sixty thousand feet up in the air... Now that she was here, it was all coming to her. She had to do something and she knew the craziest ideas hadn't even come through yet, though she knew she was close. Those first few notions of what she might do to end this scared her half to death.

They'd stopped walking now, and a brief and silent elevator ride brought her at last to a closed door. "You underestimate me," she said, looking at Jojo with eyes that said she was serious and didn't waver from his.

After a few moments, she mentally moved on, looking around and back at Jojo again. "Is this the room?"

She didn't wait for confirmation before pushing the door. The brightness outside contrasted immediately to the darkness inside. Chyna had to adjust her eyes, but she managed to surge forward, almost levitating it seemed, when she arrived at Dean's bedside. She grabbed his hand. It was cold, but her eyes could barely stop moving up and down the frame of his body. She removed her purse and threw it onto the sleep chair near his bed.

"Dean?" Chyna whispered, leaning over him as he was startled awake. He opened his eyes to her, smiling and trying to sit up immediately upon seeing her.

"Dean, I'm so sorry," she said, hastily running a hand over

her face, not realizing her tears were falling until her fingers felt the wetness on her cheeks.

"Ms. Lockhart, hello, good to see you," came a voice. Chyna looked over at the man standing at the foot of the bed. She did a double take, somewhat confused, before realizing the doctor had been there all along and she'd missed him, concentrating as she was on Dean. "I was just checking some things," the man continued. "I was about to tell Mr. Jameson here that he is very lucky. His bleeding has stopped and things are looking stable."

Chyna offered a friendly smile but continued to gape at him expectantly. The doctor was short, the capacious lab coat dwarfing him all the more, and fair skinned; he spoke with an accent. Chyna looked back and forth between Jojo, Dean and the man. She wanted to hear more, to understand the extent of Dean's injuries. When Dean pulled her hand, Chyna looked over at him.

"I'm all right."

Forgetting everyone, Chyna leaned down, looking deeply into Dean's eyes. "You better be," she whispered. "When you get better, I'm going to hurt you myself for pushing me away." He winced as he laughed. It had felt good to see him smile, but the pain at the end of it wasn't what she wanted to see.

"Has he been given anything for the pain?" she asked the doctor. "His eyes are rather glassy, and he seems weak."

"Yes, well we had to repair a tear to the muscle and that will need to heal," replied the doctor. "It was a pretty deep stab so the recovery will take some time. He has refused the narcotics but we've given him the strongest OTC meds we have. If he changes his mind, he can have something at any time."

Chyna nodded, feeling only a moderate twinge of relief. She looked back at Dean, knowing his stubbornness and unwillingness to take medication likely had something to do with his macho-man persona.

"Why no meds, sweetie?" she asked beseechingly. "Aren't you hurting? How many times did they stab you?"

"Just once."

"We found three wounds, Mr. Jameson," the doctor amended.

"I know what you found, doctor, thanks for the report," Dean retorted. "We can talk later."

"I'm sorry, Doctor," Chyna corrected quickly. "What Dean means to say is, please continue with any other information you're able to share with me and his brother." Chyna knew Dean was trying to kick the doctor out simply due to the fact that she herself was there. Limiting the information the doctor shared was the only way Dean could maintain the impression that he was protecting her, and while she might give him brownie points for his motives, she still looked at him disapprovingly. After a moment he nodded, permitting the doctor to finish without further interruption.

"Your fiancé, uh, has sustained what looks like several knife wounds to the upper torso and the lower back," the man continued, only a little hesitant. "We've done a CT scan to ensure that there was no internal damage to any vital organs. Thankfully, the weapon didn't pass through the pleural cavity so did not injure his spine. He might have injured his back slightly, maybe from falling backward, pushing the knife further in with the fall, or perhaps from struggling with the intruders."

Chyna cringed but continued listening intently.

"It looks like they - whoever did this," the doctor went on, "narrowly missed the membrane of the abdomen. If the knife had penetrated that tissue, Mr. Jameson would've needed more extensive repair and surgery; but as it stands, he's been very lucky. We are thankful for cases like these." The doctor riffled his papers. "He has been groggy but that should be wearing off soon. We gave him the strongest stuff available for the pain when he first arrived, but nothing has been administered since then. He needed some blood, too. The only concern right now is the pain and the blood loss. He is very weak, and seems rather excitable, too, but I urge you to keep him calm." The doctor turned to Jojo. "The police were here earlier. Mr. Jameson, I assumed you talked to them?" The cold return stare made the man look back swiftly to his notes once more.

"They're working on it," Jojo offered coolly.

"What?" Chyna looked up sharply from the doctor to Jojo. "What are they working on?" she demanded again.

The doctor hesitated. "I'll let – uh – well, I'm on call, so if there's any trouble... I have some other patients to see but will check back in just a bit." He hurriedly turned to leave.

Chyna grew angry: just moments earlier she'd defended this man's right to stay in order to give the full report, but now that he knew the police were involved, the doctor ran like a little child. Chyna turned as Jojo took the place of the doctor at the foot of Dean's bed, his eyes looking right past Chyna as if she wasn't even there. Instead, he fixed steely eyes on his brother, commencing some sort of silent communication.

Chyna could only stare at him in disbelief. Straightening her back, and standing as tall as she could, she took a deep exasperated breath of air and pushed it out audibly and slowly, letting both of them know that an explosion was imminent.

"One of you better start talking to me. The time for me not to be involved is long past. Look, I'm worried, okay, so what do you propose I do to help? You either help me be a part of whatever it is you have information on, or whatever you're planning, and clue me in, or I promise you will not like my going rogue. Plus, Jojo is the only one able to chase after me, Dean Jameson, so you better talk to me - *now*."

There was a brief silence. "Wow," Jojo said after a beat. "Do you feel better, Chyna? So anyway, uh, Dean has this idea that Lisa -"

"Nope," Dean cut him off. "Get out of here. I'll handle it."

Jojo raised his eyebrows, but quickly left before Chyna could protest. It was all well and good, she thought, even as her frustration mounted. She was sure she could bring Dean around to her way of thinking if she were alone. He would listen to reason. Also, she didn't intend to give him any more options.

Before Chyna had a chance to open her mouth, Dean started talking quickly. "I was thinking of telling Lisa that I love her," Dean began. "Then I'll tell her that all I want is for her to somehow trap Warren. If she agrees, we'll be able to wire her to catch him, get some incriminating information on record and put an end to all this." He paused. "The thing is, Chyna, that plan will mean you'll need to go away again. You will not be directly involved."

32

M oving closer to Dean's bed, Chyna looked down. Gently she placed her hand over his forehead and rubbed his brow. Only when she really leaned in it did she notice that his eye was slightly swollen. She looked up to find a light switch, but it was then that he spoke.

She knew how blinding the hospital lights could be: she hated when nurses and others flipped them on without warning. She'd been a hospital nurse once upon a time, and the patients' top complaints were feeling cold, harsh lighting and the constant interruptions from nurses and other sick people down the halls. Truly, it was a wonder that anyone managed to get well under such conditions.

For the moment, she ignored the need for a better look at Dean, leaving the lights alone.

With no one else to think about for a moment, and seeing him with her own two eyes, Chyna felt just slightly calmer. She continued to study him up and down, noticing the outline where the bulky bandage lifted the sheets slightly away from the frame of his chest. His eyes were hazy, though he otherwise seemed perfectly alert. He was obviously fighting the effects of the medicine; he was also likely very tired, she reasoned, having just spent that whole visit to Georgia staying up half of every night talking with his beloved family – and her.

His lip was cut, bloodied, and inflamed. From there, her mind went on and on, conjuring a thousand other injuries the naked eye couldn't see.

"How's it going?" Dean said groggily.

Chyna smiled, resisting the urge to roll her eyes. "I'm all right. I... I..."

She faltered. "Good," Dean replied and closed his eyes momentarily. Chyna sighed. She had wanted to return immediately to the idea Dean had just mentioned concerning Lisa, but he conveniently didn't seem as if he was eager to share further details just then.

"I'm so sorry this happened to you, I'm sorry," she said. "Did - did you already set the plan in motion - the stuff with Lisa, I mean?" She reached for his hand, realizing belatedly that the other one was wrapped tightly in gauze and pinned with a shiny metallic clip.

Her eyes traveled back up to his face. Not knowing what else to do with her hands, she quickly withdrew them from him and folded them together. When she couldn't stand it, she wrung them, then finally crossed her arms over her chest with a hand under each armpit. She didn't know what to say or do, so she paced. Eventually, she said, "Tell me about Lisa, and don't leave anything out."

"Tell me about your trip back here," Dean whispered.

Chyna's pacing stopped momentarily in astonishment. She could strangle him, but he wasn't deterred despite his injuries. "Fine. Okay, fine. Getting here was a nightmare," she said at last, taking a deep breath before continuing. "There was no one to talk to, babies crying everywhere, I sat by this old lady, she fell asleep, then I drank a lot of coffee and had to pee several times. Okay?"

Telling her tale, Chyna relaxed again. Looking down at Dean, she said, "Are you sure you're all right? Are you sure? Because..." She looked around for something to pound. "Because I'm. Going. To. Hurt. Someone." She accentuated each word by pounding her fist into the palm of her hand repeatedly. Running a hand over her head, she shoved back her too-long bangs when they began to tickle her forehead. "I'm going to hurt Warren and the rest of his sorry gang of crooked governmental cronies. Oh, Dean. I'm so sorry."

"Come here," Dean managed to whisper when Chyna's mouth finally closed. "Here," he repeated, awkwardly patting the small space next to his thigh with his bandaged hand.

"I don't want to hurt you," Chyna replied as she stood immobile, frozen to a spot far from the bed. Her face was tight with apprehension. When he patted the space again, she moved cautiously closer to his bedside. As soon as she came within his reach, he managed with his good hand to pry her folded hands away from her frame and pull her closer. With only a little resistance, she leaned down over him, being careful for fear she might aggravate his pain in some way.

"I'm all right, stop worrying," he said, using the thumb of his good hand to gently rub away the frown line between her brows. "Give me a kiss." Finally, she graced him with a sad smile.

"I'm so sorry you're hurt."

"Yeah, you mentioned that. Now, I said give me a kiss."

Chyna acquiesced. Bending her head down, she fleetingly brushed her lips against his.

"You must be joking, what was that?"

Chyna laughed. When she leaned in again, Dean pressed the back of her head gently. "Better," he whispered, his eyes a shade darker with desire.

She giggled. "You're terrible, even in your state..."

"I'm not dead, you know."

"Don't joke! Dean, this is serious."

Jojo returned to the room. "Y'all all right?"

Chyna nodded, but Dean was the first to speak. "I'd be better if you'd get some news, any news," he told his brother. "What did your friend say? For someone who gives orders for a living, you sure don't follow them very well."

"That's why I give them," Jojo replied seriously. "Look, I'm trying." He looked at Chyna, then back at Dean.

"Yeah, do that," Dean replied.

"Do what? - try what?" Chyna looked back and forth from one brother to the other. "Tell me about Lisa," she insisted urgently. "Have you found her?"

But Jojo had already left again. Chyna focused on Dean, holding his arm. Her fingers felt cool, but were warmed by the blood that pumped through him. She shivered, thinking of the worst alternative.

"We can't find Lisa," Dean told her. "She's skipped town, but Jojo has a detective friend on the case to see if this new plan can work."

"It's a bad idea. It's..." Chyna trailed off. "Dean, don't either of you dare try to keep things from me now. Let me know what's going on. What are you planning? She already knows you love me: how can you convince her otherwise? Are you even sure she has proof? Would she even be willing to help implicate Warren or Mr. Hardig in any of this?"

"Shh," Dean managed.

"Don't tell me to *shh!* Do you know what I went through? Do you understand what you mean to me? Now look at you, you're laid up here." She gestured toward his bulky frame, taking up most of the twin-size hospital bed. "It's all my fault, and you're still protecting me, or trying to. I can do something, I'm not helpless, you know!" She paused. "You're all I have left," she added more softly.

"And I'm still here," he replied. "Climb up here with me."

"No."

"Please."

Moments passed while Chyna stood before Dean's bedside, hands on her hips. She dragged a shaky hand across her forehead and wished for something to pin back the ever-bothersome bangs. Concerned, she watched as Dean raised his head off the pillow and when continuing to hold the position for an extended period proved difficult, he blew out his breath harshly and plopped it back against the pillow.

Chyna wanted nothing more than to pound some sense into that thick head of his, to shake him for scaring her. Instead, she moved nearer, releasing the railing to lie beside him. Turning on her side, she tried not to lay too much of her weight on his good side. She felt his uninjured arm come around her in a tight grip, and to her surprise he managed to pull her more snugly against him. With his other hand, awkwardly, he lifted the sheet and brought it around them. Chyna kicked her shoes off.

"Keep those legs still, will you? There's a drawers thief in this joint: stole my underwear."

Chyna smiled just a little and rolled her eyes. "You're incorrigible."

"I'm encouraged, that's what I am."

"Why on earth would you be that? I don't see anything encouraging about this entire situation."

"I am, though," he replied. "They continue to harm me so they can have you all to themselves, but they constantly underestimate my determination to keep you safe."

"Don't be so nonchalant about this, and stop it," she said, reaching a hand behind her to still Dean's hand as it caressed her back. She wasn't immune to his caresses. It made her want to cry yet again over what he'd been through, but she was tired of crying. They weren't going to decide to proclaim their love, try to be together, work out their issues only to have Dean killed: not if she had breath in her body.

"This gown is rather drafty - but do you find it sexy?"

Chyna couldn't help but chuckle at that one, despite the gravity of the thoughts turning in her head. Tentatively she lay her head down on his chest.

"Am I hurting you, do you hurt anywhere?" She looked at him.

"My lips."

Chyna propped herself up on her elbow to look at Dean's mouth. "They're a little chapped," she agreed. "Did they punch you?" Lightly she touched his bottom lip with her index finger. It was bruised and cut. Her thumb then brushed the cut at the corner of his mouth. She turned to retrieve a small tube of ointment she'd seen lying on the tray table and applied a small amount to the tips of her fingers, smoothing it gently over Dean's lips even as he tried to turn his head away from her.

"Busted my lip all by myself, doubling over from the pain those punks put in my side. Jeez, Chyna, I was hinting for you to kiss me again. That stuff is disgusting, it tastes awful," Dean moaned, turning his head from the smell of the ointment.

"You're not supposed to eat it," Chyna reminded him, recapping the tube and setting it aside. "They stabbed you as a warning, but I'm thankful: hardly anyone seems to use knives anymore," she commented, freshly relieved that it hadn't been a gun.

"That's why I'm telling you it's all a game."

"That doesn't make it any less serious," she replied. She lightly touched Dean's side, her fingers meeting what felt like corrugated cardboard. She placed the blanket back over him, hoping the side of the bandage touching his wound was softer.

"Little pocketknives. Boy Scout rejects, bunch of punks," Dean muttered dismissively. "How was your flight?" he added once again, trying to change the subject.

"All right," she replied, realizing her earlier description of the flight ordeal had gone unheard.

"You've had some caffeine, I smell it," he declared. "Cafe latte? Espresso roast? Or, I know, a double shot?"

Chyna nodded her head against his chest. "Actually, it was Maxwell House - on the flight. Almost six cups. They were only tiny," she added as a somewhat lame defense, wondering why she'd been so quick to admit her caffeine intake. "Listen," Chyna went on, dismissing their irrelevant banter. With her index finger she drew light circles on Dean's chest while she tried to get her thoughts together. "I want, I need you... to, to work with me on this. Togetherness: isn't that what we're about? We're supposed to be a team now. We work together." She didn't wait for a response from him, either acquiescence or protest.

"We can make better sense of everything together, pooling our facts, than we can with just you and your brother working to protect me," she continued. "I've got some information too. I plan to ask what Gah- knows about... about Warren." Chyna intentionally left off Gary's name, for now. "If, uh, he is willing to tell the authorities, then there's the proof. I could go to Warren." She paused thoughtfully. "In fact, I could do with Warren what you were going to do with Lisa. I could pretend to like him, then put on an act of realizing I loved him all along. I could wear the wire."

Chyna exhaled and inhaled deeply, ready for Dean to have a fit. She hadn't quite mapped out the plan to get to Warren Hardig, but slowly her initial idea was coming together more solidly in her mind. "Like a sting operation," she whispered finally - only to realize Dean likely hadn't heard a single word she said. He was asleep.

She wanted to cry at the apprehension she felt and the need for him to verbally forbid her to enact what she contemplated. But how else was this going to work out? She could be deterred so easily when right then, what she desperately needed was determination. She got a strong dose of it the more she continued to stare at him lying there, helpless. She got up slowly, knowing he needed to rest. She kissed the side of his mouth so she wouldn't get the ointment on her lips. "I love you so much," she whispered. "This is gonna work and we're gonna be fine, but I will fix it. Your brother will help me and I'll be careful, I promise." Chyna knew he couldn't hear her but her mind was made up.

She searched for her purse and retrieved it from the leather chair in the darkened corner of the room, digging through the contents for her cell phone. Her first phone call would be to Gary and her second would be to Warren. She removed her engagement ring, tucking it down into her purse. Then she took another breath and reviewed Dean's sleeping frame one more time before slipping quietly out of the room and out of the hospital, on a mission to finally clean up the mess of their lives.

33

W hen Dean awoke, he blinked his eyes and rolled them heavenward. He was immediately unsettled by the fact that his sleep hadn't been interrupted by Chyna's light snoring, or her constant restlessness as she tried to find a new position next to him. Instead, he'd been awoken by the irritating sound of some hospital machine with its incessant beeping noise. It was apparently daylight: he saw the light from the sun shining through the dingy white and tattered curtains of his room. What day it was, what hour, and just how long Chyna had been gone remained a mystery. He wasn't concerned about the hour so much as the fact that Chyna was no longer beside him, and that he hadn't even been able to stay awake to note whenever it was that she'd decided to leave.

Dismayed, he tried to bring his body upright as best he could, but stopped trying when the door swung open. His uneasiness increased, however, when the subject of his thoughts didn't walk through the door. He watched as Chyna's friend Charlize, also unfortunately known as Nurse Ratchet as far as he was concerned, moved briskly through the door with a tray.

"You seen Chyna?" he asked, once she'd set down the tray on his table and removed the ugly brown cover to display what looked like breakfast.

"Well, I'm sorry it's only Tuesday to you, too!" Charlize replied. "Here's your breakfast. Let's see, I saw Chyna..." Charlize thought for a moment, "for a brief moment early this morning."

"Where is she now? What time is it?" Dean questioned. When Charlize wiggled the tray in front of him, he pushed it away. Just the sight of the eggs, let alone the smell of still more unidentifiable yet supposedly edible items now escaping the cover, made his stomach quiver with disgust.

"I don't know, Dean, to your first question; and to your second, it's after nine o'clock," Charlize said testily, looking at her watch.

"Are you the only nurse in this joint or something?"

"Nope," Charlize shook her head. "But I have an invisible badge that says 'Welcome All Ornery Patients'. You have 'ornery' written all over your wrinkled forehead."

She read the data on the many monitors and noted them on the flip chart she held against her hip, then replaced the chart in the slot at the foot of Dean's bed. "I'll be back to take your vitals," she announced, "so get your attitude in check or I'll stick the thermometer in a rather less than preferable location, and note for the next nurse on duty how constipated you are, so you know what that will get you. I'm sure Chyna will be back here to fuss over you any minute, so stop worrying."

Dean would never stop worrying about Chyna: that much he knew. He wished he could have stayed awake to hear all that she was talking about the night before, but the medication had made him drowsy and he dozed off. He watched Charlize wagging her finger at him as if he'd been a naughty boy.

"There's a trick to this whole hospital thing," she began, and he rolled his eyes. "You cooperate," she continued, "you get your vitals stabilized, you show improvement — that starts with a good attitude, and being nice to the nursing staff doesn't hurt either. Then you eventually check out, which I'm sure is number one on your long list of priorities. Try some of those steps I just gave you and we'll see what I can do. It starts, by the way, with eating up all of your breakfast." Charlize pushed the tray back to where Dean could reach it. As she left the room, she flipped on the TV to send some news talk show blaring to life.

Just a few moments later, Chyna finally walked through the door, looking ten times better than she had last night. She smiled at Dean and his pulse immediately calmed. He was elated to see her but that didn't stop him for questioning her. He stabbed at the remote to turn off the television, annoyed. "Where in the world have you been?"

"Well, good morning to you too," Chyna said. "I brought you breakfast." She held up a brown bag with the famous golden arches on it. When she leaned down to kiss his lips, he held her there a moment longer.

"You look better, I'm happy to say," he said.

"And your color is returning, thank God," answered Chyna. "And Charlize says your attitude is spot on regular old Dean Jameson. I'm so happy, honey."

Dean dismissed her sarcasm. "You didn't go to the house, did you?" he asked worriedly, knowing it would break her heart to see the place in the complete shambles Jojo had told him it was. That being said, he was thankful to hear that the mess was mainly confined to the kitchen, where most of the struggling had occurred. He knew there would be some damage from the scuffle, but 'complete and utter destruction' was Jojo's exact turn of phrase - and his brother never exaggerated. He contemplated all the time they'd spent working on the Jameson family home the last few months, with its solid history, deep roots, and a story about each of their childhoods, including Chyna's, hidden in every corner. It wasn't her house, not yet, but she'd always be a part of it; so seeing some of it vandalized would upset her.

Chyna nodded and closed her eyes. She'd been there all right. Couldn't help herself from picking up just a few things and piecing them back together, or setting fallen pictures where they once had been.

"Yes, I, uh, I was there," Chyna whispered. Try as she might not to let it show, Dean knew she took it to heart. "The door was pulled off one of its hinges, and your mother's secretary was in pieces."

Dean was saddened that he'd not thought to move that precious item after it had been brought down to be painted. Dean and Chyna had worked on it together, sanding all the imperfections, patching any rotten holes, primping and painting it a nice dark maple. Now it was chipped, its legs broken, repair work virtually impossible, its sentimental value irreplaceable. It must have crashed over during Dean's and whoever's scuffle. They had, after all, caught him unawares and defenseless.

"All your hard work," she said, crying now.

Dean managed to sit up and pull her closer to him. He took the bag from her and set it aside.

"Shh, we'll fix it, Chyna," Dean said solemnly, watching the emotions flit across her face. "They're just things, material possessions."

Chyna just shrugged, as if there were no more words. "I know we will," she said quietly.

"What are you thinking?" Dean asked, as the smell of the hot greasy food got the better of him. He was starving, and though he rarely ate a lot of fast food, he could go for something greasy right about then, considering his rubbery hospital alternative.

"Oh, nothing," she said quickly. Dean noticed the way she hastily wiped her eyes as if she was moving on from the topic. This made him pay more attention and caused him to be a little more alert this time than last night. She seemed almost resolute about something.

"So, first, uh, I brought you a sausage biscuit. I even got some jelly for it. I thought you'd like that."

Tucking her lip between her teeth, Chyna looked up, replacing the cover on the hospital meal and putting it on a nearby chair, then proceeded to lay several napkins out on the little table. She took each half of the biscuit, tore open the small packets with her teeth, and squeezed a generous portion of jelly onto each side of the biscuit.

"So, Chyna, what's the plan about?" Dean said seriously, while he eyed her. A picture of interlocking gears grinding one into the other might as well have been stamped on her forehead as she turned the biscuit over to spread the remainder of the jelly.

"Well, I've decided to talk to the agent, Mr. Dunbar - you know him, right, you and Jojo are his friends? I'm going to make an official statement about Warren, but it won't be released just yet. I've called Gary and he's agreed to talk to the authorities. I don't know how helpful he'll be, or if he's just saying he will help and doing absolutely nothing: we will see."

"What did you promise him in order to get him to agree to that?" Dean asked incredulously.

"Nothing, nothing, I swear," she insisted. "He's lost his book deal, he may even give up seeking the presidential seat, but I still have my ways to get to him."

"What ways, Chyna?" Dean said solemnly.

Startling them both, the phone in Chyna's tote bag rang loudly before she could answer him. Chyna smiled falsely, wiping the corner of Dean's mouth and her own sticky hands with the paper towels, and reached for the phone.

Dean watched as she looked away from him while she spoke and he also noticed the fact that she didn't say much of anything, that she simply nodded, muttered a bunch of 'yeses' and 'I understand', then cheerfully ended the call with a bland "thanks for calling," before placing the phone back in her purse.

When she turned back to him, Dean eyed her expectantly.

"That was a friend of mine," Chyna said in response to his silent question.

"What friend?" Dean asked angrily. He knew she was up to something and, to his further agitation, knew that he was in no position to stop her. "Talk to me, Chyna! Who the hell was that? What is the plan?"

When she didn't respond, Dean took a frustrated bite of his sandwich, quickly chewing and swallowing. "Look, damn it, you better tell me, Chyna, this isn't a game. Jojo and I will handle this. I won't have any harm to you on my head."

Chyna looked at him as if he'd gone completely crazy, and her anger at his words and the entire situation rose to meet Dean's. "Oh? But I can have yours on mine, is that what you're saying?"

Immediately, she shook her head as if to retract the words she spoke. "I'm sorry, honey, I'm sorry. This is my fault."

"It's not your fault," he tried to reassure her, but when that brought more tears to her eyes he stopped talking altogether.

Running a hand down her face, Chyna moved her purse and leaned in to whisper: "Will you remember something for me, Dean?"

"What?" Dean snapped.

"That I love you, only you, okay? With all my heart, Dean, no matter what anyone else says, no matter what you hear, remember only what I'm telling you: I'll be spending the rest of my life with *you*." She kissed him quickly before he could grab her. He could tell it was her way of distancing herself from him, knowing that if he said much more, he would be successful at getting her to stay.

"Please eat your breakfast, increase your strength, and be all right so you can come home to me, so we can move on with our lives, so we can get married. Now I've gotta go. I've got something to do."

"Chyna, no!" Dean pleaded. "Listen to me, listen to me. We believe that Lisa will help us: we think she was the one who called the police after they beat me up. They were going to burn down the house. Lisa, we think, is the one we really need on our side. We've got an FBI agent to help, a friend of Jojo's, to get Lisa to trap Warren."

Dean reached farther up the railing, talking so fast he felt out of breath and lightheaded. He was, however, surprised at how well his legs worked once he managed to extract them from under the covers and get them off the bed, where they met with the cold railing. Undeterred, he used it to pull himself upright even as the pain bit into his side from the stretch. It felt as if his sutures might burst open with every inch he heaved himself forward.

"Warren is into so many different things, illegal things," he informed her. "The police and the FBI are already onto him. We're just going to get Lisa to be the decoy to do the sting on him. Chyna, please it's... he's dangerous, he is. Please don't go - please."

Dean wasn't sure why he bothered to explain all this. Chyna already knew about their FBI buddy, Trent, and she'd obviously talked to Jojo - only Jojo hadn't told him anything about that. Maybe there'd been some discussion last night, but of course he'd probably slept through it. He vaguely remembered Chyna saying something, but what, exactly, he had no clue.

"I have to," Chyna said resolutely, as she stood at the door ready to leave, gripping her bag. Dean could tell her mind was already made up. "I have to fix it."

Then she was gone. Dean could do nothing except nod in regretful acquiescence as he watched her go. The pain of breathing deeply trying to explain the Hardig vendetta in just a few minutes left nothing improved.

"Please be careful," he whispered belatedly.

Dean fell silent, trying to concentrate on calming himself and visualizing the pain leaving him even as it seemed to increase. He was thoughtful as the words 'come home to me, come home to me' repeated over and over, rolling around in his head like loose marbles. There was no doubt in his mind that he was going to come home all right - but what if *she* wasn't? He knew Chyna was planning something: the kind of thing that just might get her killed, or as close to the grave as one could get. The attempt to take on the bad guys had almost killed him, and he was much tougher than she. She'd been through enough.

Chyna was mad about his carelessness, he knew, not to mention the inflated ego that had led him to think he should even try to take on two oversized bullies with weapons while he was not only unarmed and caught unprepared but also outnumbered. Meanwhile, whoever the thugs were, they had already shown that they had means and directives to end his life.

Taking another bite of his sandwich, Dean chewed thoughtfully, trying to figure out exactly what details Chyna might know, what she would do, and how far she would go. His temper seemed to simmer, worsening with every minute that passed, until it eventually boiled over.

In a rage, Dean threw everything from his tray table onto the floor. When he looked down, the cold, black and white speckled floor wavered beneath him, but he focused and managed to stay upright. He reached for the cheap phone, wondering how he would find clothes, his own phone and his wallet to get out of there - because after this phone call, that was his only mission. Gritting his teeth at the pain and the exertion, he took a deep breath and dialed Jojo's number.

"Get over here, now!" he said the first moment the line connected. He didn't wait for an answer or even confirmation that his brother had heard him before hanging up. His fingers jammed on the receiver again, dialing a second time. Dean prayed that between Army Tactical Operations Commander Jojo and Special Agent Terrance "Trent" Dunbar, Chyna was in the right hands to protect her, and that she'd emerge unscathed from whatever plan she was trying to execute. He hoped against hope that Warren Hardig wouldn't be able to harm a single hair on her head, even if that meant he himself had to die. And as soon as he got out of the hospital, Dean resolved that he was going to personally ensure Chyna's safety with whatever fight he had left in him. He'd be sure to take his weapon this time: that way he, Jojo and Trent would all be armed and ready for whatever was about to happen.

34

Special Agent Dunbar saw the number of his long-time friend Dean Jameson flit across his phone, but now was not a good time. He was focused: too busy helping his friend Jojo get justice, and right then he couldn't be distracted for anyone. Trent couldn't take time away from his surveillance of Warren Hardig's home - or one of them, to be more accurate. The man actually had three residences including one in California, but he spent most of his time here.

Trent glanced over the sheet he had, reviewing all the details about Mr. Hardig. At that moment, as he had so many times before, he sat in a dark unmarked van to check all the cameras he'd installed in the home. So far, anyone could see that the subject definitely had issues. Much of the footage so far showed Hardig either staring off into space or doing something that looked like cooking, only he never actually ate whatever it was he made. Then there was the endless pacing that sent him back and forth repeatedly from a dark room in the rear of the large apartment to the living area and back again.

Hardig had been home a good little while now, yet Trent observed that he never took off any of his formal attire. He even kept his suit coat and necktie on, as if expecting someone. One thing he never seemed to do was to sit down for any length of time. It was exhausting just watching him, even to Trent, and he'd seen plenty of weird things in his time.

"Odd, isn't he?" commented Jojo.

Trent looked up. "Yes, very. I was just thinking there was all kinds of oddities throughout this entire thing, but thankfully all the television monitors are up and running fine."

Surveillance was Trent's specialty, and underhanded, seedy alleged rapists and monsters were also in his purview. He lived to ensure they never hurt anyone ever again.

"This is driving me nuts," Jojo groaned. "If she's bailed again, I don't have much of a plan B. Why isn't she here?" Trent just sat quietly, in his element, waiting.

"So she's not coming? If she was coming she'd be here by now. Think she backed out?" Trent said eventually. He hated to admit it, but they'd been sitting there a couple of hours and so far there'd been no contact from the female police officer who was supposed to meet up with the woman and wire her up. He checked his phone.

"Hey man, by the way, your brother is blowing up my phone," Trent added over his shoulder. "Did you touch base with him?

"Yeah, I talked to him," replied Jojo. "He's still in the hospital."

"They hurt him that bad?"

Jojo shook his head. "They tried to, but my brother's tough. He's finally engaged and getting married: he has a lot to live for."

Trent shrugged. He didn't know a thing about engagements and women and married life. This life - cameras and monitors and crackling voices on the other end of a phone line - was his life.

"Look, Trent, I appreciate your coming to help me."

Trent waved a hand, dismissing his thoughts along with his friend's unnecessary thanks. "You know I'm cool. I'll wait as long as it takes for her to get her butt in here."

Jojo nodded to his longtime friend from way back and kept pacing the limited floor space of the vehicle. As he checked his watch for the umpteenth time, his anger grew.

"Dean will be all right if we can only get this guy," he continued. "All we gotta do is ensure he stops trying to kill my brother and take his girl. Nobody puts a knife in my brother and lives to see the next hour, let alone the next couple of days. Time for this punk to pay." Trent nodded – then both sets of eyes snapped to the door as it flew open.

"Where the hell have you been?" Jojo said heatedly, but stopped cold. "Oh my God, are you crazy?"

"What?" Trent said. He took off his headphones and stood up to get a closer look.

"What's the matter? Ms. Stephens? You don't look like the woman in the photo." Trent turned to Jojo, confused. "This her? Talk to me, man."

Jojo was shaking his head at the woman in shock.

"No, this ain't her. It's Chyna Lockhart, my brother's fiancé."

CHYNA LOCKHART REALIZED that to play dirty, you had to develop an attitude that made you fearless. In the pit of her gut, that attitude smoldered like a small wildfire, but in her heart she was exactly where she needed to be. Most importantly, she was ready.

The second thing she'd learned was that you had to do something, even with fear riding your back. And the third thing she'd learned was that in order to move on with her life, she would have to become someone else entirely. All the dishonesty, the game-playing and the underhandedness just weren't in her nature: all of it went against everything she held dear in her heart. She was certainly scared that something might happen, that her crazy idea could go south; but she was more concerned that if Dean ever got into battle with Warren and his thugs, Dean would not survive. Even if this new crazy scheme of hers did not work at all, she had to try.

That was the spiel she gave Jojo on the phone.

The argument exhausted her, and now Jojo was having his own conniption fit inside the black van, unseen and undetectable several blocks away. Chyna felt really sorry for having duped the other poor detective that had helped her get set up and taped the microphone to her body, but she was determined. If she could pretend to be Lisa Stephens to fool even a highly trained detective, she was sure she could fool Warren into thinking she'd finally left Dean for him. Meanwhile, the poor woman, who'd given her some great advice and quick instructions about what she was to do, was likely now being read the riot act by both Trent and Jojo now that they knew the truth.

Chyna liked Trent from the little she knew of him, although she was thankful they'd never met. She knew him largely by reputation, and he'd quickly become Chyna's ally: despite Jojo's protests, Trent had been the one to argue that Chyna's idea might just work out even better than the one they'd planned with Lisa. According to their surveillance so far, Lisa seemed no more than a bed partner to Warren, not someone he actually cared about; whereas Chyna was someone he might actually try to protect. Chyna tried to convince herself that was the case, and armed with that idea, she would take all she could get and use it to her advantage.

In the freezing corridor of the DC high-rise, Chyna mentally reviewed everything the detectives had told her. There had been so many instructions to remember that she might just fail before she got started. "The microphone's just there," Trent had said. It was there all right. She tried to adjust her shoulders, as if that would take away the relentless tickle of the wire down one side of her waist. Gray tape held it securely to her chest just above than the elastic of her bra. It didn't stick out at all. She barely saw any protrusion as she passed several reflections of herself in the mirrored elevators and walls on the way up to the fourteenth floor and Warren's door.

Act natural. We have more microphones in his apartment too, so there's no need to be really close to him to get all that he's saying, else he'll become suspicious... All the strategic advice from Trent and Jojo echoed in her ears. *Ask open-ended questions. Don't worry about the wording or exact incriminating phrases so much as getting him to talk and just ramble naturally. That's his downfall, we'll get him on that alone...*

Chyna smiled widely and falsely when Warren opened the door, but her eyes were wet - from the water she'd sprinkled on them in the lobby bathroom just moments before.

"Warren, hello."

He looked surprised. "Chyna? What are you doing here?"

"I'm um... Warren, I'm sorry, is this a bad time?"

She turned as if to leave, but, as hoped, his hand on hers stopped her from turning completely away from him. He pulled her closer, over the threshold and into his home. When she met his gaze, she knew she'd have to pretend this was an Oscar-winning performance. The only thing that would get her through was the ultimate reward she had to look forward to, so much better than an Oscar: a life of peace and contentment with the man she truly did love.

35

"Warren, I can't be with D-Dean anymore," Chyna spluttered, in a show of overblown distress. "He's just.. He and Gary are just so, so similar. I keep making the wrong choices. I'm sorry, I hope you don't mind my coming here, I just needed someone to talk to..."

Chyna hung her head. Oh, how she hated the large, unfeeling eyes that started back at her. They were already quite scary, now that she'd been alone with him for all of ten minutes. Every time she'd encountered him prior to now, she'd wanted to get away as quickly as possible. Now that she was trapped with him for a little while, and deliberately at that, she was confronted once more with all the little things about him that had always told her to run.

Warren nodded. His hand reached out to cover hers and she fought down the urge to pull away. Instead, she turned her hand slowly and gripped his as if she were desperate.

"How is Dean doing?" Warren asked.

Chyna was caught off-guard. "Uh - what?"

"How is he doing since you told him you were leaving him?

Oh. Chyna nodded. "I... it wasn't pretty, we argued and it just, it just wasn't good. He said awful, hurtful things..."

"I'd be heartbroken at the possibility of losing you, too."

She looked around, feeling out of place, naked almost. She never wore anything so hideously provocative and revealing as her costume for this evening's performance. Dean would hate her looking so trashy. She was a casual-clothes person. Even for her job, she didn't have to buy anything other than a few fun shirts with whimsical prints: candy canes for the winter months, candy dots, cats chasing balls of yarn, umbrellas in the summer.

"Are you hungry? I could make something, or attempt to."

"No, no. I'm fine." Chyna glanced over at the large and dimly-lit kitchen area before looking back at him. It was evident he had burnt something at the stove not too long ago: noodles perhaps, now just a brown-black mess stuck to the pan.

He had the nerve to seem coy, even outright giddy about her being there: he didn't hide his elation. She worked hard to steel her own resolve to continue the charade even though, just minutes in, it already felt significantly longer.

"I'm relieved you don't want me to attempt cooking. I'm actually of no use in the kitchen," Warren confessed, almost shyly. Was he blushing?

Chyna smiled, wiping at her fake tears. "It's sweet of you to try, thank you."

"I'd do anything for you."

"Yes, I realize that now," she replied. "It's just hard to make sense - "

"Something to drink, perhaps?" he interrupted.

"Oh yes, w-whatever you have is fine."

Warren hurried to the small wine fridge that matched the other cabinets, with a black lacquer exterior so glossy it was as if someone had just polished the surfaces before she arrived.

She glimpsed every shelf stocked full, with myriad wine bottles arranged in perfect uniformity. Proudly, he showed her the label of the bottle he'd selected before announcing it aloud. "This, my love, is a 2017 Bouchard Pere & Fils Montrachet."

"Oh!" Chyna forced her face to light up, not really understanding or caring in the slightest, but doing all she could to feign interest. "That sounds lovely. It's quite an expensive vintage bottle, though, isn't it? Please don't waste that on me."

"It's no waste. You are worth everything and so much more," simpered Warren. "This is from Burgundy, France. Have you been?"

Chyna shook her head.

"No, of course not, why am I not surprised?" Warren sniffed. "That's only part of what's wrong with Gary, and Jameson too, for that matter: they never took you to see the world. There is so much to see. I will enjoy traveling with you as my companion. Their small minds were so beneath you."

I could be enjoying traveling right now if not for all the time wasted with you and Gary. We're going to Africa, to make a difference. Just in time, Chyna remembered to nod back at him despite her thoughts. "It sounds beautiful, Warren. Thank you."

"I can show you everything."

Not knowing how to get on to the other topics and feeling somewhat helpless, Chyna watched him retrieve two crystal glasses from a nearby cabinet. She was silent as he expertly uncorked the bottle and poured her a glass.

She thanked him and sipped: a very small taste, just for effect. The pungent aroma greeted her before the flavor touched her tongue. It went down and burned, adding to the already bitter taste of the experience as a whole. She smiled and cooed over the drink and his refined taste.

"Delightful, isn't it?"

"Yes."

"I don't stay here often," Warren continued, looking at her then looking away as if nervous. "I bought this place to get away from my father. I do a lot of my business here, but I'm actually in the process of moving again."

"Oh?" She tried to find an opening to address the business she was there to conduct. She tried to look as if she hung on his every word; to make her eyes reflect a love she didn't feel.

"What are you doing here?"

Quickly she refocused on what he was saying, remembering that she was there for a purpose: to get at the truth, for the sake of her future life with Dean.

"Well, I told you, I left Dean." She looked away.

"Oh yes, you did?" Warren said. "I haven't heard how bad they hurt him."

"They?"

"Yes," Warren said.

Chyna would get that part later. "Well, he got a knife wound to his upper torso. He lost a lot of blood."

"Did you really leave him?"

Chyna turned when Warren pulled her roughly into his arms. His eyes were so cold a door might as well have opened and brought a blast of cold air to her skin. "I - I did. I even gave him back his ring." She held up the ringless finger before his eyes.

"Oh, I wish I could have seen that... I wish... I knew... I knew you'd do it, I believed, I hoped that you would."

She nodded. "You did everything to make me see."

"Yes, yes," Warren shouted suddenly. "Dean, the Jamesons, they're nothing. I told my father I'd be better than him. I told him I'd succeed where he failed." Warren let go of her and took another swig from his wine glass.

"Where – ah, how did your father fail?"

"Ms. Alfreah, of course. He loves her, my father always wanted her, but he just couldn't ever seem to lure her away

from Mr. Jameson. I've always been different than him, though:
more ambitious. I succeeded where he couldn't."

Chyna pretended that that revelation didn't shock or
repulse her. "Wow," she said, pretending awe.

"Kind of like I love you," Warren said as he moved closer to
her again and placed an arm around her. Chyna did her best
not to shrug away in disgust.

"Your love, though, it's not an obsession, it's real?" she
questioned.

"Isn't it probably both?" He laughed. "I hated that Gary had
you, and when you divorced, I wanted so badly to comfort you.
Then it seemed Jameson had you, so I pulled out all the tricks
in the book to ruffle his feathers, to make him think you and I
had something going on. I just wanted him out of the picture. I
still want him dead," Warren said casually.

"No!" Chyna shouted without thinking. More calmly, she
continued: "He's out of the picture, you don't have to worry
about him anymore, we can be together now, but to k-kill him
would... take you away from me! To jail, that is, my dear." She
touched his cheek, trying not to show her revulsion at the
straggly and coarse facial hair that grazed her palm.

"I still can't believe it," sighed Warren. "And I'd never go to
jail, darling. I have too many people on my payroll for that."
Warren moved to pace the small kitchen confines. "Do you
really mean it? Do you love me?"

Chyna could only nod. "I do, I just want us to go slow. I...
feel bad for leading Dean on, by denying my feelings for you
for so long. That wasn't right."

"I know why you did it."

"You do?"

"He's stable, he has family. Here, it's just my dad and me. I'm
sorry I have nothing more to offer you in that way - but we'll
build our own family. We will be very well off. We'll move away
from my father, for a start: he's nothing but a washed-up old

man, obsessed with another man's wife." Warren laughed. "Sounds like me, I guess, but like I said, I'm better than my father. I'm going to have the woman I've always wanted: we'll be happy. Perhaps love would have made him softer..."

"Being better than your father? In the sense that you were able to bring a Jameson down when he couldn't, years ago?"

"I guess you could say that."

"The fire - that was ingenious," Chyna went on. She needed a checklist to keep track of all the things she needed to revisit. Her brain was growing scrambled. Rather than be mad about the many subjects she hadn't covered, she forged ahead as naturally as she could. "I mean, his father had just died. Nothing like kicking a man when he's down, right? It was... a perfect time to do that."

"Was it? You thought so?" Warren glowed. "It was Lisa's idea really, she said he'd made some comment about it. I just helped her thoughts come to life."

Chyna nodded enthusiastically. *This was more like it.* The wire was recording it all.

"I wish I could say I had planned it all, but Lisa took care of it for me," Warren continued.

"Well, I mean, the hassle of having him beat up then leaving him for dead. Why didn't you just finish him?" she queried.

"I tried," he replied calmly. "The men had instructions to start another fire. It would've looked just perfect: as if he'd set it as well as the first one at his office, you know? A man driven to desperation because he was in so much debt? It's a classic case, really. Anyway, Lisa went and got in the way: she actually called the police. I was going to pin that fire on her if I couldn't pin it on him. A lover scorned," he sighed melodramatically. "She is so pathetic."

"That's brilliant," Chyna choked out.

"You're brilliant. I love you, Chyna. Hey, I have something to show you. Come this way." Warren grabbed Chyna by the hand and led her to a door at the back of the apartment. A cold draft enveloped her as he opened it.

"I've been planning this for several years. It's going to be so beautiful: the second Hardig empire. Dad has no idea. I've thought it all through myself, and now at last I've set the deal in motion."

Chyna watched as Warren plugged in a cord at the wall, illuminating a big glass box filled with tiny paper structures, small stick figure-people with blank faces, green plastic trees and shrubs dotting the scene. It was like no other planned development she'd ever seen, even on television.

"This," Warren said as he came back to stand beside her, "will be the Hardigs' twin buildings, in the heart of Springfield. The mall is here, but over here will be more upscale shops: just like a piece of New York City right here in the heart of Northern Virginia. Adjacent to I-95, people can just zip off this exit ramp over here. That part will be installed after they completely demolish all this over here and cart away the rubbish, to be dumped at Jameson's old gutted building. He and one other stubborn business owner have been the only barriers to my success. Their resistance has cost me time: delays. If this last attempt on his life didn't send the right messages, I'll have to get it right the next time I try." Warren gulped at his wine.

"Do you know that I offered him a part of this space, a piece of this?" He gestured toward the model. "He didn't want it! I offered him executive positions, corner high-rise, prime real estate and even a spot on my team. And you know what, my love? All that was really only so I could be closer to you, so I could have you. I know you'd never cheat if you were to get married, but I couldn't lose you. Plus, Jameson has a lot of pull in the community; at least that's what my father says. If I could persuade him to see the benefit of this development, other prominent people, county and state officials say, would think it was a good deal. They'd support the project with tax incentives and full-on tax breaks, not to mention more favorable media attention. We're not the moneygrubbing folks we're portrayed to be," Warren rambled.

But you are killers just the same. Chyna's gut lurched and shot a zinger straight up to her head.

"Here!" Warren continued. "The lower garage. People can have their cars parked, and then spend time shopping. Over there" — he pointed to a small park that separated the retail community from what looked like apartment complexes — "is housing: apartments, community pool, gym, tennis and basketball courts, spa: a tower of very high-priced living efficiencies."

As Warren clicked a series of buttons, a waterfall sprang to life from a miniature fountain in front of one of the largest model buildings. Next to it, Chyna was shocked to see miniature neon signage bearing her name. *So tacky.*

"You'll love this: this is the Chyna Shop!" He chuckled at the play on words. "An upscale art gallery and boutique. You can sell your art pieces here, or display imports from others in your circle. These glass doors are so people from outside can look in and wish they had your creativity, wish they could get nearer to you and your mind as you produce such fabulous works. I bet you didn't know that I knew? Oh yes, I know your passion and your talent." Warren positively gurgled with delight at his own cleverness. "Gary used to invite me over, and I'd sneak up to your studio. I know that he made you lose faith in your abilities, but I used to look at your work and admire it and you. I admit I coveted a few pieces. Gary let me purchase many of your renderings when he sold them off for charity. How could you give away such precious art of your own creation, of these beautiful hands? Oh, all my fantasies are coming together. I'll make you so happy. I'll make you a goddess. Gary and Dean couldn't put you up where you belonged. Oh, and I know about the trouble you've had conceiving, but I'll get the best doctors in the world, I promise."

"Stop! Stop it." Chyna felt ill, her heart pounding as if she was about to have a heart attack and faint. She could feel her act to coax the truth from Warren going rapidly out of the window. She backed away and stumbled against the oak doors of a large bureau she'd seen on her way in. The doors flapped open and Chyna turned around.

Warren rushed in front of her to close the doors, as if there was something there he didn't want her to see. "I'm sorry, I've upset you. I'm sorry."

"It's just, it's just too fast... and how did you know about all that?" she gasped.

"Gary told me. He said he was glad you hadn't been able to have children, that you'd lost—"

"No, don't... please don't finish that."

"I'm sorry, I'm sorry I've upset you," repeated Warren woodenly.

Chyna couldn't think anymore. She watched him, but she moved on to something else quickly before she let go of whatever was in her stomach, which couldn't have been much considering she hadn't eaten in almost twenty-four hours. She made herself concentrate on the way he stood in front of the bureau, hands behind his back. "What's in there, what are you hiding?" she asked, trying to sound playful.

"Nothing," Warren said. "It's just... you'll think I'm crazy, you'll think badly of me."

Too late for that, Chyna thought silently to herself, then noticed the way he hung his head, almost like a child. "I won't," she tried to reassure him. "I wouldn't do that."

He considered her for a moment, then quickly turned and opened the doors to the bureau, sliding each one back until it fit perfectly into a groove. It was the kind of unit meant to house a television, but as Warren moved from in front of her holding a small lamp, out of the dim light there appeared a shrine dedicated to Chyna Lockhart's life.

He picked something up, a picture, bringing it out of the dark and closer to where she stood, and she looked down in horror.

"This is my vision board and this, your sonogram. Gary threw it away, but I saved it. I knew that someday you'd bear my child, our child, once we're married – oh, I'm so very glad you've come to your senses. Everything I put on this board has come true. It's all here!"

Chyna couldn't stand to see the picture of the child she'd lost and yet she stared at it for several long heart-hearing moments. A tiny smudge on an otherwise nondescript black square that looked much like a cheap polaroid print out of old. Gary had thrown it away in secret, knowing she would mourn the loss of not only her baby but the only evidence that it had even existed. She had nearly lost her mind tearing up their house to find this little picture. And Warren had taken it all along. Gary had let this deranged man into so much of their lives without a single thought for her protection. And here he stood, having tried to take her future once again just a few nights ago.

"You...you were right," she whispered, covering her mouth. The depth of his obsession with her had shaken her, making this charade much more difficult to see through to the end.

36

Nearby, with their headphones on and their eyes glued to the monitors mounted along the van's walls, Jojo and Trent sat with a female FBI detective watching the screen.

"What's she doing, man?"

"Let's go," Jojo said as he stood and moved to the van's rear exit door.

"Wait."

"No, no, let's not wait. Move it, right now. We have enough, don't we?" Without further pause, Jojo was out of the van, moving at breakneck pace. "You forget I used to do this too," he called over his shoulder.

"And you forget I'm in charge of this operation, so if anything goes wrong it's my head on the line," Trent shot back, but followed his friend to the door anyway.

When they entered the building's lobby, they found it deserted. They moved toward the elevator, but when Jojo reached the door of the stairwell, he disappeared.

Taking a deep breath, thankful that he'd dressed liked he was a maintenance person by way of a disguise, Trent made sure no one was looking before moving more casually down the hallway to follow Jojo. He caught up with him in series of long strides, taking time to remember the number of stairwell cameras he'd counted. He knew the few that were out: a major violation in the event of a security issue, he automatically noted.

Trent concentrated. Though he was in perfect shape, Jojo Jameson exhibited superhuman strength, keeping everyone on their toes. Both of their professional training programs had been intense, but the FBI academy was a one-time thing with few requirements for maintenance, whereas Jojo still trained and worked out regularly, having served a full US Army tour just months prior. Trent gritted his teeth and kept his focus on each stair as he tried to keep pace with the freaking Incredible Hulk.

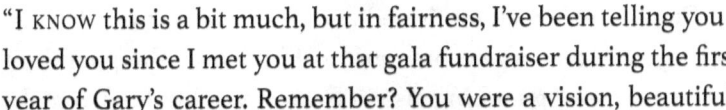

"I KNOW this is a bit much, but in fairness, I've been telling you I loved you since I met you at that gala fundraiser during the first year of Gary's career. Remember? You were a vision, beautiful, and I guess that night started my fixation on you."

"Okay, but - " she whispered. She tried to clear her brain, but she felt faint, and the planned words left her mid-sentence. Had he even heard her before, she wondered? She tried again.

"Don't you think that was a little unhealthy though, Warren?"

Chyna wasn't sure what she was doing. In some ways, she wanted him to hear her truthful thoughts now that she had the information she sought at long last. At least, with her brain now completely scrambled by the harrowing experience, she *hoped* she had the information everyone needed. In any case, it didn't seem to matter anymore. The mental weight of what she was doing was already beginning to take its toll on her: she suddenly regretted her presence there. It brought back some of her most painful moments. She was scared for herself, worried about Dean, and she wanted out of there. What more information did she need?

"Would you really end Dean's life, Warren, just to have me?" she asked weakly.

"Are you judging me, dear heart?"

Chyna looked straight at him, hoping there was hesitation around her question; instead, she seemed to witness a kind of shift in his eyes.

Warren unplugged the light from his prized development replica. Chyna hoped to God this development would never see the light of day so long as it bore the Hardigs' name.

"Did you hear me, Chyna?" he intoned.

"Yes, of course - I mean, no, I'm not judging you; and yes, I heard you." Chyna was flustered. "I just - I just was hoping to understand how far you'd go to realize your... dream? I don't think I've ever had such ambition to go after what I wanted."

"You haven't been motivated and pushed so far yet, darling. In time, you too can become just as blinded by the pursuit of your goals, seeing nothing else in front of you but how to make them happen," smiled Warren indulgently. "Just as I have. It's in all of us. I mean, haven't you a goal in coming here?"

"Yes, to be with you! And to..." Chyna stopped herself just in time. She took a step closer to the cabinet and forced herself to bend down to inspect all the pictures of herself more closely. Pictures of herself and Gary - pictures even the paparazzi shouldn't have had unless they'd been invited into her home, personal pictures that she'd never pose for: her in her bedroom, painting in her then studio, in her night gown. Then there were pictures of her and Dean at the store, and entering the Jameson house. Pictures of her in front of the Senate office building when she'd been to see Gary alone that time; then some pictures she'd seen on the news... Her hopes dashed, Chyna searched in vain for that little scrap of proof that her baby had existed. The men in her life back then had taken her entire life as well as her livelihood away from her.

There was a click behind her. As if in a dream, Chyna watched as Warren shut the doors of the little room.

"I'm afraid you know all my secrets," he said, turning to face her.

She couldn't think. He was a maniacal, insane monster, further disturbed than she or even Dean had ever guessed.

She pushed past him as gently as she could and moved quickly out of the room, back to where there was more light: where she could not only see, but also breathe.

"I just... there is just so much," she managed. "I-it would have been easier if you'd told me how you felt from the beginning, no?"

"I thought you loved Dean," he responded.

Chyna nodded. *I do, I will always love Dean, not you, you,* her mind maintained, and she nearly bit her tongue to keep the truth from leaping forth.

"I'd have anyone removed for you. Dean, Lisa, Gary: they were all in my way - in our way. Honestly, I may still have to kill Dean, sweetheart," Warren mused thoughtfully.

"What?"

Chyna knew that Jojo and Trent were hearing her every word, but although they'd told her the code word she could say to end this nightmare, she had completely forgotten it. She wanted to end this, and fast. Would they come, or would they continue to wait for her signal?

"Why, why would you still need to...?"

"Because, come on, he would never let you go without a fight," Warren chuckled. "He'd never subscribe to letting you just walk out. I'm convinced now you were only ever able to get away from that monster because he's currently incapacitated, is he not?"

She nodded mutely.

"Chyna, I would fight for you, I wouldn't ever give up. But there is just one more thing."

"What, what is it?"

She stood with her back straight. He moved closer and though she wanted to retreat, she managed to stand her ground. His hands touched her hands, then moved to caress her elbows.

"If you are lying to me, I'm afraid you could meet the same fate as Dean. You would hurt me so badly, Chyna. All these questions about Dean instead of about our future, our planning – well, all that makes me doubt you. Are you for real, honey?"

"Yes, yes of course." Panicked now, Chyna began to turn, but his arm yanked her back roughly.

"Are you sure? I mean, you've asked so many questions about Dean. How can I be sure?"

His arms dragged her closer, moving further up to grab her biceps, squeezing each arm painfully. He would have lifted her off her feet if she weren't already so tall. She saw his eyes again. Then he moved forward, kissing her roughly at first before both hands left her arms and fastened around her neck.

"Warren please, don't scare me, please," she choked out.

Just as she had a mind to knee him in the groin, the doorbell rang. Warren's grip loosened instantly. She broke free, running to the door and wrenching it open to reveal two tall men with guns. She felt frozen to the spot. Jojo was the first to move forward, pushing her out of the way and toward the door.

"You set me up?" Warren asked, confused.

"Yes! You're going to burn in hell!" Chyna said, feeling overconfident. She rubbed her neck, realizing her throat burned with fear. Now that her arms were free, they ached with the memory of his tight grip.

"I wouldn't have harmed you, Chyna - why?" Warren bleated.

"Leave now Chyna, go to the female officer - "

Warren lunged forward and tried to grab the gun but he couldn't wrestle it away from Jojo. He stopped when Jojo punched him, causing him to fall back. Looking shocked, he backed away, holding his mouth as he ran toward the back of the apartment, with Jojo and Trent hot on his heels. He slammed the door of the bathroom and there was a click as the door locked.

"There's nowhere to go, Warren - it's 14 floors down," Trent said loudly.

Chyna looked up. They were so high, too high for an escape... but then she wondered if he were crazy enough to jump.

She moved forward for a better view of the door. Trent and Jojo had guns drawn, standing taut on each side and communicating to each other silently as they strained to hear any clues to indicate what Warren was doing. Both their guns were pointed to the floor. Jojo locked eyes with Chyna long enough to implore her to leave, waving her out the front door with his free hand.

All at once, Warren's loud screams pierced the walls of the apartment. Instinctively, Chyna's hands flew to her ears and made her unbelievably nervous at the same time. The voice was almost otherworldly, so shrill and high-pitched, and he called her name repeatedly as if in agony.

"I'm gonna do it, Chyna," she heard in horror. "It's all your fault - blood on your hands!" The crazed man pounded the closed door so fiercely that Jojo and Trent reared back momentarily, as if he might tear it down with his bare hands.

"Chyna, get out of here, now," Jojo yelled over Warren's cries. Then the banging stopped, just as abruptly as it had started. The new silence was so eerie that she wanted to leave as ordered, but for some reason she remained: rooted to the spot. Jojo and Trent leaned in as one. Trent tried the doorknob cautiously but it was locked. From an inner pocket, Trent produced a long, thin piece of metal and inserted it silently into the lock.

The door opened slowly. Chyna wasn't sure what she would see, but Warren was standing there as if he'd been waiting for them to do just that all along. He looked right at her, as if he knew she's still be there. Tears coursed down his bloodied face, streaks and marks under his eyes. Before she'd even registered that he was holding one, Jojo and Trent made commands for him to drop his weapon. His eyes didn't leave hers. Sure enough, he held a gun to his temple. Then, before either Trent or Jojo could reach for him, Warren pulled the trigger.

The shot reverberated against the walls. Warren's body crumpled to the ground and so did Chyna, falling down as she blacked out from the trauma of her waking nightmare.

37

D ean was home but he wasn't alone. After pleading with the doctor to let him go, he'd had to sign plenty of paperwork stating that he was leaving against medical advice and was being released of his own free will. He'd been warned about the ramifications if he didn't take it easy and allow his body the rest and get the healing it needed for complete recovery. If he disturbed his stitches at all, for example, they could burst and start the bleeding all over again. Then there was the dressing: that would need changing, and doing it improperly could mean infection and all sorts of additional complications. Moreover, the doctors warned that if he moved too fast or exerted too much energy, he could fall and cause himself even more damage. Reluctantly, he'd been following their orders as best he could. Moving a bit slower than his normal stomp-the-ground pace, Dean shifted restlessly back and forth between Chyna's living room and the kitchen, waiting for her.

"Honey please - please sit down."

"I'm alright, Momma," he reassured her. Everyone was there in Chyna's house. Considering the family home was still a mess, it had made sense for them all to come there instead. His Mom had set to cooking up a storm, something she knew usually brought some comfort; but right now, Dean couldn't rest until he knew Chyna was safe. Nonetheless Ms. Alfreah had made all his and Chyna's favorite foods. Soon, the newly refurbished house was filled with the kind of love she had grown accustomed to providing over all these years. Whatever the trauma, the food would help to bring about at least some familiarity and comfort. His mother and the rest of his family provided a welcome distraction: Dean was glad they were all there. Plus, they'd keep him calm whenever Jojo arrived, ensuring he didn't wring his own brother's neck.

Dean understood part of what happened, but he just knew his brother had some culpability. One part of him said that so long as Chyna was safe, it wouldn't matter what went down. Another part said he'd never forgive his brother if Jojo had let Chyna place herself in any danger. They'd worked out a plan, him and his brother and Trent and that plan had clearly been thrown out the window.

"Dean, why don't you go lie down, please?" Tish stood. "You know we'll wake you as soon as she gets here."

"You should not even be here," he smiled sadly at his sister. Tisha really shouldn't travel this late in her pregnancy, but she seemed fine. Dean was thankful to Chase for driving the whole family up from Macon; but now they were all taking turns poking and prodding him to rest, even as his agitation grew by the moment. But if there was one person Dean couldn't ever be upset with, it was his pregnant baby sister.

He smiled and placed an arm around her shoulders, thinking back to a time when things were so much simpler. Dean and Tish were the youngest: the last ones to leave the house after their older siblings went off to college. Consequently, they also seemed to be the closest, thick as thieves. Dean's gaze lowered to her protruding belly. He thought about the twins she carried, then about Chase, his brother-in-law: a nervous wreck who never seemed to leave his wife's side.

Dean bent to kiss his sister on the cheek. "I'm all right. I wish you hadn't come up here in your present state, though."

"I know you do," Tish said, smiling as she rubbed her round belly. "But we're here now. The doctor said we're all doing fine. It's you we're worried about..."

Tish abruptly closed her mouth as they both noticed an unmarked car pull into the driveway. As if they hadn't been talking at all, Dean moved to the door to open it wide.

Dean stood frozen to the spot as Chyna emerged from the car and walked slowly toward the door, flanked by Jojo and Trent. She was wearing his brother's coat, much too big, and Dean's mouth dropped open as he saw her legs in sheer pantyhose: an indication she was wearing something awfully short underneath. Dean watched as Jojo ushered Chyna inside ahead of him. His brain worked hard to fill in the pieces he'd been missing. His eyes were still on Chyna, registering something he hadn't ever seen in her. As well as the fear on her face, there was a strange new skittish way she held herself. Her eye makeup was streaked as if she'd been crying, and the lipstick she so rarely wore was smeared across her face. The thoughts he conjured of what might have happened went from bad to worse: he hoped they were far from the truth.

Before Dean even asked Chyna how she was doing, he moved to embrace her, but instead of giving herself to him as normal she remained still. She shook her head, halting him from touching her, not looking him in the eye, pulling away almost as if she were afraid. Dean's brows knitted together. The striking lack of warmth in her usually gentle eyes made his heart hurt. His anger flared toward Jojo, for permitting Chyna to do whatever she had done to leave her this way.

Chyna moved further into the room and stopped short, startled to find so many people in her house.

"I'm sorry everyone, I'm sorry. I'm so glad you're here, I am. I just need a few moments. Excuse me." With that, Chyna turned and hurried upstairs.

~

EVERYTHING WAS HURTING: her feet, her head and her heart – but when Chyna saw Dean, her heart constricted with both pain and relief that he was safe. It took sheer force of will not to embrace him, to be comforted by him. She wanted to squeeze him so tight for being exactly where she needed him to be that she actually thought she might hurt him.

She couldn't touch him, though: not yet. When she entered the house, she felt as if all eyes were upon her, scrutinizing, assessing, detesting. While nothing could be further from the truth, she currently saw the whole world through a lens of guilt. Unaccountably, she felt ashamed.

She was at the top of the stairs in seconds: she had to throw up. She opened the door to her bathroom as she removed Jojo's coat. She was thankful that the family hadn't been able to see the get up she wore, although the heavy makeup plus her pantyhose-clad legs doubtless told them at least part of the story of what she had done. Looking like a cheap trick: she hated it. Disgusted, she threw the coat onto the chair outside the bathroom before ducking inside.

Sick to her stomach about what she'd tried to do and the terrible way it had all eventually ended, Chyna sank down onto the cold tile floor. Still on her knees, she removed the dress and pantyhose, shoving them into the too-tiny decorative trashcan, and pulled off the remaining bits of gray tape left behind from the wire. She'd get it together. She had a future. And, yes, to Warren's earlier point, she had ambition. Yes, she'd do anything to get justice. No matter whatever her original intention, though, tonight she had set a course of action in motion and now she had to live with the unintended consequences. Her actions had effects.

However true it was that Warren himself was to blame, for all that he had done to Dean, the fact remained that a man was dead. Numb, Chyna didn't feel justified in either her grief or her guilt. Regardless of who had been right or wrong, she herself would have to live with this day for the rest of her life, and that was going to be a bitter pill to eventually swallow.

DEAN PACED and tried to remain calm as Jojo recounted the night's events, but Chyna's reaction to him had rattled him to the core. At a loss for what else to do, Dean rounded on Jojo.

"You let her do this? Have you lost your damn mind?"

He looked to the ceiling as if he could see through it, wondering if Chyna was all right and what was going through her head.

"She came in there and asked to do it," Jojo protested. "She came over already dressed in that stuff, and she duped the female officer into wiring her, okay?"

"What, they didn't know who to expect?"

"Well, who else would sign up but the person who was supposed to show up? Chyna told the lady she was Lisa Stephens. This wasn't some kind of pageant, Deanie. Listen, if I hadn't let her in on this tonight, she would have done something stupid on her own. If she'd gone over there to meet him on her own, no protection, no one listening in..."

Jojo trailed off, leaving Dean's imagination to fill in the blanks. "This wouldn't even have happened if you had been open about what was going on," he added heatedly.

"Don't turn this on me! I was handling it," Dean retorted.

Jojo gaped. "Handling it so much you got laid up in the

hospital, lost so much blood you needed a transfusion? That's handling it all right."

"You're a stupid idiot."

"Stop it!" Tish yelled. "Stop it right now."

"You never think far enough ahead, do you, Joe?" Dean continued, ignoring his sister and disregarding the presence of his family. "You ever think beyond today, beyond right this moment? If anything had happened to Lisa in that same situation, she would've bailed fine and you'd've called the entire thing off. See, Chyna wasn't prepared for a sting operation. She's never done anything of the sort. She never even lied about anything before, but you let her talk you into this crazy plan of hers. You ever consider that maybe she couldn't handle it, once all was said and done? Of just how crazy that man was? Something went wrong, didn't it?"

Dean knew if something terrible hadn't happened, Chyna wouldn't have shrugged from his touch. She wouldn't have run as if he were the enemy and her eyes certainly wouldn't have evaded his. It was all there, in her eyes, the fact that she took on something greater than what she was prepared to handle.

"So what happened?" Dean repeated again. "If they got him on tape confessing to it all: the fire, leaving me to my damned death, and whatever else he did... if that's all that happened, why the hell is she so upset?"

"Dean, Warren killed himself," Jojo said quietly.

Before Dean could even absorb the magnitude of what he heard, his fist balled up and connected with Jojo's cheek. Everyone gasped; Jojo looked stunned. Worst of all, Dean didn't even feel any better. He watched as Jojo rubbed his jaw and stared at him.

"I wouldn't let anything happen to her, Deanie."

"Yeah, thanks."

Before anything else could be said, Dean turned and left as quickly as his now-burning side would allow. Extending his arm back to punch his brother hadn't been a good idea. Now he had to haul himself up the stairs. He moved much more slowly than he thought he would and had to stop for a breather once he reached the top. He hated all of this. Hated his condition, hated being mad at his brother, hated making a fool of himself in front of the whole family. He was wrong in this, too, he knew, and Jojo was right; but he would deal with all of that later. If Chyna was all right, he would be fine too - eventually.

38

Upstairs, the water cascaded over Chyna's body. Scalding hot, it still wasn't hot enough to wash away Warren's touch, his caresses, his disgusting kiss and the feel of his now-dead hands.

The magnitude of all this was so much greater than she had thought. He was far crazier than she could have imagined. He had some serious problems. Before, she had thought his biggest problems were his jealousy, his greed, and his need to manipulate people like pieces on a board game: moving them, repositioning, even eliminating them so he would have a better advantage. It was more than that, she now knew: it was psychological. Serious.

Turning the faucets to shut off the water, Chyna stepped from the tub and wrapped herself in a towel. She bent to pick up the remains of her outfit and dumped all the remaining garments in the silly little trash can: the frilly underwear, her bra, the cheap necklace, the lace-covered stilettos.

She froze a moment when a light tap sounded on the door.

"Yes?" she said, knowing it was Dean. She hated that he'd

come up. She wondered if he was all right, knowing stairs would be hard for him.

"Chyna, please let me in. Are you all right?"

"Yes, I'm all right," she replied, relaxing somewhat. He sounded out of breath, but at least he *had* breath - that was all she cared about. She tried to soften her voice when she responded: "I'll be out in a minute."

She opened the door and watched Dean's back. He moved slower than usual to take a seat on the bed. He smiled at her and her heart sank. She rushed to him, sitting by his side and grabbing his hand tight.

"I'm sorry, I'm so sorry," she said.

"Why are on earth are you sorry? You did something so brave."

"I'm sorry for running away from you earlier." When Chyna really looked at him, she saw that he was sweating, so she turned on the ceiling fan before rejoining him. "You're sweating."

"I'm fine."

She was up again, and this time she moved quickly to the dresser where she grabbed a bottle of deodorant, applied it and searched her drawers for sensible clothes and underclothes. She went into the bathroom again, not bothering to close the door. When she came out again, she felt only moderately better: at least now she was clean, and at least she was now wearing clothes that made her look and feel more normal. With her back to Dean, she managed to look in the mirror, thankful that the hideous makeup was all gone. She removed the long dangly earrings, too, and set them on the dresser.

"Did you get released from the hospital or did you just leave?" she asked, finally turning to face him.

"I signed some papers for my release – so both," he said.

"So you left before you were supposed to, relinquishing the

hospital of any liability?" Chyna said, reclaiming her seat beside him.

Tentatively, as if she'd disappear, Dean turned to face her and pulled her into his arms. Moments ticked by and he felt her release a deep breath before her body shuddered with sobs.

"Chyna? Baby, look at me. It's over now," Dean said. He pushed her back to get a good look at her. "You're the bravest person I know. You did it - you didn't have to, but you did."

"I did it all right. I drove him to kill himself."

"No!" Dean said emphatically. "He did that all by himself."

"If I hadn't — "

"Hadn't what? Got to the truth, tried to end his game-playing? Tried to send him to jail where he belonged? He didn't have to do any of this."

"I pushed him, didn't I?" she ventured. "He said that he loved me. I just used that against him, I just..."

"He might have loved you, but his love was so unhealthy, sick, even deadly," reminded Dean. "It was a twisted, obsessive kind of love, a love that hurt people: you, me, my family, my office, and Lisa too. We're all victims. His father is also responsible. He has a role to play in this. He could have reported his son, got him help or done *something* before all of this escalated to what we have now. Not your fault."

Chyna nodded. She knew all that was true, but still she couldn't shake the feeling that he had died on her shift or something. The sting operation had been a catalyst for Warren's mental health troubles, she was sure, and his discovery that her supposed feelings for him were phony had sent him over the edge.

Granted, a part of her had always felt that he was putting on a show. His screaming and his blame did seem an added theatrical opportunity meant only to make her feel guilty. Not to mention, she would be wise to remember the possible alternative outcomes. His issues weren't truly about her at all. It had always been about besting his father on various fronts: money, wealth, status, even marriage. In all of that, Chyna was nothing more than a consolation trophy to him. And what if he'd killed Dean? Then she wouldn't be feeling the guilt that currently weighed so heavily on her shoulders - she'd feel completely differently.

Just then, Chyna remembered. "His father knows and may have had a hand in the fire at your building, Dean," she added. Dean nodded.

Chyna couldn't believe all that had occurred: how life had changed in just a few hours. "It was sick all right," she admitted. She suddenly felt the enormity of the day's events hit her afresh. She changed the subject.

"I can't believe TT is here. She shouldn't travel in her condition."

Dean shook his head. "They are here for me and you."

"Are you mad at me?"

"No, never."

"Are you mad at Jojo?" She knew his response would be different when it came to his brother and, sure enough, his twitching jaw told it all. "It's my fault, Dean," she continued. "So, don't you dare be mad at him. I begged him to let me do it. I bought the dress, the cheap makeup, the jewelry, everything, and then I lied and told the female detective I was Lisa Stephens. I did it all, and you know what, Trent was the only one who even believed I could."

"I believe you could do anything Chyna. I believe in us," Dean said. She was momentarily silent, unsure of what else to say or how to respond.

"Listen," Dean went on, "this wasn't about that. It was about the pain you're now experiencing, and the fact that you could have been hurt: so much more hurt than you physically and mentally feel right now. You could have been killed."

"But this might not be over," she protested. "You know, what if, what if..."

Dean's hesitant nod admitted he had similar thoughts but dismissed them. What if Chauncey was angry over the death of his son – and he surely would be, especially given the way it went down. Dean had worried about that, too. He took a deep breath.

"One really horrible person can't hurt us any longer, however that reality came to be. In all these years, Chauncey has not actually harmed my family, and now perhaps he'll finally see what his craziness did to his own son. Perhaps he'll finally let it go. In any case, he'll be investigated for whatever role he played. Maybe this whole mess will help him to see all the errors he's made over the years. It's almost as if old Chauncey had projected his own perceived failures onto his son, then Warren took them and ran with them in a more dangerous way."

Chyna nodded. She wasn't sure whether she felt as optimistic as Dean about the possibility that the latest tragedy would somehow cause Chauncey Hardig to turn over a new leaf and cease his vendetta against the Jamesons. Her actions had either ended a long and complex feud or triggered a new kind of war. Only time would tell what played out, but she prayed Dean was right. Maybe he knew something she didn't.

"I told him I loved him, but I didn't, ever. I never stopped loving you."

Looking down and touching her left hand, Chyna yelped in horror.

"What's the matter?" Dean said, alarmed, but Chyna was up and rushing to the bathroom. Searching frantically through the trash, she retrieved the little black purse she had carried. She'd put her ring in there for safe keeping, intending to replace it on her hand as soon as her nightmare ended, but her fainting spell had made her forget all about it.

She heard something hit the tile and immediately dropped to her hands and knees. With a flood of relief, Chyna located the ring in the fluffy bristles of the bath mat and placed it safely back on her finger before returning to Dean.

"Is everything all right?" he asked. Chyna nodded, staring at her ring. "I tried to make it right," she blurted one last time.

"You did," Dean said, laying back against the pillows with a soft sigh. "You did." He placed an arm around her narrow waist and Chyna felt herself melt back into him. Mindful of his side bandage, she snuggled gently closer. She knew she needed rest to refresh her thoughts and eventually, she hoped, share his perspective. She was truly sorry it had ended this way. She prayed a prayer of thanks for Dean being all right and there with her before she drifted off to sleep, safe again in Dean's arms, the only man she loved.

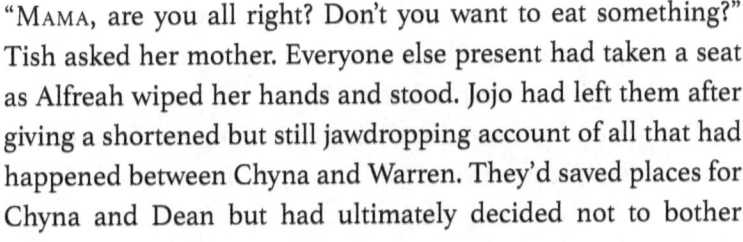

"Mama, are you all right? Don't you want to eat something?" Tish asked her mother. Everyone else present had taken a seat as Alfreah wiped her hands and stood. Jojo had left them after giving a shortened but still jawdropping account of all that had happened between Chyna and Warren. They'd saved places for Chyna and Dean but had ultimately decided not to bother them.

Alfreah smiled sadly. She had certainly understood Jojo's need to leave and had assured him that everything would be all right. While she hated to see her children fight, which was such a rarity, she always knew they'd eventually make it up and be together once more. What she hated the most about the current situation were the reasons behind the discord within her home. Dean would be okay, she knew. He and Jojo would always be close and their brotherly relationship would mend, too; but she just couldn't rest until she got some things off her chest and that meant she had to go back to the root of this mess. As much as she was reluctant to do so, she had to see Chauncey Hardig.

She should have visited him some time ago, Alfreah reflected: if she had, perhaps all of this could have been avoided. Perhaps Chauncey would still have his child, perhaps Chyna wouldn't have to live with the guilt. Then again, nobody could have foretold the lengths to which Warren would go with his sick obsession with Chyna. No one could have known that this would be the end result. Maybe all this would change Chauncey... yet she felt deep down that nothing would change him. Nonetheless, she had to speak her piece, offer her condolences and find out for sure.

"I'll be back," she replied to her daughter. "I'm all right - I need... I mean, I'm going to run an errand. It won't take long."

Alfreah moved hurriedly to the door, grabbing a light jacket that wasn't hers and dwarfed her tiny frame but would do. It had just started raining, so the unseasonably warm winter nights they'd been having would be slightly cooler.

"What?" Tish said. She pushed her plate back just a touch and looked with concern at her sister.

Returned the look, Jina wiped her mouth. "Mama, it's almost after eight o'clock. What do you need at this hour? Whatever it is, we'll go get it for you."

"No, I have to go do this. I'll be back," Alfreah said, and left through the front door without further word.

lfreah Jameson couldn't tell her family where she was going. For one, she didn't know what she'd find when she got there, and two, none of her children would believe that Chauncey wouldn't hurt her. She herself wasn't totally sure he wouldn't pull out some old tricks either, but she was determined.

In the crisp autumn air, it took only fifteen minutes for her to get to his Alexandria high-rise. Alfreah Jameson entered the Hardig building through the imposing double-glass doors, their frosted panes emblazoned with the name HARDIG in lettering so big and wide it seemed to cover most of the glass.

"Hello, ma'am. The office is closed now," a man wearing a uniform said from behind a massive desk.

"Is Mr. Hardig in?"

"Well, yes, but — "

"Then he'll want to see me," she interrupted the man, who looked nonplussed but picked up a phone and pressed a few buttons, keeping his eyes on her. "Yes, sir, there's someone to see you - ah...?"

"Alfreah Jameson," she supplied.

A brief pause. "He says to go on up. Eighteenth floor, ma'am." The guard pointed to a row of elevators along the far wall.

As she pushed the button for Chauncey's floor, Alfreah thought of her husband. If he were living, he would hate that she was here now. But she had to stop any further disruption to her family once and for all.

The door slid open and Alfreah encountered another guard, casually seated on a chair where a secretary might have been by day. He nodded sleepily to Alfreah and pointed.

Uncertain of what she would find, she cautiously pushed open the door. Behind the desk sat Chauncey Hardig, Esq.

"I knew you'd come visit me," Chauncey said, swiveling once in his seat before standing. He wasn't a tall man, unlike her Joe. In fact, Hardig was just a few inches taller than her five-foot-three-inch frame.

Looking away, Alfreah took a moment to study the pictures lining the dark interior. A conference table dominated one corner, backed by floor-to-ceiling windows with a view to the other buildings in the surrounding area.

"I must say that you look beautiful as ever," Chauncey purred. "Your hair, beautiful. It suits you so well now that it's completely gray. I wish I could say the same for my own." He patted his oiled coiffure.

Alfreah looked back at him with disdain. It was always about him. What had ever attracted her to him?

"Would you care for something to drink?" he continued. "A little chardonnay? I'm just picking at a dinner platter left over from a late business meeting. You're welcome to share it, or I can have whatever you like sent up?"

Alfreah shook her head. Somehow, this exchange reminded her of what she had seen in this man, even if for just a short amount of time in her twenties. Drive and determination had drawn her, she recalled: all his dreams, the potential for him to be something great – but being with him would have required her willingness to put up with the many other qualities he lacked. Granted, it would have been nice not to struggle for those initial years, with her husband not making enough money and having four kids; but they'd got through it, and she wouldn't trade that time for anything. Her involvement with Chauncey all seemed so long ago now: in another lifetime really, and certainly well before she met and married Joe Jameson.

Hardig, by contrast, was alone. He had money, but nothing else. He was indeed wealthy. She saw it there in the furnishings of the office, the platter of cocktail shrimp and dipping sauces on his mahogany conference table. The juice bar, metal and chrome. He had everything at his disposal.

"Free?"

"Don't call me that," she said, trying to remain focused on her purpose for being there. She was determined to pay her respects while also questioning him about his own role in his son's premature mortality.

"Chauncey, I'm sorry about your son," she began.

"Are you?" Chauncey asked, raising a skeptical eyebrow.

"Aren't *you*? My God, Warren, he was ill. He killed himself, for God's sake."

"No one knows that better than I do. I've spent almost a million dollars on his mental evaluations, to no avail mind you."

Alfreah kept herself steeled against such harsh talk. "Is that all it was to you: money wasted for time in the doctor's office that didn't work?" She'd forgotten through the years how heart-less he was and now the whole sad picture came crashing back. She thought maybe with age and maturity he would change, certainly after today's news.

"You forget he wasn't my son, he was my stepson," Hardig continued. "I spent years grooming him into something he obviously wasn't cut out to be. He had problems ever since his mother died. I could have kept my money in my pocket!"

"Grooming him? Was he a pet to you?" Alfreah replied incredulously. "Seems like you should have spent time loving him instead."

"That was my way. I did the best I could with what I had. I offered him to you - "

"First of all, don't you dare quote the words of Thurgood Marshall: you're no match for such a man, Chauncey. Secondly, I thought it best for you to raise Warren. My God, he was all you had. He was your opportunity to - "

"Well, he wasn't you," Hardig countered. "Maybe if you had helped me, both our lives would have been different."

Alfreah nodded, now sad that she'd come. He would never change, even with his only child gone, biological or not. She wondered whether, if she had taken Warren in, she would have been able to raise him. Would love have been enough from the Jamesons in that situation? Would they even have been able do as they saw fit, or would it simply have been a way for Chauncey to keep in touch with her for the rest of their lives? Hardig had even asked her if she'd raise Warren, but they could not afford another child: she was already pregnant with her own third child when he'd asked. She'd thought that by not giving Warren up for adoption, Chauncey was implicitly accepting fatherhood. She thought her prayers for their relationship had been answered, but they hadn't. Over the years, Warren was only tolerated. Money and schooling, everything paid for and bought, but he was left lacking the things he needed most: acceptance and love. Those were gifts Chauncey neither possessed nor was willing to provide.

"When love eludes you, you focus your energies on other things."

"Things? They can't love you back, Chauncey."

"And neither did you. Nothing lost, nothing gained."

"So you don't even care that he died? You're here as if the day goes on. As if nothing tragic happened just today."

"He is and was a failure," Chauncey snapped. "The police are likely on their way here right now to question my hand in all of this. Thankfully, my lawyers will be here and I have enough people on the payroll to straighten out this mess. Those people help me sleep. I never told my son to go after yours."

"People?"

"My publicist, my lawyer."

"Right, of course," Alfreah said, exasperated. "Well, I am sorry about your son. My last few questions pertain to your involvement with my son's building. You wouldn't know anything about that either, now would you?"

"Did I burn down his place of business? So what if I did," declared Chauncey. "I didn't, by the way, but my son always did take my instructions very literally, so perhaps in a roundabout way... You know very well that your husband stole that property from right under my nose almost forty years ago, anyway."

Alfreah bridled at the accusation. "He labored on that entire strip, taking extra shifts to make money for our family!"

"Still, he became chummy with the owner. I was interested in that space, me. I wanted it for you, for our future."

Alfreah shook her head slowly, wondering if she had ever truly understood him. He lived so far in the past, stuck there. Back then, a powerful rich man had chosen Joe Jameson over Chauncey Hardig, not only to sell to but to give one of the units to, free of charge. It was a big deal then, and Chauncey had obviously never got over it.

"I've apologized a million times for the years I sought after you, Alfreah, knowing you were committed to someone else. I lost my head then. I was young and foolish."

"Now? You're just older and still quite foolish," Alfreah retorted.

"I've made mistakes," Chauncey sighed. "Now I guess I'll live my life alone."

"That was your choice," she answered. "You could have had your pick of anyone, any woman you wanted..."

"But I only wanted one woman," Chauncey reminded her. "I'm guilty of having an unhealthy fixation on something that wasn't mine to have, and then I'm guilty of projecting those same unhealthy feelings on my stepson. What a vicious, cyclical web I've woven. Now tell me, Free, what did you come here for? Do you want my confession? Well, I can tell you that your family is safe now. This Hardig won't bother you any further. The only other Hardig is dead, so he certainly won't be pursuing your precious son any longer. I remember your passion, Free – Alfreah - for your family, always fighting for all of them. That passion stirred me. Even coming here to question me this evening: it takes guts to even come here at this hour. That boldness stirs me as well. Do you remember the passion we had for each other?"

"Don't go there." Alfreah shut him down firmly. "I've forgotten that. I replaced that scant handful of episodes with memories of my husband, something you were never going to become. My passion didn't drive you. Money, that's what always made you salivate. I was a mere accoutrement on your arm - nothing more." Alfreah paused. "I always wanted to be married, to have a family. That's what I sought after, and that's what I got. Just thinking of them makes me happy. Joe Jameson gave them to me and I've never regretted any of it. I never will regret the path that I chose."

Chauncey chortled derisively. "The struggle, you didn't regret that? Paying bills late, the time you asked me for money when your broke husband nearly broke his back fixing other people's homes to make ends meet?"

"Asking someone I thought was a friend for money was a mistake!" she exclaimed. "I made a mistake. And none of that matters, not at all. The final thing to say is that I'm sorry your pathetic life has come to this. I hope you're happy alone and without family to love you. You did this: you created this yourself. Your infidelity and your lies while we dated still hurt, but that's nothing compared to what you'll feel when you finally take time to review your life and how lonely it is. To know the hurt you've brought to others with your take-all attitude. My son will recover: he will move on with his life and he will be happy. All my children will be all right. I just hate that this is the way it ended for Warren. He is the one I'm really sad about. No one should have this happen to them."

"I'm going to release you from our lives," she went on. "I've lived my life, now I will reap the benefits of raising children and can now live out my days spoiling grandchildren. Meanwhile, you can live up here, work till all hours of the night, and burn in hell for all I care. You heartless, self-serving fool."

Alfreah turned and left. Her thoughts consumed her as she made her way to the bank of elevators and descended to the lobby. She kept moving purposefully, knowing she was finally free and that now the door could close on this particular chapter. Then the tragic events, the lack of remorse Chauncey had exhibited and a sudden wave of missing her own rock of a husband all turned into tears that cascaded down her cheeks. She was done with this entire scene. She mentally closed a door that had been left open for far too long.

40

H is sisters initially looked at him as if he were crazy, but Dean was undeterred. Catching up on the years he and Chyna had missed was his only goal, not to mention trying to replace a few really bad days with good ones. Eventually, Tish, his easy-going sister, and Jina, the more uptight one, would help him with a most legitimate request they could get behind. Dean was nervous, but with Jina on speakerphone and Tish across from him, he took a deep breath. "I got it all planned out, up here" - he tapped his temple. "The part I still need your help with, though, is getting Chyna to the designated spot, on time and in appropriate attire."

Even he couldn't believe what he was attempting. With the help of his sisters, Dean had conjured up a beautiful wedding. With the right motive, namely love, he was beginning to think he just might pull it off. For the moment, though, there was some stunned silence. Dean shrugged at Tish's gentle smile, noting her raised eyebrows.

"You heard me correctly," he said, sipping a cup of coffee in a pair of jogging pants and a tattered sweatshirt. "I know how you guys like to plan things. I already talked to Angie, and she agreed to do the menu, so that's the hardest part taken care of off the bat." He shrugged.

"There's no question we'll help you, it's just... well, what's all this rush?" Tisha chimed in.

The sooner they got married, the sooner they could begin the rest of their lives together. After all, Dean kept reminding his sisters and everyone else just as they'd kept reminding him that the entire production had been more than fifteen years in the making. Hadn't he wasted enough time already?

"Shouldn't we wait until Lisa is apprehended?" Jina put in, her voice crackling from the phone. Background noise from the busy wedding dress shop muffled her voice.

Dean nodded. "Yes, J, that has crossed my mind, but what if it takes forever to find her? She is nowhere to be found so far. It's like she's dropped off the face of the earth."

It was true, he'd thought about Lisa, but if she knew what was good for her she'd stay good and hidden, and if she had some sort of weird hankering for arrest she could show herself at any time. There was a warrant out, and as far as Dean was concerned, he hoped she'd stay hidden forever

"Well, okay then," Tisha said. "Just let us know what you want us to do, and we'll do it."

When the phone beeped, he picked it up and said his good-byes to Jina. She'd be by the house any moment, having sourced a selection of dresses for Chyna to choose from. Hearing water running upstairs, he whispered a few more instructions and hurriedly completed the call.

He was glad Chyna was waking up on her own. She'd been in and out of sleep for the last seventy-two hours, and he still didn't want to interrupt her. Her body and her mind needed rest and reset from the ordeal, and he was chief sanity protector until she no longer needed him to keep noise and outside news away from her. He was happy to oblige.

Her nurse friend Charlize had ordered her some special

medication and sent it over to the house. Dean couldn't remember the name of it, but it banished the makings of a flu-like cold from her body. Only trouble was, it also left her drowsy. Each time she awoke, though, she was looking, talking and acting more like herself, and for that he was thankful. The worst of the storm had passed. The Jamesons kept the television turned off until the story of their lives blew over and they could eventually move on.

Only Dean couldn't stop himself from reading the paper, mostly out of habit on his phone. He had just wanted to stay abreast of everything, just in case there was any misinformation being circulated, or something he should tell his family or Chyna about. The entire story now read like an excerpt from a novel. The latest coverage was a front-page feature-length spread in the *Washington Post*: "The Rise and Fall of Prominent Business Tycoon Warren Hardig." Uninterrupted by a single advertisement, the story had been recounted in a handful of the most popular Washington magazines, and then again in other business journals.

Thankfully yet sadly, in a city full of scandal, his death wasn't revered for long. As the world went on day by day, the usual numerous folks continued to do wrong. After a while, the inevitable lawsuits against Warren started, and many a commentator had not-nice things to say about him as well as his father. Despite the dwindling print runs of the newspapers, print copies were selling out for the first time since a Washington sports team won a national title: too long ago to remember.

Reporters sought Dean and his family for comment, but thankfully they had a savvy, veteran news person in their corner: his sister, Jina. The tactics and carefully-crafted statements she turned out sent them packing. No doubt she eased the level of scrutiny they all faced in more ways than one. The fact that they mostly stayed indoors, too, meant they couldn't be accosted unawares and unprepared by a press mob. Dean planned to keep it that way a little while longer, but the fact was they couldn't stay hidden forever.

The phone buzzed and brought him out of his reverie. He picked it up on the first ring. It was Jina. He was glad she was so helpful. She took this wedding planning seriously. He was glad everyone loved Chyna so much. They'd all do anything for her. He didn't have an exact date in mind, but it would be very soon.

"Yeah, she's fine," he responded. "Sleeping, but I think she's up now. No, Mom made enough food - there should be some left over. If not I'll see what's at the house."

He paused, listening. "I don't know but ten seems like a good number, so long as the styles are different. She's bound to like one of those... I mean, don't you think?" he asked, keeping his voice low as Chyna now stirred around upstairs. She'd likely be down any moment, so time was short. "Got it. Okay, just make sure they are something she would like."

When Chyna came down, she smiled at Tish and Dean who sat in the quiet living room. Dean stood up, thankful for once that the pain in his side didn't bite into him, reminding him of everything. Normal movements were getting easier day by day.

He leaned over and kissed Chyna. She smelled heavenly, her hair wrapped up in one of those hair cover things, but otherwise dressed in jeans and an oversized bright yellow sweater. It was the woman he knew. She looked more and more like her normal, beautiful self.

"Good morning," she whispered, still groggy from her medication.

"Good day," Dean countered. "It's a little past noon," he added, showing her his watch.

"What are you guys doing? TT, when are you going back to Georgia?" Chyna inquired.

"Oh, I don't know," Tish replied, airily. "I miss you guys so much, I might have the baby here. What do you think about that? Heck, we might move back."

"What? That would be amazing!" Chyna took a seat across from her friend, happy to just not do anything for a while. Dean returned with a cup of coffee which he handed to Chyna, having refilled his own.

"What's on the agenda for today? I can tell you've got something planned," Chyna remarked. "You have this sneaky look about you: both of you, for that matter."

"Me? No!" Dean replied quickly, but couldn't keep the laughter and the excitement from his voice. "Well, as a matter of fact I do have a couple of things in mind, but only if you're feeling up to them. If not, they can wait until next week."

"Well, what are they?" Chyna asked, grabbing a pillow and tucking her legs up underneath her. "What is it? TT, you know, don't you?

"Maybe," Tish sang, "but I am sworn to secrecy."

Dean stood, drained his coffee mug and looked at his phone.

"Oh, TT, come on now, how can you be sworn to secrecy? You're the one with the secret," Chyna wheedled; then she was thoughtful a moment. "Aren't you?"

Dean nodded. "Yep, and we swore ourselves to secrecy."

They all laughed. Dean reached for Chyna and kissed her again. "I have to run an errand but Jina should be here any moment. Will you girls promise to behave yourselves?"

"Why is Jina coming?" Chyna asked suspiciously.

"She's your friend?"

Chyna rolled her eyes as Tish laughed.

"Listen to me: be in the moment, have fun and tell me the truth. Are you all right, right now?" Dean asked.

Chyna nodded her confirmation. "Any word on Lisa?"

"No," Dean said. "But we can move on, Chyna. She won't hurt us now. We can move on with our lives regardless of whatever happened and wherever she is, okay? She can't control us anymore."

"I know, I just... I was just wondering," Chyna replied.

Truthfully, Dean would wonder, too, until the day she was caught. It'd just have to be something they'd keep in the back of their minds, staying calm yet vigilant.

"Until then, you stay here awhile. Jina is on her way and TT is here. You're on labor watch."

"Oh boy!" Chyna's eyes bulged, barely able to contain her excitement. "This is going to be so fun."

Satisfied that she had something distracting her, Dean gave his sister a peck on the cheek and gave Chyna one too, holding her tight and lovingly, remembering to thank God constantly for protecting her. He stood again, smiling at her elation over possible baby news, knowing she had no idea that, if he planned like crazy and if everyone on the team came through, she'd have more good news than ever in less than a week. He winked at her as he left.

CHYNA WATCHED as Dean left before settling into coffee with her long-time friend. She and Tish chatted about everything, and she could definitely say some of the sadness on her heart had passed. It helped a lot when she had an entire team of folks shielding her from her bad thoughts, creating a comforting bubble that protected her from everything, including the news, reporters and just about anything that had the potential to bring her down. Dean was in a good mood, as Chauncey Hardig had been arrested just the other night. Ms. Alfreah had ensured a steady source of well-balanced meals: plenty of hearty soup for Chyna's cold and lots of good proteins. And most importantly, she was facing forward and looking ahead. When the doorbell rang, she got up, smiling at her best friend and future sister-in-law. "Want to bet Dean forgot his keys, TT?"

"Hmm, I don't know, doubtful though," Tish replied.

Chyna walked to the door, and, as usual, heard Jina before she saw her.

"Hellooooo! It's just me, and uh, I got some heavy stuff in my arms. Good morning, or afternoon, or whatever the heck this is. Hey sissy," she yelled down the hall.

"Hey," came Tish's reply.

Chyna was about to close the door when someone else followed, dragging a rolling garment rack thing as well as several containers that looked like hatboxes.

"Hello, darling, hello. Glenda Pritchard, manager at Signature Bridal. It's my pleasure - the bride, I presume?"

The woman, a fair-skinned older lady with a high-pitched voice, was replete with smiles, a long black dress and lots of noisy charm bracelets that jangled on her skinny arms. Chyna closed the door in awe and offered a shy 'yes' to the woman's question. Something inside her immediately ignited, embracing the word. Of course, she had to be the *bride,* as the only one of the three women present who was not yet married.

She led the woman to the living room to join everyone else. The woman swiftly turned her various materials into a complete display case; and when Chyna saw the dresses emerging from each nondescript black garment bag, she was speechless. Today would be the day she picked out her wedding dress.

41

C hyna rose early, wondering what on earth awaited her concerning her wedding. She needed a shower and coffee, but she resolved that she'd be downstairs and ready to go before Jina came to get her this time. Her course of medicine for the cold had finished and she was glad to be done with it: it had made her drowsy. She looked at herself in bathroom mirror and smiled.

I'm getting married... well, at some point.

She blinked rapidly at the complete giddiness she felt and turned around, noticing for the first time that there was a long garment bag hanging on the shower curtain rod.

"What a sneaky little devil," she said aloud. She seized the note taped to the outer plastic and opened it quickly.

Try this on, Jina coming at 10:00 to see about alterations and other stuff. Love you, D.

Chyna giggled. She could not wait for the fitting. She was just a little apprehensive that as her wedding moved ever closer, she still had no idea where it would be or any of the heavily guarded details. Truth be told, she was laid back enough not to care. She was excited and she had enough control over all the aspects that it didn't even matter. The last few weeks had given her so much perspective. She didn't need details, nor to be super picky about everything: she just needed Dean.

She managed to get into the dress after taking a shower, ensuring she kept it spotless. She admired herself in the mirror, amazed that it fit so well. The tailor might not need to make any alterations at all: it truly was fitting like a glove.

"Signature Bridal lady, you killed it," Chyna breathed.

Just then, the doorbell rang and she had no choice but to go downstairs in her gown. She walked slowly lest she fall and break her neck: not a good look. "I'm coming," she hollered when the doorbell rang again.

Chyna opened the door and Jina waltzed in. "Hey - oh my god, I'm so glad you're not Dean," she exclaimed. "Look at me!" Her friend embraced her and they hugged, squealed and jumped around together.

Chyna couldn't believe it.

"I can't believe it!" Jina said in awe, echoing her thoughts. "What on earth did he say to get you to put that on?"

"What do you mean? He said in the note the lady was coming at ten o'clock," Chyna replied, confused. "But I really don't need her, do I? It seems to fit great!" Chyna couldn't resist turning around and parading before Jina. "I can't wait to show Tish." She laughed when she finished.

"Oh well, uh - no I think it's fine, you're right," Jina agreed.

"So I should call and cancel the fitting, right?"

"No uh, don't worry about that," Jina replied quickly. "I'll take care of it. Here, read this." Jina pulled out her phone as she handed another envelope to Chyna.

Chyna stared at it in awe. It was a beautiful cream-colored envelope, so official-looking she was afraid to open it. The little satin bow held the contents in place. She'd picked this very calligraphy, with the exaggerated curls. The lettering for the C to her name and the D in Dean dipped and rounded. She wondered how in the world they'd been able to do it so quickly.

YOU'RE INVITED TO THE MARRIAGE OF CHYNA A. LOCKHART AND DEAN E. JAMESON, AT TWO P.M. ...

Chyna's eyebrows raised and she started laughing, but sobered as she registered that the date on the card was... today. The clock said 9:55. If this obvious typo were true, that would mean she had only a few hours to get ready. "Wouldn't that be something?" she said aloud, chuckling.

"What?" Jina turned and put her phone into her purse and put her purse on her shoulder.

"This invitation you gave me. It's so beautiful, and it's the one we picked out with the script font and raised black lettering, but it's too bad there's a typo in the date. It says the wedding's today! Can you imagine?"

Jina smiled. "Actually, I can."

Chyna viewed Jina's face, but she wasn't laughing at all. Jina was evading her, which was painfully obvious for someone usually so direct.

"So you ready to go?" Jina pressed. "Momma and Tish are at the house. We figure we can do your makeup, you don't wear that much, so let's go!"

Chyna's eyes filled with tears as she finally understood. "Jina, oh, it *can't* be today, not today! I'm not ready," she breathed, feeling like she might hyperventilate.

"Okay stop it, do not cry!" Jina urged in alarm. "When I deliver you to my brother, you gotta be okay! if you're crying, he'll take one look, blame me and I'll have completely failed on my mission. Chyna, please." Jina snatched a napkin from the roll on the kitchen counter and helped her friend dab her eyes.

Chyna let Jina wipe her tears, then took the balled-up napkin from her as she continued to reread the card, heading back upstairs with a new sense of energy and elation mingling with nerves about her closer-than-expected nuptials. "I don't know what to do, Jina - what should I do?"

The last week's planning had been exhausting, but as she reviewed all the input she'd given every single day, she realized there wasn't anything left. Her days were so blurred together they didn't make sense. Tish and Jina had orchestrated one visitor after another, leaving Chyna exhausted but excited. All that selecting - invitations, cake samples, menus, flowers, color schemes - meant there was nothing else left to do.

Seeing as her biological family was null, Chyna really only wanted a small ceremony: maybe a winter evening, with dinner, nice music and just enough people to sit around an oversized table comfortably. That plus a small space for four to six couples to dance: she and Dean, Tish and Chase, Tony and Jina, and Charlize and... Chyna put a mental question mark. Trent perhaps? She hoped Jojo and Dean could invite him. After hearing about how Dean treated his brother, she hoped JoJo would still come to take part in their wedding, too. While Dean had assured her that they had talked and she believed him, she always fretted that her own actions had driven them apart, too. She didn't want that to be the case.

Moving on from such melancholy thoughts, Chyna continued down her small guest list. She thought of Bubba, who'd worked so tirelessly with Dean on her home. Now, like the house, here she was: still standing, and not too shabby for everything she'd been through. Everything felt so right.

"Okay, like, what are you doing?" called Jina, intruding on her reverie. "Just get some make-up and a change of clothes! We have that party dress that you liked that that lady brought..."

"You do?" Chyna stood from her musings. Her heart beat so fast she could barely breathe. She felt overwhelmed with the pure elation that surged within her. "Oh Jina, oh my God," she repeated.

"God would thank you kindly if you would leave Him alone," returned her friend smartly. "You are not in distress, you are fine. And everything is A-Okay, right? Dean is so happy, he worked so hard. I've rarely seen him like this. Hey, you love him, right?"

"Oh my... I mean yes, Lord, yes, of course! Of course, he is all that matters."

"All right then, let's go find Mr. Potato Head himself so we can get this thing baked!" Jina reached for her arm, and they nearly fell down the stairs but managed not to injure themselves.

"Okay, but wait, wait, where, where is the wedding?" Chyna asked breathlessly.

Jina opened the door as Chyna grabbed her purse and keys.

"At your favorite place in the entire world, of course" Jina smiled. "Momma's house. Now come on, child!"

42

"You know you sent the wrong person to do the job. She will mess everything up and you'll have one big nightmare on your hands," said Jojo knowingly.

"Thanks for the vote of confidence," groaned Dean. "I was hoping that just this one time she wouldn't spill the beans. She's gotta come through."

Resisting the urge to check his watch yet again, Dean looked over at his brother, who was heaving a garden torch into the ground like Paul Bunyan. "What was I supposed to do, send you over there? She would've known something was up for sure then. At least she's been with them the last couple weeks picking out everything. Jina is just supposed to tell her that they're going out to take pictures, then bring her over here. If she could do that one simple task, then we're home free. Heck, if Chyna agrees to marry me after all this, anything is possible."

"What on earth are you talking about?"

"I'm just saying that I feel like I may have rushed her by putting everything together so quickly. Don't women like to fuss over the details of just about everything?" Dean asked skeptically. He'd been unsure and nervous for the better part of the last week about how he'd orchestrated things.

"Do I look like a woman to you?" asked Jojo. "And no, she was a part of the process without the extra work. You've always been top of the line, Deanie. You're a cool cat. She didn't have to lift a finger: that was really nice, convenient and easy. Anyway, I think they like it when we get all sappy but still take charge, and that's what you did, for sure. Your motives were all kosher."

Dean nodded. He couldn't argue that his brother's advice was sound. He moved quickly to another subject. "I meant to thank you for what went down. I mean, I was just worried about the toll it would take on Chyna, I don't want anything to come between us... and I'm sorry I punched you."

Jojo stood from clearing the pathway of the new brick patio. It had been freshly swept and a long white runner ran down the middle. Rented white guest chairs flanked each side.

"You had every right to be mad," his brother replied. "And again, I'm the one who is sorry. I didn't realize how it could affect her. Things could easily have gone south - but I wasn't going to let anything happen to her, I'm sorry. If something like that ever happened with Angie, I'm not sure how I'd feel – all to say I wouldn't want to wear the shoe if it were on my foot. My jaw ached for an entire day, but I suppose you went easy on me. I should have thought about it more."

Dean nodded finally, glad it was all out in the open and both of them could move on.

"So, you and Angie - you sure about that?"

"Never been surer in all my years," grinned Jojo. "It's weird, though: I kind of feel rushed, you know? Like it's now or never."

"I feel that way," agreed Dean with a chuckle. "You think all of this isn't a rush?"

"Yes but you've known Chyna your entire life. I've not known Angie that long."

"It's not the length of time, it's the quality of that time."

Dean smiled as Jojo eyed him skeptically. If Jojo felt half of what he'd felt, his brother should marry Angie tomorrow. Urgency wasn't new to him, so it made perfect sense in his mind. He felt rushed by choice, simply because he didn't want to be away from Chyna another minute – let alone another night where she was in her house alone. Yes, he was just down the block from her, but there remained a threat of danger. More than that, it was about starting their life, trying to make up for lost time. So his brother and Angie didn't have the time behind them that he and Chyna did – that didn't matter. It was still whatever one felt; and no-one had any right to question what someone felt, least of all those looking in from the outside. Dean checked his watch a second time.

"Casey and Cassie?" Dean asked, referring to Angie's kids: her niece and nephew whom she'd adopted when her sister passed away.

"I realize they come along with the package, if that's what you mean," answered Jojo. "I know they won't say goodbye when we say I do. I think I love them too." He blushed. "I know, I know, my attitude..."

"Well, no, I mean, what about Case?"

"Oh, you mean his talking?" Dean nodded. "Well, Angie's been working on some sign language with him. He's had tests. He's going to have more over the summer and then they'll be presented to the school to see what's what. For now Angie's teaching them, on her own." Jojo glowed with pride. "They're whip-smart, both of them. But it's a long road ahead, I know that much."

Dean nodded again, hoping his brother did truly know what he was in for. He wasn't worried, though, because, as always, the entire family would help them no matter what life threw at them. Everything for the Jamesons was a family affair.

Now, Dean reflected with a smile, he could start building his own family, just as soon as his bride to be arrived.

With renewed hope about everything from his brother's love life and future to his own, Dean focused on what he was doing, counting the minutes and setting the stage for new beginnings.

43

Somehow, through tears interspersed with peals of laughter amidst lots of commotion and excitement, Chyna managed to pull her mind together. As silly as it was, she kept her beautiful dress on the whole time. She covered herself with the oversized terrycloth robe Jina had thought to bring over for her, and together they waltzed their way down the sidewalk to the Jameson family home. The entire situation was just unbelievable.

Unsure of what to do next, Chyna stood in the kitchen, having just entered through the side door, while Jina ran back to her car, claiming she'd forgotten something in the trunk. A million thoughts ran through Chyna's mind, chief among them the question of who in the world had orchestrated such a production. She would die from a fit of hysterical laugher if her heart would just slow down and let her, but it raced on regardless of what she did, said or thought. Chyna placed a hand over her chest as if to calm it. In just a couple of hours, she was getting married.

Chyna walked to the living room's terrace doors. The curtains were drawn: heavier, better-insulated drapery had been put up for the winter, to keep the chilly weather out of the old house. Just as Chyna was about to peek out, the door swung open and Thomas, Tish and Chase's son, bolted through. He waved quickly, not recognizing her at first, then slowly turned with a startled expression on his face to get a better look at her.

"Uh, hi, Aunt Chyna," Thomas said, thrusting his hands into his pockets and looking shiftily toward the door.

"Hi, Thomas - you look so handsome." Chyna smiled, looking him over, from his black tuxedo with a black bow tie and white shirt peeping out, down to his shiny patent leather shoes.

"Uh, thanks," Thomas muttered, embarrassed. "Uh, you might want to go upstairs. I think Mama is looking for you. And Grandma too."

"Well, all right, but uh, is Dean out there?" Chyna queried.

"Um – uh -"

Chyna smiled as Thomas stammered, unsure what to say; then the door opened quickly and Dean peeked inside first, as if checking before spotting her. "Hey!" he said and kissed Chyna on the cheek. "Are you ready?"

"I have to do my hair." She reached up and touched the hair and belatedly realized she hadn't bothered to comb it at all. Chyna then touched her face. "Oh no! And my makeup!" she sputtered. "Dean - this is it? We're getting married today?" she whispered in disbelief.

"Yes, is that all right?"

"No, no, oh no," Chyna cried, suddenly panicky.

"Okay, okay, we can do it next week – or next year?" Dean said quickly.

"No, it's just that... you're seeing me before the wedding ceremony! It's bad luck!" she wailed louder.

"Listen to me!" Dean took Chyna's face between his hands and looked over at Thomas, who watched as if he didn't know what to do or say. "T, tell your mom and grandmom that Chyna is here, and that she'll be up in a minute."

He turned back to his bride-to-be. "Chyna, look at me. Nothing can ruin this, nothing can ruin us. We've overcome every possible adversity to get to this point. All that stuff about seeing you before the wedding – well, that's just some superstition someone made up, probably the same wonderful someone who invented dieting. Okay?"

Chyna laughed and so did Dean.

"We have no room for such silly notions in our life."

Chyna nodded, then wiped her eyes. "You look so beautiful," she added in response.

Dean only chuckled. "Thank you, but guys are handsome, okay? Handsome."

Chyna laughed. "What time is it?"

"Almost time," Dean said, pulling up the sleeve to his suit coat to check his watch. Chyna nodded and turned to leave.

"Chyna, this is all right, right? I didn't take anything from you? You feel as if this is our wedding, not only mine, right?"

"This is the most spectacular thing anyone has ever done for me," she answered with conviction. "I'm just so surprised. I see everything within my grasp: everything you've given me. I'm just overwhelmed. Dean, is Bubba coming?"

Dean nodded.

Chyna reached out her hand to turn his face back to hers. "You truly thought of everything. I am delightfully overwhelmed, Dean. I'm so happy."

Dean visibly straightened and nodded, smiling. "Kiss me."

"After I say I do." Laughing, Chyna turned and ran quickly up the stairs.

ALFREAH JAMESON, dressed in a cream-mint colored suit, stood up from where she had been perched on the bed. She'd been silent while Jina applied Chyna's makeup and Tish styled her hair. Chyna was so absorbed in her thoughts that she'd forgotten that Ms. Alfreah was there at all.

When Alfreah stood, her daughters promptly left the room. "How are you doing, dear?" she asked Chyna.

"I'm really excited," Chyna said. "I love your son so much."

"I know you do." Alfreah nodded. "And on this occasion, I've got a little story to tell you. One day, many, many years ago, I was looking out the window, my Joe by my side like he always was. All of my kids were playing outside, some kind of game. Then I saw my Dean. He pushed you too hard and you fell, skinned your knee. You shed a few tears: scared more than hurt. But Dean was right there seeing if you were okay."

Chyna watched as Ms. Alfreah stroked the air to her right side, and she wondered if the older woman felt her husband beside her as she spoke.

"I miss my Joe," Alfreah said, as if reading Chyna's thoughts. "But I said to him right then: 'Honey, did you see our boy? You see him out there, acting a fool for our new neighbor? And look how hard he pushed her. I think he really likes her.'"

Both Alfreah and Chyna laughed out loud.

"I know you don't believe it, but when you get to my age your mind stops running around so much," Alfreah continued. "The clutter up here," — Alfreah tapped an index finger to her temple — "clears up eventually, long enough to listen to what God whispers into your heart. I've already heard it, because He told me. Most things He keeps to Himself, letting us figure it out, or just die waiting for Him to reveal it to us, but a few things do eventually come clear. Me, now, I see some more children in my home: grandbabies, for all my kids, more than my arms can hold. They're coming. Believe, honey, believe and pray!"

Chyna nodded. She wanted badly to believe and wondered

if her future mother-in-law knew of the fate she had already met in the baby-bearing department. It didn't matter, Chyna decided. She was getting married, and that was all that mattered to her at this moment. She couldn't think of anything else, she told herself – but she had to admit that she'd never stopped dreaming of children with Dean.

"Well, look, time's a-wastin', and I gotta get to what I have," said Ms. Alfreah, all business once again. "Blue, borrowed, new? Got all that?" The older lady ticked off the traditional items on her fingers before pausing thoughtfully.

"I have so many memories in this house. I don't want to lose it out of the family, and while I love it, I just don't think I can stay here," she went on. "Now that Joe is gone, I think I want a nice small apartment, maybe nearby. The longer I stay down in Macon, the more I think I'm turning into a small-town kind of woman, even though I was raised in the city. As I age, I want quietness. Blessed quietness! For now, I'm going to live with my daughter and Chase a bit, until the twins get a little older; then maybe I'll purchase something small down there. But I haven't chartered all that yet, honey. Besides, someone's got to keep this place up, share lots of love here, raise children..."

"No," Chyna whispered, shaking her head frantically as Mrs. Jameson removed a thick folded paper from her purse and pushed it toward Chyna's hand. "No, no!" Chyna repeated more forcefully, her throat turning as dry as the Sahara. She folded her hands so tightly she felt her recently trimmed fingernails dig into her palms.

"Since you were a child, I know you wanted to live here and be a part of this family. Even though you didn't sleep here, Chyna, you were a part of this family," said Alfreah, continuing to thrust the envelope at Chyna. "I love you like I do my own daughters. I know you had a rough time of it growing up: your mama tried and did the best she could, but you do have her to thank. You get that caretaker stuff from looking after her. You did everything you could: spent a lot of time wishing she would just get up. I know about that. It takes a special person to go into people's homes, to whip the family into shape – it's not one of the duties you're supposed to have to take on, but you do it with grace, and love, helping the family cope. Not everyone can do that. Not everyone has the sensitivity the family needs. What you did every day for your mother helped to foster that gift inside of you..." The woman stopped herself. "Listen to me! Lord, I'm so far from what I'm trying to say. The point is, you did that for Joe, for me. You helped me, and I want you to have this house," Alfreah finished with clarity. "it may be a little old and drafty, but I'd like to think it's got a lot of character and a lot of really good memories for both of us. You can fix it up, make it yours and Dean's. I just would like for you to have it. It's my - Joe's and my - gift to you."

Chyna turned to face herself in the mirror. The tears streamed from her eyes and she hastily wiped them, so as not to stain her dress with black from the mascara she wore. She couldn't believe it. She'd just been given a house, of all things. She'd expected a rope of pearls, a necklace, some antique piece perhaps; but property, a symbol of family, a place to rear another generation of Jamesons? That she hadn't expected at all. She placed the paper on the table and pushed it away in awe.

"Let's not talk about it much more now," Alfreah smiled. "If you don't marry that man downstairs in double-quick time, he might die of a broken heart. One more thing: all that happened in the past? It's behind you now. Let go, okay? One day, if you want and if you remind me, I'll tell you about the Hardigs, but not today. It's a tragic story, and it started long before you got here: nothing you did caused any of it. I won't permit that to mar your day - and they won't interfere with your future either. All you need to know is that they're gone, over and done with, okay? Hurry along now. I'll see you downstairs."

As Alfreah left the bedroom, Chyna closed her eyes and prayed, just as Alfreah Jameson had always instructed her to do. She believed in God. It was because of Him that she'd made it this far, but her prayer life could certainly use more frequency. She bowed her head: she would change that, starting today.

"Amen," she whispered aloud after a few moments. She opened her eyes and looked up to the mirror. Then, as if in slow motion, her eyes traveled up past her perfect hairdo to meet the cold, cold eyes of Lisa Stephens.

44

S uddenly, Chyna couldn't breathe. Quick as a flash, Lisa had lunged forward and wrapped a rope around Chyna's neck. She yanked hard and the vanity bench toppled. In an instant, Lisa was straddling her, applying every ounce of her weight and strength to Chyna's chest, her thumb pressing hard into Chyna's jugular.

"Please," Chyna choked out with her last remaining breath. "Don't. Lisa."

"He is mine!" Lisa yelled. She was practically standing now, with all her weight on Chyna's throat.

Chyna was blacking in and out, her vision blurred, certain this was the end. She couldn't get hold of Lisa: when she tried to grasp at something, all she found was carpet, handfuls of dress and the air she couldn't use to breathe. Finally she did manage to grab a handful of Lisa's shirt, pulling her enough to get up. They rolled tumbling on the floor, but Chyna was too disoriented and weak to get the upper hand. At last she got a gulp of air and somehow managed to scramble away on all fours. She was almost to the door when something pelted her in the back – once, then twice, the second time higher and sharper. She collapsed, her body mid-reach for the door. She screamed faintly before she blacked out cold.

DOWNSTAIRS, in the cool outside air, the sun was high, warming up the place where Dean stood. With the minister to his right and his brother at his back, Dean couldn't have asked for a more perfect wedding day. It wasn't as cold as he thought it would be, and in any case the two open-pit fireplaces he'd rented ensured that no one, even a beautiful woman in a wedding dress, would be too cold on this early winter day.

Dean kept looking to the window, a tad concerned that his bride didn't come. He eyed his sister and mother who had just left her moments ago: they'd assured him she'd be down any moment. He smiled to assure everyone gathered that everything was okay.

Suddenly, they heard a piercing scream from the house. He looked up at the window in horror, then took off in a mad dash through the terrace doors. He was up the stairs with his brother on his heels in a matter of seconds, adrenaline and God working together to give him superhuman speed, his recent injury forgotten.

Any pain of his own left his thoughts when he got to the top of the stairs and saw Lisa Stephens, a pair of scissors in her hand, poised above Chyna's limp body.

Instinctively, he fell to his knees, moving closer to Chyna and taking one of her hands. He wanted to reach for the scissors but he stopped, his hand shaking when Chyna didn't respond. He looked up, a plea in his eyes.

"Don't do this, Lisa. Please."

After what seemed like an eternity, Chyna's head rolled and she seemed to regain consciousness with a start. "Don't move, Chyna," Dean muttered to her, his eyes never leaving Lisa. He placed a hand on the back of her head as he looked into Lisa's eyes and inched closer, his hand outstretched.

"You don't want to do this, Lisa," he said coaxingly. "I'm sorry I, uh, led you on."

She almost lowered the scissors, and her slight hesitation gave Dean a spark of hope: at least the madwoman could be soothed. Still, he didn't take his eyes off her.

"Why wouldn't I want to do this?" Lisa said heatedly. "I love you. I did everything for you. You said you wanted your place burned down, so I thought I did what you wanted. Even if you didn't want it exactly, Warren said that – that at least you'd feel despondent and need a shoulder to cry on. Then *she* came back to town." Lisa looked down with hateful eyes. She raised the scissors again.

"Warren is dead," Dean intoned.

Lisa paused. "What?"

Dean nodded, still watching her. "He can't lie to you anymore. He lied to all of us. He used you to do his bidding, to handle his dirtiest deeds and business. Now, if you testify about what Mr. Hardig knows, you can move on with your life and this can be just a small thing. I will put in a good word for you. You don't want to add murder to... anything you might already be implicated in. Trust me, it will be so much worse if you hurt Chyna."

I'd kill you myself, Dean added silently, hating that he hadn't been more vigilant. He knew Lisa was dangerous, but a murderer? Her sick fixation on him was just as bad as Warren's had been on Chyna: they were perfect for another. If only they'd ridden off into the sunset together, leaving him and Chyna the hell alone.

"I'm so sorry Lisa, I truly am sorry, but this is not the way okay? We'll – we'll get you some help, and..."

Dean trailed off. He was trying to sound sincere but realized it was impossible. Any hint that he was lying to Lisa would only hurt Chyna. He looked down at her again. Her eyes strained to see what happened behind her. He continued to cradle her head but at various intervals she squeezed her eyes tight, as if fearful for how this would end.

"Lisa, I care," Dean said, trying a different tack. "I care a lot about you, but this – this..." — he gestured briefly with a sweep of his hand, wary of another possible strike against Chyna at any moment. "This won't solve anything. I would never want you to hurt anyone. I'd never want you to... kill. That's just not the way, okay?"

He saw her soften at his plea. Her hand relaxed just a little from its death grip on the scissors.

In a rush, Trent and Jojo moved forward to tackle Lisa and pull her off of Chyna. Dean pulled Chyna fully into his arms and carried her swiftly to another room down the hall.

For a moment, Chyna's head lolled, dizzy and disoriented. Dean could tell that she didn't know what had just happened. He set her on the bed, then knelt to get a better look at her.

"Oh my God... Where is she?"

"Chyna, look at me," Dean said, gently bringing her face around to meet his. He tilted her head and neck gently to examine the small welts on her neck. They weren't bloody, thank God; the skin was just irritated.

"Dean?"

"Yes, I'm here."

"She didn't like... kill herself, did she?" Chyna asked.

Dean shook his head. "She is fine. No one will harm her. The police are on their way, and this time she will go to jail. She's still alive." He allowed himself a small chuckle. "Kicking and screaming, but alive."

"Can we get married now?"

Dean laughed and looked at her, but sobered when he saw she was completely serious. "Maybe in a bit. We've got a couple more important things to take care of right now."

"Nothing is more important, Dean," she said decisively. "This isn't right. Everything's a mess."

Dean rolled his eyes heavenward, but hesitated when he saw a tear snake from her eye. "Listen, I told you, we're going to get married - we are, but first we have to make sure you're all right. Does anything hurt? You blacked out, I think. You were out cold when I came up here."

"The minister is still here?" Chyna persisted, ignoring Dean's question completely.

"Yes, everyone is still here, downstairs. Tish and Jina were eyeing the lobsters like a couple of malnourished children, though, so I'd assume they'd love to skip straight to the reception and dinner."

Her eyes shone. "We're having lobster?"

"And shrimp scampi and Maryland blue crab, plus hot wings for us men types and a whole bunch of food you love... Now, answer my question, Chyna. Are you in any pain?"

"Dean, I am so fine." She rushed to stand and Dean backed up, wrapping his arms around her. She put a hand to her head momentarily but tried to pretend nothing was wrong.

"I may have a concussion, but I want to be married right now," she said, a little slowly. "How about this: we get married, then we'll go to the hospital. This time you cannot leave me until I'm safely down the aisle." She looked at him. "Dean, please..."

Dean felt all of his resolve slipping, and despite everything, he nodded. He resolved to ask Charlize to have a look at Chyna as soon as he got downstairs. When they exited the room, they found the entire family lining the hallway, waiting for them.

Chyna couldn't help smiling. She rested her head on Dean's shoulder. "Just a little drama, people," she announced. "Now we are ready to get married."

Cheers rang out. As the happy couple made their way down the stairs, everyone followed, taking their seats again. Dean and

Chyna hung back as the processional music began. Chyna took his hands and looked deep into his eyes.

"Dean. This is our wedding day and I've waited so long to get to this point. I want you to know that I want it. I want you."

"You got me, Chyna," he answered. "Make no mistake, I'm yours."

Chyna smiled and hugged him. The door opened, and this time, instead of leaving her, he moved with her right by his side. Bubba, their longtime faithful friend, came to stand on her other side, looking awkward but proud in dress slacks that didn't fit him and a mismatched morning coat that looked to be straight out of a 1962 barbershop quartet. Smiling, the old man bent to give her a kiss.

"Y'all young folks like to do things kind of different, don't you?"

Chyna smiled and Dean raised an eyebrow. "Something like that."

"This is it. Now." Chyna stood straight as her future sisters-in-law quickly fixed her dress and fussed with her hair so the pictures wouldn't conjure visions of the Bride of Chucky, before rushing back to the front and taking their places again.

Chyna had a headache: as soon as she got through the next few minutes, she'd let Charlize take a look over her, but right then, adrenaline carried her. She was so very excited.

"Ready?"

"When you are," Dean answered, kissing her on the cheek.

"Oh, I ready," Chyna said.

They both laughed and with all the people both of them loved the most, they moved slowly but determinedly down the aisle toward the future that awaited them.

"You thought of everything," Chyna whispered.

"I was highly motivated," Dean whispered back.

EPILOGUE

Finally, after a long drive back from Georgia and almost eight straight hours at a hospital, Chyna and Dean returned to her home. Tired but elated, they removed their clothes and climbed into bed. Chyna grabbed her notepad and quickly with the charcoal pencil set she'd received for Christmas sketched an idea as Dean sat in bed looking over her shoulder.

"Can you believe it? They're here," she said.

"I can't believe it," Dean nodded. "Chase was a wreck. I thought they were going to admit him in a bed right next to my sister," he added with a laugh.

Chyna laughed. "He was just so nervous."

"Yeah. Hey, what are you sketching?"

"Their names. I'm going to paint something with their names on it. Camille Sharon Alton: she came first, right?"

Dean nodded.

"Then Karynn Sophie Alton. They were so precious - like two little tubs of honey." Chyna set aside her sketchpad, satisfied that she had at least jotted down a few ideas, then turned to snuggle closer to Dean. "Sorry I'm rambling on, honey."

"It's all right. You're just happy. I am too. I *am*," Dean confirmed, knowing Chyna didn't totally believe him.

"But you're worried, too?" Chyna asked.

"Yeah," Dean admitted.

"About Jojo?"

"Yeah."

"What kind of military calls two days after the New Year, eight days after Christmas? That's insane."

"Yeah," Dean chuckled softly. "Eight days after Christmas – what are they thinking?" And then, raising an eyebrow at Chyna's look of outrage, "Only you would think about it like that. I think it's going to be all right, I guess. I want to hope that it will anyway."

"It will, honey, it will. He's on special assignment: they're tying up some things overseas, right?" Chyna asked as she moved farther down under the covers. She wrapped her arms around her husband.

"Yeah, something like that. Does anything really ever get tied up overseas, though, in a perpetual war? Jojo didn't have a lot of details, or I guess he couldn't tell me if he did."

"It would seem so," Chyna said.

Dean grinned. "I think he asked Angie to marry him on New Years."

"What?" Chyna gasped. Dean nodded. "Wow. Well, we'll help out with the kids, whatever she needs. She's already family."

"I love you, Chyna Jameson." Dean turned to look at her. He'd never cease to be amazed by how thoughtful she was, how she was always ready to do whatever she could for anyone. His heart, even when so full of joy, was heavy about yet another tour of duty for his brother, especially now that he'd found love. It seemed the worst possible time.

He refocused on Chyna, wondering what he'd do without her.

"I do wish Jina could be a little bit nicer to Angie."

"She's hurting, what with her baby being diagnosed with diabetes, it's a lot, he's so little," Chyna put in.

"Yes, but still, that's Jojo's intended. You know she can be mean sometimes: stop defending her abrasiveness."

"Well, you know how protective your sister is over him. It was just the two of them in the family before you and then Tish came along. Plus, remember how mean you were to Chase when he first came around?"

"I was not mean to him," Dean protested. "Everyone has to go through an approval process, especially when it comes to my baby sister. I had to make sure he was the right one."

"Is that what you're calling it? Approval process? Um hmm." Chyna hummed skeptically. "Then I supposed overprotective sisters have their own *approval process*, too. All I can say is, thank God I was a shoo-in to everybody - everybody except you, of course," she laughed.

"That is not true." He hugged her tighter.

"You'll never admit it." Chyna scooted down further under the covers and pulled Dean to her.

"You don't get to be mean to me and then try to sweet-talk me, young lady..."

"You are mine, I get to do whatever I want. Fall in line, solider boy."

"So bossy, man," Dean said, commencing to kiss Chyna with longing. She was always switching up her smack talk with love, knowing he would give in to her completely and always. She sometimes let him think he was the boss, but he was clearly mistaken.

Once again, Dean told her just how much she meant to him, thinking of all they'd been through and all they would now go through with their family: together at last, once and for all. He kissed her again and again, until, at least for a little while, the complex issues of their day, their family and the rest of the world faded away. They were truly home.

The End

RESOURCES

SUICIDE PREVENTION

National Suicide Prevention Lifeline
Visit: https://suicidepreventionlifeline.org/
Call: 1-800-273-8255
Text: HOME to 741741

A LETTER TO MY READERS

Dear Reader,

   I hope you have enjoyed Chyna and Dean's story and thank you for taking time to visit with them. I cannot begin to thank all of you enough for your support through all of these stories.

   If you have time, please consider leaving a review on Amazon, Goodreads or any other book-seller platform. I would appreciate it so much.

   If you would like to ask a question, send me an encouraging note or comment, feel free to drop me an e-mail, use the "contact me" page on my website or send me an email using the contact details below. Please visit my website to review and discuss the questions I created around each book in the Jameson Family Series.

www.TraceeGarner.com
Email me: Teegarner@aol.com

Until next time, I wish you the best.
   Tracee

ABOUT THE AUTHOR

Tracee Lydia Garner is a national best-selling and award-winning author. A Virginia native, she currently resides in the northern Virginia area with her family. She is an advocate for persons with disabilities and often speaks to youth, minorities and women from all walks of life. She enjoys writing and cooking, and, of course, loves to read and make videos about her books. Tracee is a member of the Sisters in Crime (SinC) writers, and Romance Writers of America.

ALSO BY TRACEE LYDIA GARNER

Whatever May Come - Jameson Family Book 1

Fatal Opposition - Parker Brothers Book 3

Deadly Affections - Parker Brothers Book 2

Anchored Hearts - Parkers Brothers Book 1